JOHNNY'S WAR

Published July 2011

Johnny's War: a novel / 1st edition
ISBN 978-0-9837747-1-6

Library of Congress Catalog Number 2011913839
1. Iraq war — fiction   2. American politics — fiction

Printed in the United States of America

CP

Published by Cascadia Press LLC
cascadiapress@gmail.com
Portland, Oregon

Johnny's War

A novel

Jim Braly

PART I
IRAQ

1 / Welcome to the sandbox

I couldn't sleep on the 16-hour flight to Iraq. The jet engines on the C-141 Starlifter were hella loud, reminding me of AC/DC at the Clark County Amphitheater. Every song pounded you, the deepest groove in rock and roll. You heard the music and felt it: The boom of the kick drum, the thrum thu-thu-thrum thu-thu-thrum of the bass guitar. Back in black, baby. The thick low frequencies moved a lot of air. The bricks of smoke-filled air moved a lot of you. Cutting through, the tinny schoop-schoop of the high-hat kept perfect time. The C-141 was like that, a giant rhythm section, a throbbing grinding whine, building, then releasing, over and over, until you were hypnotized, shifting slowly from side to side like an old wind-up metronome encased in Jell-O. High-pitched metallic vibrations rattled on top of everything, loose aircraft rivets or something. If only I had brought a few joints, I would've been in Wynken, Blynken and Nod-off land. Too bad you couldn't spark it up on this flight.

My seat was toward the front, under the left wing. Four guys sat to my right. We didn't talk much. Maybe it was the noise. Or the nerves. This was getting from Point A to Point I. No beverage, no peanuts. Good thing they didn't charge for extra baggage because we had tons of it. After being in the air forever, you could feel the pilot throttle down. The engines backed off from a scream to a roar. I knew the guy next to me, Amerigo Taymondo, from Fort Benning. He turned and said, "Hey, Cutter, you wanna make a little bet?"

"On what?"

"On whether we go down in a screaming ball of molten steel and flaming flesh."

I looked at him. Mute. My face went all WTF.

"You know," he said, "fiery death on our first day in Iraq. Big headline: More than 200 troops killed in Baghdad crash."

"You want to bet on whether we all die?"

"Yeah, why not?"

"If you win, how am I going to pay off? Won't I be dead?"

"You can pay me in heaven," Taymondo said.

He had such a serious look on his face that I laughed, but nervously. "How much are we talking about?" I asked.

"Five bucks. I tell you what, you can pay me now. If I don't see you in heaven, then we're already squared away. If we land safely, I'll give you back your five bucks and I'll give you five on top of that."

I rolled that deal around in my mind. My mom was always telling me to watch out for scams. If you get an e-mail from Nigeria, it's a rip-off, she would say. Don't ever go into an Internet chat room because nobody is who they say they are, she would say. Don't ever take street drugs because I read about a girl whose body was turned into a block of wood by synthetic heroin, she would say. The prices aren't really lower at a going-out-of-business sale, especially a rug store, she would say. Mom would have found something wrong with Taymondo's offer, too, but the risk seemed low. I said, "OK, let me get this straight, I give you five bucks now, and if we land safely, you give me ten bucks?"

"Right."

I fished a fiver out of my wallet and handed it to him. "Deal."

Taymondo stashed the bill in his pants pocket. "I hope you win," he said.

"Yeah, me too."

"You probably will. The Starlifter carries countermeasures. Once we start corkscrewing down, we'll probably fire off a bunch."

Minutes later, the C-141's nose plunged like the first drop on a roller-coaster. High-pitched whoosh-whoosh-whooshes followed. We banked hard right. I death-gripped the cold steel armrests. "There they go," Taymondo said. "Check the flare trails. Fourth of July. The SAMs won't know what to go after."

It occurred to me that, yeah, surface-to-air missiles might be coming after our transport plane, that, yeah, if we got hit a couple of hundred guys would die. Damn, SAM, this was no video game. I knew this was a dangerous, real war — nearly 250 troops had already been killed — but this was the first time I believed it, that I imagined the possibility of be-ing one of those unlucky grunts who didn't make it. I got a funny feeling, like when I came down with the flu in high school a few years ago, and I was as lightheaded as a helium balloon. When I floated into the boys' bathroom and looked at myself in the mirror, I was all sweaty. Every drop of blood had drained from my face. Sheer trembly white. Shadows under eyes. Sickly goth-boy.

■

My name was the most important thing to know about me: Johnathan Ambrose Cutter IV. My mother liked to tell the embarrassing story about my birth, how I got crossways and didn't want to come out. In the first hint that I would have a talent for tangles, the umbilical cord snagged my neck like a noose. My tiny smushed face turned purple. When I finally entered this world ("Thirty-six hours of hard labor," Mom always added) on June 29, 1984, I let out a scream that brought an extra doctor and nurse running into the delivery room.

Mom named me right there. "Johnny Ambrose Cutter," she declared, "my beautiful boy." Her tears fell like rain on the Oregon coast. Mom said she cried out of love, mostly, and because she refused the drugs. I think she cried because Dad wasn't there. I was a month premature, and Major John David Cutter III was off on a mission in Nicaragua that he couldn't talk about. My grandpops, First Lieutenant Johnny Michael Cutter II, lay in a veterans hospital in Vancouver, Washington, two weeks away from dying of a mysterious cancer.

Maybe the ghost of my great-grandpops, Master Sergeant John Ambrose Cutter, lurked in that delivery room. Mom would always say she got a weird chill when the doctor handed me to her.

I was destined to become a soldier. With that lineage, that military blood, what else was there? Plus, once Mom quit crying, she propped me up with one hand and saluted with the other. Those were the days when she was still a military wife. She claimed I returned the salute.

■

The C-141 vibrated. I tensed up. I hoped it was only turbulence. I needed some air. The plane smelled like our high school locker room. We always thought it was sweaty shirts left in lockers, which was part of it, but later we found out there was toxic mold in the walls — all that

Oregon rain leaking in. During my senior year, the school tore down the locker room. That was the same year they dropped P.E. classes, so it all worked out.

I realized somebody was tapping me on the shoulder. "Hey, Cutter, you OK?" It was Taymondo. I heard myself breathing like a hunting dog bringing back a bird.

"Yeah, sure," I said. "No problem."

"OK, just checking. You got a little white there."

I looked at his brown face, dark eyes and acne scars. I wondered if he was part Indian, like the kids you saw around the Chinook casino. I nodded and said, "Yeah, I don't tan so good."

Taymondo laughed. "I hope you brought some sunscreen, dude, cause Iraq is like 130 degrees."

I had flown on a jet only once in my life before joining the Army, so I didn't know much about landings. This one seemed extra-rough. I got a flippy tummy as the plane slammed the runway. The engines began to whine at a higher pitch. The pilot hit the brakes. My body pressed against the seat belt.

"*Hooah!*" somebody screamed. "*Welcome to the sandbox!*" Piercing whistles and rowdy obscenities erupted. We rolled to a stop and the rear cargo doors opened. Everyone grabbed their gear, slinging 90-pound duffel bags over their shoulders. We tromped down the tailgate. It was dawn's early light, morning in Iraq. The highest temperature I'd ever experienced was maybe 95 degrees. This felt worse. I peered into the distance. My eyes adjusted to the unrelenting brown and I noticed something weird: There wasn't a single tree. I began to feel heat coming up from the runway through my boots.

Somebody tapped me on the back. I turned around and Taymondo handed me two five-dollar bills. "Here you go, Cutter. I'm glad I lost."

"Sweet," I said, stuffing the money into my wallet. "So far, I'm liking this war."

2 / Shades of Lawrence

Forward Operating Base Viper, about 10 miles north of Baghdad, was my new home. A small city sprouting in the middle of a sand plain, it resembled a prison more than a military base. Barbed wire topped a perimeter of concrete walls. Two guard towers, each packing a machine gun, flanked the entrance.

We rode in from the airport in the back of a big truck. The highway was wide and smooth. I didn't know what to expect, maybe a dirt cart path, but certainly not a real interstate that was in better shape than Highway 101 back home.

It was the first day of August. The heat stunned me. Sure, they told us in basic training it was going to be brutal, but hearing that and feeling this were two different things. Once we cleared the main entrance checkpoint and rolled onto the base, a linebacker-looking soldier pulled a meat thermometer out of his duffel bag and held its thin silver probe in the air. The thermometer beeped and he said, "It's a hundred and sixteen. Start cooking your own goose."

We single-filed out of the truck and assembled in the burning sands. I thought of the Oregon Dunes on the coast near Coos Bay, where the sand was cool and fine by comparison.

I looked around the base and saw many portable buildings, which reminded me of home. My high school was a village of portables, beige boxes with leaky roofs, which wouldn't be a problem here. No rain. In the far reaches of FOB Viper stood rows and rows of tents, like some Lawrence of Arabia subdivision. Signs of construction were everywhere, pallets piled high with plywood, bulldozers moving dusty earth, trucks ladling concrete into foundations, welders joining I-beams into skeletons of buildings-to-be. It looked like we would be here awhile.

"Ten-hut!"

We were milling around, piling up gear, gawking at the buzzing base, but when the command came, we snapped to attention like show dogs, eyes front and center. Nobody wanted to be labeled a malcontent or a screwup in the first five minutes on base.

An older soldier with a bit of a gut stood before us. His lighthouse eyes swept across our faces. Combat patches dotted his sleeve and some hardware on his chest reflected the sun as he moved. "At ease," he finally said. We exhaled as a group. You could hear fatigues rustle and boots creak as muscles relaxed.

"I'm Warrant Officer Henry Figg," the soldier said. "I want to welcome you to Hotel Viper. I'm going to do everything I can to make your stay comfortable. Let me say first, though, that if you've heard rumors about the room service being sucky, they're absolutely true. However, if you like Rip It, we've got enough to fill the Persian Gulf and I will make a solemn promise to you. There are two things we will never run out of at Forward Operating Base Viper: Insanely caffeinated battle juice and ammo, because, in point of fact, aren't they the same thing? Now is everybody ready to rip into Operation Iraqi Freedom?"

We let out a group "yes, sir," but it was tentative and, by the standards of even the first week of basic training, seriously lame. In our defense, we had no idea of where we were, what we were in for, or who this Figg guy was. Add to that the disorientation of 16 hours on a roaring jet and being dumped into a blast furnace.

Warrant Officer Figg shook his head. "That was pitiful," he said. "Your drill sergeants would be sad and perplexed to hear you now after all they went through to turn you into soldiers, into the best fighting machine in the world. So I'm going to ask you again and maybe those sergeants could actually hear you this time. *Are you ready to rip into Operation Iraqi Freedom?*"

"*YES, SIR!*" we screamed with one voice, one mind, no clue.

Figg smiled. "Better. Much better. Let's get you to your rooms."

I wanted to forget about Drill Sergeant Stoddard, who menaced us like a pit bull at a crack house, all barking and snapping and frothing. It started off comical and quickly got ridiculous. In the second week of basic, as we stood at frozen attention in a pouring rain, soaked to the bone but too scared to shiver, this Southern kid named Bobby Vigonya smiled when Stoddard accused our entire company of wearing crotchless purple panties and suggested that we get a sex change operation "to make it official." We instantly learned that a smile was a virtual death sentence as Stoddard marched over to Bobby and exploded:

"Was that a smile I just saw on your fuck-ass girl-maggot cross-dressing lesbian-sucking face, Private Vigonya?"

"Yes, Drill Sergeant!" Bobby yelled. He stood lock-tight straight, hoping to evade punishment by telling the whole truth.

"Would you like to have your maggoty homo asshole invaginated by a Pigstick from the EOD?"

"I don't know, Drill Sergeant!"

"You don't know? You *don't know* if you would like to have your bleeding hemorrhoidal asshole invaginated by a Pigstick from EOD?" Stoddard bulled in even closer, nose to nose with Bobby, and spewed a mist of spit all over his face. *"Because you look like the kind of girl who would like it!"*

"Requesting permission to ask three questions, Drill Sergeant."

"Permission granted."

"What is a Pigstick, Drill Sergeant? What is the EOD, Drill Sergeant? What does invaginated mean, Drill Sergeant?"

Stoddard shook his head in disgust and his face contorted like a constipated gargoyle. "Private Queeronya, you are telling me — and this company of soldiers who trust you with their lives — that you know nothing about Pigsticks, EOD teams or invagination?"

"Yes, Drill Sergeant!"

"Private Suckdickya, you are a sorry pathetic uneducated excuse for a cancerous open-for-business rectum. The EOD is the Explosive Ordnance Disposal team. These highly trained specialists blanket the bedsore called Baghdad looking for IEDs. Do you know what an IED is, Private Queerinya?"

"Yes, Drill Sergeant! It's an improvised explosive device."

"Well, that's a start. I will now educate you further: A Pigstick is a disruptor, a mechanical device used by the EOD to fire a high-pressure blast of water into the IED trigger to disarm it, thus saving your helpless Hollywood ass from being shipped home in a bucket of blood and foul-smelling anal pus. So I will ask you one more time, Private Poolboy, would you like to have your pink ruffle-and-lace-wearing asshole invaginated by a Pigstick?"

"No, Drill Sergeant!"

"Does that mean you understand what invaginated means?"

"Yes, Drill Sergeant!"

Hey, Stoddard, I wanted to say, I had gay friends in high school and they were all cool and never bothered anybody, but he would have shot me for knowing queers, so I kept my mouth shut.

Warrant Officer Figg led us to what he called Forward Operating Base Viper's "South Forty." The term "Hotel Viper" wasn't accurate, nor was "rooms." Our unit was assigned to the tent metropolis.

Figg said, "You'll be happy to know that FOB Viper is on level ground, for those of you concerned about shit running downhill, but don't worry, you only have to take a shower once a week." Figg delivered his cryptic remarks with a straight face and lack of tone. His logic, or lack of it, made me think of Mrs. Bayonne's class in English literature during my one semester at Coos Bay Community College. She spent a week discussing non sequiturs, and she probably hated them as much as Stoddard hated homos. Figg also said, "We get up early at Viper, with the sun, but the moon is where we pierce the darkness."

I didn't know what that meant but asking a question was out of the question. It felt like that first week of basic, when we spent every moment trying to get grounded, to avoid psycho land mines, to survive.

During in-processing at base headquarters, I found out I would bunk with five other soldiers. One of them was Sergeant Pete Klug, our squad leader. He was older than the rest of us, late-20s, and said he'd been in Iraq from Day One. Klug looked like a body builder, glistening with sweat when he walked in and introduced himself. He seemed like a no-bullshit guy. He'd just been to the gym for a workout, he told us. His head was shaved. "I recommend it," he said. "You don't have to worry about sand fleas and lice. On your head, anyway."

We newbs got our gear stowed, then we crashed on the cots. We were beyond wasted. Klug headed for the track. "I try to run at least 25 miles a week," he said. "Remember, stay hydrated. Water is your best friend, maybe your only friend."

I was lucky to be rooming with Tim Gulde, my hulking battle buddy from Fort Benning. We had forged a steel-strong friendship during basic. Tim got me through some horrible days. He came from Oregon, too, a pit stop called Burns, east of the Cascades and about as far from my hometown of Trillium as you could get without crossing into Idaho. The only thing I knew about Burns was, it got far below freezing in the winter. I welcomed any commonality, no matter how slight. My other roomies were Bodie Davis, a skinny acne-faced kid from Belle Eagle, Tennessee; Ulysses Jackson, from Sumterville, Alabama, who had trained at the language institute in Monterey and knew how to speak Arabic; and Willie Lincoln, who pointed out that he knew "how to speak street."

"I'm from *Deee*troit," Willie told me. "Everybody calls me D-Willie. If you ever need to know how to say hello in Arabic, you go to Ulysses, but if you want a translation of 'yo, whassup in the crib, muthafucker,' you come to me, OK? Cause I will be here for you. Cause you are very very white. Where'd you say you from again?"

"Trillium, Oregon."

"Oregon. That's out west, right? Is Oregon a state? I thought it was a territory or some shit like that. You got any Indians out there?"

"Yeah, Tillamook, Umpqua, a bunch of tribes running casinos."

"You got any black people out there? Any Buffalo Soldiers? Any African Americans? Any brothers?"

"Not really. Only the Portland Trail Blazers."

"Ha! I love basketball, Cutter. I think I'm gonna like you but we gotta brown you down. You are seriously pale. I'm gonna call you Ghost. You got any sun in Oregon?"

"Not really."

"Then I guess Iraq is a change for you."

"Yeah."

"You got any suntan lotion?"

I shook my head forlornly.

"I got you covered, Ghost," D-Willie said. "I'll loan you some color."

Warrant Officer Figg stuck his head in our tent a little later. "Anybody hungry? I'm taking you out to lunch. I'm buying and I don't mean Meals Ready to Eat. I mean real food for real soldiers. At 1400 hours, you'll meet your commanding officer."

The mess hall was stuffed with rows of folding tables and metal chairs. You could get meat loaf, pasta, cheeseburgers, chicken wings, peas, carrots, salad with ranch dressing, ice cream, fudge cake dripping with chocolate syrup. They had more food than I had ever seen, even more than the HomeTown Buffet, and they piled it on your tray, heaping mountains of high-octane fuel.

Figg rounded us up at 1330. "Before you meet your commanding officer," he said, "I'll take you on a little tour of the Tactical Operations Center. It's our brain and our nerve center, also our spleen, liver and colon. You'll be talking to these guys whenever you're out on a mission. The TOC can get you whatever you want, D9, Abrams, Kiowa, Apache, Black Hawk, Predator, Reaper, A-10, F-14, F/A-18, F-16, JDAM, Rockeye, M-72 LAW, Javelin, M-198 with HE and RAP rounds, ADAMS and RAAMS, white phosphorous, BLU-82, GBU-28, Tomahawk, TOW, Javelin, Hellfire, Pershing, AIM-9, anything you need to do your job, up to and including an ICBM. All right, now don't call your mother and tell her you'll be launching the Big One. That won't be up to you. Besides, why worry her unnecessarily?"

Bodie Davis raised his hand.

"Question?" Figg said.

Davis opened his mouth but it was a false start. Nothing came out. He clenched his teeth and you could sort of see scenarios spinning out in his head. Then he said, "Uh, no, sir. Sorry, sir."

We walked across the base to the Tactical Operations Center, which was jammed with more high-tech gadgets than I had ever seen in one place, like a Circuit City on steroids and meth. The scene was Christmas for gearheads, with racks of metal boxes lit up with tiny winking lights; communication modules all crackling and warm; banks of computers, their fans whirring away in a struggle to stay cool; and guys in headphones.

Figg discussed protocols and introduced us to some dispatchers and mission coordinators. Then he motioned for us to fall in behind him. We followed Figg like marching baby chicks to a brown double-wide trailer up on concrete blocks. It reminded me of the rusty cars back home, the lawn ornaments. Figg swung open a flimsy door. "You can think of this as your personal TOC," he said. There was just one big room, filled with rows of folding metal chairs, a speaker's lectern and a wide whiteboard.

Sitting in the front row, a man in camouflage rose and turned to face us. His namestrip said Dozinger. The black-and-gold patch on his left sleeve said Ranger. He had a shaved head and that made his dark thick eyebrows appear extra bushy. He was small and wiry, which I didn't expect, and surprisingly old, probably around 40. The left side of his face was mottled pink with scar tissue. Must have been a burn, the kind of ill-placed disfigurement you politely tried not to notice.

"Hooah! Welcome to FOB Viper!" he yelled, approaching us like a rogue wave that could kill us or propel us on the ride of our lives, or both. His deep powerful voice should have come from a much bigger body. He shook each of our hands with a grip like a vise. "Davis, Gulde, Lincoln, Cutter, Jackson," he said, reading our namestrips in succession. "I'm Captain Kyle Dozinger. Welcome to Bravo Company. I'm pleased and proud to meet you. We're going to make history."

His eyes made me believe him. They were steely gray, locked and loaded, focused on us like a laser.

3 / Blink of an eye

The first week at Forward Operating Base Viper flew past. Mostly busywork. A lot of in-processing sludge at the reception station had to be settled before we went out on our first mission. D-Willie Lincoln got a paper cut while updating a next-of-kin form. "If I bleed out and die," he said, "that would be like totally bionic."

"Don't you mean ironic," I said.

"I don't think so, Ghost."

Basic training had steeled us for this red-tape battle. The main snafu was my paycheck. The direct-deposit setup got lost in translation from Fort Benning to FOB Viper. After filling out a new form, I smiled so big it hurt. As a new private in the United States Army, I would make nearly $18,000 a year with the combat pay and allowances added in. After deductions, more than $14,000 of that would be deposited in my account at Oregon Savings Bank. My $20,000 infantry signing bonus was coming through and would start collecting interest. I didn't even know what interest was before that dinero hit the fan. *I was rich*. Back in Trillium, I made $7.05 an hour busing tables.

One of the great things about Iraq was, you didn't need money. There was no place to spend it. The base provided everything. When I got out, I'd be set. I'd pay cash for a two-door Scion with 18-inch super-alloys and juice it up with two subwoofers and 1,000 watts. I'd get a ring, pick up Halley Fallon, drive over to the coast for a walk on the beach, and get down on one knee and propose. Classy and classic. OK, the first thing I would do is let my hair grow back, but then the rest of that beautiful plan would kick in. I could get a job in private security right away and go to college on the G.I. Bill. Halley and I would do it like rabbits and maybe she'd pop out a bunny. I lay on my cot at night imagining our little family. Sometimes an explosion in the distance spoiled the spell.

The following Wednesday, after intense Iraq orientation classes, from geography to weather to ancient animosities to ordnance detection, Captain Dozinger was ready to turn us newbs loose. All the guys in my tent were going out. Amped. Each of us would ride in a Humvee with three other guys, experienced soldiers who had been in-country for at least three months. They weren't expecting a lot. Our job, as the captain put it in the mission briefing, was to "watch, learn and survive — and two out of three ain't good enough."

The mission would take us to Sadr City in east Baghdad. The day before, insurgents had kidnapped the son of Sheik Barzan al-Farid and were holding him for $50,000 in ransom. Al-Farid was a shadowy Shiite cleric who may or may not have been working against the coalition. "Now he needs our help," Dozinger said at the briefing, "and he came to us and asked for it. If we come through, we could turn him. He's influential in the community. Little wins add up to big victories."

We would send a convoy of five Humvees. Sergeant Klug would command the mission. Ulysses Jackson's knowledge of Arabic put him in the lead Hummer with Klug. My battle buddy Tim Gulde would be in No. 2, I would be in No. 3, D-Willie Lincoln in No. 4 and Bodie Davis in No. 5.

We skipped breakfast to assemble our gear, going over a long checklist of weapons and supplies. Our goal was to leave the base by 0800, get to the sheik's house before 0900, collect any evidence that al-Farid could give us, then fan out across Sadr City, talk to people, let them know we were looking, and make vague promises of dollars for information. If we got a tip, we would check it out. If we got a location, we would extract the hostage by whatever means necessary, including lethal force. "If it comes to a firefight and they're gonna kill the kid, kill them all," Dozinger said, evenly, without emotion. "Then render the location unusable. Sergeant Klug will call in an airstrike if necessary."

I was nervous. My stomach hurt and my brain locked. Basic training tore me up in a lot of ways, but nothing like this. Two months ago, you knew the drill sergeant couldn't touch you. Those were the rules. He could smoke you, for sure, scream, yell, roar, accuse you of enjoying sodomy, make the entire company do pushups because of your foolish mistake. But the captain laid out a lot of ways we could be seriously touched on this mission. No rules. We weren't in pushup land anymore.

I looked over at Gulde as Dozinger reviewed emergency medical scenarios and the procedure for calling in a medevac chopper. I recognized a look in Tim's eyes, from the third week of basic, when neither of us knew if we would make it.

As we headed for the Humvees, Klug said, "This will go fine, don't worry. Killdozer can get a little dramatic."

"Killdozer?" Bodie Davis said.

"The captain. It's kind of his nickname. Don't let him hear you say it, though, if you know what I mean."

Davis nodded. Killdozer. What was up with that name? Back channel Army info seemed to travel by word of mouth. Osmosis.

I was loading M-16 clips into the Humvee when Captain Dozinger walked up. "How're you doing, Private Cutter?" he asked.

"Good, sir," I answered, shifting into a parade rest stance.

"The first mission can be a challenge. You're ready to go?"

"Yes, sir."

"Who's your driver?"

"Owen Lewallen, sir."

"Are you riding shotgun with *Corporal* Lewallen?" the captain asked.

"Yes, sir, *Corporal* Owen Lewallen," I said, correcting my error.

The captain's eyes bored into me. He nodded, stepped back and looked around.

"There's a problem with this vehicle, Cutter," the captain said.

"A problem, sir?"

"That's right. Do you know what it is?"

"No, sir."

"Look at this windshield. It's filthy." Captain Dozinger ran his index finger across the glass and nearly poked me in the eye. "See? There's dust on this windshield. That's a serious problem."

"Yes, sir."

"Do you know why that's a serious problem, Cutter?"

"Because it reduces visibility, sir?"

"That's right. Never leave this base without making absolutely sure that your windshield is sparkling clean. And what is it you'll be looking for through the sparkling clean windshield?"

"The insurgents who kidnapped Sheik al-Farid's son, sir."

"What else?"

"Uh … " A falafel stand? A kebob joint? An "I ♥ Terrorists" T-shirt? I had no idea. Drill Sergeant Stoddard had furiously hammered us about the risks of faking it, so I said, "I'm sorry, sir, I don't know."

The captain prodded: "Think, Cutter."

"Any … anything suspicious, sir?"

"What would you consider suspicious, Cutter?"

"Suicide bombers, sir?"

The captain wagged a dusty callused finger at me. "That's good, Cutter. That's excellent. It's nice to know that you consider suicide bombers suspicious. I can see that the Army has trained you well. That gives me great and lasting comfort."

"I'm sorry, sir, that was a stupid answer."

"I'm reassured that you recognize that, Cutter. Forget the sir. I want to talk to you man to man."

"Yes, sir."

"Cutter."

"Sorry, sir. I mean … sorry." I unclasped my hands from behind my back and let my arms dangle. I took a deep breath and exhaled, trying to relax.

The captain said, "You had some counterterrorism training at Fort Benning, didn't you?"

"A little."

"Do you think it was thorough? Do you think they taught you what you need to know to stay alive in Iraq?"

"Permission to speak freely?"

"Absolutely. Don't tell me what I want to hear, Cutter, tell me the truth. Lies are the coward's way out."

I formulated my response for a moment as the captain's eyes locked onto mine, searching for fear. "I'm not sure if I learned enough. I didn't know anything when I got to basic training. They taught me a lot but I don't know anything about Iraq. I don't know who we're fighting, exactly. I don't know how we're fighting, exactly. I don't know why we're fighting, exactly. And that makes me a little nervous." As soon as I finished, I wished I had kept my mouth shut.

But the captain nodded. "That's good. That's smart. That's normal.

That's healthy. You *should* be nervous. A lot of the things you don't understand, neither does the Army. We're learning as we go. Sometimes it's painful. Sometimes it doesn't work and we have to switch tactics, but we've got to stay strong and smart. We've got to always be vigilant. We've got to maintain focus. If we lose focus for even the blink of an eye, bad things can happen." The captain turned his head a little. The blotchy pink burn scar entered my field of vision like a billboard. "When you go out there today, I want you to keep looking — at everything. Notice your surroundings. Look blocks ahead. Look at the people on the street. If the street is empty, ask yourself why. Look at the cars. Have you seen the same car for a while? Why is that? If there was a tripwire or a pressure plate in the street, would you see it in time to tell Corporal Lewallen to stop?"

"I hope so."

"The correct answer is yes, Cutter. Now clean this windshield and have a good mission."

"Yes, sir."

Captain Dozinger shook my hand and headed for D-Willie, who was checking under the hood of his vehicle. Corporal Lewallen walked up with the other two guys who would be in our Humvee today, Private First Class Albert Gonzales and Specialist Mike Sauderbach.

"Hey, Johnny," Lewallen said. "You ready to rock and roll?"

"Like AC/DC, sir."

"Right on. Let's do it."

We continued loading gear and Lewallen said, "It looked like Killdozer was giving you The Talk."

"Yeah, I guess he was."

"It's good advice. You'll be an extra set of eyes today."

"You can count on me, Corporal Lewallen. No blinking."

Lewallen smiled. "Call me Owen," he said. "I'm not into the whole rank thing. So you'll be on communications. You've used the FBCB2 system before, right?"

"Only in class."

"Then you know what to do."

"Yes, sir."

"Where are you from?"

I told him about Trillium and the Coast Range and the Doug firs. He told me about his hometown, Buffalo Prairie, Illinois, a "flat nothing little place" about 10 miles east of the Mississippi River. "Big cities freak me out," Lewallen said. "I've been to Chicago. It's all the way across the state. I wouldn't go back. They should call it The Dirty Crowded Windy Freeze Your Ass Off City."

The soldiers I'd met so far were a lot alike. They talked about home. Home was common ground for us.

Our convoy rumbled out of FOB Viper at 0759, a minute early, kicking up a cloud of dust. The front gate sentries saluted.

We picked up speed on the highway to Baghdad. In 15 minutes we were snaking through the suburbs. Captain Dozinger's talk was looping in my head. I looked around constantly, nervously, like an itchy-face paranoid schizo. Nevertheless, I was drinking in the sights and sounds of the city like a man stranded in a desert. The men with their long beards, tall turbans and flowing robes. Mysterious women walking behind, covered by burqas. They must have been broiling in there. Colorful awnings shaded the streets as we rolled through a clogged market area, with hundreds of Iraqis milling around, buying produce. The convoy had to slow down.

I kept my eyes on our windshield, which was building up a fine layer of dust, not bad, but I could notice it. I said, "Owen, should we give the windshield a little wiper action or something?"

"Yeah, I'll get"

A blinding flash of fire and light engulfed the street. The blast wave made our Humvee shudder for a moment. Debris rained down. The noise was awful, an instant cataclysmic roar. My eardrums felt like they'd been jabbed with a sharp pencil. I couldn't hear much. In the distance, Corporal Lewallen yelled softly, "Call in medevac."

I knew what to do. Drill Sergeant Stoddard's relentless training was imprinted on my battle DNA and it jolted me like the kick from an adrenaline shotgun. I got on the radio to the Tactical Operations Center, reported the situation and gave them our coordinates. A muffled voice said something back to me. I hoped it involved the dispatch of a Black Hawk chopper.

I found myself next to the smoldering wreckage of Tim Gulde's

Humvee, which had flipped onto its roof. With M-16s at the ready, our guys encircled the vehicle as if to protect it from harm. Of course it was too late for that. Direct hit. The Vee had been ripped open, a huge jagged wound in its side, door blown off hinges, windshield and windows shattered. Amid the smoky dusty choke-a-thon, all I could see was my closest friend from basic training, still belted into his seat, hanging upside down like meat on a butcher's hook, one lifeless surprised uncomprehending eye still open, staring at infinity, one eye gone, nothing left but a bloody pulped socket. Much of his face was peeled off, nose cartilage poking through remnants of charred skin. A shard of metal had pierced his neck; blood was draining in a steady stream.

My battle buddy was beyond dead: Burned and mutilated. Nobody should leave this world like that. The indignity was wrong. My first thought was, I will never see Tim again. When I felt tears running down my cheeks, my second thought was, Soldiers don't cry. My third thought was, Maybe I'm not really a soldier. Drill Sergeant Stoddard was in my head, though, screaming at me to shut my sorry mouth and suck it up. So I did.

4 / Seeing is not believing

We held a funeral service the next day on the base. Somebody, I couldn't remember who, told me that the memorials happen fast because the Army needs to move on, it can't dwell on the loss of a soldier, the enemy doesn't take a break and we don't either. I thought that was messed up. Captain Dozinger asked me to say a few words, give a tribute to Tim, since I was his closest friend on base. "It's tradition," he said.

As I stood in front of the guys, on a little plywood platform outside the base chapel, I managed to choke out the words, "When I first met Tim Gulde …" Then my throat spazzed. I could only stand there, vocal cords paralyzed, body shaking as my stomach churned. I had no memory of walking off. Somehow I ended up at the latrines. Puking.

I tried to raise the toilet lid with my boot but I didn't have the coordination. It kept slipping off the edge of my boot sole. *Bang … bang.* When there was nothing left to heave, not a fleck of disgusting stinking residue to expel, my body kept on heaving. Grotesque gut-wrenching *garraack* sounds. I collapsed to the dusty floor, leaning against a plywood wall. Breathing. Just breathing. Mostly through my mouth. When air came in through my nose, the stench of fresh vomit and well-baked shit and piss made me gag.

A voice came through the door: "Hey, you doing OK in there? You need any help?"

I took a big mouth breath. "Yeah, I'm fine," I said. "Thanks. I'm good." That was ridiculous and I started to laugh.

"You sure you're OK?" came the voice outside.

"Yeah." I stuck with my answer and it made me howl even harder.

"OK, but if you need anything, you know, just holler."

Amid my convulsive laughter, I said, "No, I'm good, thanks."

"All right. Good luck, man."

Yeah, I was good. Thank God there wasn't a mirror in the latrine. I could feel what I looked like, though. Red eyes, swollen and burning.

Tears, dust, vomit and snot on my face. I shook my head violently to try
to dislodge the grunge.

I sat there as images flooded my brain. Tim's M-16 standing up next
to his empty boots on the platform, his helmet perched atop the rifle
butt. A chaplain leading a crowd of soldiers in prayer for a "fallen warrior going home to God." I remembered thinking, Are you kidding?
Tim Gulde is going home to Burns in a box and no one will recognize
him because his face is gone. I wondered how they handled that. Then
Killdozer called me up to the front to speak.

And I froze.

I vaguely remembered the Black Hawk landing … our guys carrying
Tim off for his ride back to the base, or wherever you went when you
were dead. I wondered about that, too. I didn't know where they took
Tim. Before I signed the papers, the Army recruiter never mentioned
anything about that. He was great on job opportunities. He knew a lot
about training. If he knew how you got home when you were dead, he
didn't mention it.

In all of our training on mission procedures, nobody had said anything about what you do when your buddy's face is blown off and he's
hanging in an overturned Humvee that was ripped open like a piñata.

I remembered somebody saying at the scene: *"Motherfucking IED."*
The fireball. The blast concussion. Screaming people on the side of the
road. Chaos. A roadside bomb. East Baghdad. I was seeing it again but
I was not believing it. Iraqis lying in the street. Pools of blood. A soli-
tary shoe.

What happened to the other guys in the Humvee? They must have
made it. Their boots weren't up there with Tim's.

The conversation I had with Captain Dozinger before we left on the
mission came back to me: The Talk.

How did we get assigned to the Humvees? I couldn't remember that.
Why was I in the third vehicle? Why was Tim ahead of me? I didn't
know. What if the bomb had gone off 10 seconds later?

I wondered about that for a while. I looked at my boots. They were
covered with dust and puke. I imagined them up there on that plywood
platform. Would somebody clean them off first? Who would arrange
them? Where do the boots go after the ceremony? Who takes them

away? That's a supremely sad and fucked-up job, I thought.

I realized I hadn't asked that Army recruiter enough questions. What if I had said, "Is there any chance I'll be puking my guts out in a filthy stinking latrine after my battle buddy gets blown to pieces by a bomb during his second week of duty?" What would his answer have been?

I finally got off the floor. I needed to be hosed down by a fire truck. I pulled a wad of toilet paper off the roll and started wiping up vomit. Mom would have been proud of me for cleaning up after myself.

After the funeral, Captain Dozinger suggested that I take a couple of days off. I protested but he ordered me to do it. I was bummed. Our squad was scheduled for missions every day. I should have been with the guys. I had to go talk to a psychologist named Niehus from the combat stress team. Niehus wore doctor glasses, big black frames with thick lenses that made his eyes look like they belonged to a gigantic carp. His head wasn't shaved. He asked me questions about how I was feeling and sleeping and coping. I answered "fine" or "good" or "very well" to all of them. It was like talking to your parents. As those huge unblinking eyes stared at me, he said, "What was your mission?"

I hesitated, then heard my voice, almost disembodied: "It was a support mission." Weird. I said the words but I didn't know where they came from. I couldn't remember what we were doing.

Apparently it didn't matter. Niehus nodded approvingly. After a few more of my "fines" and "goods," he seemed to be satisfied and cleared me for duty.

I walked back to the tent, struggling to recall our mission. Why were we out there? I tried to page back to the briefing but I was blanking. When I entered our tent, Pete Klug was sitting on the edge of his cot doing curls with a dumbbell. "Hey, Cutter," he said, "how you doin'? Did you have fun with Niehus?"

"What, does everybody know I had to go see him?"

"It's no big deal, we've all been to his office."

"Yeah?"

"Killdozer is obsessive about mental health." Klug's eyes rolled up into his head and his tongue poked out to the side. He made gurgly wailing noises, which made me laugh. He looked so goofy, so psycho. I didn't expect that from our squad leader. "You don't have to worry about Niehus," he said. "He clears everybody. The Army needs the bod-ies."

That was like a knife. I flashed on Tim hanging upside down in the Humvee. Klug saw it on my face. "Oh, sorry, man, poor choice of words. I just mean that I'm sure Niehus will clear you."

"He already did."

"Hey, great. So you're goin' back out?"

"Yeah."

"That's excellent, Cutter."

"Yeah. Hey, Pete, can I ask you a question?"

"Sure."

"You don't have to tell Niehus I asked you this, you know?"

"We never tell Niehus anything. In fact, the more you withhold from him, the better off you are. You don't want a guy who wears glasses like that to be poking around inside your head, do you?"

"I guess not."

"What's the question?"

"Niehus asked me what our mission was and I told him it was a sup-port mission."

"Yeah, it sort of was. Why, did he have a problem with that?"

"No, but I was spacing on the details. Like, I can't remember why we were out there."

"We were gonna go talk to Sheik Fuckface, whatever his name was. Remember? His son got kidnapped? We were gonna find the kid and get him back. Then the sheik would like us, and if we gave him fifty grand, he would fall in love with the Americans and we'd all live hap-pily ever after and democracy would come to the Mideast. Who says money can't buy you love? You remember that?"

"Yeah … right … I think I do. Kidnapped. A kid got kidnapped." Hearing Klug describe it, the captain's briefing came into fuzzy focus.

"So you were right in telling Niehus it was a support mission."

"I guess I'm still a little foggy on what happened after the blast. Did we find the kid?"

"The mission was canceled. We had, you know, other things to do that morning. You remember all that, right?"

"Yeah. But what happened with the sheik's son?"

"Nobody's talking about that."

"Why not?"

"His body is still missing."

"Body … you mean he's dead?"

"Yeah, pretty much. We only found his head. We haven't given up, though. We're still looking for the rest of him. I guess if we find what's left, Sheik Faisalfuck will like us for a few minutes. If we reach out to him with some cash."

D-Willie walked into the tent then. "Hey, Ghost," he said, "how you doin', my brother?"

"OK."

"OK? You're seriously doing OK? Because if you're really doing OK, I want to give you this." D-Willie handed me a sheet of paper.

"What is it?"

"Some notes."

"For what?"

"For my funeral, in case Killdozer wants you to say some shit about me. Notes would be helpful, right?"

D-Willie and Pete started laughing. They fist-bumped. The notes were handwritten in pencil, the scrawly letters of a third-grader. I read aloud: "Your probbly wonder why its raining today. Well there 2 resons. God is cryin and Detroit William Eldon Lincoln the best dam soldier in the history of Army is kicking back in heaven eating BBQ wings and pissing on Irak."

I looked up at D-Willie. He was grinning like a Portland pothead in a medical marijuana dispensary. "Whaddaya think?" he asked. "Would that help?"

I had to smile. "Yeah, thanks, this is good," I said. "I'll keep it in a safe place. And I'll be sure to call you *Eldon*."

D-Willie held up his fist. I gave it a bump.

5 / The steely grip of irony

I woke up one morning in November and realized Tim Gulde had not been in my dreams for several weeks. I lay in my bunk, considering what that meant. A small breakthrough. It was my fourth month in Iraq. I was getting into the base routine. We went to briefings. We did our missions. We rounded up insurgent suspects. We flex-cuffed them. We put hoods over their heads. We shipped them off to Abu Ghraib prison. We gave toothbrushes, dental floss and candy to Iraqi kids.

My former life back home fell away. I didn't e-mail as much. Sometimes a day or two would go by and I wouldn't think about home. No room in my head for what I left behind. Only room for the mission. If you didn't keep the mission in focus, you could die. Killdozer was a bear on that point. Or you could die even if you did keep the mission in focus. Didn't matter. It was random.

From August to November, starting with Tim, we lost 23 soldiers from Forward Operating Base Viper. I knew six of them. Digger Malone was the only screwup. He "forgot" to wear his helmet because it was hot, but every day was hot. A sniper blew Digger's head open in Sadr City.

While doing ammo inventory, Bobby Vigonya had an accident. He fell off a ladder and broke his neck. Pete Klug said, "Somebody shoot me in the face if I fall off a ladder and die. I want to go out looking like a soldier, not a roofer. Fucking ladder was made in Jordan. I saw the sticker. That never would have happened if we had some Made-in-the-USA ladders. What the fuck? We get our fucking ladders from fucking Jordan now? That's fucked up."

Three guys were all blown up in the same Humvee: A.J. Burwick, Emilio Garcia and a specialist everybody called the Tinman. His real name was Dante Yaden.

I only found that out at the ceremony. Dante's death was especially ironic, as I'm sure Mrs. Bayonne would have pointed out in English lit class. The Tinman spent most of his free time — his own personal time — up-armoring our Humvees. You had to pass by the motor pool to get to the mess hall, and more often than not, the Tinman would be out there, his welding torch hissing like an angry snake. Sadly, not even Dante, as driven and obsessed as he was, could slap on enough scrap metal to withstand an EFP bomb.

A.J. and Emilio were burned beyond recognition. Their dog tags melted in the explosion, so who knew if their IDs got matched correctly, but at least there were blackened lumps resembling bodies to go home. The Tinman was obliterated. That was the day I realized why the base funerals had just the boots, rifle and helmet up on that platform. Metaphor for a man. Sometimes not much of the remains remained. Bone fragments, charred flesh, toenails, limbs, whatever could be recovered, the bits headed to Dover Air Force Base, which, I finally heard, was where the body bags went.

When I was vegging in my bunk, weird stuff would pop into my mind and make me laugh, in a sick way. I imagined Mrs. Bayonne leading a discussion of that last flight, "the trip home for 37 flag-draped coffins, filling the hungry maw of that airplane. Now, class, these soldiers are already dead, you see. They are merely globs of formerly living human tissue packed in what amount to double-strength resealable sandwich bags. However, if a hajji with a Stinger missile, originally built by an American weapons manufacturer, shot that plane down and killed those men again, blew them into even smaller pieces of tissue, would you consider that to be majorly motherfucking ironic?"

As much as she loved the use of powerful language, Mrs. Bayonne would never say "majorly motherfucking." Except … if she was teaching in Iraq, under the influence of the sandbox, I wasn't so sure. I thought she might have been capable of some very bad words.

Irony was on my mind a lot and that's what made me think of Mrs. Bayonne. I was also starting to see images of the first guy I killed. And the second. And the third. I had sort of put them out of my mind for a while. I never mentioned anything to anybody. I didn't want to get sent to talk to Niehus again, but after the funerals for the Tinman, A.J. and Emilio, I couldn't avoid my own internal questions.

The mission that day was to help secure a route for a resupply convoy coming from southern Iraq to Camp Victory. Our guys covered the roads through Mahmoudiyah, a city of a half-million people, most of them Sunnis, about 25 miles south of Baghdad. Killdozer told us three times during the briefing that the Mahmoudiyah area made up one corner of the Triangle of Death, like we didn't already know that. The thing about buildings in Iraq was, they all had access to the roof. On burning hot nights, families would sleep up there, but snipers could be up there too — wide awake and scoping. The captain went over these details many times. "You probably don't have to sweat too much until the convoy is coming through," he said, "especially the fuel trucks. Think of them as rolling bombs. If you see an RPG launcher or an AK barrel peeking over a roof wall, do whatever it takes to neutralize it. Unleash everything. Do not hold back. Be nimble, be quick, light 'em up with a candlestick."

But we didn't have the manpower to secure every building and it would have created a lot of heartless and mindless blowback if we had barged into homes and businesses to check the roofs. The rules of engagement were tight. So we waited, our Humvees spaced a block apart. We had D-Willie in the driver's seat, me on communications, Amerigo Taymondo as gunner on the .50-caliber, and Benjamin Benum, a private who rode with us occasionally, on utility.

As usual, Killdozer was right. As the fuel convoy came into view, we scanned the rooftops like maniacs, our M-16s off safe. It happened fast. I saw a guy in a black hood with an RPG tube on his shoulder emerge from an alley about 30 yards up the street. *"HAJJI!"* I yelled from my position behind the hood of the Humvee. My trigger finger reacted, squeezing off maybe 10 rounds, and the insurgent went down. As he fell, his RPG whooshed wildly across the street and destroyed a storefront in a flaming explosion.

That blast set off the firefight.

Black hoods and AK-47s popped up along the rooftops. Taymondo went into meat-grinder mode with the .50-caliber. I picked off two more guys but a massive explosion got Dante, A.J. and Emilio in the lead Humvee. There was nothing we could do. It was over in less than a minute. Bodies lay in the street. Civilians ran off screaming. I radioed for medevac.

We took only three casualties, somebody said, it could have been much worse. *Only.* Bitter word. I wondered whether Camp Victory appreciated what it took to get that resupply convoy through. Did anyone tell them? Specialist Dante Yaden, Private First Class A.J. Burwick and Private Emilio Garcia got to go home in body bags in the belly of a C-17, and Camp Victory got its fuel, its lights, its air conditioning, its Internet connections, its microwave ovens, its chocolate pudding.

I kept asking myself how that was a fair trade. I was glad I killed three hajjis. Taymondo wasted six or seven more with the .50-caliber, but when I considered whether that evened the score, my answer was: No way. You lose one of your own — or three — it wouldn't matter if you killed a hundred of the enemy. Nevertheless, killing people was fucking weird. Despite my training, I wasn't exactly ready to do it. When you pulled the trigger, human beings died. They were *gone.* Maybe you get used to it, I thought, and it doesn't bother you, or maybe you're never ready to kill and you do it anyway and feel guilty, or maybe it just becomes a live action video game with unlimited ammo and you keep score, or ... I had to stop thinking about it. That was easier and safer. Confusion might get me killed. Maybe there wasn't even a right answer. Or maybe it was "D — All of the above, depending on your mood and whether anyone you know has been blown up recently."

Something else weird, a couple of days later, Killdozer called us in for a special meeting. "As you know," he said, "General Petraeus toured Baghdad earlier this week. It has come to the attention of the general and CENTCOM that a lot of gratuitously offensive language is getting tossed around in this war. At several forward operating bases, including Viper, the general has seen graffiti and bumper stickers that he thinks are unbecoming of soldiers."

Every man got a you're-bullshitting-us look on his face.

"Going forward," the captain said, "the new rule is, no bumper stickers of any kind will be affixed to any Army vehicle, and we're not allowed to say certain things."

Pete Klug snapped: "Like what, sir?"

"In general, objectionable profanity. Specifically, things like motherfucker. Like camel fucker. Like goat fucker. Like dog fucker. Like donkey dickwad motherfucker."

"Sir, I like donkey dickwad motherfucker. It motivates me."

"That's too bad, Sergeant Klug, because this unit will not be using that epithet anymore. The preferred term is 'enemy combatant.'"

Over a chorus of chuckling, Klug asked, "Captain, how are we supposed to kill these enemy combatant epithets if we can't call them motherfuckers?"

"Didn't your mother ever teach you that if you can't say anything nice about your enemy, don't say anything at all?"

"No, sir. My mother is a better military tactician than General Petraeus."

The room broke into jams-out laughing. Killdozer just stood behind the lectern, frowning, but he let us kick it out. When the hilarity died down, the captain said, "I understand that you think this is ridiculous but the brass is serious about it."

"With all due respect to the brass," Klug said, "I pray to God every night that I'll be able to kill enough of these camel-fucking donkey dickwad enemy combatant motherfuckers to end this war. I can tell you that God has never once complained about my language. All he's ever said is, 'Kill as many of them as you can, son.'"

"God is not your commanding officer."

"With all due respect, sir, are you sure about that? Because God is like an eight-star general. Maybe ten. He definitely outranks Petraeus."

"He's in a different Army," the captain said. "For now, until General Petraeus leaves our area of operation, or until God himself shows up and gives me countermanding orders, that's the rule. And make no mistake, we *will* follow it."

As I lay in my bunk obsessing over the insanity — the firefight, our three dead, the polite language rule — I couldn't get it all to mesh. I wondered if Army lifers ran into this kind of puzzle as they moved up the ladder. Or did they just stop thinking about whether it made sense?

When I got home, I would ask Mrs. Bayonne for her opinion. With her deep understanding of irony and non sequiturs, maybe she could explain it.

6 / Class is seriously in session

Army education was radical. I didn't think about Trillium High School or Coos Bay Community College anymore, other than Mrs. Bayonne's class, which I truly missed. I occasionally wondered what my friends were doing at their jobs, assuming they could get jobs, probably cleaning out the deep fryer at McDonald's. Mostly I pitied their mundane lives, because I was learning extreme stuff, like how to take care of an M-16. Did it matter whether the french fry grease was a week old or a month old? Not to me. Did it matter whether sand clogged your M-16? *Hell, yeah!*

The teachers here were interesting, the exact opposite of Mr. Gargenfarger in junior year trigonometry class. We called him Gaggo because he was always coughing and clearing his throat. It seemed like the only thing he cared about was smoking. We'd see Gaggo in his car before the first bell and during the lunch period, puffing away like a madman with the windows rolled up. He never did explain when we would use trig in our actual lives. The Pythagorean theorem was the only thing that ever stuck in my head, and that was only because the dude who invented it, Pythagoras, had such a cool name. Wait. Was Pythagoras from trig or algebra? I couldn't remember. The hypotenuse no longer mattered. When we needed to get somewhere by the quickest route, we had GPS and the FBCB2 computer.

The teachers in Iraq kept your attention. They were total experts. They could be funny, too, in a grimly random way. Captain Dozinger bumbled into our weapons class one day with a white-tipped cane in one hand and an M-16 in the other. He was wearing a blindfold. In about 90 seconds, he disassembled and reassembled that gun. In the middle of the demo, he said, "Make sure you put a lot of focus on the bolt assembly" — then he threw a silver rod, the firing pin, into the air. He did a half-spin and caught it behind his back. The squad went nuts. "The pin has to be pressed all the way down," the captain cautioned as he inserted it into the bolt, "or you'll get that dead stinking meat feeling when you pull the trigger and nothing happens."

He stood there holding the assembled gun, the blindfold still on, and said, "This'll come in real handy if you're ever a prisoner of war." The half of us who got it laughed like loons on California Skunk. Then he took off the blindfold to reveal that he was wearing some bad-ass wrap-around Stevie Wonder shades underneath. We cheered insanely. He said, "The thing to remember is, treat your gun like your girlfriend. With love and affection — and a lot of oil."

Somebody yelled, "My M-16 is a lot tighter than my girlfriend." Captain Dozinger did a Clint Eastwood. He took off the sunglasses slowly, narrowed his eyes, and rasped: "Well, punk, you gotta ask yourself, Do ya feel lucky? Cause this is one of the most powerful guns in the world and it'll blow your dick clean off."

The Army was teaching us so much. The high-tech gear we got to use was amazing: Geo-positioning modules, location transponders, message encryptors, night-vision goggles, laser spotters, portable radar, the FBCB2. Everybody in our unit got some battlefield medical training. The big question: What should you do first, return fire or apply a CATS tourniquet? The choice was obvious. Now I understood triage. I could put a splint on a fracture, a dressing on an open wound, no problem. I was surely the only guy from Trillium, Oregon, population 420, who could do a needle chest decompression. It looked a lot scarier than it was. I enjoyed the hands-on learning. It meant something: Life or death.

The Army classes made me wonder what public school education would have been like if, say, Gaggo had told us, "Let me stress that, unless you do your homework and learn to calculate the cosine of the periodic function, there's about a 90 percent chance that you will die within two minutes of hemorrhagic shock on the trigonometry battlefield."

All of us would have studied harder and earned better grades. It would have helped if Gaggo had done impressions, too, maybe a Keanu or a Kanye. We probably would have cheered.

7 / Tools of the war trade

We went to bed early, preparing for a middle-of-the-night mission. Intel came in on some Sunni insurgents who had a torture chamber at a house in Baquba. We were assigned to roll on that, raid the place around 0400, and bring in anybody we found. Killdozer looked us all in the eye, though, and said, "If it feels like they don't want to come with us, like it would be a hassle to bring them in, if they resist, we don't need a reason to eliminate the problem. It might even be good advertising."

Knowing you had to get up at 0130 was nerve-racking. About five minutes after lights-out, Earl Sackenwurtz, a new recruit who took over Tim Gulde's bunk, said, "I can't sleep. Tell us a bedtime story, Ulysses."

Ulysses Jackson had become our squad's official storyteller. Not only did he speak Arabic but he also studied journalism in college and worked for the Birmingham News for a year before joining the Army. That was impressive to me because I worked for a semester on my podunk high school newspaper, which we put out on a mimeograph machine. Sheesh, talk about cub reporting.

The U-man could really make words dance and sing but he had to be coaxed. "Forget it, Sack," he said, "I'm trying to sleep here. You should too. We've got to get some tomorrow."

"That's what I'm saying. I wanna sleep but I can't."

From the end of the tent came D-Willie's voice: "Yeah, come on. One story. It won't kill ya."

"All right, one short story. Do you want a fable, a cautionary tale, a life lesson, some narrative fiction, non-fiction, or new journalism?"

"Something with sex in it," Sackenwurtz said. "That helps me sleep."

"Wouldn't it be easier to jack off," Bodie Davis suggested.

"First person, second person, or omniscient narrator?" Ulysses asked.

"First," Sackenwurtz said. "Omniscient sounds too complicated."

"Good choice, Earl. You might have trouble with second person, too. All right, buckle up. It was a June evening. I picked my girlfriend Gloria up in my '69 Camaro. She had a racing stripe, and by that, I mean G-L-O-R-I-A had a racing stripe, not the car. The Camaro had two big red fuzzy dice hanging from the rearview. Gloria had on a small red fuzzy tube top that accentuated what did not need accentuating. She wore short shorts that made her legs look even longer than long. It was around 90 degrees and muggy in Sumterville, the kind of night that made everyone moist and slippery. It was the kind of night when beads of sweat formed on your upper lip, and you needed somebody who was willing to lick them off, real slowly, somebody who didn't get prissy about a little salt and a little tang. We took off for Mobile because we got it in our heads that we wanted to make it on the beach."

"From here to maternity," Davis yelled.

"No," Ulysses said definitively. "You've got to know when to hold it, know when to enfold it. We got there around two in the morning. The only thing you could hear was the water washing in and swooshing out. It was smooth, hypnotic, relentless … in-and-out, in-and-out, in-and-out. Those Gulf waves were lapping at the shore and we were lapping at each other. Somehow, Gloria lost her tube top. She asked me to help her find it. The air was so warm and so thick, I asked her if she really needed a top. She said, 'No, I guess I don't.' The waxing moon put her naked, sui generis breasts into stark silhouette. We put down a beach towel and started to get a monumental groove on. After about 20 minutes, Gloria said to me, 'When we get married, I want you to fuck me every night until I can't walk anymore.' And I said to her, 'Won't that make it difficult for you to get around?' And she said, 'I don't care. I'll buy a motorized scooter and follow you wherever you go.' And that was the night I learned a lesson about the most important thing a woman can have. Does anybody know what that is?"

"Sweet generous breasts," Sackenwurtz said.

"Negative."

"Long legs?" D-Willie said.

"Nice try."

"A motorized scooter?" Davis asked.

"You're hopeless, Bodie," Ulysses said. "No. The most important thing to find in a woman is a sense of humor. Sweet dreams. We gotta get us some 'surgents tomorrow."

Davis wasn't satisfied. "So how does the story end?" he asked. "Did you marry her?"

"No, Bodie, we broke up. Now go to sleep."

We rolled a little after 0230, a total of 22 guys spread out over six Humvees. With our full-on gear, night vision goggles, Kevlar everything, M-16s and enough ammo to take down a minaret, we were dressed to kill. It was weird how you got used to walking around in all that shit. When you weren't wearing it, you felt almost weightless, like you could float away in a breeze.

Killdozer, Klug and Ulysses took the lead Humvee. D-Willie, Taymondo and I rolled behind them, with everyone else following. The convoy was a big serpent, a writhing target. A crucial job was to watch for spotters, even in the dark, a tiny glowing screen, dim little blips of light, the telltale LEDs of death. An Iraqi who got on his cell could be detonating a bomb or calling to alert his trigger man up the road. Making a cell phone call near American Humvees was a good way to get shot. The constant explosions were making us very twitchy. Most Iraqis knew that. The ones who called anyway were probably bad guys. What was so important that you had to talk at just that moment, as we were rolling by? What about a guy who made a hand signal or looked at us the wrong way? What if he was just an angry civilian? There were a lot of them.

I asked the captain about that. "You trust your instinct," he said. "Your body will tell you who's a bad guy. Listen to your gut. You see a guy watching you or acting like he's *not* watching you, but then he takes a peek, the wrong kind of peek, chances are good he's an insurgent. You could find a reason to take him out, not only to save your own life but the lives of your buddies. You'll know when to do it."

"What if my gut is wrong?" I said.

"First of all, never ask that question. And second of all" — Killdozer shrugged — "it's collateral damage. Mistakes happen. We'll give the family a condolence payment for their loss. They'll be satisfied. Three grand goes a long way in Iraq."

So far, I hadn't faced the collateral damage decision. I hoped I never would but it seemed like every Iraqi had a cell phone, even little kids. For sure, all the teenagers and adult males. The women were probably texting under their burqas. Cell phones everywhere. Any one of them could trigger a roadside bomb and kill you. It was easy to hate cells. Where did all those phones come from? What did the Iraqis have to talk about? Apparently you could call or text anybody in the country to give them your status update: The electricity went out again, the water dripping from our tap is brown, and the goat died, but Allah surely will smile upon us soon. Most Iraqis were unemployed, so how could they afford all those phones? Were cell phones the only thing in Iraq that actually worked?

Fortunately, the highway north to Baquba was deserted. When we hit the outskirts of the city, Killdozer got on the radio and warned us, for about the ninth time since we left Baghdad, to be alert and keep in a tight-but-not-too-tight formation. The captain was like our mom. He could be annoying, the way he repeated everything. We all had the GPS coordinates of the terror house but, yeah, OK, the convoy needed to stay within visual contact. Say a Toyota "Taliban van" cut in front of you and hit the brakes. It meant one of two things: There were jihadis on a nearby rooftop with rocket-propelled grenade launchers ready to take you out, or the van was loaded with artillery shells and ball bearings, and the driver was about to hit the fuck-me button. The blast would send the driver to Allah, and he would take a few of us with him, though the more I thought about it, the more I realized we were definitely not going with him to Allah's crib, because, logically, it couldn't be a one-track same-place deal.

Come on, if we were going to the same exalted place, then what were we fighting about? Wouldn't Allah be mightily pissed off at both sides when we got there? Seriously, were we going anywhere except in the ground, whatever pieces were left of us? And by the way, where the hell was our God? Why did he let all this shit happen? Lately he seemed like a sorry-ass excuse for an all-knowing all-powerful being. Was he so busy that he couldn't get on his heavenly cell and let us know a suicide bomber lurked around the corner, and maybe we ought to take Dog Meat Avenue instead of Saddam Boulevard? Couldn't he arrange for a dropped call from a cell phone detonator?

We were a few blocks from the house. The city was still dark and quiet, a good sign. Killdozer got on the radio again: "OK, it's going down just like we talked about. Headlights off, please. Park 'em on the street along the wall. As soon as everybody is on the ground and in formation, I'll go through the gate and you follow me in. Taymondo stays behind on the .50-cal. We're three minutes to target."

I looked at Taymondo. He gave me a thumb's-up. He loved the .50 and was a deadeye shot with it, therefore, he always got assigned to stay behind atop the Humvee and intimidate anybody who might wander around to see what the ruckus was. If there were bad guys, RPG guys out to mess with our Vees, he would take care of them.

We crept along, barely 10 miles an hour, trying to keep the engine noise down. We turned onto a stylish palm-dotted street lined with large-box houses, all various shades of Iraqi brown. With sunup about an hour away, the black of night was giving way to deepest darkest blue. Killdozer stopped his Vee about 50 yards from the end of the street and put on his left turn signal. Amusing. Wouldn't want to get a ticket. D-Willie maneuvered past on the left and parked on the shoulder, just beyond a big wooden gate to the compound. The other Vees pulled in behind us. We made a little noise as we got out — you couldn't help it, the Vees were such clangy tin cans — but it almost didn't matter. The surprise factor was going away; I noted a few lights switching on up and down the block in other houses.

So far, the terror house was dark, which was either very good or very bad.

Killdozer backed up in a little quarter-turn, aiming the Humvee at the gate. The men massed on each side of it. The Humvee's high-beams flashed on and Dozer floored it. Six-point-five liters of diesel-guzzling American motor roared. The Humvee crashed through the gate like it was a Lego model. The Vee played the role of gigantic football lineman, opening up a hole. We fullbacks rushed through it. Killdozer slammed on the brakes in the middle of a sandy courtyard. His Vee skidded to a stop with a gritty screech. The men charged ahead and we kicked in the front door. Ulysses yelled in Arabic, "Nobody move, get on the floor," or something like that.

But nobody was home.

We went from room to room, expecting to find at least a few bad guys cowering in closets or hiding under beds. They would claim to be lowly restaurant workers or goatherds — living in a ritzy Sunni neighborhood. But no. Nobody home. Ulysses made a good find, a bomb-making manual printed in Arabic. Overall, the mission was a disappointment. Also a relief. Nobody died.

Uh, nobody on our side died. We found a strange door inside a bedroom closet. It led to a hidden basement room. We threw a tear-gas canister down the stairs and shut the door. We aimed our weapons at the closet. If anyone came coughing and sputtering up those steps, we might have to give him the M-16 cure. But all was quiet. After 10 minutes, we opened the door and let the basement air out. We switched on the light and went down.

We found three dead men, presumably Shiites, and a video camera on a tripod. The tape was missing but it was easy to figure out what they were recording. Iraq was a twisted snake of a place. The concrete floor was caked with dried blood. Most of it must have come from the fattest of the three — that body was missing its head. Maybe a gallon of blood had leaked out.

"Check this out," Pete Klug said. He nudged one of the still-attached heads with his boot. The face was streaked with blood, like it had been painted by a drunk with a stick and a can of burnt umber.

"Look at the forehead," Klug said.

At first I didn't see the hole through all the gunk but then: "Oh, yeah. That must have hurt."

Klug gave the other head a nudge and said, "Got a migraine here too." He pointed to a workbench along the wall opposite the stairs. We walked over and saw a couple of hammers, a screwdriver, a chisel, a crowbar, a vise and an electric drill, which Klug picked up. He gave the trigger a quick squeeze. *Vazheerrrrrr!* Some pink goop flew off the bit and stuck to the wall.

"That's a big-ass drill," Klug said. "I hope these crunk fuckers never get ahold of band saws."

"Or wood chippers," Bodie Davis added.

8 / What's in a nickname?

When we got a day off, most of us would kick back and do absolutely nothing. The object was to clear the mind of images from previous missions. You didn't want some of those pictures to imprint. A smiling Iraqi kid giving you a high-five while on patrol, yes. That kept us going but you didn't want to carry other things home with you, assuming you made it home. Some of it was real nightmare wake-up-screaming stuff. So it was healthy to push it aside with a stupid movie on DVD or mindless weightlifting in the dusty gym.

Or with popcorn.

We were bunked out and vegging on a Sunday when Ulysses Jackson walked in, carrying a big cardboard box. It had a bunch of red "fragile" stickers on it, plus about 50 stamps. "Listen up," he announced. "If any of you jack-offs would like to live vicariously — assuming you know what 'vicariously' means — then you are cordially invited to watch me open this package, which I have been saving for a cerebral occasion such as this."

"Is it from Osama?" Pete Klug asked. "Did you find it by the side of the road? I don't want to die vicariously."

"It's from my mother."

"Does she like you?"

"She loves me."

"I'm listening," Klug said.

"Mom asked me if I needed anything and I mentioned that the food here sucks: Meals Ready to Excrete. Then this package arrived. As far as I'm concerned, there are only two things worth dying for. One is a package from home. The other is … give me a minute … I'm thinking … oh, yeah, Iraqi freedom."

"Right," Bodie Davis said. "Open that sucker up."

We gathered as Ulysses cut through layers of tape with his Ka-Bar.

"It's like Christmas," D-Willie said.

"Except it's 112 degrees out and I'm not feeling the snow," Klug said.

We pushed in close as Ulysses peeled back the top flaps.

"Oh my God," Davis said.

Ulysses pulled out a popcorn machine and maybe two dozen bags of popcorn. We let out a mighty "YEAH, BABY" cheer accompanied by high-fives.

"It's the Sunday cage match," Klug said in a deep announcer voice. "Orville Redenbacher vs. al-Qaida. Who will prevail?"

Popcorn reminded me of home but not necessarily in a good way. Mom used to make it. Dad was occasionally there in those days and we would sit around munching for an hour or so, maybe watching TV. It was the only time Dad asked me about school. He teased me because English was my favorite subject. "Good luck getting a job because you can quote from 'Remembrance of Things Pissed,'" he once cracked. I didn't get that one until later. When I understood the reference, I had to give him some respect for saying something both funny and literary. Maybe I underestimated him.

Ulysses loaded the popper and fired it up. When it really got going, Davis said, "Just like a thousand little IEDs."

"Never say that word," Klug warned, slashing a finger across his throat. "It's bad luck."

The aroma of corn and cooking oil was a nice change from diesel and kerosene. As we kicked back and waited, Amerigo Taymondo got a conversation started: "Why does everybody call the captain Killdozer?"

I had an idea: "Isn't it just a short version of his real name? Kyle Dozinger ... Killdozer."

Davis said, "Lame, Cutter. I heard snipers had Dozer pinned down in a burned-out building in Sadr City. His radio was dead and he'd been awake for 24 hours. He slumps against a wall and falls asleep with his M-16 cradled across his chest. He *dozes* off. Get it? A Mahdi army guy walks up to him and pulls out a pistol. Before the Mahdi can shoot him, Killdozer — *who is still asleep* — empties his clip into the guy."

"Mahdi go bye-bye," D-Willie said.

Klug banged a spoon on a glass to get our attention, like he was going to make a toast. "All right, enough with the speculation. Yeah, Killdozer is amazing with an M-16 but it's not the real story. You didn't hear this from me but he was about to knock down a terror house with a D9 bulldozer, and a couple of hajjis sneak up with a bomb and try to plant it under the tread. If they could blow the tread off, the D9 could only go in circles. Luckily, at that moment, Killdozer does a little backwards pivot to line up with the front of the house. Unluckily, one of the hajjis gets his feet caught. The other one runs. So the hajji is on the ground, screaming, pinned by the tread, his feet crushed. Dozer gets off the D9 to see what's up. The bomb is sitting right under the back of the D9. Killdozer points at the bomb and says, '*Qillat al-adab.*'"

Klug paused to let that scene register. We looked at Ulysses, who explained, "That means the hajji was being rude. He had no manners."

Klug nodded. "Then Dozer points at the crying hajji and says, '*Mustashfa, you want to go to mustashfa?*'"

We looked to Ulysses again for the translation. "Hospital," he said.

Klug continued, "So the hajji is screaming, '*Yes, please, yes*' — in English. And Killdozer says, 'I'll call Osama and see if he can come pick you up.' The hajji gets this Arabic what-the-fuck look. No translation needed. Killdozer climbs into the driver's seat and backs up. The D9 weighs 50 tons and it rolls lengthwise over the hajji. It squeezes him like a ketchup packet. See, there's righteous cosmic blowback here. They never got the bomb set for detonation, so the hajji is the one that explodes like a bag of blood hit with a sledgehammer. Then Killdozer bulldozes the terror house and drives off. There's nothing left of the house. There's nothing left of the hajji. The universe is in balance."

"Fuckin'-A, that's what I call a nickname," D-Willie said.

We sat there awhile, letting Klug's explanation sink in. Maybe that was the real story, or maybe it was just a story, but it was easy to imagine. Crazy shit like that happened in Iraq. If you stopped to think about it — like we were at that very moment — you could get seriously creeped out, which was bad for the mission.

Fortunately, Ulysses started handing out bowls of popcorn. We munched like maniacs, prompting Klug to say, "Anybody want to watch a zombie movie?"

We did. It would go well with the popcorn. Diversion was good for the mission.

9 / Our very special treat

At the end of a morning briefing, Captain Dozinger said, "Now I have a special announcement. We've been invited to hear Paul Bremer and Prime Minister Maliki speak in the Green Zone tomorrow. I'm all wet with a very special excitement that I have expressed in private with some personal lubricant and my howitzer."

Not everybody got Killdozer but I understood sarcasm. Mrs. Bayonne spent a week on it in lit class. Plus, I already had a well-developed internal sarcasm meter, which I got from Mom. It didn't develop, it just happened, about 10 years ago. Killdozer's expression made me remember. It was one of those cold gray rainy Coast Range afternoons. The school bus dropped me off and I tramped home. The road to our house wasn't paved, so my shoes got muddy. When I walked in, Mom came running up to greet me. She said, "Hello, my wonderful son. You're so special that I made fresh chocolate chip cookies. Can you smell them? After you have some cookies and milk, I'm going to let you play video games until dinnertime. For dinner, I'm going to make you the biggest juiciest cheeseburger you've ever had, and dessert is going to be some more cookies, along with apple pie that is in the oven right now. You'll be having homemade vanilla ice cream with your pie, too. After dinner, I'm going to put a gold crown on your head because you're the special little king of the world."

"Really?" I said.

"No, you thoughtless little brat!" she yelled. "Look at your shoes. Look at the floor. It's filthy. Now get outside and take those shoes off, then get a rag and clean up this mess. Don't you ever wear muddy shoes into this house again. Do you hear me?"

Loud and clear. I didn't get the cookies, the cheeseburger or the pie, but suddenly I got sarcasm.

Killdozer told us we also had tomorrow off but his face reminded me of Mom's, with that curled lip and the disgusted head shake. There were some hoots and hollers, like the guys might be happy about this field trip to the Green Zone, unlike Captain Dozinger. I looked around for Pete Klug. What was his face saying? Klug was in the back of the room, with the same fuck-this-silly-shit look as Killdozer.

The captain said, "I've been told that everybody should bring their cell phones or cameras. We'll meet here at 1200 for the ride to the mighty walled fortress of solitude. Don't be late, gentlemen. This is a forced march."

The Green Zone was a mystery to me. I'd only driven by it on patrols. There was nothing much to see on the outside except miles and miles of concrete blast walls, at least 10 feet tall. I'd heard that inside the perimeter blast walls, there were more blast walls, and beyond those interior blast walls, you had to get past a final layer of even more blast walls. On a busy day, it could take hours to get through security, especially for the Iraqis who worked there, but once inside, you could walk around without a flak vest or helmet. You were *safe*. You could relax. No IEDs, no suicide bombers, no snipers. Supposedly there were restaurants and swimming pools — *in the middle of Baghdad*. Amazing. Saddam's palace, on the banks of the Tigris, rose up in the Zone like a mega-marble wet dream with toilets made of gold. Maybe that was why the captain told us to bring our cameras.

I wondered if they would let us shit in the gold toilets. Klug wouldn't turn up his nose at that, would he? That truly would be special, a big upgrade from when you were on patrol. You were in bad trouble in the middle of a mission, out in the sandbox, on your way to nowhere, if your gut started to cramp up. The sweat would start to roll down your forehead, burning your eyes. It was constipation sweat, not regular Iraq sweat. Our MREs didn't seem to have fiber in them. They were more like intestinal superglue than food. You could eat six or eight of them, a couple of days' worth, and nothing would happen. Then the ninth meal would have no place to go — logjam — and suddenly your gut gave you the two-minute warning. "I gotta find a place to stop," you'd tell the Humvee driver. That was code. "Can't you hold it?" he would say. "For two more minutes," you would tell him. "Then I'll be forced to let loose right here in the Vee, if that meets with your approval." It was brinksmanship, the nuclear option, the very real threat of a bummer in the

Hummer. Nobody wanted that. The driver always stopped. Of course, if you forgot to bring a WAG bag, you'd have a shituation on your hands, maybe literally. If you had to squat by the side of the road, a sniper might put a bullet in your ass. If you didn't have any toilet paper in the Humvee, you were also screwed.

Once we had a reporter who was embedded with our unit for a couple of weeks and he was always pestering the guys for story ideas. I heard Klug tell him, "You should write about where we shit. You know, like in the middle of the desert, or the Euphrates, or the Tigris, or the reeds by a canal, or the rubble of a building, or you break into an abandoned house, only it doesn't have running water, but you and six other guys have to use its toilet anyway. You could interview the guy who's last at that party. It would be a real scoop. It's the dark underbelly of the war that nobody ever writes about. Actually, it's the dark underpants."

The reporter didn't get Klug and looked at him like he needed psychiatric help. Klug smiled and said, "I'm serious, you'd get a lot of good digestive disaster quotes. It would make great bathroom reading."

"Interesting," the reporter said, "maybe I'll check into that." Then he walked away and didn't bother Klug anymore. Mom would like Klug, I thought. I hoped she could meet him someday.

We got to the Green Zone just before 1300 hours the next afternoon. The speeches were supposed to begin at 1600, so we had enough time to get through the security maze.

Our platoon took its place in line on the road leading into the Zone. It wasn't moving. It was nearing 120 degrees. Sometimes we drank our water, sometimes we just poured it on our faces. D-Willie was driving and when we weren't moving, he would shut off the engine. "I'm trying to save gas," he said. "The insurgents blew up another pipeline a few days ago."

We creeped, stopped, started. Inside the first ring of walls, D-Willie said, "This is weird, Ghost. Something's up."

"What?" I said.

"Check out the Apaches." He pointed toward helicopters buzzing overhead. "That ain't normal."

I saw four of them, darting, hovering, meandering around the perimeter of the Zone. In about an hour, we reached the next security checkpoint. A soldier holding a clipboard asked us for our names and unit, and he checked us off. The line moved ahead and D-Willie said, "Think about it, Ghost, why are so many Apaches on the case? You think that's normal?"

"I don't know what normal is."

We went through two more checkpoints, one of them staffed by four Blackwater guards. A couple of them looked under our Humvee. "What the fuck are you looking for, Blackwater?" D-Willie asked. "You think we might have a bomb under this tin can? Guess what. We spend our time trying *not* to fucking get blown up."

Their beefy leader slung his M-16 off his shoulder and crossed it over his chest bandoleer-style. He turned his baseball cap backwards, took three steps toward the driver's side door and got right up in D-Willie's face. Their noses were nearly touching. The Blackwater dude wore a pair of dark wraparound shades so you couldn't see his eyes. His face was piggy pink, his chin was covered with a slimy goatee, and he had one of those barbed-wire tattoos around his left bicep. He was a real Mr. Cool. Disgusting. "Do you want to get in to see the man, or do you want me to send you back to your pup tent?" he said in a low growl.

"Fuck the man," D-Willie spit back. "Don't you have anything better to do than hassle the guys fighting the war for you?"

Blackwater Cool took two steps back and pointed his M-16 at D-Willie's head, but D stared him down silently. The guard said, "Why don't you step out of the vehicle, boy."

"Why don't you brush your tooth and play your banjo, Southern Muthafucker Man."

A horn honked somewhere back in the distance. I heard a metallic click — Blackwater Cool taking his M-16 off safe. "Step out of the vehicle," he said, "and don't make me tell you again, boy."

I thought he was about to kill us both. With one bullet.

"Is there a problem?" It was the amazing Killdozer, walking back from a couple of vehicles ahead of us. The captain had a special sense: He always knew where trouble was about to ignite.

Blackwater Cool's meaty head swiveled toward Killdozer like a .50-caliber machine gun. "Who the fuck are you?" he asked.

"Captain Kyle Dozinger, commander of Bravo Company, 2nd Battalion. These are my men. Let them pass."

"Assholes don't get in."

Killdozer moved closer to Blackwater Cool and whispered something. Cool said out loud, "You think so?"

The captain's left hand whipped through the air, latched onto the barrel of Blackwater Cool's M-16 and pointed it at the sky. Without mercy, sidestepping at light speed, the captain put Cool in a chokehold with his right arm. Killdozer bent backwards, lifting the burly guard off the ground, holding him there until his face turned purple. As Blackwater Cool passed out, his hand slipped off his gun. The captain released his anaconda hold. The inert unconscious body smashed into the asphalt like a 220-pound bag of warm worthless shit.

"I know so," the captain said. He took the clip out of Cool's M-16 and handed it to D-Willie, who passed it over to me. In about five seconds, the captain disassembled the gun, dropping each piece on the ground, except for the firing pin, which he threw into a lake next to the road. He turned to the other Blackwater Cools, who had moved 10 paces back, and said, "Wave my men through. And get your boy some water. Looks like the sun got to him."

Killdozer started walking back to his Humvee. The Cools stepped aside smartly as he passed between them. D-Willie tapped the gas and we were rolling. "Cracker muthafucker," he said. "Turn his baseball cap backwards on my ass? He had Mississippi written all over him. Fugly muthafucker's gonna kill somebody someday. I hate those rent-a-cop thousand-dollar-a-day muthafuckers."

"Those what?"

"Rent-a-cop thousand-dollar-a-day muthafuckers."

"You mean a thousand dollars a week."

"No. I mean a day. Those Blackwater fucks make $300,000 a year. And they don't even go into combat."

"Are you kidding me?"

"I tell ya, Ghost, those Blackwater brotherfuckers are getting paid out the ying-yang. You didn't know that? It frosts my ass."

What a shock. I was never a money guy. I hardly knew what it was. Our family seemed poor. Not that I thought about it that much, but our house was ramshackle. The paint was peeling and the front porch sagged, but every house in town looked like that. Partly, the weather was to blame, always wet, and even if the gray went away, the sun couldn't poke down through all the trees. One year, the roof started to leak. The living room ceiling got a huge water stain in December after a pounding rainstorm. Mom freaked, of course. It was maybe a year after Dad had left us for the first time. "Johnny, we've got to get a tarp," she said. "We don't have the money to fix this right now." At least we had enough money to buy a blue plastic camping tarp. Mom and I climbed up on our rusty trusty extension ladder and laid that tarp down, putting old bricks around the edge of the roof. When I left for basic training five years later, I took a last look back. That tarp was still up there, no longer blue, all the mold had turned it green, but it was holding on.

Those memories came back when we got through the last layer of blast walls, as Saddam's palace came into full view. "That's insane," I said to D-Willie.

"Yeah, it's ours now."

"The palace?"

"Yeah, we took it over."

"Have you ever seen it?"

"Nope, only heard about it."

It was 70 or 80 feet tall. The entrance had a gigantic column on each side of a huge archway that came to a point at the top. Everywhere you looked there were smaller versions of the archway. The palace appeared to be made of stone, big beige blocks. It covered an area the size of three or four football fields and was surrounded by lakes. Or was it a moat? As we rolled by, I saw a soldier casting a fishing line into the water. I wondered what he might catch. Piranha? Shark? Firing pins?

After parking, we passed another security checkpoint to get inside the palace. It rearranged my brain. I felt like a backwoods Oregon hick. Our civics class piled into a rickety old bus one time for a field trip to Salem to see the Legislature "in action." I was impressed with the Capitol, the gold pioneer statue on top of the building, the big staircases on either side of the entrance leading to the Senate and House chambers. We peeked in the governor's office. He wasn't there. We studied the big portrait of Tom McCall standing on the beach with a strange little heli-

copter behind him. We trudged up to the Senate gallery to listen for a
while. They were supposed to be talking about money for schools,
which is why we went in the first place. All we heard was video poker
this and lottery formula that. We got bored fast and booked out of
there, but the building was nice. Now, comparing it to Saddam's — I
mean, our — palace, I realized the Oregon Capitol was a broom closet.

Inside the palace, we were escorted by two more Blackwater Cools. I
started burning about how much those suck fucks got paid for strutting
around doing nothing. We passed through a huge round open area.
Maybe 30 feet above us hung a gaudy crystal chandelier. Pairs of dark
stone columns supported the top half of the building. The floor was
laid out in a geometric pattern of light and dark marble.

We walked on through a 15-foot-wide hallway that had the same
pattern in its floor. Soon we were herded into a marble hall where Bremer and Maliki were going to speak. A roped-off section at the front
was jammed with reporters and photographers. Why? Folding chairs
had been set up for the troops. Our unit grabbed seats near the back of
the hall. Hundreds of soldiers were already sitting down. We waited for
about an hour. Finally, an Iraqi in a suit came out and sat at a long table
in front, up on a stage. I guessed it was Maliki. I honestly couldn't have
recognized him, but the crowd got quiet. Then a guy we did recognize
walked out:

President Bush.

The room erupted in cheers and howls and whistles.

"Are you kidding me?" said Pete Klug. "Why is the draft-dodger
here? This is a combat zone."

Guys held their cell phones and cameras aloft to snap pictures but
our company was subdued. I looked around and mostly saw a bunch of
dissing faces. Losing guys we knew from FOB Viper made it impossible
to cheer for the man Klug called "the poser in chief." Whenever Klug
got overly frustrated with the war, he would tell the story of Bush's
timely and mysterious entry into the National Guard to evade the draft
during Vietnam. Klug had a sore spot for Dick Cheney, too, who got
five deferments back in the day. I wasn't sure what I was feeling but it
hit me that I had never thought about politics before. I had never voted.
I was too young when Bush won his first term and I didn't get regis-

tered for the 2004 election, despite Viper's relentless push advising every soldier to vote absentee — for the commander in chief. I tried to remember who he was running against but I couldn't. Maybe I should have paid more attention. Not that it would have mattered.

When the cheering died down, Bush said he had come to look Maliki in the eye to see if he was dedicated to a free Iraq. Captain Dozinger, sitting behind us, snorted at that one. "That's a long trip for nothing," he muttered. Killdozer was usually a raging gung-ho complete-the-mission Army-to-the-bone fanatic, but he could explode into cynicism without warning if something lit his fuse.

The Blackwater Cools eyed us. I guess they thought we weren't into the president as much as we should have been. The more I looked at Bush, the more his smile seemed plastered on. I wondered if the Cools would toss us out. I wondered if Bush believed what he was telling the Iraqis: "The fate of this nation is in your hands."

From what I'd seen, the fate of Iraq was in *our* hands. We were the ones out there busting our asses, taking mortar hits, running over IEDs, getting cut down by snipers. The Iraqi army, if you could call it an army, mostly stood around smoking cigarettes. It could piss you off if you stopped to think about it. Speaking of pissing, I said to Klug, "I want to go see the gold toilets. You in?"

"I don't know if we can get out of here."

"I've got a plan," I said. "I ate too much last night."

"OK," he said, smiling. "Let's blow this poop stand."

We squeezed past a half-dozen guys and plopped out of the row near the back door. The lead Blackwater Cool focused his wraparound shades on us like a cyborg. I walked right up to him and said, "We've got an emergency."

"What?" he snarled.

"We're both like 90 seconds away from shitting ourselves." I put on a googed-up grimace for his consumption.

He shook his head. "Nobody leaves till it's over."

Letting out an intestinal rumble, I latched on to my stomach with both hands and squeezed. "OK," I groaned, bending at the waist, "but I can't be responsible for what happens. The baby's coming. I'm gonna have it right here. I've got to warn you, I had three MREs last night:

Cheese and Vegetable Omelette, Chicken Fajitas and Jambalaya."

The menu was magic. Blackwater Cool opened the door and practically pushed us out. "It's down the hall," he said.

We walked around for about 10 minutes, gawking at this crazy building that seemed like the equivalent of a pyramid built for a pharaoh. The place was deserted. Everybody must have cleared out for the Bush visit. We pushed open every door we came to, offices, closets, and finally a bathroom.

"It's the yellow brick road shithouse," Klug said. "We ain't in Kansas anymore."

It was ridiculous, maybe 20 feet on each side and 15 feet tall, with a row of windows up high that let in a lot of light. The floor-to-ceiling tiles were cream-colored, flecked randomly with rainbow hues. Tilesetter must have been a good job in Iraq, because you saw tile everywhere. One wall was fronted by a green marble sink, about the size of a bathtub, with gold faucets. A gigantic mirror in an ornate gold frame hung above the sink. A massive L-shaped overstuffed purple couch filled up one corner. "What's that for?" I said.

Klug flopped down on it, lying back with his hands clasped behind his head. "Good question, since this is the women's bathroom."

An inspection of the toilet proved, disappointingly, that it apparently was made of marble, not gold, although the flush handle and water pipe appeared to be gold. There was also a smaller toilet next to the main one. It was odd — no seat, no water tank.

"What's the deal on this thing?" I said.

"You don't get out much, do you, Cutter. That's a ... you've never seen a personal face washer?"

"A personal face washer?"

"You've never used one?"

"No. I don't think we have these in Oregon. Is it just for hot places?"

"Yeah, you could say that. Give it a try. Just stick your face down over the sprinkler thingie in the middle and turn the water on full blast. I think you'll find it's very refreshing."

Might as well, I thought, when will I ever be in one of Saddam's bathrooms again? I kneeled, closed my eyes and twisted the handles. Cool water spurted up and I turned from side to side to give each cheek some spray action. "You're right, this feels great," I said. "It tickles."

"Yeah, I imagine it does," Klug said, "especially when it gets really wet." Then he burst into loud echoing laughter. I looked up and water splashed all over the marble floor. From the edge of the couch, Klug snapped a photo of me with his cell phone. "It's a bidet," he said, "not a personal face washer, although I've never seen you look more radiant."

"A bee day? What's a bee day?"

"It's a ... how do I put this? ... it's for *girls*, Cutter. They go, they move next door to the bidet, and they ... freshen up. You've almost got it." Klug snorted like a warthog and took another picture, the one that ended up on the barracks bulletin board, with my soaking wet face all confused and contorted. Right next to that shot was a photo of President Bush from the palace appearance, grinning like Alfred E. Neuman and flashing the V sign. Some smart-ass tacked a handwritten headline over the two of us:

Johnny Cutter practices
Bush interrogation techniques

10 / No power to the people

"Who wants to do a good deed tomorrow?" Captain Dozinger asked at our mission update. "Who wants to *nation-build?*" You could have heard a firing pin drop. The captain scanned the room with his squinty sniper-spotting eyes. He met vacant stares.

"Tough crowd," Killdozer said. "Let me put it a different way. There's something called the Office of Reconstruction. They're bean-counters from Washington and they're here to help. By help, I mean they're here to fuck us in the foxhole without any lubricant. I'm here to tell you that it's a real invasion of your personal space."

Dozinger expected us to crack up. Normally we would have at least whistled, or shouted "yeah, baby," or done a quick air jack-off. No way would our unit have remained comatose.

Unless …

We were punking Killdozer. Pete Klug came up with the plan after amping us for a few days on his stash of Romero and Fulci films. "Let's fuck with Dozer tomorrow," he said. "No matter what the captain says at the meeting, we just sit there like we're drooling brain-dead zombies in some whacked-out cult."

"You mean like Pentecostals?" Bodie Davis said.

"Yeah, but with less snakes and more gibberish," Klug explained. Since he was our squad leader, he would lead the zombie uprising, beginning with his signal, one quick boot stomp. We were stoked on this rebellion. Word spread quickly.

So Killdozer was looking at about 50 vacant-eyed guys, staring straight ahead at nothing, but he just kept slogging. That was his style. Nothing fazed him. This would be a test of wills. "The Defense Department needs better numbers," he said. "The bean-counters have been noticing how much electricity the Iraqis have, and the answer is, even less than they had when Saddama-rama was in power. They've also been counting up the number of barrels of oil being pumped in

Iraq, and, surprise, it's even less than when Saddama-lama-ding-dong was doing his thang-a-lang. This may come as a surprise, but they're also figuring out how much clean water the Iraqis have, and the answer is — "

Killdozer pointed an accusatory index finger at us and swept it from one side of the room to the other. "Anyone?" he said. Nobody cracked; the zombie wall held.

"OK, the answer is, even less than when Saddama-yo-mama was wetting his whistle on camel penises. Now we all know the insurgents have leveled half the country and we've leveled the other half. Still, the geniuses at the Office of Reconstruction don't understand why the Iraqis are worse off than before we invaded."

The captain laid a long interrogation stare on us and got nothing. He plowed on: "So they decided yesterday that this is a problem. Now they want us to fix it by tomorrow — because a report is going to come out and they're going to look bad. So I repeat my question: Does anybody want to do some *nation-building?* Our unit is going to provide cover in Fallujah for a very big, very important, very connected American contractor that's coming in to repair an electricity distribution station. That's the bad news. The good news is, they're going to use the power to run the neon lights at the only Islamic strip club in Iraq."

Bam! Pete Klug's boot hit the floor and he stood up. We all rose with him. "Strip club," Klug said in a guttural undead zombie voice. "Strip club." He lurched slowly toward Killdozer and the rest of the unit followed. We extended our arms in front of us and clomped our boots in unison on the flimsy floor of the double-wide. The whole trailer vibrated. "Strip club … strip club," we chanted.

Killdozer held up his M-16 and shouted: "Don't make me go Blackwater on your sorry zombie asses."

"Strip club" … *clomp* … "strip club" … *clomp.*

The zombie army kept pressing in on Dozer. We backed him into a corner. "After we complete this mission," he yelled, "everybody gets two days off."

Klug thrust his fist in the air and screamed: *"Hooah, two days off!"* The rest of us, following his lead, also began to howl: *"Hooah, two days off! Hooah, two days off!"*

After whooping and whistling and moshing around Killdozer, we settled down and returned to our chairs to listen to his description of the mission logistics. He started by saying, "I don't know who the bigger zombies are, the clueless Washington brain-eaters or you guys. Oh, wait. Let me think. Yeah, I guess I do know."

The next morning, we rolled west out of Forward Operating Base Viper at 0600 hours. The sun was rising, the golden light was beautiful and the temperature was a balmy 74 degrees. It was about 40 miles to Fallujah, an hour's drive if nothing went wrong, but something always went wrong in Iraq. It wasn't possible for everything to work. The dividing line was survival. When stuff went wrong and nobody died, that was fine. When stuff went wrong and we lost a guy, that was when we cursed God, Allah, the Sunnis, the Shiites, the Washington zombies, the sandbox wasteland. I made a mental note to ask Captain Dozinger what the point was, why were we leveling Iraq if we were just going to rebuild it? Mrs. Bayonne would have called that a non sequitur or a logical fallacy.

We'd been rolling for about half an hour when the convoy began to slow. Change was bad. We got used to the whining drone of the road noise, the throb of the engine. When that changed unexpectedly, something was up. We had about 30 guys distributed between a Humvee with a .50-caliber up front, three troop-carrying trucks in the middle and another Humvee with a .50 in the rear. We could fit only eight guys in the back of each truck because we had so much gear, food, water, fuel and weapons.

"What the hell," Klug said as our truck chugged to a stop. "Weapons ready," he ordered. "Everybody out." We grabbed our M-16s and jumped out the back. We froze in position, looking to the west. There were no cars on the highway, which was good, because maybe 10 klicks away was a monster wall of swirling brown hell.

"It's a *shamal*," Ulysses Jackson said. "That's Arabic for 'bitch plague of sand.'"

Klug said, "I don't think we're going to Fallujah today." The storm extended at least 10,000 feet into the air. It turned the bottom half of the sky brown. Above the raggedy top edge of the sand wall, the sky was blue and cloudless. It reminded me of one of those modern art paintings. A blue band and a brown band. All it needed was a yellow circle somewhere. Nature's art. The canvas was about 50 miles wide.

Klug walked up to confer with Captain Dozinger. It was a short meeting. He ran back. "Saddle up," he said. "We're gonna try to beat this bastard back to the barn."

D-Willie jumped into the cab of our truck and started the engine. The rest of us piled into the back. The convoy made a U-turn. D-Willie gunned the engine with a jolt that jerked us into each other like bowling pins. Out the back, we had a good view of the brown wall. You couldn't tell how quickly it was moving but it seemed to be closing on us. The truck had a top speed of maybe 40 miles an hour because its gearing was so low. When you gunned it, the transmission sounded like a blender full of nuts and bolts. The truck was made for carrying heavy loads, not high speeds. The Humvees were faster but they weren't going to leave us behind. We would outrun this storm together or get trapped in it together.

About 10 minutes from north Baghdad, the edge of the storm engulfed us. The wolf-howl of the wind slowly overtook the bear-growl of the truck. We pulled the canvas flap down at the back. A mile later, D-Willie shouted back: "Dozer says we gotta pull over."

The convoy rolled to a stop. Day was turning to night. The storm started to batter us. The truck shook, straining against its suspension. The howl was ferocious, the sand a screaming power tool, grinding down anything in its path. I closed my eyes and mouth so tight my face muscles ached. I put my chin against my chest, trying to angle my nostrils away from the sand invasion. Despite covering my face with my hands, I began to feel grit in my nostrils, so I breathed shallower and less often. I missed Oregon. Fuck Iraq, I thought, what kind of a place suddenly turns into a sandblast pit? Well, there was an explanation. Iraq got about four inches of rain a year. Nothing much grew, especially in the west, so there weren't any roots to hold the soil. Not that Iraq had any soil. It was mostly dust. Your boots sank into the sand with each step. On a summer day, your boots could sink into asphalt. Bootprints were everywhere. In Trillium, towering Doug firs were everywhere. My little town sat snugly up in the Coast Range mountains about 20 miles from the Pacific Ocean. It got 65 inches of rain a year. Trillium's sky was gray about nine months of the year and the temperature seldom topped 60. The differences were stark. In Iraq, I was a salmon out of water.

After two hours, the howling wind backed off. Our truck had a thick layer of sand in it. The storm moved on to ravage whatever lay east of our position. We waited half an hour to be sure it was over. Then we limped back to base, towing the rear Humvee, which wouldn't start.

There wasn't a single suicide bombing in Baghdad that day. The insurgents couldn't blow up what they couldn't see. Everybody stayed inside during storms. There was nobody around to kill.

The mission was rescheduled for Friday, giving us a couple of days to degunk our weapons and vehicles. I wished Mom could have seen me on cleanup duty. She would never again rag on me about my room.

We rolled on Friday, same time, same mission. Captain Dozinger went over the logistics again "just in case you forgot" but spent a lot longer on the procedure for calling in air support. A few of us looked at each other. Why was he making such a big deal out of it? Pete Klug stepped in: "Captain, are we expecting opposition?"

"We are not expecting any unusual opposition," Dozinger said, "but Fallujah is still a pissed-off city. For those of you who haven't been there in a while, it looks about the same as it did after we went in to tamp things down during Blackwater Bridge: Tons of rubble, no running water, electricity a couple of hours a day, 80 percent unemployment, families of wild dogs eating corpses in the street, families of people eating the wild dogs. None of that matters because the Office of Reconstruction thinks Fallujah shows a lot of promise."

"Is that good kebab place still there, on that side street by the bazaar?" somebody in the back asked.

"Negative. That street is gone."

We got to the center of Fallujah at 0715 hours. There were long lines at the first checkpoint into the city but we got waved right through. Rank had its privileges. So did nationality. We quickly passed through two others. Killdozer was so right: The place was a wasteland, like a science fiction desert planet whose sun was blowing up. It was mostly shattered concrete with exposed rebar that resembled tangled spaghetti.

We rolled directly to the electrical substation on the east side. It sat forlornly in the middle of a block, facing a street that provided access to a big iron gate that hid its innards. An eight-foot concrete wall topped with rusty barbed wire surrounded the whole thing.

Our first job was to set up a perimeter: No traffic in or out for a three-block radius on all sides. Before we could get going on that, Killdozer came back to our little squad, Pete, me, Amerigo, D-Willie, Ulysses and Bodie.

"I don't like that building," the captain said, pointing to a brown three-story structure a couple of blocks outside our safe zone, some kind of warehouse or office or apartments. Or something. It was hard to tell. No sign. One zit where it had taken an artillery shell. It looked deserted but its roof was surrounded by a wall, which triggered Killdozer's twitch-o-meter. The roof was custom-made for snipers, offering concealment and protection from fire.

We should have worried about that building but Iraq was like a pinball machine. The constant pings made it easy to get distracted, to overlook something. Except for Killdozer. Whatever he called out, whatever he suspected, whatever he predicted, it almost always happened. If his nickname wasn't Killdozer, it would have been The Oracle.

"What do you recommend we do here, Jackson?" the captain asked. Killdozer was transparent, in a good way. He was testing Ulysses and training him at the same time. The rest of us learned by watching. We loved the captain. He would let us make our own decisions but if we were going to get ourselves killed, he'd give us a suggestion, a tweak, a question that would save our lives. Like one time we were out on patrol in Sadr City, looking for bad guys, driving around to see what was up, giving soccer balls to kids, handing out candy. Hearts-and-minds stuff. Killdozer rode with us. Deep in the impoverished bowels of the slum, he said to D-Willie, "You see that piece of shit Toyota parked up ahead on the right, the one with no license plate? Why is that there? Are the rear springs sagging? Is there something heavy in the trunk? Why is that the only car on the street? Why is there nobody walking around? Why were the last two intersections blocked off so we had to go this way? Were they really doing construction back on those side streets? Did you see any construction equipment?"

D-Willie hit the brakes and we stopped half a block short of the Toyota. He did a quick five-point U-turn on the narrow street and we

roared off in the opposite direction. D said, "Let's have EOD check it
out," and Killdozer nodded approvingly.

This building situation was the same deal: Paranoia time. Ulysses
said, "Davis and Taymondo could take the Vee to the edge of the perimeter and put the .50 on the roofline of the building. If we've got
shooters up there, Tay could neutralize them."

"Good start," Dozer said.

Ulysses looked at the roofline. "We could take out the building," he
said. "An F-16 could be here from Camp Ridgeway in five minutes if
they scramble."

"You could do that," Killdozer said with no enthusiasm.

"But maybe let's start with a recon," Ulysses suggested.

"Get some eyes in there, I like it," the captain agreed. "In the meantime, Lincoln, call Ridgeway and ask them to stand by."

Ulysses said, "Klug, Cutter and I could check it out while Taymondo
covers us."

"Good plan," the captain said. "Klug will lead."

The three of us huffed to the building. The area was deserted except
for one skeevy old man wearing a tattered dusty dishdasha. He sat on a
rock at the edge of the cratered-out street. His lumpy face had a moldy
Halloween pumpkin thing going on. He lit a cigarette as we approached
and sucked in smoke like a vacuum cleaner.

Ulysses said, "*Ahlan.*"

"*Sabah al-kayer,*" the guy croaked back, or something like that.

Ulysses began asking him some questions. The guy was all "*hakeesh-
kaffahf*" and "*daakhil-yubaarik.*" There was no way I could ever learn
Arabic. It all sounded like throat cancer with extra phlegm.

"He doesn't know anything," Ulysses said. "Let's go."

We moved on but I looked back to make sure Pumpkin Man wasn't
getting on a cell. He flashed me a toothless indecipherable grin, one
that could have meant either "I love Americans because you liberated
my country" or "I want to cut out your stomach and liver and feed
them to my goat." He had his nicotine dreams. We didn't have time to
win his ancient heart and muddled mind.

Klug got on the radio to Taymondo: "What do you see, Amerigo?"

"Nothing."

"Nothing is good. Out." Klug motioned for me and Ulysses to follow him. We ducked when we passed the building's windows, even though they were boarded up. We came to a wooden door, apparently a side entrance. Klug clicked off safe and switched his M-16 to full automatic. Ulysses and I did the same. Klug said, "I'll go in first and take center, Ulysses left, Johnny right." Then he kicked in the door.

We entered a long hallway strewn with trash. An invisible fusillade of shit and piss greeted us. Because of the heat, human waste in a closed space became a biological weapon. It burned our nostrils and triggered our gag reflexes. Many Iraqi buildings and houses reeked of shit and piss, which signified the presence of squatters. Literally. Maybe Pumpkin Man lived here. Maybe he had just gone outside for some fresh air.

Reconning the first floor, we found heaps of garbage, including fast-food containers crawling with cockroaches. Soon we came to a warehouse-looking corrugated steel door about 10 feet tall and 12 feet wide, with one of those chains for raising it.

"Check this," Klug whispered, pointing to a padlock. "Why is this locked up? Interesting." He motioned for us to get up against the wall on either side, then he put a round into the lock's heart. We waited to see if the gunshot set off any movement, yelling, fleeing, whatever. Nothing. Maybe the building was abandoned, or maybe this was an ambush. No way to know except to go in. Klug raised the clanky door and we ducked inside. It was like a big garage, with a couple of old panel trucks parked next to each other. There was even a bright red Snap-On toolbox. I wondered where they got that.

"Goddamn," Klug whispered. He was beyond full-alert mode, all jumpy, eyes wide, sweat pouring down his face. He pointed to a neatly stacked pile of artillery shells. I was scared enough already but I looked to my right and on a tool bench I saw an ashtray with a cigarette in it, burned down to the filter, giving off its last whisps of smoke. Now I was terrified but strangely, I laughed, a quick "ha," because it hit me that somebody had been smoking in a bomb factory. Was that wise? Ah, the power of nicotine. Then I thought of Pumpkin Man outside, smoking like a tire fire, probably calling his friends to let them know the American infidels were snooping around. I suddenly felt full-on nausea, and not because of all the shit and piss, but because I realized that Pumpkin

Man had triggered my twitch-o-meter and I ignored it. Very stupid.

"Let's get the fuck outta here," Klug said.

"Roger that," Ulysses agreed.

We retraced our steps, ready to empty our clips in case of an ambush. Outside the building, we paused for air, for a good look around, and for Klug to radio Taymondo: "We've got a bomb factory here. We're taking it out. Tell D-Willie to get us that F-16 from Ridgeway. You mark the building."

I noticed that Pumpkin Man was gone.

Klug gave the signal and we took off like jackrabbits. Normally, all our gear was so heavy, but now I felt like a track star. I could have run the 440 hurdles with all this crap weighing me down, helmet, Kevlar exoskeleton, canteen, ammo, Ka-Bar, 9mm sidearm, the M-16 in my right hand as light as a relay race baton. Adrenaline, baby.

Then everything went into slow motion. A blizzard of .50-cal bullets *psshewwwed* over our heads — from Taymondo, who was on the case. Ulysses went down, a face-first header. I looked back at the roofline and saw a black hood and a Kalashnikov jutting over the wall. The sniper's head exploded and his rifle fell three stories into the dust. You didn't mess with Taymondo and his mighty .50-caliber. Before the sniper died, though, he got off one lucky shot. Blood spurted out the back of Ulysses' right leg, mid-thigh. Klug and I picked him up and put his arms over our shoulders.

"You OK?" Klug asked.

"My leg hurts like a motherfucker and I'm not in the mood to bleed," Ulysses said, "but other than that, I've never been better. Did you get that camel fuck?"

"Yeah, Tay corrected his ass," I said.

"I'm gonna need some help, guys. Sorry. I'm tired. Real tired."

"Yeah, my brother, we're gonna get you there," Klug promised.

Ulysses' head sagged. His eyes closed. His leg dangled like a puppet's. He was a big man, over 6 feet and probably 200 pounds, at least 260 with gear. His thigh bone was probably shattered and he might have been going into shock, especially if the bullet had severed a big artery. Seconds were crucial. Klug and I propped him up and started moving.

Klug slapped Ulysses square in the face and yelled, "Wake up!"

Ulysses looked out with glassy eyes.

Our Humvee bounded up through the potholes, Taymondo riding the turret like a rodeo cowboy. "Get in!" D-Willie yelled. "Medevac is on the way."

An F-16 was on the way, too, and its distant scream put it a minute away or less. We lifted Ulysses into the back. He moaned, a good sign; he was conscious. We jumped in ourselves and D-Willie jammed on the gas. Klug said, "Thanks for the ride, man."

We rolled back inside our perimeter, parking front grille to right front tire of another Vee to create an L-shaped blast wall. From the turret, Taymondo painted the bomb factory with a laser beam. Bodie was on the radio with the F-16 pilot.

Klug and I finessed U-man out of the Humvee and onto a back board. His eyes were open. His breathing was labored but steady. I whipped a CATS tourniquet onto his upper thigh. The F-16 blasted by in a recon pass and the pilot's voice crackled out of the radio: "There's a dead hajji on the roof."

"Kill him again," Ulysses said.

"Did you copy that, Switchblade?" Bodie asked.

"No."

"One of our guys took a bullet. He says light that fucker up again."

"Roger that."

The F-16 circled and made a run from south to north. Our position was east of the factory, maybe three klicks from the Euphrates. The pilot was giving us a safety margin. Laser-guided smart bombs were supposedly accurate but nobody trusted them.

Amid the roar of the engines, we heard the goodbye whistle of a 2,000-pound bomb. I plugged my ears and took a quick look over the Humvee's front fender. The factory erupted in a gigantic fireball. *"Holy shit!"* Bodie Davis yelled appreciatively.

I dropped back behind the Humvee. Staccato explosions followed milliseconds later, the artillery shell cache detonating. I looked up again — I couldn't help it, I wanted obliteration and revenge — and the building folded in upon itself, popping and cracking, pancaking into rubble. A gigantic dust cloud rose, filling the sky, eerily mushroom-like.

I turned my attention back to U-man but the captain had him covered. A lot was happening. A Black Hawk was setting down in the street about 30 yards from us. The F-16 blasted straight up to at least 15,000 feet, either a hotdog celebration of his direct hit on the bomb factory or an evasive maneuver in case there were any hajjis around with SAMs. It looked like fun, streaking through the sky like a psycho meth bird, never having to carry a backbreaking pack. Not like us ground pounders. Pilots had it made. Until they got shot down.

We carried Ulysses to the chopper and loaded him aboard. The Black Hawk revved and off it flew, heading for the nearest combat support hospital, probably Camp Ridgeway. We saluted our brother. His day was done. Ours wasn't.

Killdozer said, "Klug and Cutter, nice work bringing Ulysses home. I think he'll be fine. The bomb factory takedown saved hundreds of lives, I'm sure. Taymondo, that was top gunning. Well done, everybody, but let's move on. Next we nation-build. We're here to fix this electrical substation. It'll be the icing on a piece of cake. The contractor is scheduled for 1200 hours, so you've got some free time. Relax. Enjoy the rest of your morning."

I tried to follow the captain's advice. I grabbed a folding canvas chair out of the back of the Humvee and sat down. Because the sun was getting high, there was no shade to be found. The air was dusty from the explosions and smelled like oil and gun powder. The factory was still burning and the ambient air temperature seemed to rise. It felt like 130 degrees. My right hand started to tremble. I held it up and watched, in a detached way. I grabbed it with my left hand and held it, squeezed it. That helped some but now both hands were trembling a little. Finally I gave up and decided to go with it. I laid the rogue hand on my right leg and just let it vibrate. Bodie Davis walked by and said, "What's the matter with your hand, Cutter?"

"I've got magic fingers."

"Must be fun for your little friend," he said.

After about 10 minutes, the hand started to relax and I was able to make it stop shaking. Getting hungry, I went over to one of our trucks and picked out a Cheese Tortellini MRE. "It's comfort food," I said. "It'll help you chill out." Weird. I was literally talking to the hand.

An 18-wheeler rolled up around 1300, escorted by a couple of Humvees, one of them with the classic .50-caliber in its turret. The other was kitted up with an Mk-19 grenade launcher. Practically drooling, Taymondo was all over that thing like sand on an open wound. Why fire a measly bullet if you can launch a grenade that would punch through the concrete walls of a building and kill everybody inside? "If you're good, maybe Santa will bring you one of those for Christmas," I yelled.

"Screw Santa, I want it now," Taymondo shot back.

The contractors unloaded a forklift and used it to bring out a gray metal box the size of a small car. They rolled it inside the substation fence and set it down near another once-gray box that was now streaked with black, apparently from fire. Then they walked to their truck, climbed into the cab, unwrapped sandwiches and started eating. I looked over at the captain, who was standing there, arms crossed, nostrils flaring, glaring at the contractors. He walked over to them and said in a fairly nice voice, "What's going on?"

"We're having lunch," the guy in the driver's seat said.

"Yeah, I can see that. When do you think you'll be ready to start installing the transformer?"

"In about an hour. We get an hour lunch break."

Killdozer climbed onto the truck's running board and put his face right up next to the contractor's. "Let me tell you how our morning has gone," he said in a low slow death-star voice. "We got here at 0700 to set up a perimeter for you. Then one of our guys got shot by a sniper and had to be medevaced out. Then we had to call in an airstrike on an IED factory. Then we had to wait an hour because you were late. Now you've spent 45 minutes unloading the transformer. I guess that tired you out and now it's time for lunch."

The way Killdozer was steaming reminded me of Mount St. Helens, which blew before I was born, but I had seen the videos. I was in Portland on a clear day one time and could see the half of the volcano that was left, 70 miles to the north. Killdozer was magmafied to the max and ready to …

ERUPT! The captain snatched the contractor's sandwich and hurled it on a TOW missile trajectory into the substation, where it exploded in a sprazzle of roast beef, lettuce, mayonnaise and tomato. "I don't care who your sleaze-fuck CEO used to be," he said, "if you think we're go-

ing to wait around while you sit on your lazy fat overpaid corrupt contractor ass and stuff your fucking face, you've got another think coming. Get out there — *now* — *AND HOOK UP THAT TRANSFORMER.*
Otherwise, we're outta here and you're on your own."

He leaped off the truck and furiously pointed to the two Humvees.
No words were necessary. D-Willie jumped into one, Bodie into the
other, and they started the engines.

Sandwich Man stammered around and finally got some words out:
"OK, OK, no problem. OK? Sorry, we'll get right on it. No one told us it
was a rush job."

By 1700 hours they were done. Killdozer was quite the motivational
speaker. He gathered the unit for "the ceremonial flipping of the switch,
the golden spike of electrical feng shui." The transformer began to hum
and we dished out some halfhearted applause. It felt anticlimactic. For
sure, it was good to get the job done and now the people of Fallujah
could shut off their Honda generators, but overall, what a supremely
fucked-up mission.

We shuffled out of the substation and closed the gate. Sandwich Man
secured a big steel latch with some clunky medieval padlock. Then the
contractors quickly bugged out to get paid, like they always did.

One of our trucks headed to the perimeter to pick up the guys at the
checkpoints. There were maybe eight of us milling around the substation, decompressing, firing up iPods, loading gear into the Humvees
and troop carriers. With the contractors' semi out of the picture, the
substation gate was exposed, though only in the after-action review did
we understand what that meant. The thing about Fallujah, it was a pit, a
cesspool, a graveyard, and nobody should have to live like that, but
electricity would have made it marginally better. In Iraq, marginally
better would have been great. Standards were different here. Our
American brains were still not dialed in to the concept of destroying
what kept you alive, what made your life a little nicer. Back in Oregon,
we'd go to the Home Depot and get a new bathroom faucet because it
was prettier than the old one, didn't leak and wasn't rusty. In Iraq, they
blew up the Home Depot.

The city was quiet, at least in our little cordoned-off corner of it. The
guys were too tired to talk. The only sounds were the clanking of metal,

the scruffing of canvas, the clonk of boxes as the gear and weapons got stacked up and stowed. I would have been hearing jays squawking back in Trillium and the soft patter of rain. Not here. In Iraq, there were no birds, no rain. Just dust.

In the distance, I heard a new sound, an engine coughing and revving. It wasn't one of ours. The vibe was too rattletrap. Our diesels had more bottom end, more thud, more chunk. My twitch-o-meter fired up and pegged the needle. I ran 20 yards to the street corner across from the substation to get a look.

A hulking black cargo truck was racing toward us. "*INCOMING!*" I screamed. "*TAKE COVER!*"

I looked back to our guys. Only Pete Klug heard me. The rest of them were rawking to their music, putting away the gear. Klug started to run my way but I waved him off. "*Tell them!*" I shouted. "*Get the hell out!*"

I took my M-16 off safe and moved to the side of the street, against the corner of a building. The truck was 100 yards away and building speed. The sun was in my eyes but the angle was nearly straight on, so it wasn't a tough shot. I sighted in. Breathe, just breathe, I thought.

At 25 yards, I squeezed the trigger. The windshield shattered. I knew I got the guy. I couldn't have missed. I wasn't spraying and praying. There was no confirming it but I must have nailed that driver.

Unbelievably, the truck blew past. A cloud of dust and oily exhaust enveloped me. I whirled and squeezed the trigger again. Nothing. Empty clip. No time to reload. Time expired.

I saw the guys sprinting away from the substation. There were two keys to surviving a suicide bombing: Distance and barrier. If we could get enough distance between our body and the blast, far enough from the pressure zone, we would make it. If we had a personal barrier, helmet and Kevlar, or could get behind a truck, a car or a wall, we might survive, depending on the thickness of the barrier, the blast pattern and whether the bomb was loaded with shrapnel. Oh, there was a third factor: Luck. Since there wasn't a lot of luck in Iraq, we didn't count on that.

The truck's path was true. Dead driver or not, it rammed the substation's iron gate and bashed through. The gate tore off its hinges, flipping wildly through the air. A laughable thought popped into my mind: Was the driver wearing his seat belt?

My training overwhelmed everything else. I was hard-wired to react, to hit the ground and cover. About 30 yards away, I had a chance to survive the blast. But the strangest thing happened. The truck didn't explode. It lodged against the newly installed transformer, engine grinding away, steam shooting from the punctured radiator. My instinct was to go see what happened; my training was to get farther away. *Stand-off distance!* I got up and ran, putting another 10 yards between me and the smoking truck.

Then it exploded.

I didn't see it; my back was to the blast. I felt it, though, the searing heat of the fireball, the huge invisible hand that threw me down. I landed on my right shoulder and rolled, to put myself out if I was on fire. I ended up lying in a mortar crater. Woozy, I felt a sharp pain, like somebody had hit me in the spine with a baseball bat. I could still move my arms. When I realized I was alive, the pain didn't matter.

One thing Killdozer had taught us about suicide bombings, sometimes the driver was just the driver, nothing more. His hands might be tied to the steering wheel, the gas pedal might be locked down mechanically. So even if I had killed this guy, and I believed I had, the truck would have kept going, just like it did. With the driver dead, then, how was the explosion triggered? Sometimes the detonator was just the detonator, someone higher up in the suicide-bombing food chain monitoring the driver's progress from a nearby vantage point. On his signal from a cell phone: *Kaboom!* Blood, guts, flying body parts, screams, destruction.

I didn't know what to think about people who were willing to drive a bomb around town, waiting to get vaporized. Were they blissful at the prospect of killing us infidels? Did they eagerly await the big bang and the virgins? What could anyone say about the handlers who were willing to vaporize the bombers, the men willing to send them off to their deaths in rickety trucks? Were they even human? Did they care about anyone other than themselves? It was a horrible incomprehensible insanity. It was everyday Iraq.

I rolled onto my back like an old arthritic man and sat up. My legs moved; I wasn't paralyzed. I wiggled my feet; I could feel my toes. That was good. The ringing in my ears was bad. I wondered if I would lose my hearing. No more Nirvana for me, I thought, smells like teen deafness.

I looked at the substation we had just repaired. It was a mass of flaming twisted wreckage. It wasn't humming anymore. The Fallujah folks would be sticking with their Honda generators.

The captain walked into my field of vision from the left, followed by Klug. With considerable effort, I got to my feet and limped back to them. Klug and Dozer were dazed, maybe in shock, just standing there with vacant eyes, as thick black smoke billowed out of the substation.

"Are you guys OK?" I asked.

They both looked at me but didn't utter a word. They just nodded, slowly and slightly. Finally, Klug said something: "Thanks for the heads-up, Cutter. We owe you one."

"Roger that," the captain said. "We'll get you a bump to private first class." Then he threw his helmet into the ground and said: "I love nation-building. *I fucking love it to death.*"

11 / Everything's great over here

Captain Dozinger was a master scrounger. Whenever he skulked around in his anonymous look — camouflage with no namestrip, eyes hidden behind shades, chrome dome tucked deep under ball cap — he was on a quest. If he could get his hands on a hand truck, he'd push it purposefully, striding around the base with the preoccupied intensity of a supply sergeant on a crucial mission. He gave off the powerful vibe of someone who shouldn't be slowed or trifled with, lest that mission be compromised.

The previous week, a hajji mortarman had put the base phone center and Internet cafe out of commission with a lucky strike on a junction box. On my way to the latrines, staying behind concrete barriers wherever possible in case the mortarfucker was still out there, I saw Dozer in stealth mode. He put a finger to his lips, silently swearing me to silence. Later that night, I realized what the captain must have been up to. He poked his head in and barked, "Candy gram."

We were ragged out, playing poker in dim light. "Hey, Captain," Klug said. "Come in."

Dozer shook his head. "No can do. I wasn't even here. I didn't give you guys this. I need it back in an hour." He pulled an Iridium satellite phone out of his jacket pocket like a drug dealer and passed it to Pete. Then he disappeared into the darkness.

Klug held the phone up high. "Who needs to call a woman?"

Hands shot up like Patriot missiles. "Make sure it's a real woman and not an inflatable," Klug said. "OK, Amerigo, Bodie, Johnny, Willie, Ulysses. I'll go last. Everybody gets 10 minutes. For every minute you go over, you pay each of us $20. I'll give you a two-minute warning and don't think I won't be checking." Klug pulled up his left sleeve to show us the hardware on his wrist. "This isn't just a watch, it's a chronograph. The stopwatch measures in hundredths of a second. If you get a busy signal or they aren't home, you can either leave a message or hang up and take another shot at the end. That's the rules. Go!"

Klug handed the phone to Taymondo and he raced outside for some privacy. The pressure was on. Each of us had to think of exactly what we wanted to say, how much we would say, and how we would say it. Time on sat phones was rare. Mostly, we all just fired off e-mails and IMs back home, if our Internet connection wasn't down. Occasionally, some neanderthal would write an actual letter, on actual paper, if he could stand the ridicule. Only officers seemed to have Iridiums and it was understood that they were for battle use only. The Army, however, which was precise, predictable and prissy about all of its other rules, seemed to have a blind spot on calling home. Each call probably cost some serious money but, really, was anybody keeping track of the bill? Wouldn't they first worry about an Abrams tank using two gallons of fuel to go one mile? Or the $20 million every time a chopper crashed? And nobody was worried about that stuff. Anyway, the money they saved by not up-armoring our Humvees would pay for a few billion hours of sat phone time.

I decided to call Halley first, then Mom. I opened my wallet and pulled out my crumpled cheat sheet. I knew the digits, they were sort of in my head, but if I spaced, that was my backup. I also jotted down a few notes, things I wanted to tell them. That was tricky. You wanted to let them in on personal things but not so much that it sounded like you could die at any moment. Why worry them? Either I was coming back or I wasn't, and we could cross that bridge or fall in the river whenever.

Taymondo and Davis both went a minute over, so that was 40 bucks in my pocket. Bodie handed the Iridium over to me and I rushed outside, dialing on the move. The phone bleeped and blurped. I looked into the sky. It was full of stars, and somewhere a satellite was connecting me to Halley. I visualized her face and the ringlets of blond hair cascading onto her shoulders, the way she brushed bangs away from her sweet green eyes. She could almost look like a cat when she stared at you, especially if she tilted her head a little. Pale skin, a big happy smile, and when she laughed she really let go. You could hear her from way down the street. Halley's freewheeling laugh made me feel good, all smiley warm.

When the phone started to ring, my stomach flipped around and I shivered, even though the air was still roasting hot. I tapped my foot with each ring … one … two … three … four …

"Johnny? Is that you?"

"Halley! Yeah, it's me."

"Oh my God, Johnny, what a surprise! It's so good to hear your voice! The caller ID had some kind of crazy number on it, so I hoped it might be you."

"Yeah, I'm on a satellite phone at the base. I can't believe I'm really talking to you. Can you hear me OK?"

"Yes, pretty good, a little echo, but really it sounds like a regular cell phone. Hey, I miss you, Johnny Cutter. What are you up to? Are you OK? Tell me everything."

"Yeah, I'm fine. I don't have too long to talk because the captain scammed this phone and we're sharing it. So things are good. I can't believe I'm talking to you. You sound great. How are things at home?"

"They're good. I'm so glad you called on Saturday. I would still have been at school if it had been yesterday."

"Is it Saturday? I didn't even realize that. I lose track of the days. What time is it there, anyway? I didn't even think about that."

"It's going on 1:30. I just ate lunch. Hey, I really miss you," she said, her voice quavering slightly.

"I miss you, too."

"Tell me everything you've been doing."

"Oh, I don't know. You know, stuff. We went to Fallujah the other day. We tried to go. We got hit by this giant sandstorm. We had to come back to Baghdad."

"That sounds scary."

"Yeah, but it was fine. Then we went back later to fix this electric power station. We basically just stood guard while they put in a new transformer, so that was, you know, interesting. It's really hot over here. I totally miss Oregon."

"What's the temperature?"

"Well, I'm standing outside at the base right now, it's almost 2400, uh, I mean midnight … "

"Hey, I know military time."

"Oh, right, yeah, I just, sometimes I should switch into civilian mode, you know, and yeah, it's still like 95 degrees."

"Ugh. What is it during the day?"

"I dunno. Maybe 120."

"That's crazy."

"Yeah. You've really got to keep drinking water. Stay hydrated."

"Johnny, are you safe over there? I almost don't want to read the paper anymore or listen to the news. Every time Governor Kulongoski goes to a funeral for an Oregon soldier, they write about it. It seems like he goes all the time. I hate those stories."

"Oh, yeah, we're safe. We're fine. We're really careful. Captain Dozinger is always watching out for us. You know, like he got us this phone tonight."

"I'm so relieved to hear that. The funerals are sad. They make me worry. I keep reading about these bombings and all that stuff, you know?"

"Oh, yeah, there's a few but we're good. All the guys in our squad are great. We all watch out for each other. We've got each other's backs. Sometime when I have more time, I'll tell you about them, D-Willie and Bodie and Pete Klug and this guy Ulysses, who tells stories and speaks Arabic."

"Wow, Ulysses."

"Cool name, huh? He's always calling the Iraq war a real odyssey."

"Really?"

"No, I made that up, actually he calls it something less flattering."

Halley let loose with her trademark laugh and my heart quivered.

"I love you, Halley." *Whoa!* There it was. The first time. A little bit of a shock. That wasn't on my list of things to say. I swiveled the phone away from my mouth because I started to choke up.

There was an agonizing moment of silence and then: "I love you, too, Johnny. I wish you could come home tonight. I'd wrap my arms around you and hold you so tight."

I imagined what that would be like. Home. Halley driving up to meet me at the PDX airport. Me carrying a big honking duffel bag. Driving back through the trees to Trillium. Sex on a blanket at The Overlook.

"Johnny?"

"I wish I was home, too. Once everything gets straightened out here, I'll be there."

Fearing that we might be straying into awkward unplanned territory, I changed the subject and asked Halley about school. I basked in the sound of her voice as she told me about her classes — heavy in science and math — and her teachers at Coos Bay Community College. In return, I gave her an abridged sanitized version of life at FOB Viper. Soon I got a tap on the shoulder from Klug. He circled around and held up two fingers then vanished into the night. "Halley, I've got to go," I said. "I'm sorry but my time is up. The guys, we're all sharing this phone."

"Hey, e-mail me more often. I love getting your e-mails. And please be careful, OK? Stay safe."

"I will. I miss you. I'll definitely be better about e-mailing when I have time."

"You'd better. Bye, Johnny. I'll be thinking of you."

"Me you too. Bye for now."

Talking to Halley made me miss home in a visceral way. My body was all wigged out. My gut hurt, probably from nerves, though the less romantic possibility was constipation from Meals Ready to Eat. I dialed home. I probably had another minute or so. At least I could say a quick hi to Mom.

I got the message machine, so I just blurted out some stuff as fast as I could, I love you, I miss you, don't worry, I'm fine, I'm safe, I'm learning a lot of things I can use when I get out, I'm getting strong. "And I have the best dreams over here, Mom," I said, just before signing off. "Some nights it's your chocolate chip cookies; other nights, it's your lasagna."

I returned the sat phone to Pete and he handed it off to D-Willie. I ended up going a minute over but it was worth it. Secretly, I was kind of glad I didn't have time to talk to Dad. It might have been awkward, especially if he was drinking.

Besides, Dad would have known I was bullshitting about everything being great in Iraq.

12 / Bringing on democracy

We were up at a godawful hour. The captain had come through the night before, telling us to hit our bunks early. "This is a special Karbala mission," Killdozer said. "Get your beauty sleep. I don't want anybody tired out there tomorrow. Stay alert, stay alive."

"Who we takin' down?" Bodie Davis said. "Give us a taste."

"All will be revealed at 0430. Remember, it's a very extremely double-plus extra-special mission. So lights out."

I locked eyes with Bodie and he shook his head. Every mission had become special. Repairing a broken sewer pipe while standing knee-deep in a lake of Shiite shit? Special. Troubleshooting a sputtering Honda generator that was feeding a tangled web of a hundred extension cords supplying the power to every television in a Sunni neighborhood? Special. Escorting some mummified Awakening Council dude to a Karbala meeting where they squabbled for six hours in Farsi? Special. We were baby-sitters for infrastructure and crazy people.

Our digital watches began to beep and chirp at 0400, amid groans and curses. We were sitting in the briefing room by 0428. I don't know how we did it. Back home this would never have happened. I would have slept till noon, and I would have guessed the same for every guy in our squad. Those recruitment commercials on TV, you can laugh at them, how you'll become "Army strong" or "a force of one," but there's something to it. Maybe I wouldn't have slept till noon if Mom had shoved me out of bed onto the floor at four o'clock in the morning and kicked me in the ass with a combat boot, telling me I could get up or become a paraplegic, the choice was mine. Or when I told her I wanted to do my chores later but right now I was going out "someplace," if she had picked up an M-16 and pointed its butt at me, threatening to smash my face in until they couldn't identify the DNA, well, yeah, I would have done the chores now, not later. The Army was like the meanest baddest bitchiest mom you could imagine, then triple it. The

Nike slogan, "Just do it," with all those perfect people running around in their $300 Air Jordans, that was for weak pukes. The Army slogan, at least unofficially, was, "Just fucking do it or just fucking die, you fucking maggot."

Killdozer walked into the briefing room at 0430 on the dot. He was never late. He started right in: "Good morning, gentlemen. We've got a very important mission today. It's special."

That was our cue to shout "Hooah!" and laugh. I wondered if the captain always did that just to loosen us up.

"In the annals of specialness, this mission is in the pantheon of the greats. We'll be rolling south to the holy city of Karbala, where you will see maybe a million Shiite pilgrims flowing through the streets toward the Imam Hussein shrine. He was the grandson of the Prophet Muhammad. When he got killed in the Battle of Karbala, it was a real downer. Even today — 1,300 years later — the pilgrims still get worked up about it."

Pete Klug yelled, "Bring on the Holy Stampede."

"Sergeant Klug knows whereof he speaks. Because we all need to learn from each other whenever we can, I'm turning the floor over to him." Killdozer motioned for Klug to come to the front of the room. "Pete was there last year. He can tell you where to beware."

"The first thing you gotta know is, be inconspicuous," Klug said.

"What does inconspicuous mean?" someone called out.

"It means be small, be invisible."

"How do you do that in full gear standing on top of a Hummer?" someone else asked.

"With a target on your back," added another.

"First of all," Klug said, "don't stand on top of your Hummer. Stay inside the Hummer. Second, wear your Kevlar. Third, stay away from the flow of the crowd. Fourth, if the crowd goes ballistic or a bomb detonates, all bets are off. Last year, 47 of them died."

The room fell silent. Then a hand went up. It was Vig Oskierko, a medic in our company.

"Question," Killdozer acknowledged.

I could see the emergency medical wheels turning inside Vig's head. He said, "Permission to speak freely, sir?"

"Always."

"Why are we going there? How does this help our overall mission? Are we supposed to save them from themselves?"

"Because those are our orders, I don't know, and yes."

The room fell into silence again. Every man locked on Captain Dozinger, studying his face, looking for meaning, looking for … more, a shred of explanation, some reasoning.

Sometimes I didn't get Killdozer. He was unpredictable. He could do the rah-rah-rah go-Army thing, for sure. It would, at any moment, come spewing out of him. Or his latent drill sergeant persona would occasionally blow up and promise to tear off our heads and shit in our bleeding neck holes. Or sometimes he would randomly throw in an "I don't know" in answer to an explosive question. That was strange, reassuring and unnerving at the same time, because we knew he was telling the truth. He didn't know how this would help the mission — *and he said so*. The thing was, if Killdozer didn't know, then who the hell did? Probably nobody. The truth was scary.

"Sir, how can we save them from themselves?" Vig asked.

"By providing a hand on the tiller," the captain answered, "by giving them a steadying presence, by bringing on democracy."

"Sir, I don't understand how democracy and a killer religious stampede are connected."

"Oskierko, have you ever been to an after-Christmas sale at Walmart?"

"No, sir."

"When you get stateside, I want you to go to one. See for yourself. Now if it will help, if it's not enough for your commanding officer to tell you to do it, if you need a compelling mo' better reason for going to Karbala, then I will move on to part two of our mission, which is based on triple-extra-special intel straight from CENTCOM."

The captain explained that we might see a black Mercedes S600 sedan rolling through Karbala or headed north to Baghdad. "It's the V-12 engine model and this one has tinted windows," he said, showing us a photograph of the car. "There are only two of these in the entire nation of Iraq, as far as we know, so if you see one, the odds are good that it's the one we're looking for."

We were to pull the Mercedes over — "but without hurting the car in any way, box it in, preferably. All right, you can shoot out the tires if necessary but don't miss and mess up the paint job."

We were to keep any occupants of the car inside — "with a threat of lethal force, and I emphasize, only a threat. Nobody dies but have your weapon with you at all times as a precaution."

We were to look in the trunk — "if you find any suitcases, maybe as many as eight, confiscate them, and send the car and the occupants on their way without asking any questions. Contact TOC immediately and tell them you are bringing the suitcases directly back to base. Do not look inside the suitcases — I repeat — *do not look inside the suitcases.*"

Killdozer stared down the room for 10 seconds, then: "What did I just say?"

"Do not look inside the suitcases," we all parroted back.

"You're clear on that?"

"Yes, sir."

"Absolutely clear?"

"YES, SIR!"

"Good. Make sure you stay absolutely clear on that. This is not worth a court-martial and 20 years in prison."

Confused glances ricocheted around the room. A court-martial? Prison? Very mysterious. Killdozer crossed his arms and stared us even further into a box. Finally he said, "Are there any other questions."

Benjamin Benum's hand went up. Because it was Benny and because he was riding with us today, I flashed on one of his quirks. He was always saying his dream was to get out of the Army, go back home to Nashville and live next door to a Waffle House. It seemed like a random dream but, OK, whatever got him through.

Killdozer said, "Yes, Benum."

"Sir, what's in the suitcases?"

Killdozer's face morphed into mighty-mean-mother mode. "It's good that you're named Benum," he said. "It has a nice ring to it. Because, Benum, your name now means *dumb-ass.* I hope you have the intelligence that our righteous-yet-vengeful God might have given you to understand that from this day forward, nobody in the Army will ever again say: Don't be a dumb-ass. They will say: Don't be a Benum. At

West Point, first-year cadets will have a required course called Benum 101 that teaches them" — a vein began to pop out of Killdozer's forehead — "*NOT TO ASK STUPID DUMB-ASS BENUM QUESTIONS.*"

"Yes, sir. Understood, sir. I just thought that the more information we have, if our questions are answered, the better the mission will go."

Killdozer took a long slow breath, shook out his arms and rolled his head around a couple of times like a yoga instructor. I had never seen the captain try to relieve tension. What was up with that? He seemed to thrive on tension. And what was Benum's deal? I had to give him respect for hanging in there but what was he driving at? Could it somehow have something to do with a Waffle House?

"Now who taught you that, Benum?"

"You did, sir. You taught me that there is no such thing as a dumb question."

"I believe I said there is no such thing as a Benum question."

"Sir, aren't they the same thing?"

"Let me explain something to you about classified information, because I have obviously failed as a teacher. You *never* ask about classified information, you *never* show any interest in it, you *never* let your eyes gaze upon it. Do you know why, Benum?"

"No, sir."

"Because classified information does not exist. If you ever come across nonexistent classified information, you take it to your grave. Is that clear?"

"Yes, sir. So there's something in the suitcases that doesn't exist."

"Roger that."

"Question, sir?"

"Go ahead."

"Do the Mercedes and the suitcases exist, sir?"

"We believe they do, yes."

We moved out in 24 Humvees, which made a lot of noise, like a huge wounded animal. Back home one time, on a weed hunt, we came across an elk with its front right leg caught in a bear trap. That poor beast was snorting and bellowing, moaning and gasping. Our convoy reminded me of that, so I didn't think about how it ended for the elk. It wasn't even 0530 yet, so the temperature was only 70, but the sun was about to show its ugly face. Soon enough, we'd be broiling under all the Kevlar.

The trip to Karbala would take about an hour. "I ain't gonna be no leadfoot today," D-Willie announced as we left the base. "I'm drivin' for mileage, my brothers, because we got us an energy shortage."

I was on navigation and communications, riding shotgun. I looked back at Taymondo and Benum, and rolled my eyes. I thought D-Willie was messing with us but they both shrugged. We had to up the volume if we wanted to be heard over the Humvee noise, and Benum yelled out, "Good idea, D, when everybody else runs out of gas, we'll be the only ones to get back home."

Suddenly D-Willie jammed the gas pedal to the floor, then the brake, the gas, the brake. The tires screeched. The Hummer snorted and bucked like a rodeo bull, throwing us around like G.I. Joe dolls.

"Jeez, where'd you learn to drive?" Taymondo complained.

"Yo, on the streets a *Deee*troit."

"I hope you got insurance," Tay said.

D-Willie said, "Hey, Benny, whatchoo know about them suitcases?"

"Didn't you hear Killdozer? If you knew, they'd throw you in a military prison and then kill you. Or is it the other way around?"

"Word, but seriously, what up? I'm askin' you as your brother."

"Just drive, D."

"Is it drugs?"

"Just drive, D."

"Is it that porn everybody's talkin' about? I wouldn't mind gettin' a little taste. Except for the camels."

"You're missing out on some mighty fine humping," Benum said.

"Is it something to do with a Waffle House?" I ventured.

"Hmmm, no, except now that you mention it, that's an interesting, potentially life-changing idea," Benum said.

D-Willie's frustration was building. "What are you two fucktards talking about? How would a Waffle House relate to a black Mercedes and some suitcases? What, are the suitcases full of maple syrup?"

Benum slapped the side of D's helmet and shouted: "*Liquid gold, baby!*"

D-Willie swiveled around to look Benum dead in the eyes. He shifted his left foot onto the gas and was steering with his left hand.

"Hey," I said. "Keep your eyes on the road." I grabbed the wheel with my left hand to hold it steady as my heart started to jackhammer.

"Yeah, now I get it," D-Willie said. "Those suitcases are filled with gold. And we're not talkin' maple syrup. Am I right?"

I sneaked a look at Benum. He was a little freaked. Taymondo hunkered down, tightening his seat belt. I turned back up front to keep us on the road. If we swerved, if we lost it, the Humvee would probably roll and we'd all eat it.

"*IS IT GOLD?*"

Benum grabbed D-Willie's helmet and twisted it back toward the front of the Humvee. "No, it's just regular money. Shit, man, watch the road."

D-Willie took the wheel with both hands. I let go and cinched my safety belt.

"OK, so it's money," D said. "How much are we talkin' bout?"

"Didn't you hear Killdozer say that's classified?"

D-Willie swiveled again but Benum yelled, "$80 million" before he could turn all the way around. D flipped back to the front and said, "So there's $80 million in some suitcases in the back of a Mercedes somewhere out here."

"That's what I heard," Benum said.

D-Willie slapped the dashboard. "Fuck that. We gotta find that shit. The Army needs that money. That's enough to keep this fuckin' war going for five minutes. Where'd it come from? Some sheik? Is it oil money?"

"Naw, it's ours," Benum said. "I heard it came right out of the Green Zone. A pallet of Army cash supposedly disappeared."

"Bullshit. The Green Zone has $80 million just lying around?"

"Probably more. Some serious bank is getting passed out to those Awakening Councils, you know, our new best friends."

I glanced back at Benum. He made a little whaddaya-gonna-do gesture with his hands.

"Disappeared?" D-Willie said incredulously. "You're saying they lost $80 million someplace and they don't know where?"

"That's right."

D-Willie went off: "*STUPID GREEN ZONE FUCK-ASS MUTHA-*

FUCKERS. WE NEED THAT FUCKING MONEY. WE NEED THESE FUCKING HUMVEES UP-ARMORED. WHAT THE HELL, THEY MAKE US DRIVE A FUCKING TIN CAN AROUND IN A COUNTRY THAT'S ONE BIG FUCKING BOMB? GODDAMN, BUSH, GET YOUR LYING CHICKENSHIT DRAFT-DODGING ASS BACK HERE AND GIVE US $80 MILLION TO KEEP US ALIVE."

D-Willie started to sniffle and sputter and grunt spasmodically. Did he have the hiccups? Was he crying? Whatever, it was kind of pitiful. Having had my own problems in that department, I looked away. I felt sorry for him. It was the first time I understood that you never knew when a guy was going to crack. Or why.

But everybody understood that if you couldn't take it anymore, if you suddenly, out of nowhere, started bawling or screaming, it was a sign that you were likely to be killed soon. That was why, in our unit at least, nobody tried to talk you out of it or tell you it was going to be all right. Because most likely it was not. Most likely your personal flip-out meant you were going to die, and somehow your body was warning you of the impending danger with a stress overload.

The Army shrinks would have called that superstition. Easy for them to dismiss it from the safety of their big brown desks inside blast walls and barbed wire. Of course, their job was to get you back out there but I could give them a couple of cases from Echo Company: Andy Adolphson and Jerry Miller. They were both blown away right after they lost it. Andy cracked, seemingly, over the cardboard-tasting beans. He slammed his tray to the floor one night and started screaming obscenities. He stormed out of the mess hall, leaving the pile of slop behind. That's how he checked out, too, three days later: A sniper's high-velocity bullet (ironically, an American 7mm Remington Magnum, we suspected) ripped through his neck, and he left a puddle of blood and spit behind in the sandbox. Jerry, same thing, a high-decibel drama over checkpoint duty alongside the worthless Iraqi army slackers, then a roadside bomb turns him to mush the next day.

What the Army mind-benders could never understand was that there were so many ways to die. Outside the wire, the danger was constant, perverse, random, and that made all of us kind of crazy.

We racked up southbound miles on Highway 8 for a while without talking, to rest our voices. D-Willie's driving improved. He kept his proper place in the convoy — not too close to the Hummers in front or in back of us (why risk losing two vehicles to one IED?) but not too far either (if we did get blown up, help would arrive in seconds). Benum and Taymondo put in their earbuds and got lost in iPod land. They turned the music up so loud I could hear it, Nine Inch Nails, I thought, or was that the road noise? Hard to differentiate. Killdozer was always warning us about loud music, and iPods on patrol were officially a no-no, but unofficially we said yes-yes to them. We mocked a memo telling us not to crank it up. Had the Army heard an IED detonate? A mortar? A 155-millimeter shell? A burst from an M-16? A low-level F-16 flyover? There were 500 ways to go deaf in Iraq and the iPod was like No. 499. The Army was hilariously out of touch.

Halfway to Karbala, D-Willie turned to me. "I'm sorry about that, Ghost."

"What?" I said.

"Back there."

"No problem. I already forgot about it."

D-Willie's face let go a little. He was relieved. There was no evidence he had cried. In the miserable heat and dust, tears quickly disappeared into dried sweat and grime.

"It got to me," D-Willie said. "They piss away $80 million just like they're pissing away this war. Like it doesn't matter. But it does matter. Do these fuckers care? No. Shit, I grew up two blocks from Eight Mile. Our house was barely even a tarpaper shack, then we lost that and had to live with my aunt. I'm sick of losing shit. I found a quarter in the street one time and I thought I was rich. You know what I'm sayin'?"

"Yeah."

"There was no way I was ever goin' to college. I didn't have nuthin'. The Army was my ticket. They talked about all this money I was gonna get for education and this great future I could have. Look, I'm a fucking cabdriver in a dirtbag country I can't even find on a map. After we're done, it ain't even gonna be on the map."

"Wait a minute," I said, "you think you're not getting the G.I. Bill money? I've got to go back to school. I could use it, too."

"Guess what, my brother."

"What?"

"You don't go to college if you're dead."

"We're not gonna die over here," I said. "We're gonna bring democracy to Iraq, and when we're done, you and I are gonna eat a Big Mac together in the middle of Baghdad. Then we're gonna walk down to the corner with that $80 million we find and buy two cups of coffee at the new Starbucks they build where the Saddam statue used to be."

D-Willie looked over at me and I tried to lay a stoneface no-blink nuclear stare on him. It worked for a few seconds but then he splurted out a little snort-fart laugh and I cracked. We started to heehaw like donkeys.

We laughed and laughed, so loud that we disturbed Benum and Taymondo out of their 100-decibel iPod reveries. They both yanked their earbuds out and Benum said, "What's going on?"

Tears were starting to run down my face but I managed to calm down enough to say, "We're bringing democracy to Iraq."

But D-Willie and I made the mistake of looking at each other and we erupted again. A big cloud of spit-fog exploded out of D's mouth and he trumpeted like an elephant. I snorted and my nose exploded out a gritty mortar shell of a snot plug. My left side hurt so bad I had to grab it and start squeezing with both hands. I vaguely heard Benum say, "That's nice, just keep your eyes on the road and let us know when we get to democracy. Are we there yet?"

When I looked back, Benum and Taymondo were popping their earbuds back in. It was one of those you-had-to-be-there things, and even though they were three feet away in the back seat of the Humvee, they were not *there* with us. D-Willie and I had slipped inside a place where nothing made sense and nothing worked, yet everybody kept doing exactly what they'd been doing, as if it did make sense and it did work. The insanity was so great and so high and so beyond that we reached a flip point and rode it rather than fought it. Maybe that made us the crazy ones. My head hurt when I thought about the circularity of it. D-Willie and I laughed so hard and so long that we tired ourselves out and we couldn't laugh anymore. Or cry.

We rolled along for a while and then — synchronicity — we turned our heads and looked at each other. I was absolutely thinking we were both in downtown Loonville, and I saw something in D's eyes that confirmed he was thinking the same thing. Bringing democracy to Iraq … *who in the holy fuck were we kidding?*

Ironically, ourselves.

D-Willie and I shook our heads in that sad moment of shared recognition. I wanted to reach out and give him a hug but my brain flashed on an image of him losing control of the Humvee, going off the road, hitting an IED, and all four of us dying because of a hug. Iraq was like that. So I sat tight. My self-preservation instinct hadn't shut down.

We hit the outskirts of Karbala shortly after 0700. The convoy slowed to about five miles an hour. Our dust cloud was moving faster than we were. We stopped and our radio crackled to life with a last-minute recap of the mission from Bravo One, but we knew what to do, protect a million Iraqis from a hajj stampede or suicide bombers, and find a black Mercedes full of nonexistent money. Simple.

The convoy fanned out to our assigned positions. From the air, it must have looked like fireworks bursting, each Humvee a singular sparkle tracing its own path. I didn't want that explosive image in my mind, because now the serious danger started. One moment you were breathing, the next a sniper's bullet was tearing through your neck and you were drowning in your own blood. If the bullet severed your spinal cord, at least the pain didn't register. Even if you were tired, even if you didn't sleep last night, now you were *awake*. Adrenaline surged. The convoy was evaporating; so was our safety. I looked back at Benum and Taymondo to make sure they had stowed their iPods and put on their headsets.

The FBCB2 system quickly got us to our assigned street in the center of Karbala. Strangely, the city seemed deserted but that was misleading. A river of humanity was percolating through it on a wide boulevard, Maytham al-Tamar, which was coming into view less than half a klick ahead.

"Jesus Christ," D-Willie said, "look at that." We rolled another couple of blocks and stopped in the middle of the street, where we could watch the flow, also the buildings surrounding us. Taymondo scrambled to his gunner's turret atop the Hummer. One jihadi with an RPG could kill us all. The other three of us took our weapons off safe. I watched right,

Benum left, D-Willie forward, Taymondo to the rear. We had to sneak looks at the hajj, though, because it was electrifying and magnetic and incomprehensible. How far had they walked? Where did they get water? What if they had to pee?

The radio spurted static and Killdozer's voice broke through: "All units, this is Bravo One, confirm when you're in position. Over."

I grabbed the radio and checked us in, then trained some binocs on the procession. No one seemed to notice us, which was excellent. Low-profile was the game.

As other Vees began checking in with the captain, we sat in silence for 10 minutes, watching the mysterious humanity plodding toward a huge mosque with a gold dome. Why? Wasn't there anything on the tube? What would inspire such devotion?

There was no way I'd ever do this … was there?

I flashed on junior year, when a bunch of us kids packed into a van and drove up to the Clark County Amphitheater to see Metallica. There was a gigantic line of cars creeping into the place, moving about 10 feet every few minutes. Crowds of people were getting out and walking to their seats. Crazy. When the band blasted into "Master of Puppets" and followed with "The Thing That Should Not Be," even crazier, we lost our minds, metalhead madness … uh, maybe our version of the gold dome effect?

"Burqa bogey at 8 o'clock," Taymondo reported over the headset.

"Roger that," D-Willie said.

She was about 60 yards from our Humvee, approaching on a side street.

"Where'd she come from?" I asked.

"I don't know. I looked over and there she was."

D-Willie said, "The sister's probably just meeting up with her girls in the hajj. Cut her some slack till we know what's what."

D was right. It was too soon. We were just jumpy. The chances were good that she was somebody's mom, wife or daughter, that she was heading for the hajj. Hard to tell underneath all that burlap. She didn't seem to be in a hurry. At 35 yards, I thought I noticed her head swivel slightly to look at us. My meter twitched. Why was she out by herself? Without a man? I looked forward and right. If this was a setup, she might have help, a car, a van, a guy on a motorbike. But there was nobody. The hajj sucked up every living thing like a dark star.

We couldn't see her face through the burqa mesh, so how could we judge? Were her eyes nervous? Red? Weepy? Hashed? Was she Sunni or Shiite? No way to read her. Besides, the sun was at her back as she moved toward us, so we had to look into it. Maybe that was her plan.

When she was 30 yards away, Taymondo said, "D, you want me to stop her?"

"Whoa, whoa, whoa! Hold your fire!"

"I don't mean kill her, just get her to stop."

Taymondo had been to the new counterinsurgency class. The other three of us hadn't. Twenty-five yards now. "Roger that," D-Willie said. "Make her stop."

Tay spouted a couple of Arabic words and the woman stopped. Of course, Tay had the .50-caliber sighted in on her. That glowering gun overcame a lot of language barriers.

The Burqa Chick just stood there for a while, like a wax figure. Then she slowly turned sideways so we could see the outline of her belly, which was huge.

"She's pregnant," Taymondo said.

"Looks that way," D-Willie agreed. "You want to wave her through?"

"I guess so."

"All right."

Responding to Taymondo's wave, Burqa Chick took a few tentative steps toward us. My meter twitched again. What would Killdozer do? Taymondo seemed to be vibrating, too, breathing asthmatically into the headset.

Then she turned toward the hajj. Good. She took a few more steps but stopped. Bad. Thirty seconds passed.

"What the fuck is she doing?" D-Willie asked.

"I dunno," Taymondo said. "You want me to light her up?"

"*No*. We ain't Blackwater cowboys. You'll spook the hajj. You kill her, you kill a thousand. Be cool."

"Maybe she's having the baby," Benum said. "Let's help her."

There was a short silence on the headsets and D-Willie said, "You're fucking with us, right, Benny?"

"Affirmative. I'm not sticking my hands up there. You don't know what you'll find. Maybe a minotaur. That's a tough delivery, at least a week of pushing and screaming."

"What the fuck is a minotaur?" D-Willie asked.

"Heads up, she's moving again," Taymondo warned.

Burqa Chick started to walk back toward us, in slow motion. However, it might have been one of those deals where she was walking at normal speed but time slowed down.

"Goddamn," D-Willie muttered.

"Call it and she's gone," Taymondo said.

"What if she changed her mind?" I said, disregarding my twitch. "What if the hajj is too scary for a pregnant woman?"

"Put the gun on her, Tay," D-Willie said. "When I get to ten, take her out … one … two … three … four … "

D-Willie counted each time she took one of her tiny slow creepy steps toward us, like she thought we wouldn't notice them. "Five … six … seven … eight … "

"*TAKE ONE MORE STEP AND YOU DIE*," Taymondo screamed. "*YOU DIE YOU DIE YOU DIE!*"

"Nine … "

She stopped. Somehow Tay's English — or maybe just his tone — got through to her. We waited while she stood there looking at us. Or she seemed to be looking at us. If only she would show us her face. How did anybody ever know what was going on with women in this country if you never saw their faces or their eyes? How did an Iraqi man ever get a date?

"She makes any kind of move with her hands," D-Willie said, "dust her."

"You got it," Taymondo answered.

Iraqis were crazy. Or were they? If we ordered them to stop and they didn't, that was a bad sign. Usually. Sometimes they truly didn't understand what we wanted. If they had wires sticking out of their clothing, that was an extremely bad sign, but we couldn't kill them until we confirmed they were suicide bombers. If we followed the rules of engagement, we wouldn't know until it was too late. Killdozer called that a "Fuck-22." The guys didn't get the reference.

We waited a good minute while Burqa Chick stood there. Or it could have been 10 seconds. Slowly, she turned around and took three steps toward the hajj. "That's it, sister," D-Willie said.

Then she stopped in the middle of the street with her back to us and began to turn, inches at a time, until she faced us again.

D-Willie punched the steering wheel with his fist. *"What the fuck? That bitch is whack."*

"Must be the hormones," Benum said.

Taymondo had the best view from the gun turret. "I got a bad feeling," he said. "I think we should waste her."

"If she takes one more"

It was like a movie explosion, only real.

A flash of light.

A gigantic fireball.

A concussive blast wave.

A black rain of debris.

I screamed, *"FUCK!"*

All I could think was, fuck Iraq, fuck war, fuck missions, fuck heat, fuck dust, fuck sand, fuck Blackwater, fuck Halliburton, fuck Cheney, fuck Bush, fuck Rumsfeld, fuck Saddam, fuck mullahfuckers, fuck suicide bomber fucks. We were so fucking fucked.

There was probably some fancy fucking psychological reason for it, why we said fuck so much. Like, there was a chance we would never have sex again? Like, we could be dead? Like, if you were a virgin when you got to the sandbox, there was a good chance you would die a virgin? We thought about sex a lot. Thank God I made it with Halley a few times. At least I knew what it was all about. Unbelievable. Amazing. Blinding-white-light beautiful. The first time, I had no idea what to do but Halley was kind to me. Her parents weren't home. She took my hand and led me upstairs to her bedroom, to a new kind of religion.

She slipped out of her top in one smooth arms-over-head motion and she wasn't wearing a bra — *Oh my awesome God!*

She pulled my face to her and I started to kiss one stunning impossibly perfect breast, then the other — *Shout it out, Glory hallelujah!*

She wriggled out of her jeans and panties — *Holy Church of the Divine Electric Slam!*

She pushed away from me, fell back on the bed and spread her luminous legs — *Almighty Lord Jesus in heaven!*

She started wiggling her toes, which was so goofball I hurt my face grinning. Was that her way of telling me to come on down and be saved?

Halley could be so … I didn't even know what the word for her was. Maybe there wasn't one. Where did she learn to be like that? Probably nowhere. Probably she just *was*. I couldn't believe what I was seeing. I looked and looked. I stared. Impolitely. I couldn't help it. This is what everyone talks about, I thought, the grail, the epic awesome chill mysterious wonder of all glorious wonders.

Halley was the cutest wispy blonde. Beautiful beautiful beautiful beyond description. I quit breathing and had to gasp for air.

She seemed so relaxed, so free. She smiled like sunshine. She said, "You know you have to take off your clothes, too, right?"

Halley could always make me laugh. When she made fun of me, it wasn't in a mean way. "Yeah," I said. "I forgot. I got all mesmerized."

I unbelted, unzipped, undressed. My body was ready. It knew what to do even if my mind didn't.

And then …

To my crushingly deep dismay, her legs snapped together — *blap!* — like a mouse trap. She raised one eyebrow and said, "Uhhhhhhh, aren't you forgetting something?"

I looked at her in torturous agony.

"Do you have some protection?" she asked. "Because I really like you, Johnny Cutter, and I really want you to fuck me."

Did she just say that? What a majestic breathtaking incandescent obscenity. I never thought I would hear anything like that in my whole life. Yet here it was. The moment. A golden goddess. Waiting for me.

"But we really need protection. Or we can't … you know … "

I saw the flash of light and I saw Halley. Some time later — seconds? minutes? — about 20 yards in front of the Humvee, I saw a sack of potatoes in the street, burning, sending off writhing gobs of black smoke. I stared at it and realized two things: The world was silent, so my hearing was probably gone, and that flaming sack of potatoes was the top half of Burqa Chick.

Because I had mysteriously seen and heard Halley in another place and another time, I wondered if I was alive. Maybe that explained the silence. Disoriented and ridiculously mixed up, I had a thought that might have explained everything: What if dying is like a silent movie preview that cuts quickly to all the good scenes, to trick you into going, before everything fades to black? I had to get out of the theater. I had to go find Halley before the end.

I yanked the Humvee door handle. The door fell to the ground. Somebody grabbed me.

"I've got to go," I said, paradoxically, in my silent movie. "I need protection … I've got to get protection."

A muffled far-off voice whispered, "You've got all the protection you need right here, Cutter. Keep breathing. Keep it together. Medevac's on the way. Everything's cool."

It was Vig Oskierko, blocking my escape. I lunged toward the other door, but D-Willie was there, holding his hand to his bloody face, slowly pulling a dagger of glass out of his cheek. The driver's side door opened and another medic reached in to stop him. Too late. D-Willie yanked on the dagger and let out a soft distant scream.

13 / What luck's got to do with it

We did almost everything right in our mashup with Burqa Chick. That was Captain Dozinger's conclusion in the after-action review. Well, except for one thing.

"It wasn't a woman," the captain said.

D-Willie blurted out, "Say what?"

"It was a man."

"No way," Benum said. "She was pregnant."

"That was bomb weight, not baby weight."

Grabbing imaginary breasts, D-Willie said, "What about the … they were at least C cups."

The captain shook his head. "No. That was C4."

"That was a dude?" D-Willie said. "For real?"

"It was real, all right. EOD recovered the proof. They saved it in an evidence locker. You want to see it?"

We grimaced in unison. *"Hell, no!"* Taymondo said.

Goddamn, Iraq was never what it seemed, was constantly playing us. The good news was, we were all wearing our helmets and Kevlar vests. Taymondo, more exposed up in the .50-caliber turret, had goggles and gloves on, too. We didn't overreact under pressure. D-Willie was counting it off; one more step and Tay would have wasted her … him.

"You gave him a chance to walk away," Killdozer said, "and you gave yourselves a chance to survive. It was the right balance."

D-Willie suffered the biggest injury, which, by Iraq standards, was nothing. It took 27 stitches to close the gash in his face and he was down with that. "Scars give a man character," he said enthusiastically. My hearing started to come back. Taymondo and Benum were only shaken and scratched.

Killdozer gave us three days off. We needed it, he insisted, mentally if not physically. So we sat around, played video games and watched movies. We also had to do a session with Niehus.

Taymondo hated head work. "If I told my dad I was seeing a shrink," he said, "he'd beat my ass bloody with a board. To him, that's all the therapy anybody needs. And what the fuck is up with Niehus and those questions? 'How did it make you feel to see the bomber's body in the street?' Is he kidding?"

"What did you tell him?" Benum asked.

"I said I was glad it was her and not me."

"What did he say to that?"

"Nothing. He just raised one of his eyebrows. What's that supposed to mean?"

D-Willie said, "That means he thinks you're a psycho. That's exactly what he did when I told him I wanted to run over what was left of her, except the Humvee wouldn't start."

"Maybe it's good to be crazy," I said. "I feel safer the more paranoid I get. Killdozer's lectures are stuck in my head."

"I'd rather be lucky than paranoid," Benum said. "You can be as psycho as you want but if you're in the wrong place at the wrong time, you're just a dead head case. Look at the guys we lost. They were just as paranoid as the rest of us. Did it do them any good?"

There was nothing to say. We knew the answer to Benum's question and the answer applied to us.

As the months went by, I settled into a disturbing routine. With every day on patrol, every mission, every explosion, every mortar attack, every obliterated corpse in the street, my life back home slipped further away. The intensity of Baghdad became more real than the tranquility of Trillium. I knew that was destructive and dangerous but it couldn't be stopped. This new normal sneaked up on me in small daily doses. I spent 24/7 with the same guys. I needed them to survive. They needed me. We understood each other because we had all been through the same insane thing day after day after day. Sad sick stuff that shouldn't have been funny made us laugh. Bloated bodies, mass graves, bullet holes in heads. That dark bond crushed everything else.

But as long as it wasn't happening to us, everything was cool. As long as everybody kept saying we were winning the war, we could keep doing what we were doing. Maybe our luck would hold.

PART II
NOWHERE

14 / Weapons of mass reconstruction

Colonel Randall Toar kept precise, obsessive surgical records. The 47-year-old doctor had hundreds of handwritten notebooks dating back to his surgical residency at Lenox Hill Hospital in New York, which began at 7:48 a.m. on July 1, 1985, a Monday, and ended at 11:49 p.m. on June 30, 1990, a Saturday. The West Point graduate had committed to 17 years of service in exchange for his education and medical training. The newly minted surgeon reported for duty and began repaying the Army on August 1, 1990, a Wednesday.

Preparing for Operation Desert Storm, the young doctor was among the first wave of Army medical personnel to set up camp with the 82nd Airborne in Saudi Arabia, beginning September 18, 1990, a Tuesday. His case diary during the four-month buildup to the war showed various non-combat injuries and illnesses, broken arms, wrenched backs, viral infections, high fevers, persistent coughs. The war was over so fast that he saw only a few battle cases. The soldiers he treated during the ground assault mostly suffered bullet wounds from potshots by Saddam Hussein's Republican Guard before they put down their AK-47s and put up their white flags. Only one soldier died on his table, an infantryman whose large intestine was ripped open by a bullet. In that case, the medevac helicopters were grounded by a dust storm, and by the time the soldier made it to Doctor Toar's operating room, the sepsis was overwhelming. A huge dose of antibiotics failed. It was a fluky, bad luck, weather-related death beyond the doctor's control.

Fourteen years later, Toar returned for Operation Iraqi Freedom, a grindingly different war that had turned gruesome. It became clear in the first year that because Pentagon war planners had failed to secure Iraqi weapons depots as the invasion began, artillery shells by the thousands fell into the hands of well-trained former Iraqi army soldiers. These Baath Party members were denied jobs in the new government, another war planner mistake, and they turned to insurgency. Artillery shells plus military expertise equaled improvised explosive devices. A lack of armor on the U.S. Army's major form of transportation, the Humvee, equaled horrific injuries from the roadside bombs.

Some days, Doctor Toar could barely bring himself to open his case diary. Each entry caused him psychological pain, unlike the physical symptoms suffered by the soldiers, but still debilitating.

Writing down the facts of the case was hard enough, but how do you tell a gunner that soft-tissue genital trauma makes his dreams of a family "questionable," the preferred term rather than "impossible"? How do you explain pneumocephaly or necrotizing fasciitis? Do you want to describe the use of the Joe Hall Morris device or the Gigli saw? In Doctor Toar's experience, it merely induced fear rather than understanding. Better to generalize, to gloss over. How can a 19-year-old infantryman deal with the news that his transected rectum will be rerouted to a bag after IED shrapnel tore through the chassis of his Humvee? How can a 21-year-old tanker burned over 90 percent of his body comprehend his treatment? We'll start with intubation to preclude airway edema, we'll administer fluids intravenously, perform escharotomies on both arms, irrigate and debride the wounds, cover them with Silvadene, dress them with Kerlex, and ultimately we'll send you, when you're stabilized, to a Level IV treatment facility. There, the burn experts, after first trying further debridement to remove newly dead tissue, will conclude that they can save your life but not your arms. Nobody likes bilateral amputation above the elbows, but there will be no other choice.

Well, no other medical choice. In his current deployment in Iraq, Doctor Toar had seen a few despairing soldiers make their personal choice, begging to be allowed to die when they realized the extent of their injuries. However, immediate treatment by medics and a forward surgical team, followed by rapid transport of the wounded to a combat support hospital, enabled Army doctors to save them.

Toar now wondered about Private First Class Johnathan Cutter, who had just passed out on the operating table after regaining consciousness for a few moments, just long enough to begin screaming in pain.

Cutter had presented with polytrauma: An apparent penetrating brain injury, third-degree burns to his lower trunk, a severely mangled right hand and the loss of his right foot.

One of the medics who helped bring Cutter in handed Doctor Toar a metal ammo box. "We found the foot," the medic said, "so we went ahead and packed it. I don't know if it will help. We didn't have any ice. It was the best we could do." The medic shrugged, aware that this foot would most likely end up with the other feet, toes, legs, hands, fingers and arms in the limbs-to-be-incinerated pile.

"It's possible," Doctor Toar said. He opened the box and took a quick look at the severed, blood-soaked foot. It was still in the boot, with the shattered tibia and fibula sticking out, surrounded by chopped-up muscles and tendons. The shear area was contaminated with the ever-present Iraqi dust and what appeared to be motor oil or wheel-bearing grease. Remnants of gray skin showed severe necrosis. As usual, there would be no attempt to reattach the foot. It was not possible, not with this level of contamination. Beyond that, microsurgery was out of the question in a busy combat support hospital.

"Thanks," Doctor Toar said to the medic anyway. "That's good work." It was standard practice to encourage the medics to bring the pieces in, regardless of the prognosis. Hope was a precious commodity in Iraq, the scrim that provided a gauzy, tolerable view of destruction, dismemberment and death.

Doctor Toar placed Cutter near the top of a mental matrix of his other severe cases. The soldier was so young, like most of the men who showed up with their grievous injuries. He couldn't even grow a beard, merely patches of light brown fuzz. His face had turned purple and red with lumpy bruises and jagged cuts, presumably the result of some kind of impact. As the doctor irrigated Cutter's gnarled leg stump with isotonic saline, he thought: I hope this kid wasn't a soccer player.

Invariably, when Toar did the wound washout before an amputation, he thought first of the life adjustment, from bed to wheelchair to prosthetic. That was just the physical part. The psychological change often left the soldier limping more than the injury. Some men got over it better than others. Some rarely got out of bed again. When you looked beneath the covers at night and saw that your legs were gone, even though you could still feel them, everything changed. When you got into your prosthetic legs in the morning, when you rigged up your hook, when you calculated what was gained from your loss, it just wasn't worth the effort. Doctor Toar was sure of that. He had seen it in soldiers' eyes and heard it in their voices during a temporary posting in Ward 57 at Walter Reed hospital. Now, every time he took off an arm in Iraq, he wondered how the soldier would make love to his wife. With or without the hook? The musing was macabre, but Toar saw too many arms and legs separated from their bodies, lying there bloody and fresh. His mind processed, questioned, considered, extrapolated. Maybe it doesn't matter, Toar thought, maybe you can get used to anything. The doctor found it best not to think about it, to try to turn off his mind's relentless examination. That kind of adjustment was too depressing. It undermined his ability to cut. Nevertheless, he occasionally looked at his patients and wondered, How will you stroke her hair with a hook?

Toar's nurse, Lieutenant Colonel Richard Dohaben, working at the autoclave, interrupted the doctor's bedroom shadow play. "The instruments are sterilized, Doctor. Ready when you are."

"Good. We're almost there. Is Constance next door?"

"Yes, should I round her up?"

"Please. We don't want this man waking up in the middle of it."

Dohaben went to the adjacent operating room and returned with Colonel Constance O'Shaughnessy, an anesthesiologist.

Doctor Toar asked, "How's it going over there, Connie? Can they spare you for a little while?"

"I think so. They're still probing his foot. They may try to save it. I don't know, though, he can't feel it and there's not much muscle left to reconstruct. We'll see. His Humvee got blown up."

"What a coincidence," Doctor Toar said. "Same here. This is Private First Class Johnathan Cutter. We've got some real work to do. I need him to be way under. I'm going to clean up the right leg first. I don't believe we need to go above the knee. The right hand will have to come off, but the brain injury is going to be a slog, a manual craniotomy. The film shows two metallic fragments and a five-centimeter hematoma. He's out cold on his own now, but he'll need your help."

"Yes, sir," O'Shaughnessy said. "I'll start an IV."

"If he goes into hypotension, are we set with epinephrine?"

"Yes. Was his head injury high-velocity? Are we looking at pneumocephaly?"

"It's a high probability."

"Then we're putting him on a hundred percent oxygen?"

"Go for it," the doctor said.

Toar immobilized Cutter's leg in a metal brace. He added a pneumatic tourniquet just below the knee and removed the combat application tourniquet that had been applied on the battlefield. The doctor assessed Cutter's chances of survival at better than average because the tourniquet had been cinched before shock set in. The doctor wished he had realized before now that somebody, most likely a soldier, had acted quickly in the chaos. He would have given another "good work" to the medic who brought Cutter in.

Doctor O'Shaughnessy held up a white bottle and prepared to extract 15 milliliters of the liquid from it with a hypodermic needle.

"Propofol?" Doctor Toar asked.

Reading the concern in his voice, O'Shaughnessy stopped in mid-poke. "Yes?" she said.

"It has an occasional side effect?" Doctor Toar always knew the answer to the questions he asked.

The anesthesiologist looked at the dressing covering Cutter's phallus and testicles. She nodded. "Priapism."

"We're also dealing with a co-morbidity, burns to the genitalia. As unlikely as it is, if the propofol induced erection, well, let's not disturb any tissue that we don't have to."

"Of course," O'Shaughnessy said. "I'll switch to Ketamine."

"Thank you." Toar turned his attention back to Cutter's leg, drawing a line with a marker about four inches below the knee. He would take off about three inches to reach viable soft tissue. This was a balancing act, more art than science. If he took off too much, Cutter could have trouble with the fit of his prosthetic. If he took off too little, Level IV or V surgeons might have to take more later. Marginal tissue left behind could refuse to heal or lead to sepsis. The next amputation would take the knee. Doctor Toar had briefly considered going all the way right now, making absolutely certain, but Cutter's knee was in serviceable shape, mild burns and a few puncture wounds. With luck, it would be a functioning joint for many years. The Army's surgical consensus was to perform amputations at a viable distal level, to preserve maximum limb length. He decided to save the knee. Doctor Toar almost always erred on the side of giving the soldier a chance to keep more of his limb.

When O'Shaughnessy had the Ketamine running and Cutter's vital signs were stable, Toar said, "Let's go."

Nurse Dohaben handed a scalpel to the doctor and he began to separate skin from fascia to create flaps that would close over the stump. He loosened the pneumatic tourniquet slightly. If there was blood flow at the site of the cut, healing could proceed. If not, he might have to take the knee. He was pleased to note a small amount of oozing at the shear. He was ready to make the cut.

"Saw," Doctor Toar said. As Dohaben handed him the amputation saw, Toar had a morbid thought: These instruments have not changed much since the Civil War.

In the 1860s, screams reverberated like muskets, and combat surgery bordered on barbaric. Arms and legs were thrown into heaping piles outside the medical tents. The so-called doctors lost more patients than they saved. Toar found it depressing to be performing essentially the same operation.

As he made the initial cuts, pulling the saw toward him, listening for the rasping of the steel blade on bone, the doctor wondered how far medicine had really come. Certainly, patients did not suffer as much now, with modern anesthesia and mostly aseptic operating rooms, but weren't the results the same? Soldiers went to war as whole men — and these days, whole women — and the unlucky ones died or came back as single, double or triple amputees. Even quadruple. Some survived with catastrophic brain injuries or severed spinal cords. They ended up slouching in a wheelchair for the rest of their foreshortened lives, aware of little more than the sun on their skin, with 24-hour caretakers who kept them watered and fed. In darker moments, Doctor Toar wondered if the men who died were actually the fortunate ones.

"He's looking good," O'Shaughnessy said. "BP 140 over 95; pulse, 82; PaO_2, 118; PCO_2, 44."

"Surprisingly good," Doctor Toar agreed. He continued the slow sawing. After seven minutes, Dohaben moved in to support the three-inch length of leg that was about to come off. "Thank you," Toar said, "almost there."

He began to shorten his strokes. In another minute, he got through the calf-side layer of connective tissue, the outer fascia and skin. It was done. Dohaben held the section up for Toar to inspect. It was like a thick, blackened, two-bone-in New York steak, covered with crusty, co-agulated blood. The doctor took a quick look and nodded. His concern now was with the segment of leg that remained, and whether it was capable of healing. The nurse took the piece away, to a disposal bin just outside the operating room. There goes a thousand barrels of oil, the doctor thought.

After performing scores of amputations, Doctor Toar operated on one especially unfortunate soldier, and the "oil equation" was born. It was arbitrary, it was cynical, it was math he never shared with anyone else. The image of that soldier, grimly accepting his fate, came back and sent the doctor's mind spiraling off into costs-of-war calculations. The patient was a corporal, an infantryman who knew his way around but had stepped on a land mine just the same. He was conscious when he got to Doctor Toar's table.

"Hey, Doc," he said in a gurgly, phlegm-laced voice. "Can you come closer?" Tears were welling up in the soldier's eyes. Toar leaned down. The soldier whispered, "I know it's bad. If you have to cut them off, I want you to let me die. OK? Can you do that for me?"

Toar's throat tightened. He wasn't a doctor at that moment, just a human being who could see and feel another man's pain and despair. "I'm sorry," he said. "I can't do that."

"Nobody has to know," the soldier said. "Just let go. Unplug. Extra morphine. Whatever it takes."

"I'm sorry. We only save lives."

"I want to be saved *from* my life."

"You'll be all right," Toar said, though he knew that was a lie.

"I'm *begging* you."

"You're going to be OK."

The soldier knew it was a lie, too. He shook his head in disgusted resignation and said, "I hope the folks back home appreciate the oil. I figure I got them at least 3,000 barrels."

Doctor Toar performed a triple amputation to save what was left of the soldier's life. Two legs and an arm were gone. The grim number was seared into the doctor's brain: A thousand barrels per limb.

Toar looked at Private First Class Cutter's face beneath the ventilation mask. Eyes closed to the bright lights overhead. Machine-aided breathing low and rhythmic. The scene was almost peaceful. It's too bad he has to wake up, the doctor thought. He turned to the tool tray behind him and picked up a bone nibbler. He began to work on the ends of the tibia and fibula, smoothing and shaping to create a comfortable stump. When he was satisfied that the bones would not cause burning discomfort in later life, he dealt with the nerve stumps, separating them with a scalpel, then suturing them into surrounding muscle. Isolated nerves, kept away from pulsing arteries, would be less likely to regenerate into a tumorous, serpentine, pain-signaling neuroma. After half an hour of finessing the tissue, he closed the stump with skin-flap sutures. Nurse Dohaben removed the pneumatic tourniquet. The finished residual leg was a study in contrasts. The stump itself was ugly, inflamed, swollen. Doctor Toar's work was beautiful, precise, salutary.

He turned to the right hand. The blast had blown most of the meat off the bones. The heat had nearly cauterized the wound; there was not much bleeding. Time was crucial. Doctor Toar did a quick guillotine amputation midway between the wrist and elbow and moved on.

"Next up, craniotomy," the doctor said. "Richard, would you set him up in the Mayfield pins?" Doctor Toar was a modest general surgeon. Based on his battlefield experience, he knew what was possible and what was unlikely. Miracles happened on TV shows, not here. His patients never had the chance for a heart-to-heart talk about the risks of paralysis or loss of speech and memory. Most of them were unconscious and near death. The few who were awake were not lucid enough to understand what was happening. Doctor Toar would be the first to admit he was not an "official" neurosurgeon. Such an exotic specialty was rare enough in civilian life. In the military, it didn't exist, at least not on the battlefield. It couldn't. The requirements — in tools, equipment, diagnostics, staff and time — were too great. When the soldier presented with a skull entry wound, a one-inch laceration in the right temple just above eyebrow level, when the film showed two shards of metal penetrating the dura mater, the choice was clear: Operate now, even if you didn't have a Johns Hopkins neurosurgery fellowship certificate hanging on the wall of your tent. A hand drill and a Gigli saw would get you in. A probe and Bishop Harmon forceps would get the shrapnel out.

Cutter's head was already shaved. He came in that way. Bald was beautiful in Iraq, carefree and cooler. Many soldiers visited the barber weekly for a buzz cut. Doctor Toar wondered whether they realized how helpful a clean pate would be during emergency brain surgery.

Toar palpated the skin on Cutter's forehead. He detected no bleeding from the laceration. "How are his numbers, Doctor O'Shaughnessy?"

"Rock steady."

"Let's go, then. Scalpel."

Nurse Dohaben handed Doctor Toar the instrument and he made the first incision, through the scalp and temporalis muscle. It was a feel thing. The cut had to go all the way through to the bone, but there was no reason to score the skull. He quickly extended the incision into a semicircle around the cranial wound. "Retract, please."

Nurse Dohaben pulled back the skin and muscle, locking it in place with retractors and clips. He applied manual pressure above the flap to achieve hemostasis. Doctor Toar turned to the tool tray and grasped the drill protectively with both hands. A thin coating of ooze made his gloves a little slippery. "First burr hole," he said, beginning to drill about half an inch above the top of the right ear. The doctor found a comfortable rhythm in the turning of the bit. Each hole required just a few minutes of work and soon all three were done. Brain surgery in the field was less upsetting than doing an amputation. The skull bone would be replaced at the end of the operation and the scalp would heal, but an arm and a leg were gone forever.

Toar threaded the saw wire through hole one and out hole two. He began to cut, pulling the wire back and forth. He preferred to use more strokes with less pressure. It took longer, but he never got tired. Nevertheless, there was no mechanical advantage and this was harder work than drilling burr holes. In 30 minutes, he was finished and handed the bone flap to Nurse Dohaben. "Don't lose that," he said. The nurse smiled wanly.

Doctor Toar pressed on the fibrous dura mater around the shrapnel with a stainless steel probe. "Forceps," he said after the inspection. Do-haben handed him the tool and took the probe in exchange. The doctor began to pick small bone fragments out of the cranial cavity. Satisfied that he had retrieved all of them, the doctor called for irrigation. The nurse washed the area with saline from a squirt bottle.

"Scalpel," Toar called. He took it from Dohaben and made an incision in the dura along the lines of the entrance wound. After two more cuts, Dohaben was able to retract a flap. The brain, pulsing softly along with Cutter's heartbeat, was exposed.

"There they are," Doctor Toar said. "We got lucky." The two metal fragments lay next to each other, only slightly embedded in the brain matter. "They didn't cut too deeply; damage may be minimal. One of them has a sharp edge, though. Forceps, please."

Doctor Toar pinced an exposed piece of the larger fragment and pulled it out in one slow, smooth motion. The doctor had seen metal fragments like this in other brains. It was silverish in color, underneath the coating of blood, and shaped like a jagged rock. Most likely this had been part of a cheap screw or bolt, the most common bomb add-ins because they shattered into sharp projectiles. If the blast wave didn't kill the soldier, a severed artery might.

Nurse Dohaben held out a stainless-steel dish and Doctor Toar dropped the shrapnel into it. "One more to come," the doctor said. He turned to the cranial cavity again and studied the exposed tip of the second fragment. Most of the piece was submerged in the brain, but being able to see part of it, not having to dig for it, was helpful. Battle-field medicine is relative, the doctor thought. What happened to this boy is horrible and senseless, but compared with the Iraqi national from yesterday, it's fixable.

Host-nation soldiers and civilians were often brought to the U.S. forward surgical teams and combat support hospitals. Medics made the gesture to win — and repair — hearts and minds. The unidentified Iraqi, about 30 years old, had presented with two entrance wounds in the skull, the left hemisphere, and one exit wound, at the base near the C-1 vertebra. Doctor Toar ran film although he knew what it would show: One bullet was a through-and-through, but one had disinte-grated in the brain, chewing up neural pathways like a lawn mower.

Fragments had dispersed in the medulla oblongata. It was amazing the man was breathing. He died after five minutes on the table. Doctor Toar considered a trip to the Baghdad morgue the preferred outcome for this patient, dubbed Abdullah Doe. The man's family certainly could not have provided 24-hour nursing care for five years, if he lived that long, or even five days, if he didn't. Doe's timely death also allowed the doctor to work on two American IED victims who showed up just 15 minutes later. Triage worked in mysterious ways.

Doctor Toar pushed cautiously on the exposed tip of the second fragment in Cutter's brain. It gave a little, easily, which meant it might release easily, too, but the risk of cutting a vessel with a sharp shrapnel edge worried the doctor. "How's the blood pressure?" he asked.

"Steady," O'Shaughnessy said, "150 over 105. He's a fighter."

"He's young," Doctor Toar countered.

The anesthesiologist nodded reluctantly. "Maybe."

"I'm a little concerned that when this piece comes out, we might get some parenchymal bleeding. Let's be prepared for cautery."

"Standing by," Dohaben said.

"Here we go." Doctor Toar grasped the tip of the fragment with the forceps and began to pull. Encountering resistance, he let go. He considered whether to make short incisions on each side of the fragment to help it slip out. The risk was motor impairment as a result of the cuts. Had he been operating at a Level V facility, Walter Reed or Brooke, he would get a consult, but surgery in Iraq wasn't surgery in Washington or San Antonio. Doctor Toar looked at his watch. He wanted to get Cutter on the next flight to Landstuhl.

He pinced the tip of the shrapnel and yanked.

The twisted metal popped out with a soft pudding-slurp sound. Toar dropped the shard in the steel dish. Dohaben set it aside and handed him the cauterizing needle, taking the forceps in exchange. The doctor watched for bleeding. There wasn't any. "Wow," he said. "That went surprisingly well. Let's evacuate the hematoma and get out of this soldier's head. He's got a plane to catch."

15 / What happened?

The droning went on for a long time. I was inside … an air condi-
tioner? A factory? A factory in a dream? Machinery was humming all
around. I was part of it. Floating in the machinery. No sense of gravity.
I felt light. Hollow. When I first became aware of the noise, it was dark,
but every now and then a light would flash, a small star blipping on the
horizon. Out there somewhere in the blackness. Then another light.
And another. Tiny novas. Then more blackness, wide and deep. More
star bursts, random and bright. More machinery, pulsing and humming. Then nothing. No time. No stars. Not even a sense of the blackness. I didn't know where I was, because I was … nowhere.

I began to think I was dead but how could I be dead if I was thinking? Yet I had no sense of my body. Just my mind. After a while, I
thought my foot moved. I couldn't feel it but I believed my foot was
floating away from my leg, walking on its own, separate from me. My
leg was light. The little novas returned to my deep wide empty black
landscape. I tried to determine if I was standing, sitting or lying. In the
blackness, there were no markers, no up, no down, no sideways.

Some days or hours or minutes later, I realized I was alone in the
blackness. "Hello?" I said. Except I didn't hear myself. "Where am I?"
Still nothing. Nobody answered. I seemed to be talking only in my
mind. "Halley, are you here?" Only the machinery spoke to me, with its
insistent thrumming, covering me like a blanket. If I could only talk to
Halley, she could tell me if I was alive. Suddenly I wanted to touch Halley but she wasn't there. That confused me. Where was she? I started to
wonder who Halley was. I didn't even know where I got the name. It
just appeared in my mind. I listened to the machinery, hoping the answer would come, or that Halley would appear. She didn't. I began to
think she was gone. Then I wondered if I knew her. I didn't know how
the name came to me. I tried to think of somebody who could come get
me. Take me away from here … wherever here was. After a while, I un-

derstood there was no word for where I was, which, really, was beyond nowhere. Maybe I was dead, a black mind existence. I considered that. How do you see movies here? Ha! That thought popped into my black mind. Wasn't God supposed to greet me? Give me a tour? Where was he? Where would I live? Did I have a … a … a what? What was the word? I puzzled over that one. I looked around for God. I could see nothing but blackness and that reassured me. If God appeared, he would definitely stand out against the blackness. Then I saw myself, standing across from me, separate from me. I was holding a sign that said, "God." What a good idea. Ha, a *God* idea! He could find me now. He could give me a ride in that … thing he rides around in. I couldn't think of the word for it but God would be driving. Except I began to doubt my theory. It didn't make sense. There was no … no … I didn't have the word for where God would be driving in the blackness. Besides, he didn't have a driver's license. I seemed sure of that. I wondered whether God carried a wallet and ID, or did everybody just know him? Maybe I could find some people who could tell me where he was.

My search for God made me tired. I watched the little star explosions for a while but I just wanted to sleep. My other self with the sign vanished. God would have to find me on his own. I began to think I wasn't going to find him. I began to wonder if God could find me in the middle of all this blackness. I would just have to stay here. Then I began to think that I went backwards, that I was somewhere before I started to think about all these things, about God. Had I thought about anything? Was everything still waiting to be thought? My head began to throb, throbbing that matched the noise of the machines. The same tempo, the same thrum. Slowly rising and falling. I wanted to run, to get out of here, but where was here? That was the question I kept coming back to. I couldn't move, though.

"Help!"

I tried to shout. I thought I shouted but I barely heard myself.

"HELP! PLEASE! HELP!"

Better. Louder. But garbly and mushy.

"It's OK. You're OK."

I heard a voice. Not mine. Whose?

"Are you waking up? Good. You can do it. Just open your eyes."

Somebody touched me in my dream, on my arm, and it crackled, like it had fallen asleep. Bolts of electricity shot through it.

"Come on. Open your eyes, Johnathan."

The voice got louder, closer. The machinery receded. It was a man's voice. Above me. "I know you're in there."

I saw him, sort of, a dim figure as he slowly appeared out of fog. I could make out the fuzzy swirling outlines of glasses and a face mask.

"Excellent. Outstanding. Welcome back, Private First Class Cutter."

I heard the words but what did he mean? Back? From where?

"Don't try to move. Relax. I'm going to step away for a minute. I'll be right back and I'll bring the doctor."

Bring the doctor? What happened? "WHAT HAPPENED?" I tried to say. I heard the words in my mind but they didn't come out right. What I heard wasn't what I said. It was messed up, like my tongue was wrapped in tape, or my mouth was stuffed with cotton.

"Hold up, Cutter. I don't want you to talk yet. I want you to relax. You're going to be fine but you've had an accident. I want to get the doctor and have him look at you. Do you understand?"

"Accident. What accident?"

"OK, you want to talk, that's good. Say that again, just a little slower. I'll listen real close."

He couldn't understand me. That seemed to make sense. It was the first thing that made sense to me in a long time. I couldn't even understand myself, except in my mind. I focused on my tongue. I moved it. Up and down. Side to side. It wasn't taped up. I held it still. Then I spoke. "*What ... happened ... to ... me?*"

"Good." The man smiled and nodded. "That's great. I got that. You're going to be fine, Johnathan. Just fine. I'll be right back. I want to have the doctor talk to you. OK?"

Why did I need a doctor?

The man said, "We'll be landing soon and your vital signs are getting stronger by the hour." He pointed to blinking lights on machinery at the bottom of the gurney. As I raised my head to look, a shooting pain exploded up through my neck and practically ripped my skull open. I could vaguely see what the man was pointing at ... machinery ... a computer screen. There were tubes sticking out of my arm and leg! My vision got a little better. Beyond me lay another … soldier? … yes … a soldier … on a gurney … *A gurney!* I was lying on a gurney, too, I realized. *Why?*

It hit me. The man had said my name before. I was Johnathan Cutter. Private first class. In the Army.

But where was I? What happened?

16 / Show me my foot

"You were injured by a bomb."

I was looking up at somebody new. His face came in and out of focus. He didn't have much of an expression when he said the words. *Injured by a bomb.* Maybe he was used to saying this. The phrase echoed
in my mind. You've got me mixed up with somebody else, I thought.
The new man studied my face. He must have been trying to figure out
if he had the right guy. A bomb?

"There's no need to talk right now," he said. "We're going to land in
less than an hour. You're doing well. You've been under heavy sedation
but we're reducing the medication and bringing you out."

I looked around, as much as I could, and realized I was on an Army
cargo jet. Now I understood the noise in my dream, the constant whine
of the engines. It reminded me of the flight to … *Iraq.* That realization
jolted me. The man was right. I was coming out of whatever this was
but I was still confused. I said, "A bomb? That's not right. I don't feel
anything."

"It's a lot to take in," the man said. "You're on an intravenous painkiller. That's why you don't feel anything. You're being transferred to the
Army medical center at Landstuhl, Germany. They have facilities we
don't have in Iraq."

"I've never heard of … Lan … where am I going?"

"Landstuhl. They have the facilities and the staff to fully treat your
wounds, Johnathan. You were injured in a bombing. You were stabilized by a forward surgical team and treated at a combat support hospital but there's more to be done."

I realized at that moment that my left nostril had a tube in it. I tried
to think, to remember, but my brain was fogged up. "More?" I said.
"More what?"

"I'm sorry but you also suffered some burns and the loss of part of
your right leg."

Those words did not register. How could they? They made no sense. Was I still dreaming? "Am I … awake?" I asked.

"Yes. You were out for nearly 12 hours."

"Part of my … leg?"

"The blast severed your foot. Your right hand was badly injured, too. I'm sorry, they couldn't save it."

What?

I couldn't breathe. I didn't understand. I tried to sit up, to look down at my legs, to see for myself. Both legs were there. I was sure of it. They had to be there. They *were* there but my arms were tied down and I couldn't rise. The man put his hand on my chest. "It's not a good time to exert yourself," he said.

"Show me my foot."

"You should rest."

"Show me my foot. I WANT TO SEE MY FOOT! *SHOW ME!*"

The man stared into my eyes. I was looking for a sign of hope and maybe he was, too, but I didn't see much, just a man doing his job. "OK," he finally said. "We can show you. If you think this is the right time. I just want you to be prepared."

"Show me."

"OK, I'll be right back."

He returned with the other man and said, "We're going to elevate." They pulled apart straps that secured me to the gurney. They each put a hand behind my head and under my shoulders. As they lifted, I became aware of other soldiers on the plane, pitiful passengers, lined up two by two. Beyond my gurney, in the bowels of the jet, twinkling dials and glowing computer screens kept tabs on the others, tangled up in tubes like fallen puppets.

Something was off. Wrong. My legs were covered with blankets. I could see the shape of my left foot sticking up but not my right. I wagged the left foot. It hurt but it worked. I tried to wiggle the right. The blanket didn't move.

I raised my right arm. The blanket sagged just beyond the elbow.

Half of my arm was gone.

Instantly, my body became ice cold. I was nauseated. My skin seemed to be pricked by electric needles. I looked up at the man.

"I'm sorry," he said.

Dazed, I looked at the blankets, at their sickening outline, at the negative space, and vomited all over my chest. Whatever they were feeding me through the tubes, my guts had turned it into putrid slop. My throat burned. I lost mental control. My body took over, screaming in physical protest. I shit myself.

They lowered my head back to the gurney. "It's OK," the man with the glasses said. "We'll clean you up."

It wasn't OK. My head grew light and everything went black. My body knew what to do. Black was peaceful. Black was painless.

17 / How do you feel?

I was back in the machinery dream, floating on a thrumming river. It was hot, like summertime. I didn't know how much time had passed and slowly I became aware of being awake. My eyes were open and focusing again. I saw not the summer sun but the innards of the Army jet, hauling lacerated human cargo. Consciousness, creeping up, halted my escape into sweet blackness. Sweat burned my eyes. I blinked as hard as I could and shook my head. *Oh, God!* My leg, the leg that I didn't have anymore, what was left of that leg, it felt like somebody was holding a blowtorch to the stump.

Stump.

The word made me sick. I had a *stump*. I was missing a leg. And a hand. *Two stumps.* How did this happen? I smelled like diarrhea and vomit. My stomach convulsed. My body wanted to throw up again. I had two stumps. What could I do? Go back to … where?

"Hey, you're awake. That's good."

The man with glasses was back, holding towels and a bucket.

"I'm Mike Kowalek," he said. "I'm an air ambulance nurse."

He began to wipe puke from my chin and the blanket. I stank like a dead animal.

"You're sweating," the nurse said. He put a hand to my forehead. How could he stand to touch me? "You're warm. I'll be right back." He brought a thermometer and placed it under my tongue. "Hold that steady. We'll see if you've got a fever." After three beeps, he pulled it out and frowned. "A hundred and three. I want Doctor MacBride to take a look at you."

Mike and the doctor returned, both wearing surgical masks. Maybe I had something bad and they didn't want to catch it.

"Mike tells me you've got a fever," the doctor said.

I shrugged.

"How do you feel?"

"Does it … matter?" Everything was beginning to hurt. My legs throbbed, my head pounded, even my dick burned. I was falling through the sky.

"I'm going to have Mike give you a couple of pills. There's an infection that's becoming more common in battlefield injury cases. I'd like to get you started on some antibiotics before we land at Ramstein. Can you take a couple of pills for me?"

I had become just another common battlefield injury case? A leg gone, a hand gone? *Common?* I nodded. I imagined two suicide pills. I'd take them.

"Great. I'll be back when we get you to the air base." The doctor left. I wondered if there was someone back in the plane worse off than me.

Mike helped me sit up to get water into my mouth from a paper cup. He shoved a couple of pills between my lips. I took my medicine with a hard swallow. The water felt good on my throat but only for an instant. "That should help," Mike said. "I'm going to clean you up now."

Mike went to work. He took the blanket off my leg and a half. He undid my … pajamas? What was I wearing? When did I put these on? I shut my eyes. I didn't want to know anything about it. Mike said, "If this starts to hurt, let me know. I'm going to try not to disturb the catheter."

Catheter? What was he talking about? I strained to lift my head, to look. What I saw, what I hadn't noticed until now, shocked me: A tube sticking out of bandages on my crotch. I threw up a few final chunks. I screamed and writhed. Mucus shot from my nose. I wanted to plunge off the plane but each move I made unleashed fire and knives. I howled between gulps of air made acrid by my own filth.

I felt a poke in my left arm. Through sweat and tears, the doctor's face appeared.

"You're going to be all right," he said. "We're going to help you."

As nowhere beckoned, my eyes closed and his face vanished. "Please don't," I whispered.

And everything went black.

18 / To sleep, perchance to survive

The difference between Landstuhl Regional Medical Center in Germany and the 28th Combat Support Hospital near Baghdad was firepower. Landstuhl, a Level IV Army facility, functioned like a 155-millimeter howitzer, while the 28th, at Level III, was more of a mortar. Both could do the job, but Landstuhl did it definitively. Working together with Level I and II, they were a formidable force. A wounded soldier could move from battlefield medic to forward surgical team to combat support hospital to Landstuhl within 48 hours. Only one in 10 of the wounded died.

Colonel Hiroshi Matsuo, an orthopedic surgeon at Landstuhl, wondered if Private First Class Johnathan Cutter would be the one. Matsuo, a balding, stocky man with bulging forearms, was given to snap diagnoses. Part of that was the need for speed. "Commit and cut" was his motto. However, he followed the progress of his patients, both those who returned to Iraq and those who needed the stateside care that only a Level V facility, like Walter Reed or Brooke, could offer. In more than 700 surgeries, Doctor Matsuo noticed a pattern that had nothing to do with the number of limbs lost.

What explained the death of a man who had suffered a traumatic battlefield amputation, his leg blown off by an IED? What explained the survival of a man who had lost both legs, both eyes, an arm, and three fingers on his remaining hand?

For Doctor Matsuo, the answer was clear: The will to live. The organ that held the key to survival was the brain. The doctor, though, would be the first to admit that not all cases followed his rule. He was a man of science and statistics, but there were exceptions. Some men who wanted to live did not; some men who wanted to die survived.

Dodging gurneys in the hallway as he strode toward the operating room, Matsuo scanned Cutter's chart. The numbers met the stability criteria for air evacuation: heartbeat, 94; systolic blood pressure, 105;

hematocrit, 33 percent; pH, 7.5; platelet count, 53,000. His temperature, 103, was too high, but the spike had occurred on the flight from Baghdad. The fever was almost certainly due to an acinetobacter infection of the right-leg stump, but a regimen of trimethoprim-sulfamethoxazole and a new amputation above the knee would take care of it. Now was the time to cut.

The doctor was honest to the point of being brusque. His view was that in the long run, self-delusion about the extent of injuries would be futile or fatal. Since his posting at Landstuhl, he had seen how a few steadfast true believers never wavered. They repeated over and over that a leg or an arm — whole or partial — would heal, if only you invested more time, more hope, more surgery, more antibiotics, more titanium rods, more shunts, more bone grafts. Just prop up the shattered leg a little longer, they preached, stay the course, until next year or the year after, and it would become functional. However, to survive in Doctor Matsuo's world of unemotional calculation, you had to be realistic, as painful and embarrassing as that was. Festering and dysfunction would continue forever if you refused to re-evaluate. You had to cut your losses.

You had to *cut*.

Yet even after you saved many soldiers' lives, the arrogant true believers crawled out from behind their safe, insulated desks to insist you had cut too soon, that in another six months all would have been peachy. Their neo-analytic skills were laughable and dangerous.

The doctor scrubbed in quickly and joined his team in the operating room. He would be assisted by a nurse and an anesthesiologist. They had already prepared Cutter for surgery. Colonel Hudson Pennington, a urology specialist, was on the assignment board as well, due in at 1100, and he would be operating on the soldier's genital burns after the above-knee amputation.

"Hello, Doctor," said Major Odette Vickers, the anesthesiologist. She was in her second tour at Landstuhl after assignments at both Walter Reed and Brooke.

"Hello, Odette. Hello, Dawn," Matsuo said, also greeting his nurse, Captain Dawn Ketteredge, who had been wounded herself in a mortar attack on the 31st Combat Support Hospital at Balad during her tour of duty in Iraq. Ketteredge was a highly coveted nurse in the hospital, partly because she stayed cool under stress during long hours in the operating room, but also because she had a special rapport with wounded soldiers. When they saw the jagged reconstruction scars along her left jaw line, which she never covered with makeup, they understood she had been through it, too, and they followed her orders without complaint. In the warrior culture, she achieved instant respect. It also helped that she was 5-foot-10 and had auburn hair that cascaded to the middle of her back when she unleashed it. However, Nurse Ketteredge rarely revealed the full expanse of her mane, and usually only to men who were strong enough to leave Landstuhl and deal with their self-doubts and deformities. On departure day, when she walked into their rooms to say goodbye, now 6-foot-2 in red high heels, it was like a jolt from a defibrillator. The sendoff hug crackled with electricity. It was Ketteredge's way of planting a seed of hope.

Doctor Matsuo moved close to Cutter's face, hoping to get a feel for the strength of this young man. There wasn't much to go on. Major Vickers had already hooked him up to the ventilator, so there was no way to tell how strongly he might breathe on his own. He looked pale and frail and small, but every amputee did. Minus an arm and a leg, a soldier's weight dropped by 30 pounds or more, and the tissue trauma had a way of shriveling up what was left of the man. Matsuo wondered whether a psychologist should be called in to greet Cutter when he woke up to discover that he had even less of his leg than before. The doctor tucked that idea away for now. He had to get moving. After Cutter's amputation, he was on the board for three more before day's end.

"Are we ready?" Matsuo asked.

"Yes, sir," Ketteredge answered.

"Vitals are stable," Vickers added, monitoring two screens of digital data and charts.

Matsuo peeled back the sterile drapes to have a first look at Cutter's stump. No surprise, it was purple, violet and black, a flaming neon sign that screamed infection and dead tissue. "Yes," the doctor said, "this must come off."

Nurse Ketteredge, knowing this would be the diagnosis, had already completed the prep, setting out instruments, applying a proximal pneumatic thigh tourniquet, and rigging Cutter's leg with a fixator.

Matsuo took a moment to inspect the previous operation. The skin flaps were well done with precise suturing, and the stump itself had a pleasing, symmetrical taper that most likely would have been comfortable in a prosthetic. Someone had put a lot of work into this one — unfortunately for nothing. Matsuo guessed correctly that the surgery had been performed by Colonel Toar at the 28th Combat Support Hospital. At least once a week, Matsuo had to take off another seven or eight inches after Toar had done the initial amputation. "Someday I'm going to make Randall Toar buy me a beer," Matsuo said with an opinionated sigh.

Nurse Ketteredge gave him a sharp look. "Maybe he owes you," she said, "but I understand why he does it."

Doctor Matsuo nodded. Though he outranked Ketteredge and she often contradicted him in her subtle way, he could never disagree with anything she said. Her hazel eyes and seductive smile kept his superior-officer prerogative in check. In addition, at 5-foot-6, he literally looked up to her.

"Tourniquet, please," Matsuo said. Ketteredge inflated it. The doctor grabbed a #12 scalpel and began a circumferential suprapatellar incision. When he was finished slicing through skin, subcutaneous fascia and muscle, and crafting his flaps, Nurse Ketteredge mopped up a surprisingly small amount of blood leakage, mere droplets.

Pleased with how the tourniquet was holding, Matsuo said, "Powermaster." Ketteredge handed him a large-bone pneumatic oscillating saw. The doctor gave the trigger a quick squeeze to test the air pressure. The blade screeched to life and the doctor laid into the femur.

Matsuo preferred working in the controlled conditions of Landstuhl, where staffing levels were adequate, he didn't have to improvise, and power tools were available. Taking a leg off with a Gigli saw on the battlefield was such a slog.

At this point in Doctor Matsuo's career, at age 49, with his wife back home in Virginia and his daughter in her first year of medical school at Johns Hopkins, he didn't feel the need to prove his manhood again on a forward surgical team, where time, chaos and danger influenced medical decisions. Also, he had come to enjoy German food. The town of

Landstuhl even had a decent sushi bar, Schmecken von Tokyo, tucked away on a side street below Nanstein Castle. Why eat Baghdad dust when you could get California rolls and sashimi? Ultimately, though, Doctor Matsuo wanted to do definitive work rather than go-go assembly-line stabilizations. Damage-control resuscitation felt like a half-measure. It was not at all satisfying to send a soldier on to the next level with wounds still open, a shredded abdomen packed with gauze, arterial shunts exposed, diversion of rectal injuries. Matsuo's distaste for barbaric maimings and on-the-battlefield medicine had coalesced during a fill-in stint with a forward team during the battle for Fallujah. He wasn't a prissy man, but after 23 cases of lacerated bowels with the concomitant fecal contamination, the doctor grew weary. At that point, he could identify which MRE the soldier had eaten the night before. Chile and Macaroni was the most disgusting, followed by the Sloppy Joe. When an obnoxious, cocksure surgeon named Yenche began calling the worst IED cases "hamburger and fries," referring to their raw, ground-up faces and burned fingers covered with "ketchup," Matsuo began pressing hard for an early reposting at Landstuhl. He was ready to resume practicing real medicine and not, as Yenche put it, "food preparation."

At 1105, as Doctor Matsuo wrapped up the amputation, Doctor Pennington poked his head into the operating room. "Do I have time for a smoke?" he asked.

Nurse Ketteredge glared at him. "I thought you quit."

"I did. Then I started again. I'm trying to be more Sino-European."

"Ha-ha," Ketteredge said mirthlessly. "You won't be as witty when Stage IV metastatic cancer puts you on the table to have a lung removed."

"You're right, Dawn, as usual. It's hard to crack wise when you're short of breath and coughing up blood."

"I'm just finishing the sutures," Matsuo said. "I'm turning him over to you, Hudson, if you have the lung capacity to take it from here."

"What have we got?" Doctor Pennington moved to the table and lifted the drape covering Cutter's genitals. "Goddamn that fucking Rumsfeld," he muttered. "When is that cheap bastard going to up-armor the Humvees?"

"I think you should ask him to his face," Ketteredge said.

"If that cold-hearted son of a bitch ever visits, I will."

"Maybe you could get him to spring for Kevlar nut cups," Matsuo suggested.

"I doubt it. You remember what he said at that press conference, don't you?"

Matsuo, Ketteredge and Vickers looked at each other, all mystified. "No," Matsuo said.

"'You go to war with the testicle you have, not the testicles you wish you had.'"

"Rumsfeld said that?" Matsuo asked.

"Yeah."

"I guess I don't remember him saying that, not that he wouldn't."

Realizing what Doctor Pennington meant, Nurse Ketteredge grimaced. "You're doing an orchiectomy."

"Yes," he said, "for starters."

Doctor Matsuo headed for the operating room door. "I'm leaving. I've seen this movie. I know how it ends."

Pennington put on his magnification loupes and went to work on Cutter's scrotum with a mini-scalpel and a scraper. After 20 minutes of scooping out what remained of the soldier's right testicle, mostly mangled purple pulp, the doctor said, "Odette, how far did you put him under?"

"I can assure you, we're all feeling more pain than he is," she said.

"How long will he be out?"

"As long as you want."

"How about 30 days?"

"Really?"

"Yes. I'd like to induce a coma. I need to do some scrotum and phallus reconstruction, but because of the burns, it's going to be a loose approximation. Once scar tissue begins to form, they'll need to take it down and make adjustments. This boy has a long, difficult road ahead and it starts by getting him to Walter Reed."

"We can do a coma," the anesthesiologist said.

"Good. It would be best if he doesn't wake up for a while."

PART III
AMERICA

19 / Out of the void

I'm not sure when I became aware of … myself. Of … thoughts. My brain seemed to turn on slowly slowly slowly. There was nothing and then there was … existence. Somehow I crossed a threshold. I moved from a black void into a black void that included rudimentary consciousness. If I was dead, at least I knew it. Strangely, to know that was comforting. It was my first thought, that I must be dead. No sound, no sight, no feeling, no body. Wouldn't death be like that? Time didn't pass, didn't even exist, but that seemed right. Wouldn't death last forever?

It was pleasant. I had no responsibilities, nowhere to be, nothing to do. I floated in the blackness, weightless, both physically and mentally. After an indeterminate while, I realized that my theory about time was wrong. Time must have been passing because I began to have more thoughts and they came in succession. I began to fantasize about food, fixating on a peanut butter and grape jelly sandwich. I wondered when I would eat something. I realized I hadn't eaten in a long time but if I was dead would I need food?

One night — it was always black; I never saw a speck of light — a question came up: Who was I?

I didn't know. I didn't even know *what* I was. Or where I was. I fiddled with those riddles for a while and got nowhere. Later, it hit me that maybe I was waiting to come back, but from what? And to what? I concluded that I was nothing but a thought, a disembodied consciousness. That theory proved to be wrong. I did have a body, because one night I began to feel pain. Not all at once but slowly, progressively, evolutionarily, the same way I had become aware of myself, whoever or whatever I was. It began with warmth. My right leg and my right arm and the right side of my head heated up. Yes, absolutely, my body exists, I thought. I was more than a floating consciousness. However, I still existed only in the black void, so there was no way to prove I had a body, no way to see my arms or my legs. After a few of the black nights — or 10? … or 20?

— I was on fire. Burning pain. Branding iron pain. Seared flesh pain.

Then I heard a distant murmuring.

I began to come out of the black void.

Shooting stars of light flashed across the inside of my eyelids. *I had eyelids, which meant I had eyes!*

An insistent voice grew louder: "Johnny Cutter … Johnny Cutter … Johnny Cutter … it's time to wake up … you can wake up now, Johnny … I know you're in there … wake up, Johnny."

Then I screamed. The pain, the awful fire, was horrible. I wanted to return to the peaceful black void.

The voice said, "That's good, let it out, let it go, breathe."

I began to see blurry features of a face above me. Apparently I was alive, although I wasn't sure of anything about life or death or limbo. I tried to say, "Help me." It should have been simple but it wasn't. Mostly I gargled incomprehensibly. Then my eyes focused enough that I understood why it was so difficult — a tube was rammed down my throat. I could see it snaking off someplace. I tried to turn to follow it.

"No, Johnny. Don't try to move. Can you hear me? It's too soon."

It was a man's voice. He was right. However long I had been wherever I was, it was way too soon, way too painful.

"It hurts," I gargled.

It was like having my skin ripped off in sheets with pliers. Whoever was talking must have known how I felt. "I know," he said. "I know it's bad. We'll get you back on painkillers but for now we need you to wake up. It's time to wake up, Johnny."

So my name was Johnny. I wasn't dead, only sleeping. I thought dead would be better. The pain came in waves, like a tsunami of lava washing over me. My eyes squirted tears. I wasn't crying — I didn't have the strength. It was more that my body needed liquid to put out the fire. "Where am I?" I said. Tried to say. It came out as pathetic groans. My throat vibrated but it couldn't form the words.

"That's good, Johnny," the man said. "Keep talking. Say it again."

"Where am I?"

"Air fly?"

He didn't understand. I moved my head from side to side, slowly, two times. I tried again to cough up the words: "Where am I?"

"Say it once more, Johnny. I'm listening but I can't quite get it."

"Where am I?"

"One more time, slow and easy."

I took some breaths. I concentrated. I puffed my lips out and pulled them back to sound out "where." I stretched my mouth sideways and brought my lips together slowly to form "am." I opened wide, a big circle, and pushed as much air through as I could to make "I." It was hard and it hurt. I tried to remember when I talked last but there was nothing to remember. Nothing there.

"Where are you?"

I nodded once. I couldn't manage twice.

"You're at Walter Reed Army Medical Center, Johnny. It's a hospital in Washington, D.C. Do you know where Washington is?"

"Yes," I rasped.

"Don't worry about talking, Johnny. It's too early. We'll have you talking soon enough. It's all going to come back to you in due time. I'll ask you a few questions and see if we can get you oriented. You don't have to talk or move, just blink your eyes. Give us one blink for yes and two blinks for no. Is that OK?"

I blinked once.

"Excellent. Do you know your name, Johnny? Your full name?"

It wasn't there. I didn't know my own name. What was wrong with me? I shut my eyes and tried to remember.

"Is that a yes? You know your name?"

"No," I tried to say, shaking my head.

"Don't talk, Johnny. There's no need to talk right now. Just blink, remember? One blink for yes and two blinks for no. OK?"

I blinked once.

"Great. That's a yes. OK, your name is Johnathan Cutter. Your mother said you go by Johnny. Do you remember that name? Johnny Cutter?"

I blinked twice.

"That's all right, Johnny. That's not a problem. No problem at all. You will remember, I promise you. OK, next question, do you know that you're in the United States Army?"

I thought about that one for a long time. It wasn't that I knew it, more that it didn't feel wrong.

"Was that a blink yes, Johnny?"

Oops. I blinked but it was just a blink, not a yes-blink. I blinked twice for no.

"OK, so that's no, you don't remember that you're in the Army."

It was too complicated. It was making me tired. My eyes hurt and I couldn't really control them. I hunched my shoulders up, an attempt at a shrug.

"I understand. This is a bit much right now. Let's take a break. I'd like you to get some sleep. Some regular sleep. I'll be back tomorrow to see you. My name is Major Travis Campbell. I'm a doctor at Walter Reed hospital. I'm going to have the nurses look in on you until I get back. I'm going to give you a couple of things to think about, though, while you're sleeping. You were in Iraq, Johnny. That's where you were stationed."

Iraq … that didn't feel wrong either.

"You were injured in Baghdad. That's why you're here at Walter Reed. That's why you're starting to feel so much pain."

Injured? When? How? Was that why I felt like I was on fire? "What happened?" I said. Tried to say. I was still croaking like a throat cancer patient. I could understand myself only in my mind.

"I don't want you to talk yet, Johnny. We need to get some of your strength back. There's going to be a lot of time for talking. We'll be talking a lot."

So how was a lot of talking going to help me? Too bad I couldn't talk well enough to ask him.

20 / Memory lame

I woke up and my head was slightly clearer, like one layer of fuzz had been peeled away. I remembered the guy named Travis. I remembered that my name was Johnny Cutter. I could see better than … yesterday? Is that when I was awake? What was going on? Where was I again? The hospital? Something was supremely fucked up. I began to get scared. Was this real? How could it be?

"Hello?" I said weakly. "Is anybody there?" Whenever I had the strength, I called for help.

After a while, a woman's face appeared above me. "You're awake," she said. "Good. How are you feeling?"

"Like I got hit by a truck."

"I'm going to get Doctor Campbell," she said. "You should talk to him." She walked away, leaving me looking at the ceiling.

"What happened to me?" I said, but my words were too feeble to make her stop. I wanted to get out of here, back to black, but I was so scared I couldn't nod off. My left arm was trembling, like I had pure adrenaline surging through my veins. Maybe I did; the arm was connected to a tube. Strangely, my right arm was calm. I squeezed my eyes shut. It was as close as I could get to black for now. I lay there for a while, trying to remember what happened to me.

"Hello, Private First Class Cutter."

I recognized the voice. I opened my eyes. It was the man from before, short-cropped hair and round-wire glasses, and the woman who had gone to get him.

"Do you remember me? I'm Doctor Campbell."

I nodded.

"Good. This is Nurse Jillian. She's going to be working with you."

It hit me at that moment. I might as well have been smashed in the face with a hammer. They were both wearing Army uniforms with all the hardware. I knew their ranks. She had a captain's silver bars; he had a major's gold leaf. That went all the way back to basic training, when they drilled us to death on how to recognize officers. I remembered. Yes, I was in the Army and I was seriously fucked up, but why?

"What happened to me?" I asked. My words sounded clearer.

"You were injured in Iraq."

I could visualize sand. Was I imagining it or was it a real memory? "Am I going to be all right?" I asked. "Because everything hurts."

The major looked at me blankly. I tried to read his face. He was cool. He gave up nothing. I looked at the captain. Same thing. Her face was a mask wiped clean of emotion. Of course, I realized, they're Army officers. They don't want me to know anything. "Please, you can tell me, am I going to be OK?"

The major eyeballed me like a ... *drill sergeant.* Yeah, that snapped into place. I had seen that before, the probing for ... *weakness.* After the assessment, he said, "We'll do everything humanly possible to help, Private Cutter, but ultimately, a lot of it will be up to you. Your willingness to work in rehab ... "

Rehab?

" ... will be a big factor in your recovery. Long term, you're going to have to learn to use prosthetic limbs ... "

Prosthetic limbs?

" ... and that takes determination and training. When you get down to ground level, it takes the Soldier's Creed."

I am an American soldier ... I will never accept defeat ...

My basic training graduation ceremony flashed in my mind ... shaking hands with my battle buddy, Tim Gulde ... the late nights helping each other to memorize the Creed ...

Oh my God ... I got cold and sick ... *Tim Gulde is dead.* Goddamn, I thought, goddamn goddamn goddamn. I realized then that the two faces looking down at me showed something I had missed before: Pity.

It was in their eyes. They tried to hide it but couldn't. "I want to see," I whispered through pooling drool and dripping snot.

They got little frowns and clenched jaws. They didn't want me to look. "I have to know, right?" I said, trying to steel up. What did they want to hear? Then the magic words came out: "I need to know so I can start rehab."

They looked at each other. The captain turned back to me and smiled. The major nodded approvingly. I had come around. I was a good American soldier.

… I will never quit …

I became all they wanted me to be.

"OK," the major said.

"Do you know what happened to me? Because I don't remember."

"You were injured by a bomb, an improvised explosive device."

"Where?"

"In Baghdad."

"Was anyone killed?"

"Yes. Some civilians and one soldier."

"Was it somebody I know?"

"I'm sorry. I don't know."

"When did it happen?"

"Five weeks ago."

Five weeks ago?

"You were airlifted to Landstuhl Medical Center in Germany."

I knew that name. Landstuhl. I heard it in a dream.

"They put you in a medically induced coma after the treatment at Landstuhl and you were transferred to Walter Reed hospital. We brought you out of the coma yesterday. You're making excellent progress, Private Cutter. Your parents have been notified that visitation can begin. Your mother will be here soon. She'll be staying at Mologne House on the hospital grounds. It's a lot to take in, I know, but the sooner we put everything in motion, the quicker your recovery will be."

A lot to take in? Was he kidding? It was impossible to take this in. I felt lightheaded. My insides spun.

"If we're going to get started, I should have a look."

"Yes," the major said.

The nurse walked to the opposite side of the bed. Together, they peeled back a couple of blankets and the bed sheet. I felt cool air. I was naked. The major unfastened a loop holding down my right arm. I raised it.

My God. My fucking goddamn God.

I didn't know what was more shocking, that half of my arm was gone or that it took so much effort to lift such a stubby little limb. But I knew this shriveled thing. I had seen it in a nightmare. The flesh was blotchy, red and black and purple. Was it healing or rotting? For sure, it was godforsakenly ugly. I waved the stump around like a symphony conductor's baton. Then the weirdest thing happened: I laughed.

It was insanely inappropriate. The horror on their faces told me that. "Are you OK?" the major asked.

"I'm sorry, you mentioned the Soldier's Creed and … I just thought of 'I always maintain my arms.'"

"Oh. Yes. Well, of course that refers to your weapons."

"Of course."

The captain and the major perked up with little smiles. They thought I was coping. Now I knew what they needed. They needed me to accept this, but I looked at my stump and I couldn't see a future for it. I tried to remember why I enlisted in the Army. Nothing came.

"Do you want to see the leg, too?" the major asked.

"Yes."

The woman pressed a button on a small box connected to the bed by a cable. Motors whirred and the top half of the bed began to rise. My left foot came into view. My right foot never appeared. Neither did the lower half of my right leg. *Gone.* I felt sick, like food poisoning. I tried not to show it and I managed not to vomit but my face must have given me away. The woman lowered my bed. She was right to let me down. I also saw, before the view was lost, a plastic tube coming out of a mass of bandages that wrapped my penis. Urine was draining through the tube.

I was pissing and didn't realize it.

I asked God to send me back to wherever I'd been for the last five weeks. Please let me drift into nothing, I prayed, but nothing didn't happen. I remained conscious. I kept thinking. I was still here. The Walter Reed ceiling was still up there. I was still in a motorized bed. I was still missing an arm and a leg.

A bomb, he said.

I couldn't remember, yet it felt searingly familiar.

21 / Rochambeau

I must have fallen asleep after the doctor and nurse left. When I awoke, it was dark. I lay there for a while. It wasn't like I could go anywhere. They had tied me down again, so I couldn't fall out of bed and hurt myself, I figured, or struggle up on my elbows and look at my injuries. I couldn't comprehend what had happened. I said it silently many times: My arm and my leg are gone.

I kept wondering how this could be real. Could my body tell me anything? I tried to listen to it, to feel every ache and pain. There were many of them but they had nothing to say.

I worked on remembering. Slowly, some things came back. The first images were from home: Mom and Halley, their faces. *"Your mother will be here soon,"* suddenly that registered. I saw Halley and myself at The Overlook. She can't ever see me like *this*, I thought.

Then it got worse. I had to go to the bathroom. I had no idea what to do. "Help," I called out. "Could somebody help me, please?"

What had happened during the five weeks I was out of it? Did I just shit the bed like a baby? That was a disgusting thought. I looked around the room as best I could. In the dim hallway light, a guy rolled by in a wheelchair. Would I be in a wheelchair eventually? What would that be like? Pushing those wheels until your hands got raw and bloody … until your *hand* got raw and bloody. How would that work out? Wouldn't you go in a circle all the time? Fuck that. Better to drive it off a fucking cliff.

A big woman entered my room. She was probably six feet tall and three feet wide, wearing Army fatigues. She flipped on a light switch and walked over to the bed. "Hello, Cutter," she said. "Welcome to Walter Reed hospital. I was wondering when I was going to get to meet you. My name is Rochelle Rochambeau. I'll be your nurse tonight, and probably every night. I don't have the seniority to get off the late shift. How are you feeling? How can I help you? For starters, let me show you how to use the call button." She guided my hand to a cold metal box on the side of the bed. "Feel that? The button in the center? You just press it and talk to us out at the nurses' station. You know, for a TBI guy, I thought I'd hear from you before now. You must be tough."

… I am disciplined, physically and mentally tough … the Creed … it was in my head again. "TBI guy?" I said.

She reached down and touched the right side of my head, so softly that I barely felt anything. "Traumatic brain injury, Cutter. Did Doctor Campbell and Nurse Jillian tell you everything that's wrong with you? Sometimes they don't. Sometimes they sprinkle a little sugar on top."

I studied her dark eyes but there was no hint of pity. Her voice was smooth like good coffee. She was upbeat in the middle of Downerville. I didn't get her at all.

"Are you going to say anything, Cutter? Or do I have to do all the talking?"

"I have a brain injury?"

"Well, they fixed it in the field and I think you're doing damn good for being fixed in the field. Your chart says you had a subdural hematoma, bleeding, but they got the shrapnel out and fixed it. You don't use very much of your brain anyway."

"How do you know how much of my brain I use?"

"Not you personally. Everybody. None of us use much of our brain. Maybe 10 percent. The other 90 percent is just waiting to get worked over by television or a bomb. Pop quiz: Do you know my name?"

"No."

"Why not? I told you my name when I walked in here, Cutter. If you used more of your brain, you'd know."

"I'm sorry. I forgot."

"You didn't forget, Cutter. You weren't paying attention. I'm going to tell you again. Rochelle. Rochelle Ro … cham … beau. *First Lieutenant* Rochelle Rochambeau. I outrank you, Cutter, so I want you to remember my name. Besides, it's just common courtesy. It's the polite thing to do, especially since I clean up after you."

"Understood, First Lieutenant Rochambeau … you clean up after me?"

"Yes, I do, me and the orderlies," she said, giving me a hard look.

I wondered what she meant by that, exactly.

"Like I said, I'm a first lieutenant. You're a private first class. Aren't you going to salute?"

"Salute? With what?"

"Have you got a stump?"

"What?"

"Listen up, Cutter. *Have … you … got … a … stump?*"

"Yes, ma'am."

"You can salute with that."

"It's tied down, ma'am."

She pulled the covers down and yanked the strap apart. "How about now?"

"Requesting permission not to salute, First Lieutenant Rochambeau."

"Permission denied but you get points for remembering my name."

Warm tears were rolling down my cheeks. My stomach hurt. "I don't want to see it," I mumbled.

"Like I said, Cutter, permission denied."

I raised the stump to my forehead. It was fucking ugly, a mass of dents and bruises and red flaky flesh. "I just want to go to the bathroom," I whispered.

Rochambeau saluted me back and said, "Permission granted."

I squinted up at her. What the hell did she mean? She walked over to the door to my room and closed it with a metallic bang. She came back and said, "Piss or poop?"

I turned my head away from her and closed my eyes.

"This is no time to get shy about your privates, Private. I've already seen everything, so it's not going to be a surprise. If you have to piss, you can just do it the way you've been doing it for the last month, through the catheter. If you have to poop, you can also do it like you've been doing it for the last month, all over the bed, and we'll clean up after you. Oh, look, there's a bathroom." She pointed to a door on the opposite side of the room. "Maybe it's time to start using it."

"I don't know how, First Lieutenant Rochambeau."

"Look, I'm gonna call you Johnny and you call me Rochelle."

"OK, but please, I really have to go, Rochelle. How do I even get to the bathroom? I don't know what to do."

She reached for the tubes in my nose and pulled them out. "Can you still breathe?"

I nodded.

"That's good. Now do you want to take the catheter out, or do you want me to do it?"

"Are you kidding?"

"You know I'm not."

"You better do it."

"All right, but I want you to watch. You need to know how to do this, just in case I die some night. My cholesterol is equal to my weight. It's a big number. I could go at any moment. Do you know how to do CPR."

"I don't know."

"You do know. The Army taught you. You'll remember when the time comes. I'm going to count on you if you ever find me face down in the hallway." She pulled the covers off me.

"What are you doing?"

"Watch and learn." She reached across and hit the button that ratcheted up the head of the bed. She moved down to my crotch. She put her left hand around the mass of bandages and gripped until I yelped. Then she grabbed a clear plastic tube between the thumb and forefinger of her right hand and began to pull.

Nothing could have been weirder than that. *Nothing. Not ever.* I watched but tried not to think about what was happening. Unless you've already seen tubing being extracted from your penis, trust me, you won't be ready. A total mind-fuck. A demented magician's trick.

I realized I wasn't breathing and quickly sucked in air, hyperventilating. I felt dizzy as Rochambeau quickly disconnected the dangling tubes from my arms. She was crazy efficient.

"You're free to go," Rochambeau said. She pointed to the bathroom door on the other side of the room, maybe 10 feet away.

"How do I get there?"

"You walk, just like anybody would."

"How do I walk? *I can't walk.* I'll never make it. I have to *go. Please.* Will you help me?"

She scowled, her jaw jutting out. "Do you mind being carried by a very large, very sweaty black woman?"

"Look at me. Do I look like I mind?"

"This is just between us, but I'm also a lesbian."

I didn't know why but that made me laugh, the ridiculousness of it maybe. Society was so fucked up that she worried about that detail at this moment? What would Jesus do, huh? Really, what the fuck would he do? I would rather have been dead than going through this but there I was, holding back a fearsomely engorged bowel, and a big black lesbian was worried about how a little white boy with one leg, one hand and a brain injury would react if he got touched by a dyke. God. Sad.

"First Lieutenant Rochelle Rochambeau," I said when I got caught up on thinking and breathing, "I don't ask, I don't tell, I don't give a fuck. You just pulled a tube out of my dick. We're pretty close now."

I gave her a no-problem shrug. I could have told her that there were eight or nine gay couples at my high school, that we knew about, *and nobody cared.* We straights saw girls sneaking a kiss in the hallway between classes, *and nobody cared.* We saw guys holding hands in the far corner of the parking lot, *and nobody cared.* I could have told Rochambeau that when my generation took over from the old racist bigot faggot-haters — assuming my generation didn't all get killed in the old racist bigot faggot-haters' wars — we wouldn't care who fucked whom.

Facing imminent disaster, I clenched my rectum as tightly as I could with my atrophied ass muscles. There was no time for a discussion of bigots and their warped sexual fears.

"OK, Johnny, if you're cool with it, let's go for a ride," Rochambeau said. She slid her beefy arms under my back and thighs and lifted me like a rag doll. I couldn't hold my head up. I wrapped my stump around her neck for extra support. It was gnarly gross but I had to do it. Moving was unbearably painful. My whole body hurt, like being stabbed with red-hot pitchforks. Maybe Satan was after me because I didn't hate gays. So what? What could he take from me at this point?

As we got to the bathroom door and Rochambeau reached for the handle to open it, I pulled myself up with every ounce of strength I had, close to her ear, and whispered, "For the record, I think lesbians are hot."

We both lost it but in different ways.

Rochambeau erupted with a hoot-laugh that reverberated in the room like a grenade. Her spasming belly pummeled me like a battering ram. Then my sphincter gave way and I exploded in a galactic shit nova. She should have dropped me but she didn't. She should have thrown me across the room but she didn't. She just stood there, the colossus of Walter Reed, holding me like a baby as I geysered excrement, coating her undercarriage and the floor with a nauseating layer of brown and yellow baby ooze.

When my bowel finally emptied, we looked at each other for a little while in silence. Rochambeau held on to me even tighter, because I was so slippery. I wished she would just crush the life out of me. "What have you got to say for yourself?" she said.

"I didn't make it."

"No shit," she said, shaking her head and grinning so wide that I saw some gold crowns in the back of her mouth. Her two front teeth had a little gap between them.

"I'm sorry. I couldn't hold it any longer."

"That's all right. I've seen worse."

"Really?"

"No, not really. This is the worst. Let's get you cleaned up." First Lieutenant Rochambeau carried me into the bathroom shower stall and put me down on a ledge that must have been tailor-made for amputees like me. She went back into the room and called for an orderly. "Bring a bucket, a jumbo mop and a 55-gallon drum of disinfectant," I heard her say. "It's a war zone in here." She returned to the bathroom and washed her arms off in the oversized lavatory. I sat there stewing in my own filth. The orderly arrived and Rochambeau said, "I'll be right back. I'm going to get him started."

When Rochambeau returned, she was carrying two big buckets and a thick stack of white towels under each arm. She set everything up in the far side of the shower. It was easily big enough for two people plus a wheelchair. She slid my T-shirt over my head and began to work, scrubbing and rubbing, dunking clean towels in the water bucket, tossing soiled towels in the empty bucket. I was an ungodly embarrassing stinking mess.

After a while, the orderly bailed, announcing that he was finished with the floor and had been paged to deal with another "incident."

Maybe that was true, maybe it wasn't. I figured he just wanted to get the hell out of the shitting field ASAP.

Rochambeau was embarrassingly thorough. She finished with the towels and pulled a hand-held sprayer off the shower wall. She fired it up and said, "OK, soldier, remember your basic training exam? You're going to have to bend over."

"What?"

"You heard me, Cutter. We're not done here. I need access."

"How can I bend over?"

"You stand up, you turn around, you bend over."

"I can't stand up."

"Yes, you can. Use the grab bar to steady yourself and stand up as best you can."

"Can't I just get back in bed?"

"I guess so. If you want to be reeking of shit."

"OK, OK. I don't know if I can stand up, though. Can you help me?"

"You know I can."

Rochambeau raised me up off the ledge, put her hands on my shoulders and maneuvered my ridiculously unbalanced body through a slow-motion pirouette. I tottered dangerously on my left leg but every time I began to fall, she caught me. Finally, I was able to assume the position.

"This might tickle a little," Rochambeau said, "but tickling is good." She began hosing me off with the handheld sprayer. "Is the water too hot?" she asked.

"I don't know. I can't feel all that much. I'm kind of numb."

She concentrated on different areas for a few minutes, washing away remnants of excrement. Finally, she let me turn around and sit on the ledge again. I was hella tired. Standing up on one leg required tremendous effort.

"Good job," Rochambeau said.

Reality was slapping me across the face. I couldn't go to the bathroom by myself. How was I supposed to live like this? But the worst was to come. The only damage I hadn't seen since waking up from the coma was to my genitals. They were wrapped in many layers of gauze and tape. I didn't want to know what was under all the bandaging. It was easy to look elsewhere. The colors of the leg stump drew my eyes away magnetically. I studied the crackly flesh. I did a math problem, estimating the distance from my hip to the end of the leg at maybe 15 inches. I didn't think of it as my leg anymore, just the leg. Maybe it wasn't technically a leg. More of an appendage. An afterthought.

I touched the arm stump. I pressed a few times near the end with my left index finger and watched the skin move. I traced incision lines that hadn't healed. Then a freakoid thing happened. The hand began to hurt. Not my left hand, the *right* hand. The missing hand was starting to burn.

I looked up at Rochambeau and said, "I think I'm losing my mind."

She continued to wave the sprayer up and down my good leg. "Why do you say that?"

"Because my right hand hurts."

"That's normal."

"The hand is *gone*. How can that be normal?"

"It's phantom limb pain. It comes and goes. The nerves get confused. How bad does it hurt?"

I held up the stump and looked at where the hand should have been. "It feels like the hand is sitting on a hot stove." I waved the stump around, trying to get away from the imaginary burner. That didn't help. The fire remained.

"I could give you some Demerol."

"That would be great. I hate pain."

"It may or may not help."

"I'll take the chance."

"Can you wait five minutes?"

"Why?"

"We need to wash your genital area and apply new dressings."

I threw my head back and frowned. I studied the shower's ceiling. I wanted to look anywhere but down.

"It's not a big deal, Johnny. We've been doing it every day for the last month."

"Yeah but I wasn't awake. I didn't know what was happening. I wasn't covered with shit."

"Sure you were. How do you think you defecate when you're in a coma? I'll tell you what, you don't get up and walk to the toilet."

Shitting the bed like a baby. There it was. Confirmed. Goddamn.

"You weren't exactly hitting the call button so we could bring you a bedpan, either."

"I'm sorry. I apologize, Rochelle. I had no idea."

She shrugged and turned the handheld sprayer on the big lump of bandages for a while. I watched as the gauze soaked up water.

"What's under there?" I finally asked.

"Let's find out, why don't we."

"You already know."

Rochambeau nodded somberly. She hung up the sprayer and began to peel off medical tape, which had been loosened by the warm water. I looked away and closed my eyes. "It's not pretty," Rochambeau said, "but you have to start dealing with it."

I wanted that Demerol. I felt feverish. I also felt Rochambeau's hand on my chin, directing me to look down. I opened my eyes and she went back to removing the bandages. I put my hand on her right arm to interrupt her work and said, "Can I have the Demerol now? Everything hurts. *I need something.*"

"OK." She stood up and left the room. When she returned, she offered me a glass of water, which I took carefully. She opened her left hand to show me two pills nestling in the palm, little white diamonds in search of a setting. She placed them in my mouth and I followed up with a big swig of water. Down they went. She reclaimed the sprayer and wet down the bandages again. "Are you ready?" she asked.

"No."

"That's all right. Nobody is." She went back to work, peeling off tape and gauze.

I started to think about how I first got in touch, literally, with my body: Masturbating in the shower. At some point — maybe around age 13 — I discovered how awesome it felt to wash my penis by hand, with lots of slippery soap. I lathered up like a maniac. I must have had the cleanest genitals in town. I worried constantly that Mom might discover evidence of my passionate devotion to personal hygiene, but I didn't worry enough to quit.

When Rochambeau got down to the final layer of gauze, she stopped peeling and said, "The thing about genital injuries is, guys have every-thing, their whole sense of themselves, wrapped up in their package. I don't understand it."

This was not a conversation that I ever wanted to have with anybody, especially not with a woman. "No disrespect intended, First Lieuten-ant," I said, though I didn't exactly mean that, because I thought she was insane, "but there is no way you can possibly understand it. Any-way, do we have to talk about this now? Can't you just put me back in a coma?"

Rochambeau plopped down onto the floor of the shower stall with a thud. It sounded ungraceful but once she got situated, she looked se-rene and Buddha-like. "Cutter, I'm just sayin', you know how the Inuits have a hundred different words for snow? Guys have a hundred differ-ent words for their penises: Cock, johnson, peter, dick, dong, dingus, rod, tool, man scepter, tent pole, trouser snake, party ferret, little howit-zer, bunker buster … "

"Bunker buster?"

"You're Army. That's an Air Force thing. Cutter, you're not married, are you?"

"No."

"Do you have a steady girl?"

"I don't know."

"You don't know? How can you not know that?"

"I used to. Now I don't know. I mean, look at me. Nobody would want me now."

"That's not true. That's not true at all. Thousands of guys like you go on to have perfectly normal lives."

"Bullshit. You and I both know that's total Army bullshit."

"No. I don't know that. You don't, either. Anyway, you are basically on Day Two of the rest of your life. You just woke up, Johnny. You don't know how your injury is going to play out. You're still in the Army. You've still got a job here if you want it."

"Huh?"

"You're a highly trained soldier. The Army would re-up you in a hot minute. Two legs, one leg, no legs, it doesn't matter."

"The Army did this to me."

"No, the Army didn't do this to you. That's wrong. Those insurgent bastards did this to you. You and every guy and girl in this hospital are heros. You're on the right side of history, Johnny. You did what we asked you to do. You did what was right. When the war books are written, everybody will understand your sacrifice. You'll look back on it with pride and so will everybody in your life — especially your girlfriend or your wife."

"Hooah," I said, bitterly echoing the cry that went all the way back to the first day of basic training.

"See? You're Army. I know you can't realize it now because, yes, this is hell and it's going to be hell for a while, but I guaran-damn-tee that you will get through this because you're a soldier, a survivor. You're not going to let a little rain stop you." Rochambeau grabbed the sprayer, angling the stream of water into the air so it cascaded down on both of us. I was already wet all over but she wasn't. That didn't last long. She waved the nozzle around and soon her fatigues were soaked. I could see the seams in her bra, which strained to contain her. Being such a large woman, she had enormous breasts. The wet clingy clothing only served to point that out. "Has the Demerol kicked in?" she asked. "If it has, we can do this now. Or if you'd rather, I'll make an appointment for you with a shrink but you have to face this, Cutter. The whole rest of your life is ahead of you." She squirted the crotch bandages like she was watering flowers, then laid the sprayer on the shower floor.

I looked down into her brown eyes and they were kind. Maybe the Demerol put me in a space where I could deal with it. I was woozy. I closed my eyes and flashed on a dark room and saw myself sitting in the middle of it, from the right side, naked, alone, in a wooden school chair. A shaft of light illuminated the stumps of my missing limbs. Psycho strangeness. I wondered if you could have an out-of-body experience if you didn't have parts of your body. Was this some kind of religious sign? Was this real? Was I insane? I reached down with my hand and rested it on Rochambeau's breast. It was real.

She put her hand on mine and slowly pulled it away. She said, "I'm sorry, Johnny. I go by the rules most of the time. Remember, don't ask, don't tell. Guys are not my thing. If they were, though, you're really good looking … even if you are all beat to hell."

She smiled halfway and I returned it. She meant it in a good way. She didn't think I was a freak, I could feel that much. I wanted the moment to last, because I wasn't so sure about what other people would think. "OK," I finally said. "Show me."

Rochambeau didn't say anything, she just scooted closer, oddly and unnervingly near my wang, wiener, whatever. She peeled off the last pieces of medical tape and began to unwrap the gauze. When she got down to the last layer, crusty skin was showing through the bandage fibers. She met resistance, where the gauze adhered to the skin, so she tugged gingerly, working the fibers back and forth until they released.

And there it was: My penis … a knobbly mass of bruised flesh held together by dozens of stitches. I was shocked, sickened, nauseated. Sweat beaded up on my forehead.

"Are you all right?" Rochambeau asked. "You don't look so good."

I closed my eyes and hyperventilated, slumping against the shower wall, bracing myself laterally against the glass with my stump.

"Johnny?"

"I'm trying not to pass out," I gasped.

"It's all right if you do. I'll catch you."

I stayed hunched up against the glass for a while, gulping air, thinking about what it would be like to take one last breath and die, the comfort of the blackness. My head was full of automatic weapons fire, explosions and yelling. Maybe that was the sign that I should die.

"*Cutter!*" Rochambeau's voice penetrated my interior battlefield. I opened my eyes and looked down. Her hands were grasping the top of my thighs. I could see that but I didn't feel much of anything, an odd non-sensation. In between, there was the lump. That's what it appeared to be. A lump of purple scabby sewn-up flesh. I wanted a 9 millimeter. I wanted to put a barrel in my mouth and fire one last shot.

Then I lost it: "*Fuck the ragheads who did this to me. Fuck the Army and those worthless Humvees. Fuck Bush for sending us to that fucking sandbox. We never found a single WMD. All we ever did was baby-sit the Iraqis and the oil and wait to get blown up. I'm so fucking stupid.*"

Rochambeau let me melt down. I squeezed my eyes shut. I wanted nowhere. But she touched my shoulder, too soon, and said, "Your memory's coming back. That's a good sign. You're going to be all right."

"Goddamn it! Look at me! Would you fucking look at me?"

"I've seen worse," Rochambeau said.

I stared at her. "Bullshit. You haven't seen worse."

"Yes. I've seen worse."

"What could be worse than this?"

"Gone."

That stopped me. She seemed to be stone serious. "Gone," I pressed, "you've seen guys … gone?"

Rochambeau didn't say anything, she just nodded in confirmation — because it was unspeakable. When I thought about that, yeah, the Army recruiter didn't speak about certain things, either. He never said anything about what you could sacrifice for your country and $20,000. He never said you could lose an arm or a leg. *Or both.* He never said you might get a brain full of shrapnel. He never said you'd see dead guys in a basement with holes drilled in their heads. He never said a suicide truck bomber would take out a power plant you just repaired. He never said a burqa bomb would detonate in your face. Rochambeau was right. My memory *was* coming back.

Yeah, it was one of those endless baby-sitting missions, the kind that drove us crazy. Nothing more than guard duty, protecting important fucks. Two American VIPs were flying in. Our unit had to get them from the airport, across town to the Green Zone for a palace lunch with a bigwig U.S. ambassador and the Iraqi oil honcho, then back to the Oil Ministry. Killdozer called it "top-secret shit." He couldn't tell us who they were or why they were there, only that they would be in a big black bulletproof bombproof fuckproof limo and that we were to lay down our lives for them, if necessary. Pete Klug raised his hand and asked, "Are we going to get any oil out of the deal?"

"That's classified information," Killdozer told him.

"That's good to know," Klug said. "That makes me feel better."

It was the middle of a hot afternoon and the city was busy. Traffic in Baghdad could tie itself into a knot over nothing. If the Iraqis were doing their jobs and stopping cars at checkpoints, there was no hope of getting anywhere fast. Our convoy — six Humvees plus the limo — crept along. At Al-Arabi Square, we bogged down even worse. Every driver, it seemed, laid on the horn. Something was up on Al-Mansur

Street, some kind of backup, so we headed southeast on Dimashq, past the Arabian Knight Monument. It was all according to plan; this was an alternate route to the Oil Ministry. D-Willie was driving our Humvee, third in line, just ahead of the limo. I was riding shotgun. We turned right onto Al-Fallujah Street, then made the next right. Just ahead, to the north, the Grand Mosque loomed on our left, the Oil Ministry on our right. We were almost there but the street was deserted. Why wasn't there any traffic? It was too easy. The bomb must have gone off early. They didn't get the limo, they got me.

Now, missing an arm and a leg, with only my memory intact, I was sitting naked and shivering in a shower with an upbeat nurse who insisted that the rest of my life would be fine.

"You're lucky," Rochambeau said. "You're alive."

"Hooah," I said softly.

22 / Bedpan blues

Walter Reed put me in charge of the PCA — "a step toward self-reliance," the doctors said. Why they used the word "step" was a mystery. I wouldn't be taking a step anytime soon.

PCA stood for patient-controlled analgesia but everybody simply called it "the button," which was a lot easier to remember. Which would you rather push, "the button" or "the patient-controlled analgesia"? I thought of it as FSM, or "free streaming morphine," and I liked it immediately. It was way better than weed. Whenever my stumps caught fire, whenever my head was about to explode, whenever I wanted to take the edge off with a smooth warm dreamy little high, all I had to do was press the magic button and soon the hospital became a lot more hospitable. The only downside was the no-overdose mechanism, not that I didn't try to override it. I pawed that button like a Pavlov dog in the beginning, practically drowning in my own drool.

I got the button just before Mom arrived, which was happy timing. When she walked into my room for the first time, she broke into sobs. I could relate. She shuffled to my bedside and leaned in, putting her arms around my shoulders as best she could, staying clear of my tubes. Some of her tears dripped onto the bed sheets. It was fortunate I was covered up. If she had been confronted with the real me, what was left, I don't know how she would have reacted. She might have needed her own self-serve morphine drip. She appeared haggard and gaunt. Lines and furrows crisscrossed her face. I had a flashback to the day I told her I was enlisting in the Army. I remembered her whirligig energy, the yelling, the cursing, the crying. It felt like forever ago. She shocked me then with her language; she shocked me now with her appearance.

I almost started to cry with her but why bother? It only made me angry because it didn't do any good. It wouldn't change anything. If I got too depressed about things, I could turn to the button, the bedside connection that was always there for me. Soon, I began to worry about how my room smelled. There was always some unpleasant bodily function going on and I was used to it, but did Mom notice? I hoped not. I always hid things from her. Drugs. Sex. Even rock and roll. I never played metal in front of her. This room, though, had to be putrid. Maybe she'll just keep crying and her nose will plug up, I thought. Satisfied to be coasting on a painkiller high, I quit worrying. There was nothing I could do. That was my new thing: I couldn't do anything about anything. It was a kind of freedom that really rang my bell.

Mom finally calmed down and said, "Johnny, I love you so much. I'm so thankful you're OK."

I didn't know how to respond. OK? She thought I was *OK?* Was she looking at me? Did she realize I was in Ward 57 at Walter Reed hospital, the ward for amputees? Did she understand that one of my tubes was a direct morphine feed and the others were various antibiotics to wage war with the Mideast microbes attacking my stumps? I tried to smile at her but there was no way I could pull that off. I half-nodded instead, without any commitment. She must have known it was fake. How could she not? She didn't know what else to say, so she didn't say anything. I just looked at her for a while. Mom had never been one to wear much makeup, if any, but she had on lipstick. I wondered what was up with that. I had never looked at her eyes up close — it felt weird to do it now — but they were a soothing milky blue, and I could see where mine came from. We had the same nose, too, a little too wide but turned up at the end, reasonably straight. I had always thought my face was too round, like a moon pie, and now I realized that I also got that from Mom. Finally, I couldn't take the wordless staring anymore. I said, "I'm not OK, Mom. Did they tell you what happened to me?"

"You're alive, Johnny. That's all that really matters. You're safe now."

Rochambeau had made a special point of telling me how lucky I was, and now my mother. It kept coming back to that. Everybody was so convinced it was great that I was alive. Their standards for being alive were too fucking low. I pressed Mom: "Did they tell you that I lost my arm and my leg? Did they explain that to you?"

"Johnny, please, don't say that."

I laughed a little at that one. Apparently she thought that if I didn't mention it, we could just ignore the fact that I was a double amputee.

"The doctors told me you're a hero."

I laughed at that one, too. "Yeah, I heard that from a nurse. I guess everybody who gets blown up is a hero."

Mom didn't say anything. I guessed she didn't want to encourage my bitterness. Some things in life, in polite society, couldn't be talked about. My mind wandered in the silence. I wondered where my heroic arm and my heroic leg were.

Mom and I did begin to talk a little more after a while. She told me all about where she was staying, Mologne House, the snappily dressed desk clerk, the bar, the cafeteria. "I want you to come visit me there just as soon as you can," she said. "The room is nice."

"I will," I promised. "I definitely will." I could tell from her pinched smile that she knew it would never happen, that I was just being polite, but it got us through.

Changing the subject, Mom asked whether I had been in touch with my friends back home. I said I hadn't. She asked about my squad. I told her about Captain Dozinger and the guys and described life at FOB Viper, up to a point, but I had to stop because it was too painful. We ventured, instead, into a few "do you remember the time" conversations.

Then Nurse Jillian came into the room. I was thankful. Even though she was my least favorite day nurse, it was a merciful interruption. My talk with Mom was getting smaller by the minute. "Hello, Private First Class Cutter," Jillian announced. "I see you have a visitor."

I introduced her to Mom, and the rave reviews of the Mologne House accommodations began, which got me off the hook for a while. I smiled secretly as Nurse Jillian's eyes began to glaze over. When Mom described the luxurious sheets — "I think they might be 400 thread count," she enthused — I flashed on Iraq and a night we spent in a deserted cinderblock house during an IED stakeout. "The garbage was so plentiful and fresh that we had rats the size of cats," I could have said, but I kept my mouth shut and let Jillian suffer.

Finally she reached her breaking point, saying, "It's very nice to meet you, Mrs. Cutter. I'm afraid I have to go to work now. I'm scheduled for a training session with your son but visiting hours last until 2100 if you'd like to come back a little later."

"I'm so pleased to meet you, Captain Jillian, and yes, I will definitely be back this evening," Mom said. "I'm still learning my way around but I've got the route from Mologne House to the hospital figured out." She rose from her bedside chair, leaned over and kissed my forehead. "I love you, Johnny. I'll see you a little later."

"I love you, too, Mom."

After Mom left the room, Jillian shut the door. Why? That was unusual. And what was she holding? Some kind of tray? "Your mother is really sweet," she said.

"Yeah."

"Family is the one thing we've always got to fall back on. It's why we do what we do."

I wasn't sure where Nurse Jillian was going with this. If she was justifying the fact that I was lying here with misshapen stumps for an arm and a leg, and I was supposed to be happy my mother came to see me in my time of need, I wasn't buying it. So I didn't respond.

"Now that you're on the road to recovery, we're going to raise the standards for personal hygiene. We'll be introducing more solid food into your diet, and I want to go over the procedure for using a bedpan."

So that was it. Fuck. "Couldn't I just stop shitting?" I said angrily.

Nurse Jillian frowned. With short brown Army hair and cold squinty snake eyes, she looked scary. "Private Cutter," she snapped, "do you think your mother would like to hear you using language like that?"

"I don't know. She seemed to be happy that I'm alive, so maybe she'd cut me some slack."

"Don't you think you're aiming a little low? Why don't you try to make her proud of you. You could start by learning to urinate or have a bowel movement in this" — Jillian held up a rectangular white pan — "instead of soiling your sheets."

Jesus Fucking Christ! Jillian was bagging me for something I couldn't control, something I hated as much as she apparently did. Fuck comas, I thought, better not to ever wake up.

"Have you ever used a bedpan before?" Jillian asked in a now-perky saccharine voice. Suddenly she was not the bad-ass accusatory drill sergeant anymore. Jekyll and Hyde action. Spooky woman could turn on a dime.

"When would I have used a bedpan? I used to be normal."

"It's a simple question, Private. I don't know the answer to it. What I'm looking for is a yes or a no."

"No."

"All right. Next question: Do you think your body is capable of producing a bowel movement now?"

"No."

"Are you sure?"

What a bitch. *"No, I'm not sure,"* I yelled. *"How the hell should I know what my body is capable of? Half of it's gone."*

Nurse Jillian stepped forward, bent down and thrust her face to within six inches of mine. It was too close, too much information. Her clenched jaw jutted out. She reeked of nicotine. "Private Cutter," she growled, "just so we understand each other, your injuries notwithstanding, you are still a soldier in the United States Army, Walter Reed hospital is still an Army base, and right now, when it's just you and me in this room, I am your commanding officer. If you want me to rip you a new asshole and give you a colostomy bag so you can have a bowel movement, I will do so. In the meantime, I am going to teach you to use this bedpan. Do I make myself clear?"

I asked God to give me a 9 millimeter. He didn't. If he had, I would have shot Jillian and then myself. Her eyes glared so hot she looked like she might demand that I drop and give her 50 one-armed pushups. She had me. All I could get out was a feeble, "Yes."

"Yes what?"

"Yes, Captain Jillian," I answered, wondering if there was a limit to how much I could be jacked.

"I'm glad we understand each other. Now the first thing to know is, we need about a five-minute warning before you have to evacuate. So when you feel the urge building, hit the call button and let us know. One of us will be here to assist you. Don't wait until it's an emergency."

I began to drift while she was talking. I wanted out. I thought about my life, my old life, the life I had two years ago. I closed my eyes and asked God to please let me go back to it.

"Cutter, where are you? I need you to focus. *I'm going to help you!"* I opened my eyes. The voice belonged to Jillian, of course, and not God. There weren't any miracles happening. I wasn't transported back to my old life. I still lay bereft in this bed. This nurse was still teaching me to use a bedpan. I gave the morphine button a whack. With God missing in action, drugs were looking like my only salvation: The First Church of the Holy Painkiller.

Nurse Jillian pulled on rubber gloves, taking the time to painstakingly adjust each finger, which I took as a bad sign that we would go through with this mission whether I had to "evacuate" or not. She pressed the button that cranked up the bed, putting me in a half-sitting position. Then she pulled the bedcovers down to my ankles.

"Can you get your dressing gown off by yourself?"

"No."

"No what?"

"No, Captain Jillian."

So she helped me remove my hospital gown, a staggering indignity and a hellacious energy burn. My stomach knotted up with the effort. I felt lightheaded. I came close to passing out but didn't make it. I just sat there, hyperventilating as my forehead broke into a clammy sweat.

"You look pale."

"Everything hurts."

"What do you mean 'everything'? Where does it hurt?"

"Everywhere."

"Cutter, you can get through this. You're not the only soldier who's ever had to use a bedpan. It's no big deal. It's just how you're going to have to go to the bathroom for a while, until we get you up on your feet."

"My *feet?*"

"Yes. Your feet. Eventually we're going to give you a new leg. A prosthetic. And, yes, you will have two feet. Just like you used to. Now I want you to try to roll over on your left side. I'm going to put my hand under your back and help. Let's go."

With no arm, I had no leverage, no ability to push. I tried torquing my shoulders to the left, which helped a little, but what got me onto my side was a shove from Nurse Jillian. "Good," she said. "Now hold that position. I'm laying down a waterproof pad now … the bedpan goes on top of the pad … this is called a fracture pan. It's wedge-shaped, thinner where it goes under the buttocks to make it more comfortable … OK, now I want you to roll back to your original position and try to keep your legs apart. You'll feel the pan underneath you."

Once Nurse Jillian took her hand away, I plopped down. The edges of the bedpan dug into my lower back.

"Well done. Now I'm going to cover you up so you stay warm. If you'd like some privacy, I'll leave the room for a bit."

"What now? Should I just … go? In this?"

"That's right. Just like you normally would."

I snorted.

"What?" she said.

"This isn't normal."

"Sure it is. This is perfectly normal."

So *this* was normal. Good to know. I got sad and sick again. My forehead continued to sweat. My stomach started to cramp up. In a minute, I realized that, yes, I probably could poop because I was constipated like a bastard, and my gut lock couldn't go on forever, and I might as well try out the new normal. "You'll leave the room?" I said.

"Yes. Say, 20 minutes?"

"OK."

"I'll see you in a little while, then. You can always buzz when you're ready, too."

I just nodded. I was tired of talking. Nurse Jillian marched out, shutting the door behind her.

So here I was, lying on top of a bedpan, missing half of my body, my guts tied up in a godawful Gordian knot, sweat pouring down my face. I couldn't imagine that this was real, or that this was my life. Where was God? What the fuck was he doing when I got blown up? Sitting on his ass having a smoke with a slacker from the Iraqi army? I hope you fucking get lung cancer, I thought, so you can understand what people down here go through. I hope you get your legs blown off by an IED in heaven or wherever the hell you hang out. I was way beyond pissed.

I thought about the times that Mom and I had gone to church. It wasn't that often, although we were both official members of First Presbyterian in Trillium. Maybe that was my problem, not enough pew time. Mostly I had a few vague memories of going there as a kid. It was restful somehow. Something about the organ music and the minister's

voice would carry me away. In the early years, I would fall asleep holding Mom's hand but I quit going as a teenager. Maybe that was it. If I
had just joined the Christian youth group, I'd be off ministering to
wayward teens instead of lying on a bedpan, a one-leg wonder trying to
shit. Instead, I joined the Army. That was some motherfucking fork in
the road.

I was still sane enough to know that I needed to turn off my mind. I
was here, now, a lopsided amputee cripple, and that was not going to
change. *Never.* It was permanent. *Forever.* I had to quit thinking about
the what-ifs but I couldn't. Mom wanted me to stay in college. Too late.
Too bad. I didn't do it. I wondered if she would mention that. Maybe I
should just tell her she was right, get that out there and over with. I'm
sure she was thinking it as she looked at me lying here. I guess I'd be a
junior now, majoring in … something. It didn't matter. I'd be walking
around — *walking!* — between classes, going to the library to study.
Hanging out in the student union.

"Stop," I said out loud. "Just fucking stop." I tried to clear my head.
Maybe it made more sense to try to clear my bowel. A distraction. Anything to shut off my mind. I planted my left hand on my abdomen and
began to massage. That was the problem, though. I couldn't escape the
shock of what I had become. Every time I did anything, the smallest
movement, it made me think of what I had lost. There I was, rubbing
my stomach with one hand, not two.

After a couple of minutes of kneading, I managed to move the pain
along from my right side to my left. Another few minutes passed and
then the urge hit. My colon let loose. Like magic, the pain vanished.
The rest of my body still ached but the gut knot was cut and my head
quit sweating. Sweet relief. I lay there for a few minutes, listening to my
breathing, thinking of nothing. An empty mind, like an empty bowel,
was a beautiful thing.

For good measure, I gave myself a hit, a little reward, a bliss kiss for
my burdened brain. If people knew how warm and fine and great and
smooth and shiny and spectacular morphine was, they would never
pray to God. Why bother? I was semi-living proof that he was absent
without leave. Why worship a slacker who doesn't come through for
you? I bowed down to my problem-solver, the great god morphine, the

reliable giver of peace and tranquillity, the true chill deity.

"Cutter. *Hey, Cutter. CUTTER! WAKE UP!*"

I didn't exactly hear my name, it was more experiencing the sound waves, feeling them ripple across me from the depths of deep space. Nurse Jillian had an insistent way of drilling through. She also slapped me a couple of times across the face and I returned to the room.

"Nice job, Cutter," she cooed. "You kept it in the pan. Well done." She made me feel like a pooping Pomeranian who just passed his paper-training test. "OK, next step, I want you to rotate away from me onto your left side, just like you did before, and I'll pull the pan out. Can you do that?"

No, I could not. I grunted and groaned. I lifted my leg stump into the air to try to get some momentum. I flexed my right shoulder off the bed. But I was stuck.

"What's your problem?" Nurse Jillian snapped.

"I can't do it."

"All right," she said, "I'm going to give you a little help but I want you to do most of the work. Your muscles have atrophied and we've got to start building them back up." She placed her icy rubber-gloved hand under my back and lifted. I heaved as best I could. I felt the bedpan slide away. Good riddance. I flopped back down like a mackerel on a boat dock. Nurse Jillian went into the bathroom. She came out armed with a roll of toilet paper, a bucket of water and towels. It took her 15 minutes to wash away my filth. As she poked and wiped and scrubbed, I wished that bomb had killed me. I imagined my boots, rifle and helmet standing in for me on base, and the guys paying their last respects. So simple. So clean. So done. Nothing else to endure.

Unfortunately, I survived. The doctors saved me. Now I couldn't wipe my own ass.

23 / Tell me if this hurts

I didn't know what was killing me more, the excruciating visits from
Mom or Nurse Jillian's obsessive attention to my toilet habits. I must
have slept 16 hours a day but whenever I was awake Mom was there.
When she wasn't doing needlepoint, she was trying to find out every
little thing about my time in Iraq. What did you eat? Who were your
friends? What did you do? Where was your room? How big was the
base? It was like an Abu Ghraib interrogation, only without the black
hood and snarling dog.

I wanted to forget all the details but ironically my memory had
kicked into overdrive. I knew everything and now I had to deal with it.
Then, when Mom left, Nurse Jillian followed up like a tag team wres-
tler. Do you need the bedpan? Are you sure? Are you ready to have a
bowel movement on your own? Can I leave the pan with you, or do you
want me to help? Is this enough toilet paper?

New doctors came in each afternoon to check my stumps, along
with eager residents or interns who took notes and stared. Could they
see my cage? I was like a new zoo animal. An Army chaplain dropped
by, too, and gave me his vigorous assurance that "God loves you."

"He has a funny way of showing it," I said.

"You may not understand it now," the man of God said, "but there's a
reason for this."

"Yeah, it's called a fucking Humvee that doesn't have enough armor.
It's called driving around in fucking circles till you fucking get blown
up." My anger was corrosive but I didn't care. Now I saw Iraq as a stupid fucking waste of good men and women. Now I saw what it did to
me. Did this church clown not understand that my life was over?

"Someday," the chaplain said, "everything will become clear. There
truly is a reason." He held up his Bible and tapped it.

"And what would that reason be?"

"It's not for me to say."

"So who could tell me?"

"God will tell you when you're ready."

"I'm ready now. I'd like to hear God's reason right now."

"Well, I don't know if God is ready for *you*."

"Are you in touch with God?"

"I like to think that I am, yes."

"That's good, because the next time the two of you have a conversation, I'd like you to tell God that when he's fucking ready, if he's got the fucking time to spare, he can fucking find me right here in Room 5731. You know, in case he's lost track in the fog of war. Would you do that for me?"

"Yes, I will." Then the chaplain got the hell out of my room, promising he would drop by again soon "to continue this important dialogue." He must have ratted out my bad attitude. An hour later I got a visit from an Army psychologist who wanted to set up an appointment "at your earliest convenience."

"How about the third of Never," I suggested.

"So now is not a good time for you?"

It seemed to be a seriously stated question, with not even a hint of post-modern irony. Therefore, I laughed. Loudly. Like a lunatic.

"I'm sorry," the psychologist said, "did I say something funny?"

"Yes, you did, and when you figure out what it was, come back and see me. I'm looking forward to you telling me how to be proud and happy about losing my arm and leg."

The psychologist bugged out then, like the chaplain. Fuck, I thought, where do they find these guys? Whatever, my shock and raw campaign was working. Enemies vanquished.

Walter Reed was a bullshit place. As insane as Iraq was, I missed the guys and their no-nonsense ability. That night, when Nurse Rochambeau stopped in during her rounds, I said, "I need a sat phone. I've got to call Captain Dozinger."

"You don't need a sat phone for that," she said. "I'll just put his call through to your room."

"What do you mean?"

"He calls three or four times a week."

"Killdozer's been calling here?"

"Yes."

"Jesus, Rochelle, why didn't you tell me?"

"You were unconscious for a month and now you're usually just out of it. He calls late, our time. I'm not going to wake you up if you're sleeping. You need to rest but I told him you're getting stronger. So next time, OK?" She cocked her head and unleashed that big gap-toothed smile. Rochambeau had a good heart.

"OK," I agreed. I smiled back, which hurt my face, like being shot in the jaw with an arrow. It didn't matter where a muscle was located in my body, or how small or how large it was, if I moved it, it hurt.

The next day I had my first real meal. Nurse Jillian disconnected my feeding tube. An orderly wheeled a food cart in and placed a bowl of chicken noodle soup on a tray over my lap. "Tah-dah," Jillian said. "Semi-solid food. Are you ready for this?"

"I don't know."

"Give it a shot."

I raised a spoonful to my mouth with an awkward case of the shakes, which reminded me, again, that I was a right-handed guy who did not have a right hand. The broth was warm and golden. My mouth crinkled up as natural flavor assaulted my taste buds. "Oh, my God," I said to Jillian, slurping a little more. "I'd forgotten what it was like to eat real food. Thank you."

"You're welcome, Cutter. We're going to try to make MREs just a distant memory for you."

"I'll never forget Chicken Fajitas."

"Few soldiers do."

Maybe I was too harsh on the hospital. Everybody there wanted to help me. I knew that in my head but my body didn't understand. What could they do for me? I was beyond help. Every time I wondered if I might have a life ahead of me, I would look at those two stumps, which was a bad idea. At least six times a day, randomly, I would pull the blankets down and just stare at what was left of my leg. In the periphery of my vision, I could see my arm stump. I would wiggle it, just to confirm that, yes, this was mine, I controlled it. This stump was connected to my shoulder. This wasn't a horror movie or a nightmare. The wounds were so goddamned ugly. It was sick and obsessive and depressing to look at them. I couldn't help it. I should have looked away, like any normal person would have. Averted my eyes. If you didn't see it, if you didn't look, it wasn't really there. If you ignored it, it would go away.

Except for one thing: If you're the sucker with the stumps, they never go away, no matter how many people call you a hero. You're a hero with two missing limbs, that's all. There was no escape for me. The rest of the world could carry on with its normal daily life. I couldn't. I had to find a way around that reality.

My latest doctor said he could help. Colonel Douglas Kendrickson was an orthopedic surgeon. He came in to examine me in the afternoon. He didn't have interns trailing behind him like ducklings, which I appreciated, and he shut the door to my room, which I liked even more. It kept the outside world out. His head was shaved and shiny, a classic Army head. He had the standard-issue ramrod-straight bearing but his voice sounded weary. When he shook my hand — with his left, not his right — he nearly crushed it. No mercy. His dark brown eyes never seemed to blink. He stared me down like a drill sergeant. He probably sensed weakness, especially in my anemic grip.

Kendrickson asked me a few bio questions, age, hometown, family, chitchat stuff. He wanted to know how I got hurt. "It was random," I told him. "I won the IED lottery."

Then he said, "Tell me if this hurts." He put pressure with his right hand on the end of my leg stump.

I screamed. It felt like a blowtorch on raw bone.

"So, yes," Kendrickson said, pulling his powerful hand away.

"*Hell, yeah, yes,*" I said, gulping air like an asthmatic. I wiggled the stump back and forth, hoping the little breeze it created could cool down the fire.

"Cutter, you need another operation. I know that's the last thing you want to hear but we want to fast-track you for a C-leg. They did a good job on the amputation but your stump could use some reshaping."

"What's a C-leg?"

"It's the latest technology, a computerized artificial leg that absorbs impact, maybe even better than your original leg. It's got an intelligent knee joint but it has to fit over your stump perfectly, without any pressure points. Otherwise, you won't wear it. I wouldn't want to find it in a garbage can over on Georgia Avenue."

"Assuming I could get to Georgia Avenue on this C-leg, how would I get back if I dumped it?"

"How far can you hop?"

I couldn't believe he said that. I wondered if I heard him right but, yeah, that was what he said. He kept staring at me, all serious. Then his face cracked a little and he smiled.

I had to laugh. The guy had some stones to fuck with a cripple. Major sickage. I should have asked the Amputee Civil Liberties Union to file a lawsuit against him but this Doctor Kendrickson made me laugh. I didn't foresee that happening very often. "Not very far," I said. "I can't even get out of this bed."

"Then a C-leg is just the thing for you. However, you do need to be motivated. It's a $50,000 leg."

"The leg I had was worth more to me than that," I said, with as long a stare as I could muster.

"Understood," Kendrickson said. "Nevertheless, I'd like you to come in for a discussion of your options, one of which is more surgery — and again, I know that nobody wants more surgery — but the upside is, it would make the odds of success with a C-leg much higher. Beyond that, the anesthesia is more powerful than a speeding .38-caliber bullet. Everybody loves it."

What a mind-fuck thing to say. My off-balance reply was pretty witless: "Really?"

"That seems to be the consensus."

Yeah, Kendrickson was an interesting guy. He knew the way in. I agreed to the appointment.

24 / Marry-go-round

"Ask her to marry you, Cutter!" Killdozer barked. "That's an order."

Like I didn't have enough to worry about, Captain Dozinger was encouraging me to charge a machine gun bunker. That was the military, for you: Giving orders that would change your life. Things were happening too fast. Mom let it slip that Halley was coming to visit me. It was supposed to be a secret. Thank God that Mom told me. At least I had 24 hours to think about what to say. Then Rochambeau brought the phone in that night, Killdozer calling, just like she said he would.

"I am so goddamned sorry about what happened," the captain said. "If I could go back and put myself in that Humvee, I would. We got the motherfuckers who did it, though. Two brothers and a friend of theirs. They were all al-Qaida. We got some intel on where they lived. We took them out two nights later."

"Thanks, Captain," I said, "but who died?"

"What do you mean?"

"Somebody in the unit died on the Oil Ministry escort mission … isn't that right?"

There was a long deep dark silence on the line. I wondered if the captain would bullshit me for the first time. Then he said, "Yes, that's right. Amerigo Taymondo."

"Fuck this goddamn war. Just fuck it."

"Yeah. I'm really sorry. He was a good man. Nobody handled a .50 the way he did. We're going to win this thing, though. Someday it'll be over, if the folks back home can stick with us a little longer." Like he knew what I was thinking, the captain added, "It won't be a waste, Cutter, it won't be for nothing, I can promise you that."

Was *that* the first time the captain had ever lied to me? Was he telling me what he thought I wanted to hear? He sounded like he believed it, kind of, and maybe he did. Whatever.

So Amerigo was gone. Three more hajjis were dead. I was trapped

6,000 miles away in a hospital bed, missing my arm and leg. What had been gained? The war steamrolled on, crushing American soldiers, Iraqi insurgents, civilians, men, women, children, camels, donkeys, dogs, cats, goats, chickens, anything that was alive. And if the folks back home stuck with us, we could continue the killing. For years. Anyway, how could Killdozer have been sure they got the right guys? They didn't have targets on their backs like we did. They all looked alike. I didn't ask him the question. What could he say? Of course they got the guys who did this to Amerigo and me. I didn't tell him that when you were shitting in a bedpan, pissing through a tube, looking at what was left of your body, wondering why they bothered to save you, the war — and retribution — seemed beyond pointless. Patriotism was for suckers and poor people, tools and fools. The folks back home showed their support for the troops by shopping, following orders from the commander in chief.

We talked for a while about Bravo Company and what the guys were up to. Same old thing, stay out of the way of suicide bombers and watch for signs of IEDs. Blow up buildings. Rebuild buildings. Hand out candy. Get the oil flowing. The usual missions. When I couldn't take the hopelessness anymore, I blurted out, "My girlfriend is coming to visit me, Captain, and I don't know what to do."

That's when he snapped out his marriage advice, which was kind of a slap in the face and woke me up. I realized I had to tell him the truth and admit that I might have overstated things.

"What do you mean?"

"Maybe I should have said my *former* girlfriend. I'm not sure if she still is."

"Have you talked to her since you got stateside?"

"No."

"Does she know what happened?"

"She knows I got hurt. My mom was in contact with her."

"What's her name?"

"Halley Fallon."

"Pretty name. What kind of a girl is she?"

The first thing that popped into my head was: "She's fun."

"Fun is good. In fact, that might be the most important thing."

"And she's really beautiful."

The captain said, "That's good, too. How long have you known her?"

I had to think about that, the math part of it, anyway, but I remembered the first day of Mrs. Bayonne's English lit class at Coos Bay Community College, when Halley walked in, weighed down by a gigantic backpack, her long blond hair soaked from the rain, and she looked like she didn't care. She sat nonchalantly in the front row, dug a notebook and pen out of her pack, and started taking notes like a book fiend. "Maybe a few months," I said, "if you just count the time we were actually together."

"Do you love her?" the captain asked.

"Yes," I said at first, without hesitation, but then: "I mean, I think I do, if I even know what love is."

"You know, Cutter. You know it when you feel it. The other side of that is, Does she love you?"

I didn't say anything for a while. I had to think about that one. Finally I said, "I don't know. I think she might have. Maybe. I don't know."

The line was pretty much dead except for some background static. Killdozer, I was sure, wanted to be upbeat but he had proved, probably, that he would never lie to me. I couldn't take the silence for long, so I filled it in with the truth, or as much of the truth as I could admit to myself: "The thing is, when she sees me, I'm not going to be the same guy as when I left."

"Of course you are. A man doesn't change because he gets injured."

Killdozer may or may not have believed that. I decided to call him on it one way or the other: "With all due respect, sir, if you could see me lying here in this bed, if you could see what I've lost, I doubt if you would say that. The fact is, I've changed."

There was another long silence. When Killdozer said nothing, he said a lot. I made sure the connection hadn't cut out: "Captain?"

"You're right. I'm not there, so maybe I should just shut up, but the Army *will* take care of you. I know that for a fact. Injured soldiers can get $3,000 a month in disability pay. You'll always have money coming in."

It was comforting to know that when I got back to civilian life, I would be able to afford a double-wide trailer on a brown rocky lot somewhere in eastern Oregon and maybe a tall TV antenna to pull in a signal from Boise. In July and August, I could sit outside and bathe my stumps in the 110-degree heat. In the winter, after surviving the summer, I could venture out on a 10-degree January morning and lie down in the snow. Killdozer had artfully changed the subject from Halley. I silently thanked him for that. I couldn't think about her, or what she might think of me. I especially couldn't bring up the real question that I had buried so deeply since the shock of waking up.

25 / Another kind of pain

Rochambeau came in around 0200. I was just lying there, eyes shut, thinking. The phone was sitting on my chest, cradled in my hand. Rochambeau began to peel my fingers off of it, which reminded me of another late night, when I was a kid. I was awake then, too, pretending to be asleep. In those days, I had a little blue blanket that I clutched like a lifeline. Dad came into the room and tried to pull that blanket away but I held on with all my strength and made a bad dream noise. He gave up and brushed his hand across my forehead instead. "Good night, little man," he said.

I made the same noise now and Rochambeau whispered, "Johnny?"

I opened my eyes and gripped the phone. "Things get taken away from me," I said.

"Sorry, I thought you were asleep."

"And I don't know what to do about it."

"I have to return this phone. Did you have a good talk with the captain?"

"Can I just hold onto it for another minute?"

"The phone?"

"Yeah."

"Why?"

"I don't know."

Rochambeau looked at me. She scrunched her mouth to one side, quizzically, trying to figure out the moment.

"I haven't seen my dad for a long time," I said, like she was not even in the room. Maybe I was talking more to myself than to her. She must have sensed that, because she didn't say anything, but she did take her hand off the phone. At least I could have that for now. "They got divorced when I was 16, and I don't really remember seeing him after that except right before I left for basic training. He said he was proud of me. I got him to come back, at least for that one day."

Rochambeau touched my shoulder. "Johnny, are you OK?" she asked.

"I don't think so."

"What do you mean?"

"I don't think I'm OK."

Rochambeau put her hand on my forehead, testing for fever, but it made me think of Dad. "What's the matter?" she asked.

"I don't know yet."

"Do I need to call somebody? Do you want to talk to somebody?"

"Like who?"

"Like Doctor Brannfors."

"What could he do?"

"He's a psychologist. He could talk to you."

"But what could he *do?*"

"I don't know."

"I don't either."

"You're worrying me a little, Johnny."

"I know. I feel the same way."

"What did you and the captain talk about?"

"Stuff."

"Any particular stuff?"

"So I have this phone in my hand and I could call anybody in the entire world right now." I turned the phone on and the display lit up. "But I don't have anybody I can talk to."

"I don't think that's true."

"You're a nurse. You have to say that. Isn't that some kind of oath you take? Don't they make you promise not to tell the guy missing an arm and a leg that he's really fucked up?"

"You are getting way too existential for me, Cutter. You want me to call Brannfors? I'll get his fat ass out of his overstuffed bed if you want me to. Just say the word. Maybe *he'll* tell you that you're really fucked up but, yes, you are correct, I will not. Because I don't think you are."

"My girlfriend is coming to visit me tomorrow. Or today, actually."

"Ohhhh," Rochambeau said, nodding her head. "Why didn't you say so?"

"I didn't know how."

Rochambeau crossed the room and grabbed Mom's chair. She dragged it over next to my bed and sat down. "So that's good news, isn't it?" she said. "Girlfriends are cool. I wish I had one."

"Am I disgusting, Rochelle?"

"What?"

"You've seen me. Am I disgusting?"

"No."

"You have to say that, right? The medical oath?"

"You think you're disgusting because you're missing two limbs?"

"I never wanted to be different. I just wanted to fit in."

"Let me tell you, Cutter, there's plenty of guys out there with two arms and two legs who are slimy disgusting. Anyway, we're gonna get you a new arm and a new leg. You just have to give it a little time."

"I want my old arm back. I want my old leg back."

Rochambeau didn't say anything. I stared at the ceiling, wondering what her silence meant. I listened to the hospital's night sounds, the whirring motors, the occasional buzz from down the hall, the electronic beeps of the machines supplying my tubes with nourishment and drugs. I wondered if they had cut back on my IV meds without telling me. I had been high, I thought, since I woke up in the hospital. If I ignored where I was, if I drifted, if I *forgot*, it came close to being pleasant. Morphine, methadone, Dilaudid, Demerol, Percocets, Quaaludes, Lexapro, they had it all, a medicinal arsenal. The war on soldierly pain was well-waged by Walter Reed. We could win that one with overwhelming force. Still, maybe I was coming down. Maybe that explained why I was thinking about another kind of pain. Where would I go? What would I do? Would I ever ... the question I could not ask.

Rochambeau must have been thinking, too, because she finally spoke the truth: "I wish you could go back. I wish we could all go back. The reality is, we can't. This is it. We have a mission to carry out. This is where we are. It's awful and it breaks my heart and we need to figure something else out but until we do, this is it."

The truth was hard to hear. And tell. Nobody liked it. I gave the morphine button a perfunctory press, which was disturbing. If I lost interest in meds, what else was there? I went back to listening to the mechanical conversations of the hospital. I wondered if my new leg and arm would make noise. I wondered if people would listen and stare.

"Tell me about your girlfriend," Rochambeau said.

"I don't know."

"You don't want to tell me?"

"I don't know if she's my girlfriend."

"She's coming to see you, right?"

"Yeah."

"Well, she must be something more than girl-*acquaintance*. She's coming from Oregon?"

"Yeah."

"That says girlfriend to me."

"It does?"

"I'd say so. That's a long way to go."

"I just don't see how … how she … you know."

"How she what?"

"How she's going to … " I pulled the covers down to expose my arm stump.

"OK, now we're getting somewhere," Rochambeau said. "You don't know how she's going to deal with this."

"Right."

"Are you worried about it?"

"I'm scared shitless."

Rochambeau smiled. "Shitless is good," she said.

"Yeah, what if she can't handle it?"

"That's a possibility. Some women can and some can't. It takes love and strength and perseverance, that's for sure, but trust me, I've seen it work."

"So you've seen it not work, too."

Rochambeau shrugged. "I wouldn't dwell on that if I were you. Shouldn't you be getting some sleep? It's late. She's coming today?"

"Yeah."

"You should definitely get some sleep."

"I don't think I can sleep."

"You want me to get you something to help? We could start with Ambien. If that doesn't work, we have other options."

"That would be great. Yes, please, put me to sleep."

26 / The highest high

The sleeping pill didn't do it for me. My eyes refused to shut. In the dark, the hospital gurgled away, digesting its patients. Some of them, chewed up like me, were in the mouth, about to be swallowed. Others, I imagined, were sloshing around in the stomach, being broken down. Still others were ready to be shit out. I hit the morphine button a few times and it didn't help. In a lucid moment around 0400, I realized something: Emotions are the most powerful drug.

I thought back to the time I had been the highest in my life. It had nothing to do with killer weed. The drug was sex. The high was happiness, elation and joy.

Thank God for Halley Fallon.

The full-on rapturous rush came near the end of my semester at Coos Bay, about three miles from Trillium and a million miles from my current life. I used to ride my beater mountain bike up an old logging road into the Coast Range. When the road ended, I continued on, beyond the clear-cut and into the forest that remained. One day, near sundown, I followed the sound of a wild ruckus, some crazy blue jays squawking like they'd just heard a hilarious bird joke. I emerged from the Doug firs onto a cliffside with an amazing view to the east across the Trillium River canyon. I called it The Overlook. I stayed long enough to watch the light fade through red to purple to gray. I went back to that secret spot a bunch of times because it was so beautiful, so natural, so peaceful. Like Halley. A week after that first time in her bedroom, I suggested that we take a hike. "Sure," she said with a wicked grin. I was prepared this time, with a huge backpack full of water bottles, blankets, sandwiches and two condoms. Halley, it turned out, loved The Overlook. I loved her nature.

But that was then. Now, at age 22, would I ever have sex again?

That was the question.

I couldn't ask it, I couldn't think about it, and yet it never left my mind. Realistically, though, if *I* couldn't stand to look at my stumps, how could a woman? I couldn't get past that. Further, if somehow a woman's acceptance was possible, would I even be capable of it? Based on what was hidden under the bandages, the answer was no. It was terrifying to think about looking, because I *knew*, and then confronting it, *seeing* the purplish, bruised, stitched-up, lopsided, misshapen mess, what other conclusion was there?

Those bandages were coming off in two weeks and I would see a urology specialist, Doctor MacMilland. I doubted that he would tell me the truth. Bad news was banned in the Army. Even a grunt like me had learned that much. A mission might fail but only on the battlefield. In the report, it succeeded. Why would it be any different with MacMilland? He was Army. He would lay out a battle plan, more drugs, more therapy, more surgery, more rehab. More *more*. He would redefine success to give me hope. I could hold onto that for as long as I wanted. Maybe I would be gone from Ward 57 before reality grabbed me by the throat and crushed my airway. There were moments when I thought I should just deal with it, soldier up. Basic training was still in my bones, the ones that hadn't been shattered. I even said the words to myself a few times: Deal with it. I sustained that attitude for five minutes. Then I pulled down the covers, took another long look at my stumps and asked: How do you deal with this? It's done. It's too late to deal.

The sun came up, like it annoyingly always did. I was still awake, thinking, wondering, fearing. Mom showed up soon enough and began her game of 20 questions.

"How did you sleep, Johnny?"

"Fine," I lied.

"How are you feeling?"

"Fine."

"How is your leg?"

"My leg is gone, Mom."

"I mean, does it hurt? Are you in pain?"

"No, Mom, I'm not in pain. I get morphine whenever I need it."

"Are you taking too much? Could you get addicted?"

"No, Mom, morphine is not very addictive, and besides, I'm only taking it every half-hour."

"That seems like a lot."

"Every five minutes would be bad, Mom, but I think every half-hour is nothing to worry about. I think that's the official dosage."

"Do your doctors know what they're doing?"

"I doubt it."

"You don't think your doctors know what they're doing?"

"I don't know, Mom. It sort of doesn't matter, does it?"

"What do you mean, doesn't matter?"

"Either they're going to save me or they're not, and if they do, I'll probably still die of a morphine overdose."

"Is that supposed to be funny, Johnny?"

"Yeah, a little."

"Do you think it would be funny to die of a morphine overdose?"

"I think it would be mildly amusing or at least ironic."

"I don't think irony is very funny."

"You're right, Mom. It's not."

I felt like a POW. Mom should have been an interrogator at Abu Ghraib. The jihadis would be begging to go to their 72 virgins: *Allah willing, I want to die right now rather than be subjected to this woman's unrelenting questions. Please kill me, Allah. Kill me now.*

Then she hit me with the mother of all mom questions: "Are you ready to see Halley?"

No! *Please, God, since you so skillfully and thoughtfully watched over me in Baghdad, could you help me one more time and kill me now?*

Mom tried to get inside my head for another hour or so. I fought her off with shrugs, non-answers and misdirection.

Then, in the doorway, Halley Fallon appeared, the real and glowing embodiment of my memories, hopes and dreams.

I was terrified. My stomach knotted up. I trembled. My skin tingled like I was lying naked in fresh snow. Even though I had been obsessing over this moment all night, or really, since I first woke up at Walter Reed, imagining it, rehearsing it, I didn't know what to say. I forgot every word I had tried out in my mind but our eyes locked and that made Mom disappear from my consciousness, which was a good start.

Halley's beauty made me ache. I hadn't seen her since I left home. Of course, we had e-mailed back and forth and sent photos but I wasn't ready to see her standing there for real. Goddamn, I *did* desperately want to die, because I needed her more than morphine. I craved her touch but I knew, somehow, that I couldn't have it. I knew it wouldn't work out. And that might as well have killed me.

She walked in the room and said, "Hi, Johnny." Then she started to cry. It was so simple and so complicated. As tears streamed down her flushed cheeks, my jaw clenched shut. I almost reached up to give it a quick squeeze and pull it open so I could speak but I didn't want to make a move that called attention to the covers. Anybody looking closely would know something was terribly wrong under there.

"Hi, Halley." Horrifying. It was Mom. How could she do that? She was talking for me.

Halley moved to the bedside and reached out, putting her palm to my face. I flinched, though, and she pulled away. Tears continued down both sides of her face. Finally I found my voice: "Thanks for being, Halley." The slip-up made cosmic sense. Nonetheless, I quickly corrected myself: "For being *here*."

My mind jumped, fixating on the position of the bed. Why didn't I ask Rochambeau to move me to the other side of the room, so my stumps would be against the wall, less conspicuous? I berated myself for not thinking of that.

"I would have come sooner," Halley said, "but they told me, well, I didn't know what to do and they said it would probably be better to wait a little bit."

Mom stood up. "I'm going to excuse myself," she said, "and let you two kids talk for a while. I do have an errand to run. It's so good to see you, Halley." Mom gave her a big hug. It ripped me up to watch them because I couldn't do the same.

"You, too, Mrs. Cutter," Halley said.

"Honey, I'll come back later tonight before I go to bed, OK?"

"OK, Mom."

As crazy as Mom made me, I didn't exactly want her to leave the room. She was a buffer between me and uncertainty. I didn't know what to say to Halley or how to act. If it was just the two of us, I might freeze up. Then Mom walked out. So there we were. Halley moved Mom's chair up close to my bed and sat down. We looked at each other for a while. Her eyes were sad. She had the lightest thinnest eyebrows, almost invisible. She wasn't curling her hair anymore and it hung straight down upon her shoulders. Her skin wasn't perfect, she didn't care, and somehow that made her even more endearing.

"I wish I knew what to say, Johnny. I thought about it and thought about it but everything just felt like … I don't know." Halley shrugged and smiled slightly, biting the left side of her lower lip. It was how she dealt with awkward moments. I tried to imprint the image on my brain in case I never saw it again.

"I really screwed up." The comment surprised me. I was thinking it but I didn't intend to say it aloud. The words, sharp, with serrated edges, just popped out.

"No you didn't." Halley reached for me. She put her hand on my shoulder. She was so kind, staying as far away from my stump as she could. She knew the arm was gone. The covers lay flat where my hand and forearm should have been.

"No, I did. I never should have left Trillium."

"Johnny, you'll be OK. I know you will. You did what you had to do."

"That's just it. I didn't have to. I don't even know why I did. When I think back, I don't understand it. I never had any idea of something like this, that this is where I would end up." I locked onto Halley's eyes and tried to see into her mind. I wondered if she would say anything. She didn't, not at that moment, and I took that to mean she agreed with me. How could she not? How could anybody?

"You're a hero."

There it was.

It always came down to that, the conclusion that other people — they — drew to make me feel better. Loss of arm and leg equals hero. I should be proud. Of what? Handing out candy to make Iraqi kids like America? Wasn't that merely bribery? Trying to stop Sunnis and Shiites from beheading each other? Why was that my job? I was convinced that they wanted me to accept what had happened but I couldn't. Because it was my life that had been ruined, not theirs. I wondered how they would feel about lying in a bed in Ward 57, saying goodbye to their girlfriend?

Halley started to sniffle. Her original tears had dried in salty tracks down her cheeks. "I've been crying since I first heard you were injured. Your mom told me. It makes me so sad, Johnny." Then she let loose with heavy sobs. I wanted to wipe away her new tears. I forgot and started to reach for her — with my missing arm. The blanket raised up about a foot from my shoulder, at the end of my stump. Halley saw its outline. Her face crinkled up and she started to shake. I pulled my left arm out instead and reached for her. She grabbed my hand and squeezed it hard. We stayed like that for a long time, a couple of minutes or more, an eternity. I found myself doing a mental calculation as the moments passed, counting off seconds that ticked by, imagining how long an hour would be, a day, a week, a year. The rest of my life.

Halley let go of me. "I'm sorry," she said, "I have to … " She reached into her purse and pulled out a tissue. She wiped her eyes, which were red and puffy, and blew her nose. "Is there a place?" she asked, holding up the tissue and making a little face. I pointed to the corner, toward a trash can at the far side of the room. While Halley's back was to me, I pulled my stump close to my body, in its hiding place, and maneuvered my left arm back under the covers. It was better if she saw me from only the neck up. I wanted to pretend for just a little longer.

Halley sat down again and said, "Sorry, I'm a mess."

"I've got you beat there."

She managed a crinkly smile and all my hopes fell apart. Her lips reminded me of the old days, when we laughed all the time. She would say something funny and crack me up, then she would join in. Or she'd get a mischievous grin right before she kissed me. I loved those grins. And those kisses. If I could erase all the memories of two years ago, maybe I could deal and at some point accept but how could I forget the things we did on The Overlook? Maybe with enough morphine …

"What happens now, Johnny?"

God, what a big fat open-ended question. Yeah, I wondered, what the hell happens now? I didn't have a clue, though I didn't say that. There were so many things I didn't say now. Bleak grim sad angry things. Who could stand to hear the things I wanted to say? Nobody.

"Mom told me you just started going to Portland State," I said.

Halley's eyes brightened. She looked relieved. There was only so much of this mopey shit we could wade through. "Yeah," she said, "it's my first semester. I transferred from Coos Bay and got into the computer science program."

"So you moved up to P-town?"

"I did. I got into student housing, this cool brick high-rise near the Park Blocks. It's about a three-minute walk to class. It's tiny but I'm on the eighth floor, up above the trees. I have this amazing view of Mount Hood. Well, OK, I've seen it once so far. It's pretty gray up there. Not nonstop like the coast but, yeah, gray rules in Portland, too."

I had changed the subject to help Halley. Now I wanted to change it to help myself. All I could think of was how I had quit school and she had continued. Now she was up in Portland and I was trapped in a military hospital bed, failing the bedpan curriculum. Could we have been any further apart?

Halley and I moved on, talking for a couple of hours about the people we knew, about what they were doing, about bands we liked, about clubs and cafes and food carts and coffee she had discovered in Portland, about her mom and dad and sister, about changes back home. About *her* new life. I knew we were winding down when she described, in great detail, a frozen yogurt shop that had opened near campus. Her favorite flavor was Hood River strawberry but marionberry was great, too. In wintertime, they mostly served lattes. You could get extra foam. They had eight different kinds of pearl tea. The cookies were really good, especially peanut butter chocolate chip and oatmeal raisin.

Small details kept us away from big ones. Halley must have known we had ignored the real topic as long as we could. After a long silence, she asked again, "What happens now, Johnny?"

I had to answer this time. I couldn't change the subject. I had to decide how narrow my answer would be. I considered Halley's choice of words. She didn't say what happens to *us*. Just what happens *now*.

"When I get a little stronger," I said, "they're going to fit me for an artificial leg. Later I'm supposed to get a prosthetic arm. It's a lot to do all at once, so they spread it out. They say it's easier that way. They told me I could live a normal life."

They. I wondered if *they* believed that. Because I didn't. I wondered if Halley did.

27 / Head in a bed

The rest of my life rested in two doctors' hands and, maybe, in the hand I had left. I went in for surgery on my leg stump a month after Halley left Washington. Doctor Kendrickson explained in my preliminary appointment that he would do a "routine" reshaping of the muscle and tissue surrounding the thigh bone so I could wear a prosthetic leg without pain. Also, if he found any dead or dying tissue, he would remove it.

"How routine is it?" I asked. "Have you done this a lot? Is there a chance I could die?"

Kendrickson wasn't much fun anymore. Where were the offhand comebacks? He gave me a colonel look, the glare reserved for a grunt who asked a stupid question. I didn't care. What could he do? Make me police the latrines? "You're not going to die," he said coldly.

"How many times have you done it?"

"I don't keep track."

"A thousand?"

"No, not that many."

"A hundred."

"Yes, maybe a hundred."

"So a hundred guys have come in here with their legs blown off by IEDs."

"That's right."

"Do you think it's fucking worth it?"

"I don't like profanity, Cutter. It's unbecoming of a soldier."

"Does that mean you don't like this fucking war?"

"If you have a problem with the conduct of the war, you need to take it up with the Pentagon."

"It's a little late for that." Trapped in Ward 57, I was getting angrier by the day. Maybe not at Kendrickson but at *somebody*. Whoever, Kendrickson didn't react. Why would he? He'd seen a hundred guys like me. No big deal, another amputee. "So you're going to knock me way out for the surgery," I said.

"Yes."

"Good. I want a lot of that super-epic anesthetic." I liked the sound of that. I began a singsong chant, "Super-epic anesthetic, super-epic anesthetic," waving my arm and stump in time like a symphony conductor. Colonel Kendrickson scowled at my musical ability.

Apparently the operation went all right. That's what they told me. What else would they say? Supposedly they took care of something called ossification. My leg stump didn't look much different, though. It was still ugly and red and purple and bruised and swollen and had a lot of stitches, mainly more of everything. When the drugs wore off, it still hurt like a flamethrower. At least more drugs could mostly fix that, for a while. Sometimes it felt like the rest of my leg was still there. The sensation pissed me off, because it was mean and cruel and mocking. It made me think about the leg. I could never have even a minute when I didn't know the leg was gone and would always be gone.

Two weeks after they tweaked the leg stump, I got a visit from Doctor MacMilland. He gave me a complicated explanation of how they would rebuild my urinary tract so I didn't have to piss out of a catheter. He used bigger words but that's what it came down to. I mostly tuned out and thought about how you can be a functioning human being one moment, and then something happens and you're a head in a bed waiting for your next surgery. If people understood this, they would never leave the house, and the Army would have to pay way bigger bonuses to get idiots like me to enlist.

"Do you have any questions?" MacMilland asked, snapping me out of my personal nightmare.

"No." No questions? Was I coming to terms with my injuries? Or did I just not care anymore? Or maybe I understood it was pointless to care. Actually, I still had one question but MacMilland was getting up, apparently content to leave without digging.

"Fine," the doctor said, looking pleased. "Then we'll do this. I'll have Nurse Jillian schedule it."

"Wait, sir. One other thing. Yes, it would be great not to have to pee out of a tube. OK, this is not easy for me to ask because it scares me.

Still, I can't stop thinking about it. I can't keep it inside my head any longer ... will I ever ... be able to have sex again?"

There. The Question.

MacMilland didn't say anything. He looked down at his clipboard. Was the answer in his notes somewhere? I thought he was stalling for time. He didn't want to give me bad news. The Army would — and did — kill to ignore bad news, so I wasn't surprised.

"Because I don't know if anybody would ever want to have sex with me like this but I'd like to know, if I ever found someone, would it be possible? When I see myself, when these bandages are changed, I don't feel like it could ever happen. Do you understand?"

MacMilland looked up from his notes. He hesitated, thinking of the least awkward way to put it, probably. He had to answer, because I had been honest to the point of physical pain. My guts were torn up. I asked The Question, even though I feared the answer was going to snuff any shred of hope I may have had. Consciously, I had no hope. I was as low and lacerated as it was possible to be but what if there was something deeper that I didn't know about, or that might be there in the future? I was close to giving up but I wasn't quite there.

"I don't know," MacMilland finally said. "That's one of the goals of the surgery, of course. Quite frankly, with injuries like this, the results are mixed. It partly depends on skin grafts and whether we can success-fully rebuild the corpus cavernosum, which was transected by a piece of shrapnel. Nerve damage can be a problem as well. It's too soon to know about that because it usually becomes apparent over time. I wish I could be more conclusive. I would encourage you to talk to the psy-chology staff. They would say there's more to sex than merely physical performance."

"Like what?" I asked.

"Again, I would encourage you to talk to a staff psychologist but the short answer is that intimacy is more than the act itself. Intimacy takes many forms."

I took that as a no and vowed never to speak of it again. I hoped that what I could not have, if I refused to acknowledge it, would not tear me up like that bomb.

28 / Independence day

Along with my mother, Walter Reed began to drive me even crazier. It was like a conspiracy. Mom was Big Mother, the constant all-knowing presence that monitored my every move, not that I could go anywhere, other than shifting positions every hour or so to alternate the pressure points. The hospital assisted her in my subjugation, with its regimen of doctor appointments, the pharmaceutical blitzkrieg, meal schedules, filing of paperwork, a check-in with a shrink, and my toilet training. Walter Reed was the 10th circle of hell.

Rochelle Rochambeau came in at the start of her shift one night and said, "I'm taking your bedpan away, Cutter. You're too old to use it."

"How am I supposed to go to the bathroom?"

"Just like you used to. You get out of bed, you walk to the bathroom and you go."

"That sounds good in theory. I hate that motherfucking bedpan. If they'd told me about that motherfucking bedpan before I enlisted, I never would've signed the motherfucking papers."

"So that's a *motherfucking* yes? You're ready to get rid of that *motherfucker?*" She stood there with a pouty lower lip and hands on her hips.

I had to smile when Rochambeau mocked me because she was having so much fun. A few drops of anger drained out of my infected attitude. "You think I can do it?" I said.

"You know I know you can."

"OK, show me what to do, First Lieutenant."

"I'll be right back," she said, double-timing out of the room. Rochambeau returned a few minutes later, walking with a crutch under each arm, her right leg lifted off the floor. She got to the middle of the room and did two revolutions on her left foot, a graceful pirouette, the crutches whirling above my face like the rotor blades of an Apache.

"You're a medevac chopper," I said.

"That's me, a 237-pound angel of mercy flying in to gather up the wounded. You want to know how I got so good on these, Cutter?"

"You know I do," I said, thinking that the mockee could also mock.

"Practice. I was on these for three months with a shattered tibia. A sniper took me down in Ramadi."

"You were in Iraq." It wasn't a question. Suddenly I understood. She'd been there.

"Not for long, a few months at the end of '03. Then I got injured and reassigned here. My daddy gave me these crutches just before he passed. They're old school. Wood. They don't make 'em like this anymore. Hundred-year-old oak. Hand-rubbed with linseed oil. Look at the grain. That's God's work. Aluminum is too cold, too sterile, too clangy. Aluminum never had to persevere through bad times, like a tree, through wind and rain and lightning and thunder. These crutches know what it's like to stand up, Cutter, through hell and back. They know what it's like to *fight*. I want you to have them."

"Huh?"

"I'm giving you my daddy's crutches. Here." Rochambeau thrust them toward me, one in each of her big hands.

"I can't take those," I protested. "They're too beautiful. They should be in a museum."

"You *can* take them and you *will* take them. That's an order. Because you do not want to disappoint my daddy. He was a feisty master sergeant. He'll come after your ass if you don't take 'em. He'll go AWOL from heaven and chase you down — and he's only got one leg. And it still has some shrapnel in it."

"Your dad lost a leg?"

"Yes, sir. Tet Offensive."

"Shit. Gimme those things. Thank you, Rochelle. *So much*." I pulled my arm from beneath the covers and reached out. Rochambeau grinned and handed the crutches over. I could only balance them against the edge of the bed. I didn't have the strength to do more.

"Let's practice, why don't we?" Rochambeau said. She stripped the covers away, levered me up and swung my left leg around off the bed so it could flop toward the floor. My body was board stiff. The movement stabbed muscles in six places. Both stumps started to burn. I gasped for air. "Good," she said. "You're still breathing. Now we disconnect The

Man." Rochambeau removed the hold-down tape, pulled the drip from my arm and laid the tube aside. "Do you like morphine?" she asked.

"Yeah. I like it a lot."

"Roger that. I still miss it myself sometimes. Are you going to be all right without it for a little while?"

"I don't know."

"Let's be cool for a second and figure out the next move." She looked across the room at the bathroom door, then back at me. She grabbed one of the crutches and stuck it up in my left armpit. "Put your hand here and hold on," she said, motioning to the crosspiece. "I'm not gonna lie to you, Cutter, you may or may not make it to that bathroom but this is a glimpse of your new world. You're going to have to learn to do everything you took for granted in a new way. It won't be easy but I know you can do it. Are you with me?"

"I guess."

Rochambeau placed the other crutch in my right armpit. "OK, I want you to lean forward and feel the crutches supporting your weight. Then I want you to figure out what to do with your stump because it's going to have to do some work."

I tried that and got dizzy. Rochambeau noticed and put a hand on my left shoulder to steady me. I squeezed my scrawny right bicep against the crutch to try to hold it in place. The stump felt like wasps were stinging it, constant pinpricks of fire.

"Can you anchor the stump against the forward strut?" Rochambeau asked. "Somehow, you've got to get that right crutch to move forward."

"I'm off balance. It would have been easier if I'd lost my left arm instead of my right."

"Yes, it would have but you didn't, so you need to figure out a way."

"Can you pull me off the edge of the bed to get my foot on the floor?"

"You know I can," she said, mocking me mocking her.

With three points of contact, the foot and the crutches, I felt slightly more secure.

"Can you slide the right crutch forward with your stump but clamp onto it at the same time?"

I did it but barely. The crutch moved only a few inches. I was still leaning against the bed, though, and I was afraid to push off of it.

"Good," Rochambeau said. "I've got an idea." She took off her belt and used it to lash my stump to the crutch, giving me more leverage.

"That hurts like a bitch," I said through clenched teeth.

"I'm sure it does but you'll get used to it. Can you move the crutch around now?"

I tested it gingerly by making a tiny circle. "I guess so but if I'm supposed to do this by myself, how will I tie my stump to the crutch?"

"You'll figure out a way. OK, take a step. Let's see what happens."

I gave Rochambeau a bilious glare like Drill Sergeant Stoddard used to ream us with in basic training. Then I angrily went for it, pushing off the edge of the bed. My foot didn't move, though, and my body pitched forward in free fall. *"FUCK!"* I yelled.

Halfway down, I prepared for impact, squishing my eyes closed and whipping my head hard left so I wouldn't break my nose and knock my teeth out.

But Rochambeau caught me. Her powerful arms wrapped around my chest like a lasso and jerked me upright. "Cutter, what in the Sam Hill is your problem?" she barked.

"Gravity," I said sullenly.

"I'm glad you're not the guy in charge of the domino theory. Goodbye, Thailand, Cambodia and Laos. Try it again but this time *actually take a step.* You've got to put weight on the crutches and swing your foot forward."

"I'll try. You'll catch me, right?"

"You get one for free. The next one's on you. I won't always be here."

"Isn't this something they're going to teach me in rehab? Don't they have crutch classes or something?"

"Sorry to say, rehab for you is every minute of every day, whether you're in an official session with a physical therapist or trying to turn over by yourself in the middle of the night so you don't get a bedsore. It's all rehab all the time."

Sometimes Rochambeau could be a hard-core cheerless MP. I hated my reality and sometimes she rubbed my nose in it. The hard part was, I respected her honesty. At least she didn't spout bullshit about my soon-to-be-normal life like everybody else. I started breathing hard through my nose, like a stupid bull going after the red cape, not realizing the matador was about to stab him in the neck with a sword. I lifted those beautiful old oak crutches and planted them six inches in front of me. I pushed off from the bed, lifted my foot and swung through an arc. My toes touched down on the floor again and I had forward momentum. Now I was committed. Momentarily resting on my left leg, I swung the crutches forward again and moved through another arc. And again. And again, picking up speed as my body weight propelled me forward.

"*Yee-haw!*" Rochambeau yelled. "*Go, Cutter, go!*"

The bathroom door rushed up to greet me. In a millisecond, disaster struck. The belt came loose and my stump lost control of the right crutch. My weight shifted and I crashed to the floor — *KA-DOOF!* The crutches clattered around me in a tangled mess. "*Fuck!*" I cried out.

"Sweet Jesus!" Rochambeau exclaimed. "Are you all right?"

"*If I broke my leg, I'm gonna be so pissed.*"

Rochambeau got down on all fours and looked at me. Then she exploded in laughter.

"What?" I said.

Rochambeau was hysterical. "I'm sorry ... I can't help it," she said between hiccupy yelps. "If you could have seen yourself. You had it goin' on. I mean you were *moving*. Like greased lightning. And then" — she held her heaving stomach and har-har-harred some more — "*you really stuck the landing!*"

With her eyes misting up, Rochambeau flipped, going off in a whole different direction. Now she started to cry. She rolled over on her side and lay there, looking at me. After creating a small puddle on the floor, she said, "These tears are coming from my daddy. He would be so proud of you, Cutter. So very proud."

29 / Emptying the nest

On my three-month anniversary of consciousness at Walter Reed, I had a long talk with Mom. You need to leave the nest, I basically said, in an ironic echo of what I had told her two years ago when I announced that *I* needed to leave and would enlist in the Army.

I was getting around all right on Rochambeau's dad's crutches. They were stunning oak works of art for the handicapped, and I finally learned how to use them after a couple of weeks of bruising tumbles. The third time I crash-landed in the hallway outside my room while taking a so-called exercise walk, one of the day nurses said, "Cutter, if you break your neck, there's not a thing the Army can do for you."

"That's OK," I fired back, "the Army has done enough already."

I remembered something Mom told me once, about how she had been worried because I was slow — still crawling on my first birthday. I finally got up on my own two feet for a few wobbly steps at around 15 months. She was terribly relieved. Here we were, 20 years later, and she could see that I had learned to walk — again — and could get around on my own one foot. Now she was able to leave the hospital. It was complicated by three new friends she had made at Mologne House, other mothers. I understood the power of a bond forged amid fear and uncertainty but she'd been away from her bookkeeping job for too long and couldn't miss any more work. It was time. To reassure her, I got out my book of doctor and psychologist appointments, and let her thumb through it while I explained what each one was for. I tried hard to sound upbeat. She cried a lot as we said our goodbyes. I walked with her down to the front entrance, doing everything in my power not to fall.

"I want you to come home soon," she said, "and we'll figure everything out. I love you, Johnny. I love you so much. You're my son, always and forever."

"I love you, too, Mom, right here," I said, patting my heart as best I could. "I *will* come home soon. I'll get better and I'll be there, I promise. I want to see some real trees again."

She smiled at me in a way that wrenched my insides. It was her face from years ago. I tried to engrave that image on my brain. That was the way I wanted to remember her. She was a great mom, I realized now, and would have done anything for me. Any differences we had when I was growing up, the scalding arguments and brutal misunderstandings, they were all small and stupid compared with this. I didn't understand it then, as a teenager, but now, as a cripple destroyed by a bomb and my own decisions, I had a different perspective.

Mom kissed me on the forehead, then the cheek. She threw her arms around me and squeezed. I did what I could with my left arm, a feeble crutch hug. She walked to her taxi, pulling a gigantic wheeled suitcase behind her. She waved continuously as the taxi drove off and finally disappeared in traffic.

I hobbled back to rehab and lifted a two-pound dumbbell for a few minutes, until my arm cramped up. I wanted to hug Mom at least once more and do a better job of it next time.

30 / Off the hook

A month later, I got a hook.

This had been in the works for a while — it was one of the appointments in my book — but I never wanted to think about it. Everything that anybody at Walter Reed did to try to help me was disturbing. Every checkup, every prosthetic fitting session, every shrink visit — everything forced me to stare at my stumps and contemplate them. I wondered how I could ever get past the shock of having lost my arm and leg. Everyone gave much the same answer: Move forward with life, day by day. Every time I heard that, I wanted to go backward. To the moment before I signed the enlistment papers. To my semester at Coos Bay Community College. To Trillium High School. Even back to the memories of Mom and Dad yelling at night. At least they were still together then. Before, I always thought of it as a fucked-up life, a purgatory to escape. As it turned out, I had no idea what fucked up was.

My prosthetic technician was named Chance Zignon. Talk about a name that fit the job. Everybody who came to see him was there because of … chance. I mentioned it during my first fitting appointment.

"Yeah," he said, "a few guys pick up on that."

Every time I came to the shop, I thought about our mission to the Baghdad Oil Ministry. Why did our unit get chosen? Bad luck? Possibly. Why was I in the third Humvee? Fate? Maybe. Why did the bomb go off at that moment? Chance? Definitely. Obsession grabbed ahold of me and shook my brain until it hurt. I invented a hundred little details that might have changed the outcome of that day.

But Iraq was random. You could randomly die. You could randomly survive. You could randomly lose an arm and a leg. Iraq was maddeningly unpredictable. You never knew what your odds were.

Chance brought out the hook. "This is going to change your life," he said enthusiastically, presenting the prosthesis in its box like it was the featured item on a dessert tray.

"It's already changed."

"I mean in a good way. Once you learn to use it, you'll be able to pick up a Susan B. Anthony dollar."

"So I could make about a dollar an hour?"

Chance laughed. "Sorry, that's not funny but it's funny," he said, applying Army logic. "At least you didn't lose your sense of humor."

"Yeah, this whole thing is very amusing."

"It's too soon but you'll figure it out someday. Hooks are sexy."

I stared at Chance in disbelief.

He smiled as he pulled the prosthesis out of its box and began lengthening the shoulder straps. "That's all I'm going to say."

"Hooks are sexy? What the hell does that mean?"

"Look, you know and I know and every guy who cycles through Ward 57 knows, the first thing you think about when you're dealing with the loss of a limb is, How the fuck do I have sex?"

That shut me up. Chance was a better shrink than Doctor Brannfors. Chance just slammed it right out there on the table with his fist. None of that vague Brannfors "coming to terms with your disability in your own time" bullshit.

"Pussy got your tongue?" Chance said, archly raising one eyebrow.

Well, yes. I still had no response. Chance had smallish wide-set dark eyes. I studied them, trying to figure out if he was playing me, but I couldn't tell.

Chance stared right back and said, "The thing is, you don't know what it can do till it does it." He picked the arm up and without warning shoved it in my face, grabbing my nose with the hook.

"*Fuck!*" I yelled, all nasally.

"Hook got your nose?" he said. Then he unclamped and put the arm down on the bench next to me. I indelicately stuck my pinkie in my nostrils to open them up.

"All right, let's see how this baby performs. Here's the sock. You know what to do." Chance handed me a cotton tube. I fumbled with it at first but managed to get it rolled over my stump. "Point towards me," he said.

I extended what was left of my arm. As Chance maneuvered the upper leather half of the prosthetic around my emaciated bicep and the harness around my shoulders, the carbon-fiber socket slid onto the stump. "You'll be doing this on your own but I'll help for now," he said.

I got a stabbing pain right down to the bone as the socket fully seated. "It hurts. It's really tight."

"That's what she said."

"Chance, you know you're insane, right?"

He shook his head. "No, I didn't. The Army says I'm normal."

"Roger fucking that."

With the prosthetic in place, Chance snugged the harness a little. I looked down at the hook. I placed my left hand next to it for comparison. I looked at my hand. Then the hook. Then back at my hand. The weirdness slapped me in the face. *I had a steel hook on the end of my stump.* I was in a bad horror movie. I would scare little kids. Suddenly the hook snapped open and clanked shut. I jumped. *"What the fuck!"*

"That was me," Chance said. He demonstrated by yanking a few times on the steel cable that operated the jaws. The hook snapped like a hungry metallic piranha. "That's how you grasp. To open it, you put tension on the cable, either by tweaking the position of your shoulder a little or moving the hook away from you. Flex the elbow joint enough to put some tension on the cable and release the tension to grasp. It's simple. It's classic. A myoelectric hand may have the electronic sizzle but a hook has the old-fashioned steak. No batteries required. It never fails." Chance pulled a dollar coin out of his pocket and dropped it on the bench. "Give it a try. If you can pick that up, you can keep it."

I pushed the hook away from my body and it opened. I pulled it back and it shut. I did that a few times to get used to the motion. Then I went after the dollar, which was harder than it looked. When I reached for the coin, the hook opened too wide or wobbled. I tried various movements but the hook awkwardly refused to grab in the right spot. With the pincers shut, I tapped the dollar a few times to get the feel of bringing the hook down on it. "Couldn't you just magnetize this thing?" I said.

"I like that idea. That's good. You're thinking creatively about solving problems but think about this one in a different way: Backwards."

"Backwards?"

"Move toward the coin when you think you've got it, not away."

"Huh?"

"Experiment. It'll come to you."

I moved the hook forward and backward in the air. It opened and closed as the cable tightened and released.

"So what's the opposite of that?" Chance said.

I moved the hook from side to side. Again, it opened and closed. "What am I supposed to do? Just tell me."

"Leave the hook where it is but move your body."

I looked at the hook and I looked at the dollar. I flashed on those county fair games that always miss as you try to grab a cheap prize with a mechanical claw. I slowly lowered the hook down to the dollar, positioning the pincers in the center. Then I pulled my body away while leaving the hook in place. The pincers opened. I tweaked my shoulders slightly to release tension on the cable — and the pincers grabbed the Susan B. Anthony. I had my county fair prize.

"Nice," Chance said.

I hated my hook already. I wanted to kill it. I wanted to beat it with a hammer until it was broken and unrecognizable.

31 / Mano-a-stump

Rochelle Rochambeau blew into my room like a hurricane and turned on the light. "Cutter, are you awake?" she whispered.

"No, I'm sleeping." That was nearly true but not quite. I was just waiting for the Nembutal to turn on and my mind to turn off. I had popped a couple of tabs a few minutes earlier.

"Well, wake up," Rochambeau said, moving to the bedside. "Something is going down. Did you ever get your Purple Heart?"

"I don't know."

"Don't bullshit me. Did you get one, or not? You would remember if you did. It's a medal in the shape of a heart, it's purple, it's got a gold George Washington on it. Sound familiar?"

"No. I didn't get one."

"That doesn't surprise me. The paperwork has to work its way through the Army python. Do you want one?"

I didn't know how to answer that. I didn't even want to think about it, in the abstract, the big picture, about what it meant to have a Purple Heart. I already thought about it a hundred times a day in small specific ways. I couldn't put on a shirt or feed myself or go to the bathroom without thinking about it. A Purple Heart was the grand final metaphysical nail-in-the-coffin reminder. It meant you had official recognition, the hardware to prove you got randomly blown up for your country and your life would never be the same. I needed to think about it less, not more. I shut my eyes, hoping the Nembies would knock me out cold with one sweet sucker punch.

"Don't get all introspective. I just heard that the Secret Service came by the hospital, asking about you and your schedule for tomorrow."

"The Secret Service? Why?"

"It's supposed to be hush-hush but it means President Bush is coming to present your Purple Heart to you."

"You're shitting me."

Rochambeau shook her head forcefully. "No. I would never do that. This is how it happens. Initial phone call. Secret Service visit. Plans for lockdown. Bush shows up. You were on the books for prosthetics tomorrow morning at 10. That appointment has been canceled. The whole ward is buzzing. This is a big deal, Cutter. Think about it. The president. The commander in chief. He's coming to visit *you*."

I thought about it. My heart started to pound. I could feel the bump-bump-bump of my pulse. The rush. I was on full alert, ready for combat. The room suddenly felt hot. I death-gripped the bed rail with my hand. "Why me?" I finally said.

"Because the commander in chief wants to thank you personally for your service to the country. Because you're a hero, Johnny."

"I gotta sleep on it, Rochelle."

Rochambeau locked on me with her contorted are-you-crazy look.

I shrugged. "I'm just really tired."

"All right. Get some rest. Jillian will be briefing you first thing tomorrow. Wait, it is tomorrow. She'll be in here at 0800 today. So go to sleep. It's a big day."

Rochambeau walked over to the light switch and flicked it off. "Good night," she said in the darkness. By then the Nembies were kicking in. The night would be all right.

Captain Jillian had trouble waking me. I resisted consciousness. Eventually she won, with the application of a cold washcloth and loud talk. She quickly went over protocol for the big visit. "You need to be in uniform for this, dress blues, completely squared away, so police your personal hygiene. That's an order, Private Cutter. Quite frankly, you stink."

"I had an accident," I explained groggily.

"Why didn't you call for an orderly?"

"I was sleeping, ma'am."

"You slept through defecation?"

"That's correct, ma'am."

Jillian shook her head in disgust. She spun around and double-timed out of the room. One of the cool day orderlies, a bulked-up guy named DeShawn, appeared in less than a minute.

"Hey, DeShawn," I said, "are you here to terminate me?"

He chuckled. "Yeah. With extreme Alabama prejudice."

"I guess Jillian is really pissed."

"You gotta quit shitting yourself."

"I wish I could. Sometimes, you know, it just happens."

"Yeah, yeah, yeah. Couldn't you a waited till the commander in chief got here? Make him clean up a mess for once."

"That's not his job."

DeShawn snorted. "Affirmative."

"I am truly and totally sorry. I was really out of it last night. Rochambeau told me about the big visit and I kinda freaked. I had already popped a couple Nembies, one thing led to another, man, I was lucky to wake up at all."

"I hear ya. Let's get you to the latrine."

Nurse Jillian stormed in at 0920. Thanks to DeShawn's scrub-o-matic efficiency and his tweaking of my uniform, I passed her inspection. She left at 0930, when four Secret Service agents started searching the room. They were a well-oiled silent team in dark suits. They examined the medical gear at the foot of my bed. They prodded my IV bags. They peered beneath the bed and lifted the blankets off me to get a look. One of them unscrewed the vent on a heating duct and shined a flashlight inside. Another agent lifted the top off the toilet tank.

"What's going on?" I asked. "Are you searching for IEDs? They're in Iraq."

The leader, a burly agitated crew-cut dude with an earpiece, looked at me with suspicion. "You haven't been informed that the president is coming?"

"Oh, yeah, right. I did hear something about that. When will he be here?"

"In about 30 minutes."

"I have an appointment then. Can he come back later?"

"That appointment was canceled."

"I don't think so. I have a fitting for an artificial leg. Do you think the commander in chief would like to help me pick out a new leg?"

The agent's eyes slitted down into sniper mode. "Is that a joke?"

"No."

"The president is very busy. So, no, he would not."

"The way he supports the troops, I thought maybe he would have an opinion on my new leg. I can't decide whether to get oak or pine."

The agent eyeballed me like a drill sergeant. "The president does not have an opinion on your new leg," he said. "You should get the one that complements the paneling in your trailer."

"We're clear," the vent inspector said. The agents flew out of the room in formation, like the Blue Angels, and stationed themselves in the hall.

I started to burn. Partly it was stump pain, because the morphine wasn't doing much, but partly it was my mind. Until this moment, I hadn't thought much about President Bush. Once in a while, back in Baghdad, he would come up in a WMD joke: "What's the difference between Bush and weapons of mass destruction? … You can find Bush in a bunker." Even the Iraqi army slackers made snide comments about him in their broken English: "Bush say meeshun accompleesh. Time to you go home now?" Mostly, we were just soldiers trying to do a job and trying to survive, without giving much thought to the command structure, which didn't appear to want to help us with either of our goals.

Now, face to face, I was going to meet the man who sent us to Iraq for nothing, the man who put my body in this bed. I lay there, sweating, as fury descended on me like a sandstorm, clouding my vision and leaving my mouth dry. The president was going to honor me with a medal, make up for my pain and suffering and loss with a few minutes of his time and a trinket. I wanted to scream for Nurse Jillian and tell her, "Fuck it. Forget it." Too late. Outside my doorway, the Secret Service honcho was talking into his earphone and flashing a hand signal to the other agents. I heard him say, "They're 10 minutes out."

I tore the buttons off my uniform and unzipped the fly. I reached under the covers and pulled the trousers down as far as I could. Then I began to wriggle. It was something I did well, with constant practice in changing positions to avoid bedsores. By bending my foot back, grabbing the fabric with my toes, and then extending, I worked the leg down. By skooching my butt around, I was able to maneuver out of the trousers. I kicked them to the bottom of the bed and shimmied out of my underwear. Naked from the waist down, I went to work on getting out of my coat and T-shirt.

The lead agent was preoccupied with communications, so he didn't notice my Houdini act. My arm stump began to prickle and burn, na-palm hot. Normally, I would have reached for a handful of pills but the scorching pain kept me furiously focused. I got my arm stump out of the sleeve quickly. That was the easy part, because the flipper limb was so short. In another minute, I managed to yank the T-shirt over my head and use my stump to push it down over my left arm. Sweat was pouring down my face. I breathed in and out deeply, trying to relax. I pulled the covers up around my neck. Just as I got situated, Jillian rushed officiously in. "Private First Class Johnathan Cutter, you've got a visitor," she said cheerily.

Moments later, President Bush entered.

God, that grating gratuitous grin, the same stuporous happy face from Saddam's palace. Sickening. An aide trailed him. They were fash-ion twins, both wearing dark blue suits, white shirts, bright red ties and, of course, American flag pins on their lapels, which proved they were patriotic. Two Secret Service agents in wraparound shades followed them into the room and took positions on either side of the door like garden gnomes.

"Good morning, Private Cutler," the president said, "I'm George W. Bush and I am honored to meet you." He reached for a handshake. I met Bush's eyes with my own but peripherally I could see Nurse Jillian grimacing. Nobody had briefed Bush on my condition. Hey, fuckups happened. All the time. I pulled my stump from beneath the covers and offered it to my commander in chief.

Bush's grin disappeared and he looked at his aide, who maintained a stony face as his glance darted between Bush and me.

"It's OK," I said. "You can shake it."

Bush looked at his aide again, then back at me. After a moment, he gave the stump a tentative little squeeze. His hand felt cold and soft.

"*YOW!*" I yelled. I wasn't totally fucking with the president. It did hurt. Well, not *that* much, so yes, I was fucking with him.

Bush's head jerked back and his neck stiffened. He dropped the stump like he'd touched a hot scaly dead fish, which he sort of had.

"Sorry," I said, "I haven't had my morphine today."

Nurse Jillian glared like she wanted to stab me in the neck with a hypodermic needle. Or a red-hot pitchfork. I gave her a puckish smile.

"I understand," Bush said, "I haven't had my coffee, heh-heh. Well, Private Cutler, I want you to know that me and every American appropriate beyond measure your service to our country. It's men like you who keep us safe, protecting our American freedoms and our American way of life, and we sincerely thank you for your American heroism. Your sacrifice will be remembered forever with gratuitous and heartfelt thanks."

"That's so comforting," I said.

Bush pulled a small black box from his trouser pocket. He removed the top and lifted the medal between thumb and forefinger. "I would like to present you, Johnathan Cutler, with this tribute of honor from the United States Army: The Purple Heart." The president returned the box to his pocket and grasped the lanyard with both hands. He made a move to put the medal around my neck. Instead of lifting my head, I pressed it into the pillow. Bush didn't know what to do.

"Could you put it on my stump?"

Bush recoiled. He stood there frozen, glassy-eyed, wax-like, the Purple Heart dangling on the lanyard in front of him.

I threw back the covers. "Either one would be fine."

Bush's aide grabbed the medal out of his hands and quickly draped it across my leg stump. "Mr. President, we need to get going. There's that emergency meeting of the Joint Chiefs of Staff. Remember?" The aide tugged on Bush's jacket sleeve.

"You have our ... our ... professed ... our most ... great gravitude," the commander in chief stammered. "Thanks for all you've done."

"Yeah, our dead guys thank you for all you've done, too."

As Bush bugged out of my room, I started to shake with rage. "The Tinman is begging you to up-armor our Humvees," I yelled after him. *"Oh, it's too late, the Tinman is dead! THANKS A LOT, YOU LYING DRAFT-DODGER!"*

Out of nowhere, I didn't see it coming, Nurse Jillian caught me flush in the face with a roundhouse slap. *"Ungrateful bastard,"* she shrieked. *"What the hell was that for?"*

"That was for Tim and Amerigo and Dante," I said.

32 / The wheel deal

I got back from a psych appointment to hear these words: "Hey, Cutter, it's Pete Klug. What up?"

Stunned, I pulled the phone away from my ear and looked at it in shock. Then I got it together and blasted: *"Yo, Pete, dude, it is great fucking awesomely chill great to hear your voice! Where you calling from? Are you in the sandbox? How are the guys? Are you winning that war?"*

Klug let out a hog grunt. "Yeah, we're all good. We're winning. That's our story and we're sticking to it like glue. Oh, yeah, and the Iraqi army is a force to be reckoned with. They're really standing up. All we need is 50 million nicotine patches so they don't have to take an eight-hour smoke break every day."

I loved Klug. "Goddamn, I miss you, Pete," I blurted out, with just enough choke in my voice to be embarrassing.

"Listen, I want to come visit you up in D.C. I'm on leave. I just got home to Shiloh, so I'm only about an hour south of you."

"Are you joking?"

"I would never joke about being on leave. I'm gonna take a trip, get out on the open road and drive like crazy, without having to worry about IEDs. I need to clear my head."

"Roger that. The only visitor I've had since I got here was my mom and I kind of went insane. I wanted to kill myself. She went back home, though. I'm still crazy but not as bad. I would love to see you. A friendly face would be … I don't even know what that is. There aren't any here. There's a nurse who wants to get me court-martialed."

"What the fuck? What are you talkin' about?"

"I sort of had one other visitor … the poser in chief."

"Bush?"

"It's a long story."

"Jesus."

"Yeah, this captain nurse doesn't believe in free speech, only Army rah-rah. You should definitely get here ASAP and buy me a beer."

"What are you doin' tomorrow?"

"Same thing I always do, tripping on morphine and lying in bed."

"Sounds like R&R."

"You have no idea."

"I'll be there tomorrow night, my brother."

My brain began to work throughout the afternoon and into the evening. Walter Reed felt like jail. With Jillian all in my face about the Bush faux pas, I wanted to get the hell out. I didn't believe she would pursue a court-martial of a double amp — how would that make the Army look? Then again, she was a firsthand witness and a true believer, and there was no way to know how far a true believer would go when she saw a protest she disagreed with. Maybe crazy far. I wore the Purple Heart during the day so that whenever she came into my room it might ward off her evil spirits. At least she could see I cared enough to fake it. After she left the hospital, though, I took the Heart off. Rochambeau asked me why.

"It's too heavy," I said, and she did her arched-eyebrow thing. She didn't press, though, so she understood what I meant.

I skipped dinner so I could think. A plan began to coagulate. I levered myself out of bed and got situated on Master Sergeant Rochambeau's crutches. I hobbled down the hall to visit Eugene Dekowski, who was transfixed by television.

"Hey, Eugene, what are you watching?" I called out.

"'Survivor.'"

I took a few steps into his room to get a glimpse of the screen above his bed. "That's a reality show, right?" I said.

"I don't know how real it is but it's got chicks in soaking wet bikinis, so who cares? Until they give us a porn channel, it'll have to do."

"They should make a reality show called 'Ward 57,'" I suggested.

"If I had to watch that, I'd blow my brains out."

His comment knocked me back on my heel. He sounded deadly serious, not a hint of sarcasm. So ... he was *living* the Walter Reed life but if he had to *watch* himself living it on television he would blow his brains out?

I decided not to point out the incongruity but I did say, "That's why

the show would be so compelling." Eugene looked at me blankly. He
didn't get satire, didn't get farce, didn't get the war, like so many Army
officers, like the doctors and nurses at Walter Reed, like the gung-ho
blab jammers on cable TV and, really, like just about everybody.

Eugene had to be a hard case. Driving down the hall, he gave off a
scary intensity and sense of purpose. He was still on the mission. He
was the first guy I ever saw in a chair and he turned me off the whole
wheels-of-freedom thing. In the early weeks, as a prisoner of my bed, I
watched the procession of other amputees rolling down the hallway
outside my room. Those wheels were a spiteful substitute for missing
legs. Those chairs symbolized dependence. They were a constant reminder that I would always need some kind of mechanical device to
make me, as the doctors put it, whole. When I woke up in the middle of
the night, though, when it was impossible to delude myself, I knew I
would never be whole. No machine, motor or prosthetic could give me
back my own leg and my own arm. It always came down to that.

Eugene was Special Forces, with a fierce combat-hardened face. He
had lost both legs when he stepped on a mine in Afghanistan. Now it
was killing him not to be out there leading his guys. It was also killing
him to have been out there. The irony burst forth like tracers in the
night sky. His eyes were locked on the tube, so I moved a little closer.
"Eugene, is there any chance you could do me a favor?" I asked.

"Depends on what it is."

"Could I borrow your wheelchair for a while?"

"Why?"

"An old friend of mine is coming to visit me tomorrow and I'd like to
be able to get around better."

Eugene muted the sound with his remote and turned away from the
television. "It's not that chick, is it?"

That hit me hard. "You mean Halley?"

"I haven't seen any other chicks visiting you. No offense to your
mother."

"No ... she's ... Halley is kind of ... out of the picture."

Eugene's head bobbed emphatically. "I figured that wouldn't last."

"Really? Why?"

"I passed her in the hall when she left here. I saw it in her eyes."

Everything clicked into place. I remembered something else Rochambeau told me about Eugene: He had done some recon behind Taliban lines. He must have been good, because he was right-on about Halley. I was shocked to hear the truth from a stranger who figured it out during a two-second drive-by. It had taken me a month and a letter.

"Why don't you get your own chair?" Eugene asked.

"I told them I didn't want one."

Eugene shook his head. "I don't think I can help you, Cutter. I need the chair myself. I might be getting C-legs but not for a few months. There's an issue. I've got to deal with bone spurs first."

"All right. Thanks anyway." I turned to go.

"Hold on. You're gonna give up just like that?"

I spun around on the tip of one crutch. "What do you mean?"

"Don't you have something you could trade me for the chair?"

"Like what?"

"Like those crutches."

"These are Rochambeau's."

"Don't you mean they're her dad's?"

"You know about these?"

"Yeah. I also know she gave them to you."

"That's right. But what are you saying? You would trade the chair for the crutches?"

"Absolutely. They've got more heart than Dick Fucking Cheney."

"I guess I would have to think about it."

"Work with me here," Eugene said, holding up his right middle finger and poking himself in the forehead. "I want those crutches and you want a wheelchair. That doesn't sound like a deal to you?"

"So you could use these? I mean, don't you … "

"*What? Need at least one leg?*" Eugene suddenly had the thrash, the hurricane eyes. He thought I pitied him — which I didn't. How could I? Nevertheless, I was standing there, on one leg and two crutches, in a figurative minefield.

Eugene's stare was like the barrel of a .50-cal, daring me to utter another word. I didn't. I looked down at my foot instead. Finally, he chilled and said, "Thing is, if I ever do get those C-legs, if I ever get out of here, if I ever get to re-up, I wouldn't mind having a backup plan. C-legs don't always work out, you know? What if the bone ossification comes back after they scrape my spurs off? Maybe I could use those crutches. I've still got two arms and good balance. If nothing else, I wouldn't mind hanging them on my wall. They've got a history. We all know the story. They mean something. What would you rather have on your wall, some spastic modern painting or those? I'd look at 'em all day long and think about my life. That's what art is supposed to do. Make you think. Not that I want to. But those are righteous crutches."

Where in the hell was God when you needed him? Couldn't he hook us up? Send some dope crutches down from the sky or something? Was that too much to ask? Apparently so. Nothing magical happened. Eugene was killing me. He thought the crutches were art, just like I did. He could see their horrible beauty, too. He was my brother. I wanted to give them up. He *deserved* them, yet all I could lame-o say was, "I don't know. I'd have to talk to Rochambeau about it."

Eugene nodded. "Yeah, I understand. Let me know."

Dejected, I headed for the door and swung into the hallway but Eugene called out, "Hey, Cutter, I got an idea."

I went back. Eugene sat up precariously on the edge of his bed, in his jockey shorts. The question in my mind was now staring me in the face and rephrasing itself: Does he have enough left to handle prosthetic legs? His bulbous purplish stumps barely protruded beyond the edge of his shorts, like a guillotine had come down almost at the hip joint. I thought he could be in a chair for the rest of his life, with no chance of walking again.

"You don't go to rehab very often," Eugene said, "so maybe you don't know that there's an electric chair down there."

"Are you serious?"

"Like a fucking RPG is serious."

"You think I could borrow it?"

"Hasn't the Army taught you that you either take or you get taken? It's just sitting there, Cutter. They made it for Jarmaine but you know how it goes." Eugene shrugged listlessly. "Infection. His arm left the building. He was a lefty, too, just like you."

"I'm a righty."

"You mean you *were* a righty."

33 / Freedom

My new mission was coming into focus. Around 2330, my head down, I rolled furtively toward a rendezvous. The Army had trained me to improvise, and here I was, monkey-wrenching a plan. My first instinct — to protect Pete Klug — had kicked everything off. I never told Eugene who was coming to visit. Klug had called from Shiloh to tell me he was running late and wouldn't get to Walter Reed until a little before midnight. To avoid the possibility of visitor paperwork, I said I would meet him outside at the Georgia Avenue entrance to the hospital grounds. "I'll find it," he said. "Keep your eyes peeled. I'm driving a black Chevy pickup."

"Roger that," I told him. "I'm driving a wheelchair. Is there any chance you could bring a few two-by-fours?"

"What for?"

"A ramp."

"A ramp."

"Yeah, for my chair."

"No problem." Pete was the king of cool. He didn't sweat the details. He just took care of them.

Then disaster struck. As I rolled along Dahlia Street, a car drove by and slammed on its brakes. It backed up and the passenger window whirred down. Unfortunately, I looked and made eye contact with the driver. It was Rochambeau. "Hey, Johnny," she yelled.

"Hey, Rochelle," I answered, trying to sound casual.

"Is everything all right?"

"Yes, ma'am." I hunched down a little to try to cover the duffel bag on my lap.

"What are you doing out here? Where did you get that wheelchair? Is that Jarmaine's old chair?"

"Yeah. I'm just practicing. Eugene showed me how to drive it."

"Great. That's all we need, another hallway menace."

"No, no, watch this." I jimmied the joystick and did a couple of 360s.

"Yeah, that's bow-chicka-wow-wow," she said. "Bust a move."

Shutting off the engine and the sarcasm, Rochambeau started to get out of the car. I putt-putted away from an overhead street light and ditched the duffel in the shadows by a tree. Then I rolled back to head her off in front of the car. "What's going on?" she demanded.

"What do you mean?"

"Why did you throw your duffel bag over there? Why do you need a duffel bag out in the parking lot?"

"All right, you got me. I was going to smoke."

Rochambeau folded her arms across her chest — bad news body language. She eyed me up and down like a sentry, taking a few steps back and forth as she looked for holes in my story. I wondered if she had ever been in special ops, because she was stealthy. She knew how to use silence to interrogate. My hand started to fidget. Finally, she said, "Cutter, you are a bad, bad liar. Very bad. Unskilled. You've got so many tells it's ridiculous. *You don't smoke.* I would know if you smoked. You've been here what? Four months? Five months? In all that time, you have not smoked one cigarette. You've given off gobs of stink, God almighty, but it was never the stink of tobacco. I know the stink of to-bacco. You want to know the real stench of slow, agonizing death? It's jaw cancer and lung cancer and brain cancer rotting away whatever tis-sue you have left. Nicotine necrosis. My daddy smoked three packs a day, four at the end. What a 155-millimeter shell couldn't kill, the ciga-rettes did. I know the stink of cigarettes. It is burned into me. I've got the scars, the mental pictures of my daddy wasting away, to prove it. You're not a smoker, Cutter. I would know. Now we can do this the easy way, and you can just tell me why you are out here, the whole truth. Or we can do this the hard way, and we will start by me going over and picking up that duffel bag and looking inside. If I find provisions, if I find clothing, if I find anything that makes me think you are about to run, you are going to be in some hot damn water."

"I'm not going to run."

"What is it, then? Are you gonna go looking for hookers down on Parker Street? Because it is my duty to tell you, Johnny — you are *not* ready. Nobody is ready for those girls but you, in particular, are not ready. Sorry to be so blunt but you are my patient and I will protect you like a junkyard dog. You are not going to get torn up on my watch."

"No, it's nothing like that. You're right. I'm not ready. I know that better than anybody. I'll never be ready."

Then Rochambeau kicked me in the face. Not literally and not on purpose but her eyes turned sad. She said nothing. She couldn't dispute my assessment of the future. She pitied me and that was the kill shot, because it confirmed everything. It really was all over for me. She made a move, scrunching down and putting her hands on my shoulders. Her eyes glistened, reflecting the ugly phosphor light. I flinched and tried to twist away. Who would want to touch me? "Please don't," I told her, but she held on like a bear.

"This will pass," she whispered. "I promise you, it won't always be like this."

"I don't think so. I think this is it. Besides, Jillian wants to court-martial me."

Rochambeau let me go and said, "The day nurses are wrapped way too tight and Jillian is the leader of the pack. Trust me, she will not get anywhere with that. What you did, many people completely understand, they just can't say so. There will be no court-martial. Unless you leave. You are still in the Army. Do you know what happens if you go AWOL?"

"Why am I still in the Army? What can I do for the Army? What does the Army want with me? Why would it matter if I left?"

"Because the Army wants to fix you."

I had been wondering for weeks whether I was crazy. I went back and forth on it. Sometimes I was reasonable but on big med days, I would lie in bed and stare at the water stains in the ceiling, and they would become moving pooling puddles of brown blood. Even now, Rochambeau was kind of swirling around in front of me. So, on the down days, maybe I was correct. Maybe I *was* gone. I started to laugh. It was random. Gone is good, gone is great, I thought. Rochambeau looked at me like I was insane. I couldn't stop laughing. The more she didn't understand, the funnier it became. I flashed back to D-Willie on the drive to Karbala, when we laughed until we almost died. That made it worse now, because it was all mixed up inside me; in a way, I was still back there, in the craziness, which made no sense at all. Because I was here at Walter Reed. Unless I was dreaming or dying or already dead. I didn't know anymore. The only thing I could do was keep laughing. My stomach began to hurt and the pain slowed me down. I had to stop occasionally to breathe, too, but I couldn't stop the laughter. Just like I couldn't stop the slaughter.

Rochambeau gave me one of her confused hound-dog looks and said, "What is so dang funny?"

Tears were running down my face and I gasped for air. I grabbed my right side and massaged, which reminded me of the stitches we got in basic training after killing ourselves in the timed runs. I could barely talk but I managed to stammer out the words, "The Army ... already ... fixed me." Then I started laughing again.

When I could get my eyes to open, Rochambeau was still standing there, so this wasn't an uproarious hallucination, and she was at least a little tickled by my hysteria. "Yeah," she said with a grin and a head bob, "I guess we did, didn't we. Look, I gotta take you inside now. I think I need to get you something. I think I need to bring you down. I mean that in a good way, not a bad way. I think you're high."

She reached for one of the handles on the back of the wheelchair but I grabbed her wrist with all the strength I had and stopped her. *"No, no, please,"* I shouted. *"Don't ask, don't tell."*

Rochambeau jerked away and said, "What does that mean?"

"Don't ask, don't tell. I'm begging you, Rochelle. Don't ask, don't tell. You know what I mean. You have to know. You know better than anybody. Don't ask, don't tell."

"Don't ask what? Don't tell what?"

"This is the Army. Don't ask, don't tell. It's better if people don't know what's going on. Then it can go on."

"Cutter, you're not making any sense. Are you gay?"

"No. I'm not anything. I'm just saying, Don't ask, don't tell. You will understand. Just go. Please let me stay out here for a few more minutes. Everything's fine. There's nothing to worry about. I need to think. I need to clear my head. I need to stop laughing. Step away from the wheelchair. Move along. There's nothing to see here."

Rochambeau smiled at my imitation of a cop. I knew then that I had talked her down. The alarm drained out of her face. She took two steps back and leaned on the fender of her car but she continued to study me. I returned her smile and let her look until she was satisfied. I finally raised my hand and wiggled my fingers in a little wave. "Bye-bye," I said. "I'll see you soon."

"Like how soon?"

"Soon."

"Like 2400 soon?"

"Yep, midnight soon."

"So you'll come back inside by 2400 hours?"

"You don't have to sound so skeptical."

Rochambeau glanced at her wristwatch. "OK, Cutter, it's 2340 now. I want you back by 2400 hours. Promise me?"

I held up my stump and pledged, "Midnight. Pinkie swear. I'll be there."

"Yeah, I hope so but maybe you will and maybe you won't. Good luck."

At first, I didn't get what Rochambeau was saying. I wondered if she had picked up on my use of "midnight" — civilian time. Or that my pinkie swear wasn't exactly official, what with the missing hand and all.

Then she saluted me. Amazing. A first lieutenant saluted a private. Why? "Don't ask, don't tell, don't forget your duffel bag," she said with the slightest smile. She got in her car and drove away without looking back. Now I understood.

Pete Klug arrived at 2355 but I didn't have to run. Rochambeau had set me free.

34 / Swords, cannons and ghosts

Pete Klug pulled up right next to me and was out of the truck like a shot. *"Johnny Cutter, my man, my brother!"* he yelled. His balls-to-the-wall exuberance transported me back to the guys and the camaraderie of our unit. He rushed to the sidewalk and grabbed me in a headlock.

"This is epic, Pete. You are a ridiculously good dude."

He let me go and stood up. Our eyes locked for a second, then he took a look at the rest of me. The dim light could hide my deformity for only so long. His face changed quickly; he wasn't ready for it. "What the fuck?" he said. "What happened to your arm?"

"I lost it."

"Fuck. We knew about the leg, but the arm, too?"

"Yeah, it's gone."

"Goddamn motherfucking IEDs."

"Yeah. Hey, did you get the two-by-fours?"

Pete nodded solemnly.

"You got room in the truck for my chair?"

"If we move some of my camping gear around."

"Can we load it in? I've got about five minutes to get outta here."

"Let's rock and roll. Where are we going?"

"Doesn't matter. I'm up for anything."

"You want me to buy you that beer?"

"I don't know. I don't get around so well without my crutches."

"Jesus, they don't even give you crutches here."

"Yeah, they do. I mean, a nurse gave me some but I left them behind. I'm giving them to another guy on the ward. He doesn't know it yet. He will soon. I left a note. They'll figure it out."

"Can't you just give him the crutches when you get back?"

"Yeah. Maybe. Maybe not. We'll see. Who knows?"

Pete got all perplexed on me, his face screwing up into a question mark.

I motioned to the truck. "Let's load up the chair and I'll explain everything when we hit the road."

"I'm headed for Yellowstone Park," Pete said.

"That's cool. I've always wanted to see it." I jabbed the joystick and rolled off to pick up my duffel bag. When I returned, Pete was still frozen with uncertainty. "Really, there's nothing to worry about," I reassured him. "I'm totally ready for a road trip. My nurse gave me permission to go. This is good therapy."

"So you can just take off?"

"Yep. And I do need to get going."

"Well, I've got 15 days. What about you?"

"Three weeks," I said, adding a little cushion.

"What about medical care?"

"No problem. I've got everything I need right here," I said, patting the bulging duffel bag.

Pete's lips squished off to the side as he considered my kit, which I had scrounged like a Killdozer Junior. He gave me one hard questioning look. When I didn't flinch, he shrugged. "All right, saddle up."

We headed west on Interstate 66. As we passed through Arlington, Pete rolled down the window and shouted into the wind, *"Save me a spot!"* He turned to me and said, "I want to be buried here, not right away, but someday."

The drive was fueled by Pete's stories from the past few months. Starved for news about the guys, I ate up every detail and asked a hundred questions. I didn't miss the war but I missed my buds. I began to ache, literally and figuratively. We zagged north on Interstate 81 and finally stopped for gas around 0300 in a town called Chambersburg. While Pete was out pumping, I popped a Lude. He went inside to pay and returned with a couple of ham sandwiches and the directions for a side trip. "We're going to Gettysburg," he announced. "The guy at the register asked if I was in the military — the haircut, I guess. Simpatico dude. He gave us the gas for free but he made me promise we would go see the battlefield. It's only half an hour from here. You up for it?"

"They got IEDs there?"

"No, just old cannons."

"Let's roll."

We had no idea where we were when we got there. Pete pulled off
the road, some road, a road, whatever road we were on, and parked the
truck in grass. It was pitch black, the moon was missing and we were
lucky not to have ended up in a ditch. We flailed out of the truck,
wrapped ourselves in a couple of old camping blankets and crashed on
the ground. The fresh air was glorious. The decaying stench of Walter
Reed was gone.

I got maybe two hours of sleep. I woke up before dawn with a bomb
in my gut. The sandwich was ready to detonate. Bad ham, probably. Or
spoiled mayonnaise. Or salmonella lettuce. Or moldy bread. Or maybe
remnants of Walter Reed cuisine from several days ago.

Pete was sleeping like a dead man. I urgently needed a latrine. A
couple of fir trees about 40 yards from our position offered some cover.
I did a raggedy one-leg crawl to the back of the truck and levered myself up by grabbing the bumper and then the tailgate. Once I got steady
on my foot, I rummaged through the gear. I was kicking myself, only
figuratively, for not bringing a couple of rolls of toilet paper. I finally
found a grocery bag. The paper was clean and sturdy, better than anything we ever scavenged in Iraq. I hopped about 30 yards before my leg
gave out and I hit the deck. The ground was weedy and rocky, which I
would take any day over the sandbox. I crawled to the trees and got my
boot and pants off. I tossed them as far away as I could, out of the splat-
ter zone. Although I had learned how to take care of my personal
needs, it never got easier. I always ended up speckled with filth. It never
got faster, either. During the months of lying in bed, my intestinal muscles had atrophied along with everything else. In my new personal war,
constipation was an implacable enemy, impossible to defeat. Only when
I filled to the bursting point would the dam break.

I didn't eat much anymore because it led, eventually, to shitting. The
last time Rochambeau had forced me onto a scale, it whispered 119
pounds. "I'm going to hook you up to a feeding tube again if you don't
start chowing down," she warned. I promised her I would but I was
lying. I lied to Rochambeau a lot. I felt bad about that, because she only
wanted to help me. I couldn't see how it mattered, though. Most days, I
languished beyond her huge capacity for healing and compassion.

When I got back to our camp, Pete was sitting on the hood of the truck, reclining against the windshield, peacefully gazing at the landscape. Two klicks out, gently rolling hills gained muted colors, red and brown and purple, as dawn shouldered the night aside. A few hundred yards away, a serpentine ribbon of trees provided cover for the ghosts of soldiers past. Boulders, rocks and pebbles assembled everywhere in their own platoons. Birds called and chirped giddily, welcoming the new day. I leaned on the front fender and took it all in with Pete.

"This is hallowed ground," he said.

"I just shit all over it."

"You know," Pete said, "if people knew how much shit armies leave behind, if they knew what they were breathing in the smoke from burning WAG bags, nobody would ever go to war. We'd all build sewage treatment plants instead."

"I just thought of a good bumper sticker: Defecation is desecration."

"True dat. We ripped Iraq a new asshole."

We turned into tourists later in the morning. Gettysburg had a serious eerie factor. Every plaque, every statue, every gravestone connected to death somehow. The swords, the muskets, the cannons, they all led to the same thought: Men killing men, spilling their blood. Even though the weather was mild, I shivered occasionally as we looked out over a battlefield. A depiction of Pickett's Charge caused Pete to shake his head disapprovingly and say, "They were crazy insane."

We stopped at the Lincoln Speech Memorial and Pete propped me up as we read the Gettysburg Address. I remembered a little of it from high school history class. Still, seeing the sculpture of Lincoln and the plaque, I got all tingly. Maybe my stumps were just acting up but I attributed it to the words.

"That dude could really talk," Pete understated. "We need a speech like this about Iraq."

"Four score and seven years ago," I said, "we invaded a country and started a war. We're still trying to stop it."

We looked at Lincoln for another moment and Pete said, "How many years is that?"

"Eighty-seven."

"I guess I better have some kids."

"And some grandkids."

35 / Crutch time

"I was an idiot to think that wheelchair would do me any good," I told Pete somewhere on Interstate 80 in Ohio. "It's a hassle to get it out of the truck. I've got to get some crutches."

Because Pete drove with such focus, I needed to plant that thought in his brain a little early. He seemed entirely capable of driving straight through to Yellowstone without stopping. "How about when we get to Toledo, we look for a Goodwill," he said. "They always have crutches. If they weren't named Goodwill, they'd be called America's Crutch Superstore."

"Yeah, why is that?"

"I don't know. Doctors should study it, though. I think Goodwill rehabs more broken legs than most hospitals. Come for the crutches, stay for the dishes and shirts. It's a miracle."

"Talk about a miracle, I got a bike helmet there for two dollars one time."

"See this belt," Pete said, tapping a big silver buckle.

"Yeah."

"Goodwill. Fifty cents. Marked down from a dollar."

"Nice."

Pete was right about Toledo. It was Goodwill nirvana — two stores within a mile of each other. We ended up at the bigger one. He insisted on carrying me inside on his back. "Come on, saddle up," he said. "It's the last chance I'll have to give you a piggyback ride. Once you get those crutches, you'll be all independent and I'll never see you again."

Pete walked right up to the first cashier, an elderly woman with a bun of silky white hair, and said, "Good afternoon, we're from out of town, could you direct us to the crutch section, please?"

The cashier peered over the pearly rims of her glasses. She had probably seen a bunch of weird characters in her day but this might have topped the list. There I was, hanging on Pete like Quasimodo's hump, my arm and flipper wrapped around his neck, my leg around his waist. Yet she didn't flinch or call security. "I certainly could," she said in a milk-and-cookies shaky old-lady voice. "Just follow me."

Her name was Rose, according to the tag on her blouse. She bobbed along with a severe limp, leading us back to the far corner of the store, where a barrel overflowed with crutches and golf clubs. Pete put me down and I grabbed the edge of the barrel to maintain balance. "Here we are," Rose said. "Are you looking for any particular features?"

"Not really. Just something to get me around."

Rose grabbed a pair from the front of the barrel and hoisted them out. "If I could make a suggestion," she offered, "these are top of the line Easy Walkers, very lightweight. They have nonskid tips and push-pin adjustment of the height, so they will accommodate anyone from 5-foot-1 to 6-foot-2. As you can see, the underarm is heavily padded and contoured for extra comfort. They're low mileage, too. They were formerly owned by an uncoordinated woman who naively tried to ride her great-grandson's skateboard. She only got as far as fractures of her femur and hip."

"Wow," Pete said, "you know a lot about crutches."

"Yes, I do. If these might work for you boys, I'm looking for a good home for them. I'll put a red tag on them, too. That gives you 50 percent off, so, five dollars for a pair of crutches. It's a smoking deal, as the kids would say. Medicare paid $279 for them. I'll even throw in a Sam Snead autograph driver."

"That is incredibly kind," I said. "I'll definitely take them. I won't be playing much golf, so I'm sure you can find a better home for the driver, but thank you so much for the crutches. I'll take good care of them."

"You're very welcome. They'll take good care of you."

We rolled into Chicago that night around 2300 and took a walk down by Lake Michigan. It was pleasant. A frigid wind whipping in off the water suppressed the crackle in my stumps. The crutches worked great. They had a lot of Rose's mojo in them.

36 / A life like this

We blew out of Chicago after downing scrambled eggs at a little grease hut. The miles whizzed by. The open road was peaceful and safe. I didn't take that for granted. The only thing that could have killed me was a tailgating trucker. Or a question. As we crossed the South Dakota state line, Pete asked about the Bush blowup, so I recounted how I had made a bitter enemy of Nurse Jillian. "She tried to deck me," I explained. "I would have been down for the count, except I was already down for the count." Klug loved the story and made me tell the part about the Purple Heart again, with more details. "Man, I wish I could have seen the chickenhawk's face," he said.

Then he followed up with the bomb:

"Hey, Cutter, you haven't mentioned anything about your girlfriend. What's going on? Are you getting married? Killdozer said he thought you two would hitch it up. Are we getting invitations soon?"

My stomach convulsed and my throat tightened. I couldn't speak. I looked out across the vast hypnotic plain, to the horizon, and imagined pushing north in my chair, putting enough distance between me and the past two years that eventually I would forget. If I could scrape my mind clean, make it resemble the land, empty and barren, maybe I could keep rolling all the way to nowhere. I hadn't thought about Halley since the day she walked out of Walter Reed. That was what I told myself. The truth, though, was complicated and not what I wanted to hear. Every night before I fell asleep, I forced myself to stop wondering what her life was like. Sleep helped. So did a Nembie or Lude, and Rochambeau hooked me up to get me through, bless her gigantic heart.

Pete didn't say anything else. For a couple of miles, I concentrated on the gruff grind of the engine. Without warning, the truth tumbled out: "She wrote me a letter." There. The words had been waiting for a chance to escape. I didn't look at Pete but I could feel him looking at me.

"You mean like a bad letter?" he said.

"Yeah."

"I'm sorry. I didn't know."

"There's no way you could."

"Is there any chance of getting back together? Have you talked to her in person?"

"She came to visit me in the hospital, so, yeah, we talked but I'm really fucked up. There was no getting around that. We tried to get around it. We talked in circles trying to get around it, around all those tubes, around my stumps. How do you get around that? That's the reality. It doesn't exactly give a girl a rosy picture of the future. There's talking and then there's *really* talking."

Pete's old truck was a bouncing noise machine, a blender on wheels. Metal clanked against metal, tires whined on concrete, wind whistled past windows, rattles and squeaks battled for supremacy. The racket was intense, making it hard to sustain a conversation. After a few more miles, Pete dove in again: "Well, did you *really* talk?"

I shook my head. I should have felt sad but I didn't. "No. You can't *really* talk about this stuff. If you did, the hopelessness of it, the crushingness of it, if you were sane, if you could look at it from outside yourself, you'd just lie down and die. Wouldn't you?"

The truck was our referee. Anytime we got close to a knockdown punch, the noise could step in and separate us. We passed a sign that said: Sioux Falls 16. Pete didn't say anything else until we got to the city limits: "So you don't think it would help to go see her one more time?"

"She made it pretty clear that she couldn't handle it, she wasn't strong enough. I don't even blame her. I can relate. If the shoe was on the other foot … uh, bad figure of speech. The thing is, I don't know if I could take care of her for the rest of her life. Please, don't ever tell anybody I said that. I know that is the wrong wrong wrong thing to say. I know you should be strong and dive in and go for the Hollywood ending but I never envisioned a life like this. Who could? Maybe I don't love her enough. Maybe I don't love myself enough. Maybe I love her too much to ruin her life. Whatever. I don't know. How could I ask her to do what I don't think I could do myself? Anyway, I never thought about it two years ago. Now here I am. All I do is think about it."

That explanation satisfied Pete. He let the subject drop. So did I.

37 / Road warriors

We left Sioux Falls at sunup, powering west. "We're just like Lewis and Clark," I told Pete, "except they did 75 miles a month."

We were making good time, doing 75 miles an hour to keep semis from mowing us down. The truckers — even the triple-trailer maniacs — tailgated like bastards, rolling thunder right up to our rear bumper, like insurgents, except their rigs were loaded with food and soft drinks instead of artillery shells. The ones that passed us often had bumper stickers that said: "How is my driving?" Mrs. Bayonne would have called that ironic.

Just west of the Missouri River, Pete looked in the rearview at a raging red rig bearing down on us. "I wish we had Taymondo and a .50-caliber in the back," he said. "They'd back off."

I felt a knife twinge. "Yeah," I agreed, "I wish we had him." Amerigo Taymondo … at least he lived in our memories.

After blasting through the town of Kadoka, we saw a sign that announced: Badlands 16. Pete and I looked at each other. He knew what I was thinking. "Yeah," he said, "let's go."

I had the urge to see more stuff. I had never really traveled, except in the Army. Gettysburg was cool and I started to think I should visit a few natural wonders. We took the turnoff and headed south. It was a relief to get off Interstate 90.

We drove a few miles and crested a hill. A jagged red-brown panorama stretched out ahead of us to the horizon. "Un … fucking … real," Pete enunciated, slowly and reverently. "What the hell is this place? It's like God's art studio."

"Heavenly earth tones," I said.

We pulled into the Pinnacles Overlook parking lot. A few clouds jostled for position in the vast blue expanse of sky, occasionally jousting with the sun. The land was all craggy and carved, pugnacious and proud, majestic beyond words.

"I want to live here," Pete said.

"I want to die here," I one-upped.

Pete laughed but I didn't know if I was joking. Was it that crazy an idea? Everybody kicks. The only questions are when and where. As for the where, the Badlands, ironically, felt good. I could visualize it. Back forever to beautiful Mother Earth.

"Hey, Johnny, look at those steps," Pete said, pointing to a descending staircase. "You want to check out the overlook?"

My insides twitched as I thought of a different overlook. The stairs looked dicey. It always came back to what I could accomplish. I had to think everything through, even the smallest physical action. Could I button my own shirt? Sometimes I could and sometimes, if the button-hole was tight, I couldn't. My life was a constant series of evaluations. "You go," I said. "It looks like a great view from down there."

"Aw, man, you can make it. That's why we got the crutches, isn't it?"

"Yeah, I guess but I don't know."

"We could do a piggyback. I'll carry you down, if you want."

"I know you would but I can see it from here. Really. You go, OK?"

"You sure?"

"Totally."

"All right. I'll just bounce down for a couple of minutes. I want to snap a picture. I'll never see anything like this again."

Pete got out and jogged down the stairs. I would have slowed him down. It reminded me of how much time he used to spend on the track at Viper base. I stayed in the truck. There were small kids around with their moms and dads. No use giving them nightmares.

When Pete returned, he jogged *up* the stairs, too. He was a running maniac. "That is freaking amazing," he said. "It's like … I don't know. They should have named it Badass Lands. I wish we were fighting for this instead of Iraq. It would make more sense. Damn, let's protect *this* from terrorists. You think this area is protected?"

"I don't know. Probably. It's a national park."

"I forget, do we strip-mine the national parks now?"

Pete was great when he got all drolled up. We headed north to a town called Wall. Pete managed to shame me into getting out of the truck for a little exercise and a tour of the crazy Wall Drug Store. "Don't be a lazy ass," he said. "After passing a hundred signs for this place, you don't want to see it? Come on, I'll buy you an ice cream cone." I wasn't too bad on the crutches, didn't fall down once, and I got a double-dip chocolate chip.

We rolled on through Rapid City and up to a little place called Sturgis. On the outskirts of town, we passed a motorcycle shop: Hawg Heaven.

"Whoa, stop, we gotta go there," I yelled.

"Where?"

"Hawg Heaven. Did you see that sign and those bikes?"

"I haven't seen anything for the last 50 miles. I'm takin' a nap, man."

"All the more reason to stop. Come on, hang a U, it's just back there."

"Copy that."

We pulled in amid a phalanx of Harley-Davidsons parked on the lot, calling to their future owners. To our left, a platform rose about 10 feet in the air. Two gleaming chromed-out Harleys with custom paint jobs sat atop the riser like beacons. They had caught my attention first but back on a metal building I had also spotted a sign: Custom repairs.

"I gotta do something about the chair," I said.

"What's wrong with it?"

"It's for old farts. It's slow. It's a Florida wheelchair. It screams, 'Look at the crip pissing his pants because he can't make it to the bathroom in time!' I hate the fucking thing. I think the battery is dead. At the very least, it needs a couple of extra batteries so I don't have to charge it up all the time. I want a hard-core mechanic to work on it."

"Maybe this is your guy," Pete said, pointing to a man in greasy blue overalls who was lumbering toward us. He was roughly the size of a huge grizzly bear rearing up on its hind legs. With his long hair and beard, he could have been Jesus, except he was smoking a joint. Then again, what would Jesus do to mellow out nowadays?

The big man came around to Pete's side of the truck and said, "Howdy. My name's Junior Jett. What can I do for you fellas?"

"My friend's got a bug up his ass about his wheelchair."

"Well, let's just see what we got here," Junior said. He took a final deep hit off the joint, tossed it over his shoulder and walked around to the back of the truck. Pete got out. I fumbled to get the rusty door open and finally managed it, awkwardly planting my foot on the ground.

"This is uptown," Junior said. "The guys I knew in chairs didn't have a joystick, didn't have a motor. They had to push it their own selves."

When Junior saw me hopping over on one leg, my arm stump flapping in the breeze, he said, "But technology's cool. There's a place for it."

Pete grabbed the crutches from the bed of the pickup and handed them to me. I got myself situated so I wouldn't fall down on the asphalt. I extended my hand to Junior. He shook it with his left and looked me square in the eye.

"Have you got a bathroom I can use?" I asked.

"Sure do." He pointed toward the metal building. "It's through those double doors on the left. You want us to get the chair down for ya?"

"No. I don't have time for that." I hobbled off, hoping the Hawg Heaven bathroom would be one of those filthy road-trip holes, so I wouldn't leave it in worse shape than it already was. If I had thought praying would do any good, I would have asked God to make sure it had toilet paper. Instead, I left that up to fate, like everything else.

I was probably gone a half-hour. To their credit, Pete and Junior just waited and never came banging on the door to see if I was still alive. I apologized: "Sorry. I'm slow."

"No biggie," Junior said. "OK, I'll see you guys in two days."

"Huh?" I didn't get what was happening. The wheelchair was unloaded, parked next to the pickup.

"Pete told me everything I need to know," Junior said. "So I'll see you back here on Thursday."

"What did he tell you?"

"Don't worry. It's taken care of."

"How much will it cost?"

"Maybe 50 bucks. Maybe less. We'll see."

"That sounds low."

"Naw, I got it covered."

"Let's roll," Pete said. "We're on a mystery mission now."

"A mystery mission?"

"Yeah, let's go."

"Where're we going?"

"I said it's a mystery. Saddle up."

We drove back into Sturgis and turned south. I tried to pry the target out of Pete with intense interrogation but he would only repeat his name, rank and serial number. He was a brick wall and I was banging my head against him. After we'd been on the road for just a few miles, a sign appeared: Mount Rushmore 32.

"Where'd you say we're going, Pete?"

"I *didn't* say. Anyway, that's classified information."

"So we're going to Rushmore."

"No comment."

"Cool. I've only seen it in photos."

We got to the park entrance just after closing time, so we drove on down the road until we found a gravel turnout underneath a gnarly half-dead Halloween tree. "I guess this is as good a spot as any to bivouac," Pete said. "I don't see any tripwires."

One thing about the Army, it prepared me for squatting. No place to sleep in the middle of nowhere? No bathroom? No electricity? No running water? No food? No toothbrush? No nothing?

No problem.

After Iraq, everything else was a motel. It was good to be in the open air, anyway. Pete and I hadn't taken a shower since we left Washington.

We were bunking in the back of the truck. Pete made a couple of sandwiches out of stuff in the cooler. About half an hour after sundown, the temperature began to drop ferociously. That didn't stop me from sweating. I got on the crutches and hobbled around a little bit, working out the road kinks. The exercise must have pumped some blood to my stumps. Usually they were gray-white, like dead fish scales, but they sparked up with a little color in the areas that weren't scarred. After a few minutes, they started to burn and sting. Blowtorch time again. I wanted to hack them off with a machete but I was still sane enough to know that wouldn't end the pain. I gropped over to the truck to get my fanny pack.

But it wasn't there. It was getting dark. Maybe I just didn't see it. I left it on the seat. I was sure of that. I couldn't wear it when we were driving, so I always put it on the seat next to me. It had to be on the seat. So where the hell was it?

"Pete, goddamn, I left my fanny pack in Sturgis. Fuck. *Fuck! FUCK!*"

"Are you sure?"

"*No, I'm not sure.* Maybe I left it in Wall. I don't know. *Shit!* I could have left it anywhere! *I need that fucking pack!* Can we go back to Sturgis and look for it? I need it, Pete. *I really really need it!*"

"Yeah, we're definitely going back to Sturgis to pick up the chair."

"*No! Tonight! Can we go back tonight! I think I left it at the Harley shop! Maybe I left it in the bathroom!*"

"Johnny, chill, my brother, we're going to Rushmore first thing tomorrow morning. Besides, the shop is closed by now. We can't go back tonight."

"*Please, Pete. We gotta go back. Maybe we can get Junior to open the shop for us.*"

"How would we do that? We don't know how to get ahold of him."

"*We'll just find him somehow. Come on, Pete. Please, I'm begging you.*"

Pete came around to the passenger side. "Let me look," he said.

I stepped out of his way, holding onto the door frame to keep my balance. He peered into the truck. He opened the glove compartment. Not there. He reached under the seat. "I feel something," he said.

"*What do you feel? Pull it out!*"

"It's caught on the springs."

"*Careful! Be careful! Don't rip it!*"

"OK, OK. Get me the flashlight. It's by the cooler."

I threw the crutches on the ground and pogoed to the back of the truck. It was faster that way. I grabbed the flashlight, flicked it on and brought it to Pete. He shined the beam under the seat. "Yeah, Johnny, that's it. Must have gotten shoved under here."

"*Oh, thank God!*"

Pete extricated the pack and handed it out. I reached for it but lost my balance. I instinctively grabbed for the door frame with my stump. Sometimes I forgot I had no hand. I splatted in the gravel like a jellyfish. "*Fuck!*" I yelled. "*Get me some pills outta there! Please!*"

He unzipped the pack and shined the flashlight into it. "What kind? There's blue ones, red ones, green ones, yellow ones, white ones, purple ones."

"They're all good. How about a red, a white and a blue."

"Is it all right to mix them?"

"Oh, yeah. We call that an Old Glory."

Pete handed me three pills. He didn't offer to help me up first. He understood it was more important to get me the drugs than to get me off the ground. Priorities. I worked up a little spit and gulped those sweet things down. Soon I was drifting dreamily into the no-pain zone, snugged up in my blanket, tripping on a swirly parade of the brightest smiling stars I had ever seen. As I faded to black, a wolf howled and an owl screeched somewhere in the distance, or maybe just inside my own head, and I wanted to kiss them.

I loved the way meds made me sleep. I had never slipped all the way under in Iraq. You had to keep your edge at all times. Now I could sleep like a dead man, let go, float upon an oblivion sea, drift so far out it was spiritual. Of course, waking up became harder. That was the tradeoff, which was well worth it.

The next morning, I surfaced to consciousness only when Pete threw a glass of icy water in my face. *Splash.* "Wake up, soldier," he growled. "We gotta report to the commanders in chief."

"What time is it?"

"0950."

I did the math. "More than 11 hours of shut-eye. Not bad."

"I got up with the sun," Pete bragged. "I already ran 12 miles."

"I ran 13 in my dreams." To remind myself I still had half of a body, I wriggled like a worm. I was stiff but nothing hurt too much. Maybe it would be a good day. Pete and I had become efficient at breaking camp and moving out. We were gone in 10 minutes.

Mount Rushmore was pure shock and awe. There they were, Washington, Jefferson, Roosevelt and Lincoln, glaring stone giants confronting us tiny miserable ants. "Unbelievable," Pete said. "I don't believe this. This can't be real. Do you believe this?"

"No. How was this even possible?" We stood there for a long time, gaping. It was hypnotic. It silenced us. I studied every detail, wondering about the stone carvers, how they got up there, how they knew what to chip away. I tried to imagine a plain mountain but couldn't. This monumental undertaking crowded out all other thoughts. Around us, people carried on their own conversations of disbelief, their eyes riveted on the huge, literally and figuratively, presidents. After a while, I realized nobody was staring at me. That was nice. For the first time in months, I didn't feel self-conscious.

"Let's go to the visitor center and learn something about Gutzon," Pete said after we'd been out on the viewing deck for an hour or so.

Gutzon Borglum baffled me. The guy joined the Ku Klux Klan and carved a big Robert E. Lee head into Stone Mountain near Atlanta. Then he put a six-story-tall Lincoln — the man who ended slavery — on the Black Hills. How did that add up? Was he schizo? Gutzon and his crew spent 14 years sculpting Rushmore with dynamite. I tried to understand that kind of commitment. I theorized that he was OCD, a real head case, struggling to accomplish something to inspire people forever, or at least until erosion wiped everything — the mountain and us — away. When you die, I wondered, do you look back on your life and say, Yeah, it was worth it? Or is it more, Why did I do that? I guessed that Gutzon didn't have any regrets. How could he? He had climbed to the mountaintop and transformed it. Then again, he died before it was finished. That might change your mind about whether it made sense.

Pete disappeared in the museum for a while but when I saw him again, he said, "We gotta go down the road. These hills are like mega-sculpture heaven. I heard they're working on this insane Crazy Horse mountain."

Insane was right. Crazy Horse's head was massive and mesmerizing. He made the Rushmore Four look shriveled. So far, only Crazy's face existed but his long pointing arm and his gargantuan horse would be carved into the mountain someday. Nobody knew when. We picked up a pamphlet that explained how the dude who started it, Korczak Ziolkowski, had worked for Gutzon on Rushmore for a while. Then he began blasting away on Crazy Horse in 1948. He died in 1982. Then his wife and 10 kids took over the project. So they'd been working on it for like 58 years. Talk about commitment.

"It's kinda like Iraq," Pete said. "They're gonna need more time."

"And more dynamite," I added.

The thing about Iraq was, it never left our heads. It could flare up at any moment, like multiple sclerosis or something. We couldn't escape. It shaped us like messed-up DNA. Iraq was our defective gene. I imag-

ined that Gutzon and Korczak were prisoners, too. Eventually, relent-
lessly, the biggest thing in their lives, the stone, would kill them. Maybe
that one big thing happened to a lot of people.

    We needed food, gasoline and a place to camp for the night, so we
drove down the hill to Custer, population 1,860. "What?" Pete said.
"This is it? Just a tiny little town? The general doesn't get his face on a
mountain? Not even a giant arrow?"

    "The last stand is a bitch," I said.

38 / Pimped ride

The wheelchair glistened in the morning South Dakota sun, sitting high atop the riser along with the two Harleys that originally had caught my attention. As we pulled into the Hawg Heaven lot, Pete said, "That's hilarious."

A hand-painted cardboard sign sat in the chair seat. It said: Electric. Lo miles.

Junior saw us roll up and rushed out of the shop like a Pendleton Round-Up bull. "Hey, Army," he yelled, "I got some ideas while you were gone. I think you're gonna like what I did."

Pete grabbed Rose's crutches from the pickup bed and brought them around to me. We followed Junior over to the riser. "I kinda just wish you sold it," I told him.

"I had a guy come in about half an hour ago and asked me what I wanted for it. 'Forty-five thousand,' I says to him. 'Dollars?' he says to me. 'Yep.' '*American* dollars?' 'Yep.' 'I could get a Softail and a 'Lectra Glide for less than that.' 'Yep.' I wasn't gonna sell your chair, Army. I just put it up there to send a message: We're all in this together. Two wheels, four wheels, two legs, one leg. It don't matter. Black, white, conservative, liberal. Don't matter. Just get on your bike and ride. Get in your chair and roll. OK, enough of my dream world. Let me show you what you got now. You better back up a little."

Pete and I looked at each other. We moved back six steps. Army training: Put distance between yourself and the blast zone. Junior nodded approvingly at our caution. Then he lowered the riser's hydraulic ramp and lumbered up to the chair. Junior weighed at least 300 pounds. I smiled as he wedged himself into the seat. I hated that fucking chair. Maybe Junior's girth would rip it apart. The big man flipped the on-switch and a powerful whine filled the air, like a turbo spooling up. He did a snap 180 to face the ramp. He jammed the stick forward. A screech assaulted our ears. A puff of smoke from each big wheel signaled Junior's takeoff. The chair shot forward and went airborne for a moment as it came off the riser.

"*Jesus!*" Pete shouted. I just stood there, uncomprehending, anchored to the crutches like a lump. Junior zoomed down the ramp and raced off toward the shop. Pete and I looked at each other with our jaws agape. In the distance, Junior made a hard right turn and ripped past a row of Harleys. He disappeared behind the shop. In a few seconds, he roared back around the other side and headed straight for us. Pete summed it up: "He's a maniac."

Junior rolled to a stop right in front of us, a gigantic grin putting his front gold tooth in the best light. "Whaddaya think?" he asked.

I didn't know what to say but some lame words came out of my mouth anyway: "Junior, that's a government-issue wheelchair."

"Not anymore."

Junior had installed two extra batteries. He replaced the joystick with a cut-down shifter from a wrecked 1966 Corvette. The man was an oxyacetylene artist who really rocked a welding torch but he didn't stop there.

"Is that a new motor?" I asked.

"Yep. Dyno 1000. Around 75 foot-pounds of torque. It came off a tugboat winch. I did a gearing mod to drive the wheels. Don't forget to check out the headrest." Junior slammed his meaty head back into a square cushion covered in stripes of black and red leather. "It came outta Mickey Fontaine's Top Fuel dragster. This was about the only thing left when it blew. I think Mickey would approve of using it on this machine."

"You mean … "

"Yeah," Junior said, "but you know, life is not very long, so you gotta make sure it's wide. Mickey's life was triple-wide. You wanna try it?"

"What have I got to lose?"

Junior levered himself out of the chair with some difficulty. I positioned myself in front of the seat and Pete took the crutches. I plopped down. The leather was still warm.

"The thing to know," Junior instructed, "is that she's touchy. Go easy on the throttle and you should get several days off one charge. I reckon up to 150 miles."

I flipped the on-switch and took a deep breath.

"We better stand back," Junior advised.

"We better get a fire extinguisher," Pete added.

"Hardy har har," I said, pushing the Corvette joystick. The chair leaped forward. I yanked my hand away and the stick reset to neutral, halting the chair.

"See what I mean?" Junior said. "Hair-trigger."

"No kidding." This time I barely nudged the joystick and the chair began to roll at a controllable speed. I would need to recalibrate my hand. I rolled around the lot for a while, in what I began to think of as first gear, doing a few lazy figure eights to get a feel for the steering. As I shifted my weight into the turns, I noticed that on each side of the chair, Junior had welded stabilizer bars with little skateboard wheels a couple of inches off the ground. I took a lap around the building and rolled back to Junior and Pete.

"What's the deal with the training wheels?" I asked.

"Stability," Junior said. "I overbuild everything."

"Makes sense," I said. "If I flipped this rig, I probably wouldn't get up. What's the top speed?"

"Our cop pulled me over in the school zone and claimed he clocked me at 26. He let me off but I was definitely pushin' it."

I had to chuckle. "Escape velocity," I said, visualizing the space shuttle blasting into orbit, breaking the bonds of Earth.

Junior nodded seriously. "Gettin' there."

"What's that on the back?" Pete asked.

"A parachute. It's an old reserve."

I twisted around in the chair as best I could to get a look. Sure enough, a brown squarish canvas container was mounted on the back of the chair. "Is that thing functional?" I asked.

"Oh, yeah. Here's the rip cord." Junior pointed to an O-ring attached to a steel cable threaded through two eyelets that were spot-welded to the right arm of the chair. "Maybe it's overkill but if you ever need to make an emergency stop, it's there. Just remember, you pull it, you pack it. Chutes are kind of my signature. I was 101st Airborne in 'Nam."

"No shit!" Pete exclaimed.

"I've put on a few pounds since then but I used to be able to jump."

"Screaming Eagles," Pete said. "They had everybody's back."

"That'll never change."

Junior fist-bumped us both and put his gold tooth on display.

"The chair is amazing," I said. "I love it. I mean, I hate it but I love it, if you know what I mean."

"Yeah, I know."

"How much do I owe you, Junior? This is way more work than I was expecting."

"It's on the house. You don't owe anything."

"Why?"

"You already paid."

I wanted to protest. I had about $200 in my wallet. I would have given him all of it but Junior's eyes told me he wouldn't take it. He stuck out his left bear paw and I shook it. "Thanks," I said. "Thanks a lot. I'll never forget this."

"Hey, what did you think of Rushmore?" Junior asked.

Pete and I answered at the same time, with the same word: *"Awesome."*

"I hear ya. First time I saw it, I wanted to quit bikes and switch to stone carving. Turned out I was better with steel. Once you chip a 100-foot nose off, that's it."

The three of us loaded the chair into the back of the pickup and Pete and I hit the road. As we rolled away from Hawg Heaven, I looked back. "Junior just flashed us a peace sign," I told Pete.

"Too bad it ain't that easy," he said.

39 / Yellowstoned

We pushed hard across Wyoming. Yellowstone National Park was pulling on Pete like an electromagnet, aligning his inner iron filings. "I saw pictures of it when I was a kid," he explained a few miles east of Cody. "They just stuck with me for some reason. Especially the buffalo's eye. That eye looked into mine and I told myself I would see one someday. Look the mighty beast in the eye for real. That day is here, Cutter."

The little town of Cody was like something out of the Wild West. With a name like that, honoring Buffalo Bill, how could it have been anything else? "I don't think my belt buckle is big enough to make it in this town," Pete said.

At first we decided to go to the hassle of unloading the wheelchair, so I could take a spin down Sheridan Avenue. The more we looked around, and after two cowboys clopped by on actual horses, the more it seemed wrong. "No offense," Pete said, "but it ain't an electric wheelchair town. Do you think?"

"No, it's not," I agreed. "I'll use the crutches. Nobody'll draw on a cripple." We walked the length of the town, ending up at the Irma Hotel for burgers and beer.

"What are you gonna do when you get out?" Pete asked.

That caught me epically off guard. "Huh?" was all I had.

"When you get out of the Army, what are you gonna do? Are they helping you figure anything out?"

"Are they supposed to?"

"Seems like they should."

"I guess they're trying. They're talking about a new leg and I got a new arm. A hook. Which I hate. That's why I didn't bring it. Killdozer said I could get $3,000 a month in disability."

"Does that shit really work?"

"What?"

"New arms, new legs, that kind of shit."

"What do you think?"

Pete took a big swig. He clanked the mug down on the bar. "I try not to think about it," he said.

"That's good. Don't. Seriously don't. Don't ever think about it. Because if you do, you will be very fucked up for a very long time. Obviously, if you lose your arm, you will be fucked up forever physically. Because an arm made out of plastic and steel cable is not going to help you. If you think about it, you will also be fucked up in the head. Don't think about it. That's what I've learned in the last few months."

"I'm sorry I brought it up. I'm an idiot. You want to get some onion rings?"

"You're not an idiot. Somebody *should* bring it up. I wish somebody would have brought it up to me two years ago. Live and learn. Learn and die."

We drove the 40 miles from Cody to Yellowstone and only said about five words. Maybe less. I didn't blame Pete for not wanting to talk to me. I was depressing to be around. My downer outburst at the hotel was all the proof I needed, confirming what I knew in my heart. Hell, I depressed myself. Too bad I had to be around myself all the time. No escape. I dipped into the pack for a pill to supplement the one I had taken in Cody. I didn't feel the need to sneak it. I only felt the need. Pete noticed, looking away from the road for a moment, but he politely didn't mention it. By now, he knew I had a painkiller problem. He also knew it was better and easier not to talk about it.

The park goosed my spirits. We rolled through the east entrance shortly after sundown. Above a mountain peak in the distance, swirling red and purple flames streaked the clouds. I imagined some raving wild-eyed painter doing a celestial number with insane incendiary pigment that was so rich and gooey it had to be outlawed. I was high, yes, but drugs or not, this was an artistic throbbing sky that was as close to God as I would ever get.

It wasn't just me. Pete saw it too. "Props to Mother Nature," he said. "It's like she set off a nuclear warhead, only we're still alive to appreciate the fireball."

"No radioactive wasteland," I added. "Gotta love it."

As the light fell, the road rose. The old truck began to chug a little and Pete downshifted. He pulled into a gravel turnout and said, "I have no idea where we're going and I'm beat. What if we call it a day right here?"

"I'm down with that."

We must have been at a decent elevation, maybe 8,000 feet, because the air chilled fast and hard. I still had Baghdad in my bones, thin blood or something from all those 100-degree nights. This felt like a refrigerator to me. Shivering, I dove into the duffel bag and pulled out every shirt I had and my other pair of jeans. Pete helped me put everything on.

We found a level patch of ground, maybe a little too rocky, and spread out Pete's sleeping bag as an under layer. Then we piled all of his old camping blankets on top of us. After half an hour or so, I began to warm up. Stars came out like popcorn in a skillet. Moonlight silhouetted fir trees on a ridge a couple of klicks away. Nothing could have been more beautiful than this.

Unless you added a soundtrack.

"Did you hear that?" Pete said.

"No. What?"

"Listen."

I lay as still as I could. I quit breathing for a moment. A breeze whispered in the trees but that was all. And then …

"There."

… faintly at first but growing louder …

"Whoa, a wolf," I said.

"Yeah."

The cry was miles away, most likely, skipping on the wind, bouncing off the sky, dodging mountaintops, floating over our campsite. Then another joined in. And another, adding a lofty yapping counterpoint. They went on for a long minute, sometimes together, sometimes back and forth, staccato yelps, mournful wails.

"I wonder what they're talking about?" I said.

"I'll find out." Pete cupped his hands around his mouth and let out a howl of his own — "awwoooooooooooooooooooo."

"Hey, not bad," I said. "Were you raised by wolves or something?"

"Yeah. *Awwwwwoooooooooooooooooooooooooo!*" Pete sat up and did some feral yip-yap-yelping. Then he stopped to listen.

And the wolves answered.

"Come on," he said, "I need some help to invite them over."

"No way."

"I can't do it by myself. Let your inner wolf loose." Pete threw off the blankets, jumped up and let out a manic howl, loud and proud. I got up, balancing precariously on my knee, and managed a scraggly utterance, like an undercranked siren.

"Damn, Cutter, you sound like a squirrel with a kidney stone. Wolf it up, my brother. Put some teeth in it."

As I tottered, I thought about my leg. Not the leg I had left but my missing leg. And my arm. I wondered where they were. Nobody ever told me what happened to them. Did they end up in a trash dump? Or rot in a Baghdad alley? Or pass through the digestive tracks of wild dogs? Nobody cared enough to tell me. Maybe nobody knew. Maybe they figured it didn't matter. That arm and that leg didn't belong to them. That arm and that leg were gone and would never come back but they mattered to me. They would goddamn motherfucking matter to me every day for the rest of my life.

I threw my head back and let out a sky-shattering howl that came from dust, from bullets, from bombs, from blood, from funerals, from body bags.

And from tears. From a torrent of tears. I started to weep. My body shook. Every muscle in my face clenched. I doubled over and fell to the rocky ground. I continued to howl until my breath was gone.

40 / Land of a thousand trances

I woke up with a sharpened ax blade embedded in my right shoulder, or maybe I just slept on it the wrong way. The pain was ambiguous. I groaned like a bear full of buckshot for a while and finally got it together enough to roll onto my left side. I made slow circles with my stump to try to loosen up the shoulder joint.

Birds were chirping and squawking dramatically. Avian opera. I heard footfalls in the distance. A couple of hundred yards off, Pete was sprinting up the road like a madman. When he got to camp, he leaped over me, trailing a whirl of dust and small stones. He chugged to a stop near a couple of pine trees. After doubling over to heave-breathe for a solid couple of minutes, he walked back, his 3rd Infantry T-shirt and camo shorts drenched in sweat. I tried to remember when I had last moved fast enough to even perspire.

"You woke up," Pete said. "That's good." He dropped and began doing pushups.

"How far did you run?"

"Thirty minutes down and an hour back up. I'm going to say 10 miles. The mountain air is brutal, though, pretty thin. It's noticeable. How you doing?"

"Got a knot in my back but other than that, not too bad."

"When we get to the village, we'll see if they have any yoga classes."

"I'd be good at the half-lotus position."

Pete stopped in mid-pushup, looked over, and gave me a bemused little head shake. "Cutter," he said, "you're Army fucking strong."

I nodded reluctantly and bent forward to try to touch my foot, going for a spine stretch. Pete plunged back into his pushups. When he had done a hundred or so, he stopped and rolled over onto his back. "So what was the deal with last night?" he said.

"What do you mean?"

"The whole, the, uh, you know, the howling thing."

"You mean the crying thing."

"Is everything all right? Do you need any help?"

"I don't know. I think it might be too late. I'm trying to figure it out. It kind of feels like help wouldn't really help. Like, what is the point?"

Pete had brown probing sergeant eyes. I wondered if he thought I was compromising the Yellowstone mission. I resolved to suck it up and quit complaining. What good did complaining do, anyway? It changed nothing. I would be heading home soon. I just needed to get through another day or two.

"You think you'd feel any better if we broke camp and headed for Old Faithful?" Pete said. "I haven't seen anything blow up for three weeks. I'm starting to miss it."

"I'm there, Sergeant, reporting for duty."

A short drive later, as we crested a hill, a gigantic shimmering lake slapped us right across our faces. "My God," Pete said. "That's something you don't see in Iraq."

"Water is a beautiful thing. Especially when you smell like a dead camel."

"Hey, this is pure running sweat," Pete protested.

"I'm talking about me. Do you think it's too cold to take a dip?"

"If it ain't frozen solid, it ain't too cold."

As we found out later from a plaque at a scenic overlook, we bathed in Yellowstone Lake, one of the park's crown jewels. I felt guilty about contaminating such an insane natural wonder with my caked-on body gunk but we had arrived at the point, living the no-budget road life, where filthy desperation outflanked environmentalism. Though a lot of stuff didn't mean anything to me anymore, getting clean still mattered. The frigid water was good for my stumps, too. The arctic shock seemed to cut down on nerve pain. I decided to see how long I could go without hitting the medicine cabinet.

Back on the road, Pete rolled down his window, stuck his head out and sucked in the clean mountain air. "This is just like what I imagined it would be," he said. "I might just stay here."

"Really?"

"I wish."

We drove the perimeter of the lake to the village of West Thumb and headed west to Old Faithful, crossing the Continental Divide on the way. The geyser was a mecca for tourists and their conveyances, sticker-covered RVs, kayak-topped SUVs, hulking motor homes, peace-signed VW buses, cars, trucks, trailers, motorcycles, even half-dead guys on touring bicycles tricked out with humongous saddle bags.

"It's like the ultimate vehicular convention," I told Pete. "They're only missing one thing."

"What's that?"

"A supercharged Top Fuel wheelchair."

"Oh, yeah," Pete said, punching the air. "Begin countdown."

We settled in a far corner of one of the Old Faithful Inn parking lots, as far away from people and cars as we could get, in case something went wrong with the launch. Pete laid down two-by-fours between the tailgate and ground, jury-rigging an off-load ramp. I wormed up into the pickup bed and skooched my way into the chair. LEDs lit up as I flicked the on-switch. "We have ignition, Houston."

"Slow and easy, big fella. Let's not get into a medevac situation."

"Been there, done that, won't do it again." I gave the Corvette joystick the slightest touch and the chair rotated to face the ramp.

"One second," Pete said, "I want to make a little adjustment." He pulled one of the two-by-fours out of the middle and placed it at the bottom of the ramp, anchoring all the other boards. "I'll stand on this to keep anything from slipping. Don't run me down."

"Roger that."

"Hit it straight on and you should be golden."

I nudged the stick and started to roll. The small front wheels bumped up onto the two-by-fours and the chair lurched forward. Pete jumped out of the way and suddenly the chair was on the ground. It happened so fast. I was amazed to still be upright. Junior Jett's modification, the extra stabilizer wheels, worked beautifully.

"Cleared for takeoff," Pete said.

"Bye-bye." I leaned into the stick and the chair bolted like an F-16. I roared through the parking lot, getting the feel of the controls. The wind in my face felt extra fine. I passed some families who gawked like I was a creature from another planet. They were kind of right. "New dilithium crystals," I shouted above the whine of the engine.

I zigged and zagged for a while, calibrating joystick pressure, practicing spins, smoothing out starts and stops. Gaining confidence, I made a few runs to the outer reaches, where the motor-home mastodons dwelled. When my hand had everything down, I returned to the truck. Pete was standing on the roof like a lookout. "Far fucking out," he said. "You were a raging cyclone out there. We gotta think of a name for the chair but let's go see Old Faithful first."

"Lead the way."

Pete and I turned into tourists as we joined the onlookers massing in a huge semicircle around the geyser. While I was marauding in the chair, he had done some recon and knew when the next blast was expected: "They're saying 1437, roughly every 90 minutes." He looked at his watch nervously, like we had a battlefield rendezvous to make.

"Coming through, thank you," Pete announced in his natural-born leader voice as we edged into the crowd.

"Pete," I protested.

He knew what I meant. "Chill, Cutter, this is our only chance. You'll never see it from the back."

A few people looked annoyed but when they saw me, the waters parted and then they looked away. One guy, though, considered my stumps somberly and said, "Thank you for your service." I mustered a polite nod but thought, Maybe someday you'll know what happened over there and reconsider.

We rolled to the front, up to the concrete curb at the edge of the viewing area. A couple of hundred yards out, a chalky gray mound gave away the geyser's position. Here and there, stubby clumps of grass looked for a foothold in the earth. In the distance, pines stood at attention on rolling hills. "T minus five and counting," Pete said. "You might want to put on some Kevlar."

"It's a little late for that."

Pete shrugged and gave a little tilt of his head. "Suit yourself."

The crowd grew restless as the minutes passed, with conversational murmuring turning to anticipatory buzzing. Small children and cameras were hoisted and aimed. Pete continued his countdown: "Brace — 30 seconds."

With moments to go, nobody made a sound. Even the breeze died down, eerily on cue. The cloudless sky provided a fine blue backdrop for an explosion.

But nothing happened.

Unfulfilled expectation quickly gave way to scattered mumbling and muted disappointment in the crowd.

"Maybe my watch is fast."

"I want my money back."

"Just my luck, this'll be the one time it doesn't erupt."

"How long should we wait?"

Even Pete joined in, leaning over to me and whispering, "I'm guessing faulty cell phone detonator."

Minutes dragged by. Somewhere a baby began to cry. Conversation picked up again. At last, a puff of steam escaped. The geyser began to spit and sputter. An igneous gurgle hushed every mouth.

Then Old Faithful blew for real — a hissing scalding 150-foot-tall gusher of water and steam. The pregnantly pent-up crowd popped too. Ooohhhs and aaahhhs wafted up in unison with the geyser's mini-mushroom cloud. Cheers and applause mixed like rum and coke. The intoxication continued for several minutes. Finally the geologic belch subsided and the crowd melted away, satisfied with the show.

"That must be a relief," Pete said. "Every hour and a half, just let it rip. Get it out of your system."

"I guess. Seems like it might get tiring, though. After a thousand years, don't you just want to kick back?"

"Not me. I like the constant banging of my head on the rocks. It keeps me focused."

We grabbed lunch at the Old Faithful Inn snack bar and embraced the road again, heading north, with stops at Biscuit Basin, Fountain Paint Pot and Firehole Falls. The stunning beauty made me feel small and insignificant. That was comforting. I could gaze off in any direction and fall into a pleasant trance. With these boiling steam vents, these majestic mountains, these canyon-carving rivers in the world, it didn't matter if I remained. They would always be here, in transcendent glory, regardless of whether anybody was around to look at them.

41 / Buffalo chill

We did our usual crash-anywhere thing, setting up camp on a flat patch of dirt next to the far north end of the parking lot at Steamboat Geyser. I held the flashlight while Pete loosened one of the battery cables. "If anybody tries to kick us out of here," he said, "our story is, the truck won't start but we reckon — make sure you say 'reckon,' not 'think' — we reckon we can fix it when daylight comes. You got that?"

"I reckon we hail from these parts."

"Exactamundo."

Judging by the position of the moon, it was after midnight when my stumps began to prickle. I tried to resist. I lay there, unable to nod off, concentrating on the Milky Way. With the absence of artificial light, it resembled a grandiose white sash across the sky's midsection. My warm tingling turned to fiery scraping-by-cheese-grater. I had to give in. Three Darvons later, the twinkling stars began to whisper, "You're feeling sleepy … very sleepy … so sleepy."

Sleep was the greatest gift. Nothing better. OK, maybe professionally administered anesthesia was better, if you wanted a blank slate, no dreams, if you wanted to wake up in a cotton-brain daze with no recollection of the previous 12 hours. Still, sleep was damned straight-ahead good. It made almost everything go away for a little while.

I did dream, though, despite the painkillers. I dreamed of the burn pits back in the sandbox. I dreamed of the grunting bulldozers as they pushed heaping piles of used-up cast-off junk and garbage into the ring. I dreamed of the putrid stench. I dreamed of the billowing black clouds of smoke. I dreamed of the acrid air. I dreamed of a sloppy wet washcloth wiping grime off my mouth and nose. The vivid sensation awakened me. My eyes snapped open.

It was dark, no stars overhead anymore. Hot reeky breath continued to flow up my nostrils. Then the washcloth hit me with a long gooey swipe. Huh? Was I still dreaming? Or was I awake? Oh, yeah, I was definitely awake — *and a big freaking buffalo was licking my face.*

The Army had never trained us for this. My first instinct was to run. My second instinct was to laugh at my first instinct. My third instinct was to shut up and not move. I went with that.

I closed my eyes tightly, to keep buffalo saliva from running into them. Besides, I didn't want to see exactly what was going on. I instantly understood how blind people adapt, how their other senses become super-aware and take over. As the buffalo bathed my face in spit, I felt the tiny bumps on his tongue, the sandpapery texture, the warmth. He was in a groove, it seemed, with three licks in each spot, covering every inch of skin, moving from my forehead, to my cheeks, to the bridge of my nose, to my mouth and chin. Then it hit me: He craved salt and I was filthy with it.

"Hey, Cutter, are you awake?"

At that moment, I couldn't answer. Mr. Buffalo was planting a wet one right on my lips. God, what a tickle!

"If you can hear me," Pete whispered, "we've got a bison in camp, so stay cool. I've got a plan."

I opened my eyes slightly, peering up through the lashes. With dawn maybe half an hour off, a deep blue light was nudging the night aside. I didn't see much, mostly matted ringlets of fur. The massive beast smelled like spoiled meat. In a moment, I got my bearings. Mr. Buff stood to my right, angled toward Pete, so I had some room to maneuver. I wasn't pinned down by a straddle, at least.

"When I take the bull by the horns, I want you to roll toward the truck," Pete said.

The buffalo was working the side of my neck now. I whispered, "You mean literally?"

"Yes, I want you to literally roll toward the truck."

"No, I mean you are literally going to take the bull by the horns?"

"Yes. On three … one."

"Please don't."

"Two."

"Fuck."

"Three."

It happened fast. Mr. Buff shoved his tongue in my ear, then grunt-snorted explosively. His head jerked back and he reared up. Juiced on adrenaline, I whirled out of the way like a coked-up dervish. Just in time. The beast's front hooves pounded down like twin sledgehammers. He galloped off, with Pete dangling from the horns, bare feet dragging on the ground for a moment. Unfortunately, Pete was more rodeo clown than bronc rider. He lost his grip and went flying.

"Pete!" I yelled. "Are you OK?"

"No. I think he broke my foot."

"Jesus." I got up and hopped over to where Pete lay writhing in the dirt.

With a two-handed pressure grip just above his right ankle, Pete tried to stop the pain from radiating up. "You see any bones sticking out?" he asked, breathing hard and fast through his mouth. "I think he stepped right on it. That guy was solid."

"Yeah, I hope he's not coming back with his pissed-off friends."

"Bison insurgents."

"Totally."

"What do you expect, we're on their land."

"I don't see any bones. Does it hurt?"

"It hurts like a bitch."

"You think you can walk on it?"

"No."

"OK, chill for a second. I'll see if there's any ice." I pogo-bopped back to the truck and improvised an ice pack out of a towel and the remaining chunks in the cooler. As I began to wrap it tightly around Pete's foot, I said, "This is gonna hurt you more than it does me."

"It always does." Pete made a face but not a sound.

"Hey," I said, "between the two of us, we have two good feet."

Pete laughed. "It's my fault. Remember, I said I wanted to look the beast in the eye."

"What did you see?"

"He was as scared as I was."

42 / Grand Canyon, great kids

Our last stop on the grand tour would, fittingly, be the Grand Canyon of the Yellowstone, the big breathtaking daddy of the park. It took some Army improvising to get there. Pete's foot swelled so badly he couldn't depress the gas pedal without severe pain, so I was forced to drive the truck, which was a stick shift.

We were scared to get out of third gear and we held the speed to about 30 miles an hour as we chugged east from Norris toward Canyon Village. We divided the labor, melding two broken bodies to make one that worked. My leg depressed the clutch. Pete scooted over next to me so his left foot would reach the gas pedal and the brake, while keeping his right foot elevated on the cooler. Our left hands anchored the steering wheel and Pete shifted with his right. Leaving Steamboat Geyser had been a disaster. Every time we came to a complete stop, getting started again made the truck buck like a methed-up mustang.

We drove straight to Inspiration Point, not wanting to risk figuring out how and where to park at the jammed village. The Point was crowded too. After some herky-jerking around, we squeezed into a parking spot in the hinterlands. We managed to get the wheelchair unloaded and Pete took over the crutches. "I'm ready to rock," he said.

I dropped into the chair. "Let's roll."

We headed for the Point, two gimps on a mission to see nature. At the first set of steps leading down to the observation deck, I stopped to consider the options: Go or don't go, whip it or wuss it. Pete stared me down but offered no verbal judgment. In his eyes, though, there was only one choice.

"Little Jet," I said.

"What?"

"The chair's name." I hit the joystick and plunged down the stairs, *bump-bonk-bump-bonk-bump-bonk*. Miraculously, Junior Jett's training wheels kept the rig upright. I mentally thanked him for the safety innovation. At the landing, I whizzed a 180 and looked up at Pete. "It just came to me," I yelled to him. "We should name the chair after its dad."

Pete nodded vigorously and bombed down the stairs, two at a time, swinging like a newly lubed pendulum. As he sailed over the last step, Pete planted the left crutch to stop and nearly speared my foot. "Yeah, Little Jet," he said. "I like it."

Near the edge of the canyon, we got in line to work our way to the railing for an unobstructed view. Up ahead, a beefy fried dumpling of a guy said to his well-breaded wife, loud enough for everyone on the platform to hear, "Good God almighty, Daisy, get a load a that scenery. I hope they never discover oil here." The crowd cracked up. Everybody but me. There was nothing funny about oil.

It took a good 15 minutes before we got to the front for the ultimate look. Pete began to snap pictures with his cell. "The fat guy was right," he said. "Awesome, man. Freaking awesome."

We gazed and gawked and marveled. We were two kids in a rock candy store. The Yellowstone River snaked its way down the canyon like a parade of glistening jewels, proudly etching its signature into the red and yellow escarpment, carrying off spoils to a secret dumping ground. Spindly pine trees grubbed for a home on the steep walls but, given enough time, sulfurous emanations would most certainly evict them. And there would always be enough time. Yellowstone National Park, almost every plaque reminded us, was conceived of volcanic activity millions of years ago. The very spot where we stood was inside the caldera, at its northern tip. There was the remote possibility that an untimely eruption would swallow us whole as it reduced our bodies to ash. Again, I began to feel small and ephemeral. Yellowstone was unfathomably bigger and bolder and badder than any speck of a human being. I scanned across the craggy rocks, the roaring falls, the fuming vents that led directly to the molten heart of the planet. I tried to lock the image into my brain, to implant a small piece of wondrous earthly joy to resurrect in another life and another place, or just to carry inside me until the end.

"I hate to break this party up," Pete said, "but it's gonna take us a while to get back up those stairs and I've gotta be on a C-141 to Baghdad in a week. You ready to head back?"

"You don't want to hike the rim trail?"

Pete laughed. "Yeah, I do. In my mind, we already did."

"All righty, then."

By going off the path, I was able to get around the stairs on the way back up. Little Jet's engine had plenty of torque and the wheels' knobby treads clawed into the rock like an ATV. It was guerrilla goodness until we got to the last set of steps. The craggy land sloped sharply away on both sides. It was impossible to go around. I looked at Pete and he looked right back, adding a shrug. "You want me to push?" he asked, gingerly testing his foot by putting some weight on it.

"Naw, I think Little Jet can take this hill. Let's see what happens." I inched forward until the chair's small front wheels were up against the first step. Then I leaned into the stick. The big wheels spun and screeched and smoked but went nowhere. The wheelchair groaned and chattered. People coming down the stairs retreated or moved sideways to the railings to give me room. I tried again. Same result, only the smoking tires began to give off a burning rubber smell. The people remaining on the stairs cleared out. I tried again. The engine whined but the physics of the situation weren't giving in. I let go of the joystick.

Pete came over and said, "What if I try to lift the front wheels onto the first step to get you started?"

"No, this thing is heavy and your foot is messed up."

"Do you guys need some help?" someone called out.

I looked up. Three kids were standing at the top of the stairs. Judging by their backward baseball caps, they were probably juniors or seniors in high school. None of them were missing any limbs or limping around on crutches, not yet, anyway, so I blurted out, "Yeah, we do."

"No problem," said the tallest kid, probably a basketball letterman. He loped down, followed by the other two.

"Hi, where you guys from?" I said.

"Powell, east of here. It's not too far from the park."

"Thanks for the help. I was doing all right till these steps."

The tall stickly kid said, "My name is Ryan. This is Chuck and Ronnie. How about if we lift those front wheels and give you a push?"

"Sounds good."

The kids dipped their shoulders to get in position. When I felt the chair flex as they put their backs into it, I applied the joystick. The front wheels popped up and leaped forward — *bonkity-bonk-bonkity-bonk-bonk* — and the chair crested the steps onto the landing, like a cork bobbing to the top of a concrete wave.

"Thanks, man," I said to the tall kid. I held out my hand. Somehow, he knew to shake with his left.

"Were you in the war?" he asked.

"Yeah."

"Which one?"

"Iraq."

"Did you know a guy named Elwyn McCandlan?"

"No, I don't think so."

"He went to our school. He got killed in Mosul."

"I'm sorry."

The kid nodded. "Yeah. Well, I hope Yellowstone is treating you right. We're proud of it. Maybe we'll see you around."

"Yeah, maybe. Thanks again."

"No problem."

The kids melted off toward Inspiration Point as Pete and I headed for the truck. "No more stairs for you," he said.

"Hey, with guys like that, I'm covered."

"Yeah," Pete said. "Those are great kids. It was kind of an Iwo Jima moment."

43 / Going home

Pete got out the map and began to study it like he was trying to pass a final exam in advanced geography. I sat silently in the truck, trying to figure out how to tell him I needed to go home. I also did a math problem, dividing my pill inventory by the number of days I estimated it would take to get back to Trillium. I wondered how much juice was left in Little Jet's batteries, and how far the wheelchair would take me, and where I could get it recharged.

Pete folded the map in half and pointed toward the squiggly lines, tracing a route. "So I'm thinking we head south out of the park and pick up Interstate 80 to Cheyenne and dip down to Denver. Then we do a loop back to D.C. on Interstate 70. We'll cruise the mighty American heartland. You ever seen Kansas?"

"No."

Pete looked up from the map. "Do you want to?"

"No."

"What, are you allergic to wheat?"

"I'm going home, Pete."

His face crinkled up, uncomprehendingly. "What do you mean?"

"I can't go back to Washington."

"What are you talking about?"

"I'm not going back to Walter Reed."

"That's crazy, Cutter."

"This was the greatest trip ever, Pete, and all I can say is thanks and I really owe you. I mean, really, more than you can possibly understand. I know you have to get back. I don't want to hold you up. So I'm just going to drive the wheelchair home."

Pete's head snapped back and he snorted. "Ha! Good one. Nice. You had me going."

"I'm AWOL."

Pete fixed me with a stunned stare.

"Seriously. I'm AWOL from the hospital."

"Are you fucking with me?"

"I'm sorry, Pete. I'm really sorry. It's just that ... I can't even explain it. I need to get home. I need to see my mom. I can't go back to that hospital. I'm done with that. Totally done."

Pete put his right hand to his forehead and squeezed the skin into folds. His head tilted back. After a while, he looked at me like a friend, not a commanding officer, and said softly, "This is fucked up, Cutter."

"I know."

"We should call Walter Reed right now and tell them there has been a gigantic misunderstanding and you'll be back in three days."

"You're right, we should, but a lot of things are fucked up and those things can't be fixed. It's too late. They're fucked up in stone. There's nothing I can do to fix anything. You know that, right?"

Pete looked at me for a long time and his face changed. He didn't argue the point.

"I know you have to go," I said. "That's cool. I totally understand. This has been amazing, the trip of a lifetime. You saved me, Pete. I thank you for that. I owe you. Now I need to get home and see some people, decide some things. There's nothing back there for me."

"They'll court-martial you."

I laughed, picturing myself in a military courtroom with my wheelchair and my Purple Heart, popping pain pills and asking for "a one-hour recess so I can go use my bedpan."

"They *will* bring you up on charges. Going AWOL is serious shit."

When I finally stopped laughing, I said, "Yeah, they probably would. That would be fun. That would be the most fun I've had in the Army. That's the best reason for me to go home: A court-martial. Bring it on."

I wrenched the door open with a loud metallic scrape and stepped out of the truck, sprawling onto the asphalt. I landed mostly on my leg stump. The blood vessels that were left would probably bleed. I imagined a pool of my blood on the courtroom floor and the Army prosecutor objecting that it was irrelevant. I got up and hopped to the back of the truck to unload Little Jet. Pete was there, waiting at the tailgate. He grabbed my shoulders to steady me.

"I'll take you home," he said.

44 / Escape velocity

I probably could have made it home on Little Jet. That rig was more an unstoppable tank than a cripple's wheelchair. The battery life was an unknown but wasn't that true for all of us? I realized that much as I headed up the trail to The Overlook above the Trillium River canyon.

Wherever I ended up, even if it was nowhere, which I was kind of hoping for, I would always remember Pete Klug. Do-anything-for-you warrior didn't begin to describe him. I couldn't comprehend that he would rig up a rock and a rope to hold down the gas pedal and drive for nearly 16 hours straight — 967 miles — from Yellowstone National Park to the front door of my mom's house to drop me off, like it was a run to the store to get milk. Words like gratitude, awe and respect were insufficient to describe my feelings.

Pete left immediately. He absolutely could not stay an extra minute. He had to make his rendezvous with that C-141. "I hope you'll get to meet my mom someday," I told him. "She would really like you."

"I hope I do, too," he said.

The last thing I ever said to Pete was, "Tell the guys that I miss them really bad."

"We will all miss you, my brother," he said. "You're a fine soldier. You served your country with valor, devotion and heart. Nobody could ask anything more." Pete's kind and laudatory words were, of course, hyperbole, if not downright false, but this wasn't the time to challenge them, because as he spoke he stood at attention and saluted me. I also stood at attention, as best I could, precariously leaning on one crutch, and returned that final salute with my stump. My hand was still there, at least in spirit. As Pete disappeared down the road, heading back to the sandbox, the pain I felt was sharper and deeper than anything I endured in Ward 57.

Mom was surprised to see me. All right, I should tell the whole truth, finally. The truth was always hard for me because it was unpleasant, because it upset everyone. Only on this last day, though, did it become possible for me to understand that, and to see the folly in it. Mom wasn't just surprised to see me, she was shocked and drained and sad and fearful and overwhelmed. She was terrified by the phone call she had received from Walter Reed informing her that I was "missing." She didn't know what to do or what to say. That was fine. There were no actions or words that could have changed anything.

"I love you, Mom," I told her. "I love you so much." And that was the truth. Now I realized it had always been the truth.

Her eyes wandered across my face and she touched my scabby cheek with two fingers, lightly, the slightest brush. She wept. That was a rational response. About 10 hours earlier, I had seen myself at a gas station in Boise. The bathroom had a shiny steel vandal-proof mirror. I was a skinny lumpy misshapen mess. I looked so long that I scared myself. Dark puffy circles underneath sunken eyes. Light brown beard growing in scraggly patches. Skin breaking out in a blotchy purplish rash. Dry crinkly lips splitting open. Hideous.

Mom wiped her eyes and said I would feel better if I took a shower. She always said that but this day, it wasn't true. I felt worse. This was the cramped little stall where, in another life, I had learned to masturbate. Now, when I looked down at the scar tissue, I wanted to cry too, just like Mom. I couldn't. I was hollowed out. I had no tears left. I just stood under the hot water, leaning against the slick fiberglass wall, discovering that it wasn't possible to wash away the grotesque grime and lousy luck and dumb decisions of the previous two years.

Later, Little Jet's tires were grinding in the mud, splattering my clean white T-shirt with brown dots. Finding clothes had been easy. Mom had kept my room the same as the day I left for basic training. Same old Pearl Jam poster. Same old skateboard in the corner. My favorite old jeans were too big for me now but I wore them with my old brown belt cinched down. I found a bungee cord in the closet and tied up the right pant leg. I kissed Mom and told her I was "going to see some friends." In a way, that wasn't a lie. In my mind, it wasn't the coward's way out.

Little Jet got stuck about a mile from The Overlook, where the trail became narrow and steep. I listened to the birds, their beautiful songs, for a long time. I thought about my life. I studied the majestic Doug firs. Sitting there, mired in mud, unable to move, I wondered if it was some kind of sign. It probably wasn't. I didn't believe in signs. It felt like one more random thing that was happening for no reason other than it had been raining for a couple of days before I got home. The birds chirped and flew and chattered on, like they'd done pure ecstasy, a feathery rave. I checked my own supply of drugs, not that I needed to, it was just habit. I knew exactly what I had left: Three pills, a Percocet, a Quaalude, a Neurontin. Nice mix. I downed them. Then I waited. I looked around, taking comfort from every rock, each tree, a ranting bluebird, the cloudy sky. My stumps had been feeling like broken glass coated with hot tar but the Neurontin chilled them out. The Lude came on with a dreamy overlay, masking pains in my neck and back. When the Perc party began, adding a dizzy little buzz, I was good to go.

I rocked Little Jet, alternating touches of joystick, pushing and letting off, forward, back, forward, back, until the wheels grabbed. The chair lurched ahead and I was on my way again.

Fifty yards from The Overlook, I popped out of the forest and gave Little Jet a well-deserved rest. I figured that over the three miles from my house, we had gained 1,000 feet of elevation. That made me think about how far I had risen in my own life. Not very.

I tried to remember my childhood. Mom had some early photos she sometimes would get out. One was cute, this chubby-cheeked little guy in tiny blue overalls with chocolate icing on his face at his first birthday party. I recalled playing baseball a few times. I rode around on bikes a lot. I bought bubble gum at the store. I played with a friend's train set. What else? I blanked.

My school days were a blur. Mrs. Bayonne was the only teacher who stood out. Her literature class reigned as my all-time favorite. I felt bad that I didn't go say goodbye to her. We could have had a rocking discussion of irony, satire, metaphor, theme and conclusion, but I didn't want her to see me like this. It would have been rude to inflict myself on her. I was tired of making everybody uncomfortable. She would have offered support, of course, and said, "As long as you can pick up a book and read, as long as you can put pencil to paper, as long as you can think, you can do anything you want. Transcendence is a state of mind." When she first said that halfway through the semester, it knocked me back. Then, it felt right. Her vocabulary gave everything she said some extra heft. Now, though, three years beyond English literature class, I didn't find her argument persuasive. I probably would have countered her encouragement with a simple statement, not big words, just something like, "Sometimes your life ends before it ends." Mrs. Bayonne might have peered over the top of her reading glasses and called that a logical fallacy but it felt true enough to me. Beyond that, I would have borrowed from Junior Jett. My life was not very long. Or wide.

I tried to think of things about Dad. We played catch a few times. He showed me how to change the spark plugs in an engine once upon a time. I didn't think he was very happy with Mom and vice versa. Overall, I didn't have many memories of him.

The Oregon sky can change at any moment. To the west, above the ridgeline, a ribbon of blue poked through as the swirling white curtain of clouds parted in the wind. The sun was sinking. Brilliant red rays angled across the landscape, warming my face. It was going to be one of those crazy coast sunsets that lasted a minute or two.

I didn't want to think about Halley. I tried not to, but my gaze drifted to the spot, our lofty lair. I said out loud, "I wish you a good long wide happy life, Halley Fallon."

Then I rolled to the edge of The Overlook.

I took a last look around. Far below, the Trillium River burbled and danced through the canyon on its merry way to the sea. It had somewhere to go. I did too. At the moment the sun disappeared below the horizon, I jammed that 1966 Corvette joystick forward. Little Jet's mighty engine roared. Its wheels spun for an instant, then gained traction. The chair launched.

Escape velocity, my brother.

45 / Mourners remember Oregon soldier as 'warrior who believed in the cause'

By Jerrold L. Sievert

The Portland Times

More than 200 people packed the gymnasium at Trillium High School in Coos County on Wednesday to mourn the death of Private First Class Johnathan Ambrose Cutter IV, a 22-year-old Army veteran who was seriously injured late last year in the Iraq war.

Wiping away tears as she spoke, Amanda Cutter, the soldier's mother, told the crowd, "I was surprised and scared when Johnny decided to enlist, but I grew to understand that he was a patriot, like his father, his grandfather and his great-grandfather. They were also Army veterans, and ultimately my son decided to follow them into battle."

Governor Ted Kulongoski attended the funeral and said, "Private First Class Cutter believed in liberty and freedom, and he put his life on the line every day to ensure the safety of all Americans back home. He was a soldier who represented the very best of Oregon. I know we can all agree that he was a true American hero."

Mr. Cutter served with the 3rd Infantry Division. He was wounded Dec. 11, 2006, by a roadside bomb during a mission in Baghdad. He was riding in a Humvee as part of a security detail escorting American negotiators to a meeting at the Baghdad Oil Ministry when an improvised explosive device was detonated by insurgents, according to U.S. Army spokesman Lieutenant Colonel Mack D. Nicholas. One soldier, Private First Class Amerigo Taymondo, died in the blast. Mr. Cutter lost his right arm and right leg in the explosion and spent nearly five months at Walter Reed Army Medical Center in Washington, D.C., for rehabilitation. President Bush visited Mr. Cutter in the hospital last month to present him with a Purple Heart.

At the time of his death, Mr. Cutter was on a two-week furlough from the hospital to visit family and friends in Trillium, Nicholas said. He died in an accident, according to Nicholas, when his motorized wheelchair apparently tumbled off a cliff in the Coast Range, about three miles south of Trillium.

"Johnny had a great passion for the tall trees and the mountains," his mother said. "I believe he was happiest when he was outdoors in nature. I know he found peace there."

Mr. Cutter was reported missing on June 3 and a search for him began the next day. A county sheriff's search and rescue team located his body in a ravine last Thursday.

Mr. Cutter grew up in Trillium and graduated in 2002 from Trillium High School. In his senior year, he wrote stories for the school newspaper and served as an assistant editor on the yearbook. He worked locally in food service and attended Coos Bay Community College for one semester before enlisting in the Army. One of his instructors, Elizabeth Bayonne, who taught English literature at Coos Bay, remembered Mr. Cutter as "a stellar student whose curiosity led him in many different directions. He embraced each book wholeheartedly, looking for meaning beyond the surface. Johnny was the kind of student every teacher dreams of having in class, and from what I've heard, he was the kind of soldier every general dreams of having in the Army."

Army Sergeant Pete Klug said, "My friend Johnny Cutter never shied away from danger, never had second thoughts about a mission. He was always on the front lines of the battle. He was a warrior who believed in the cause. Though I only met Johnny's parents today, I want them to know, and I want to say publicly, what a tremendous honor it was to serve with their son."

Concluding the ceremony, Mr. Cutter's father, Major John Cutter III, said his son "made me prouder than I ever imagined I could be. He stepped up, on his own, to defend this country from the forces of tyranny and darkness. His memory will burn brightly. I hope that his time in the United States Army will remind all of us that freedom can never be taken for granted."

As a bugler played "Taps," six soldiers in full-dress uniforms carried Mr. Cutter's flag-draped casket from the gymnasium to a hearse.

Mr. Cutter is survived by his mother, of Trillium, Oregon, and his father, of St. Maries, Idaho. He will be buried in Willamette National Cemetery in Portland.

About the author

Jim Braly worked for 33 years as a reporter and editor, for The Arizona Republic, The Santa Barbara News-Press, The San Jose Mercury News and The Oregonian. This is his first novel.

Acknowledgements

To research military medical scenes, I referred extensively to "War Surgery in Afghanistan and Iraq: A Series of Cases, 2003-2007," edited by LTC Shawn Christian Nesson, DO, U.S. Army; Dave Edmond Lounsbury, MD, COL, U.S. Army (Ret.); and Stephen P. Hetz., MD, COL, U.S. Army (Ret.). In my opinion, this book is a towering achievement for reasons that go beyond its immense value as an emergency surgery tutorial. For background on the Iraq war, I turned to hundreds of stories and photographs from The Washington Post, The New York Times and The Associated Press. The foreign correspondents and photographers who cover the war provide a profound public service.

www.ingramcontent.com/pod-product-compliance
Lightning Source LLC
Chambersburg PA
CBHW081145170626
46809CB00011B/3151

* 9 7 8 0 9 8 3 7 7 4 7 1 6 *